New Medieval Literatures 25

New Medieval Literatures

ISSN 1465-3737

Editors
Prof. Laura Ashe, University of Oxford
Dr Caroline Batten, University of Pennsylvania
Dr Philip Knox, University of Cambridge
Prof. Wendy Scase, University of Birmingham

New Medieval Literatures is an annual of work on medieval textual cultures. Its scope is inclusive of work across the theoretical, archival, philological, and historicist methodologies associated with medieval literary studies. The title announces an interest both in new writing about medieval culture and in new academic writing. The editors aim to engage with intellectual and cultural pluralism in the Middle Ages and now. Within this generous brief, they recognize only two criteria: excellence and originality.

Founding Editors
Prof. Rita Copeland, University of Pennsylvania
Prof. David Lawton, Washington University, St Louis
Prof. Wendy Scase, University of Birmingham

Advisory Board
Hans Ulrich Gumbrecht, Stanford University
Jeffrey Hamburger, Harvard University
Christiane Klapisch-Zuber, École des Hautes Études en Sciences Sociales, Paris
Alastair Minnis, Yale University
Margaret Clunies Ross, University of Sydney
Miri Rubin, Queen Mary, University of London
Paul Strohm, Columbia University
Jocelyn Wogan-Browne, Fordham University

Submissions are invited for future issues. Please write to the editors:

Laura Ashe (laura.ashe@ell.ox.ac.uk)
Caroline Batten (battenc@english.upenn.edu)
Philip Knox (pk453@cam.ac.uk)
Wendy Scase (w.l.scase@bham.ac.uk)

For submission guidelines and further information please visit
http://www.english.ox.ac.uk/new-medieval-literatures
For information on the New Medieval Literatures Scholars of Colour Essay Prize, please see https://www.english.ox.ac.uk/new-medieval-literatures-scholars-colour-essay-prize

New Medieval Literatures 25

Edited by Laura Ashe, Philip Knox, Caroline Batten and Wendy Scase

D. S. BREWER

© Contributors 2025

All Rights Reserved. Except as permitted under current legislation no part of this work may be photocopied, stored in a retrieval system, published, performed in public, adapted, broadcast, transmitted, recorded or reproduced in any form or by any means, without the prior permission of the copyright owner

First published 2025
D. S. Brewer, Cambridge

ISBN 978 1 84384 741 0

D. S. Brewer is an imprint of Boydell & Brewer Ltd
PO Box 9, Woodbridge, Suffolk IP12 3DF, UK
and of Boydell & Brewer Inc.
668 Mount Hope Avenue, Rochester, NY 14620–2731, USA
website: www.boydellandbrewer.com

Our Authorised Representative for product safety in the EU is
Easy Access System Europe – Mustamäe tee 50, 10621 Tallinn, Estonia,
gpsr.requests@easproject.com

A catalogue record for this book is available
from the British Library

The publisher has no responsibility for the continued existence or accuracy of URLs for external or third-party internet websites referred to in this book, and does not guarantee that any content on such websites is, or will remain, accurate or appropriate

Contents

	Illustrations	vi
	Abbreviations	ix
1.	Ælfred Grammaticus *Megan Renz Perry*	1
2.	Wicked Wolves, Culpable Sheep: Animal Lessons in Medieval British Fables *Linnet Heald*	33
3.	Medieval Networks of Memory: Writing the Mortuary Roll in Thirteenth-Century Britain *Elaine Treharne and Mateusz Fafinski*	59
4.	Domestic Politics/Insurrection Politics: Parables of Obedience in the *Mesnagier de Paris* and the Revolts of 1380–3 *Michael Sizer*	90
5.	Bishop Henry Despenser and Manuscript Production in Late Medieval Norwich *Holly James-Maddocks and R. F. Yeager*	121
6.	Accumulating Easts: Ancient Geographies and Genealogies in John Gower's *Confessio Amantis* *Amanda J. Gerber*	169
7.	Arthur in the Mountains: The Multivalency of Mont-Saint-Michel and the St Gotthard Pass in the Alliterative *Morte Arthure* *Stephen De Hailes*	200

Illustrations

Ælfred Grammaticus, Megan Renz Perry

Table 1.1: Outlay of the Harley *RP* gloss programme   13

Table 1.2: Relative similarity of construe markers in contemporary grammatical manuscripts   16

Table 1.3: Syntactical emphases in the Harley *RP* Fragment in context   18

Medieval Networks of Memory: Writing the Mortuary Roll in Thirteenth-Century Britain, Elaine Treharne and Mateusz Fafinski

Fig. 3.1: Cambridge, St John's College, MS N. 31, entry for Egglestone Abbey   69

Fig. 3.2: Cambridge, St John's College, MS N. 31, entries for Southwark Priory and Westminster Abbey   73

Fig. 3.3: Cambridge, St John's College, MS N. 31, two successive entries for Furness Abbey   75

Fig. 3.4: Cambridge, St John's College, MS N. 31, entry for Barking Abbey   78

Fig. 3.5: Cambridge, St John's College, MS N. 31, entry for Westwood Benedictine Priory, Worcestershire   81

Fig. 3.6: Cambridge, St John's College, MS N. 31, entry for Wroxhall Priory   83

Fig. 3.7: Cambridge, St John's College, MS N. 31, entry for Pinley Priory   84

All figures by permission of the Master and Fellows of St John's College, Cambridge. Photographs © Ian McKee.

Bishop Henry Despenser and Manuscript Production in Late Medieval Norwich, Holly James-Maddocks and R. F. Yeager

Fig. 5.1: BL MS Additional 34114, fol. 164r, *Roman de Thèbes*. © The British Library   142

Fig. 5.2: Cambridge, Trinity College, MS B.11.7, fol. 6r, Hours. By permission of the Master and Fellows of Trinity College, Cambridge   143

Fig. 5.3: BL MS Cotton Claudius E.viii, fol. 43r, *Flores historiarum* (detail). © The British Library — 144

Fig. 5.4: BL MS Cotton Claudius E.viii, fol. 71v (detail). © The British Library — 145

Fig. 5.5: BL MS Cotton Claudius E.viii, fol. 77r (detail). © The British Library — 146

Fig. 5.6: BL MS Cotton Claudius E.viii, fol. 137v. © The British Library — 146

Fig. 5.7: BL MS Arundel 74, fol. 2v, Bede, *Ecclesiastica historia*. © The British Library — 147

Fig. 5.8: Oxford, Bodleian Library, MS Hatton 1, fol. 181v, Missal. © Bodleian Libraries, University of Oxford — 148

Fig. 5.9: Cambridge, Trinity College, MS B.11.7, fol. 8v. By permission of the Master and Fellows of Trinity College, Cambridge — 149

Fig. 5.10: BL MS Additional 25588, fol. 109v, Missal. © The British Library — 150

Fig. 5.11: Oxford, Bodleian Library, MS Hatton 1, fol. 120v. © Bodleian Libraries, University of Oxford — 151

Fig. 5.12: Oxford, Bodleian Library, MS Hatton 1, fol. 148v. © Bodleian Libraries, University of Oxford — 152

Fig. 5.13a: BL MS Additional 57534, fol. 96v, Processional. © The British Library — 153

Fig. 5.13b: (inset) Oxford, Bodleian Library, Hatton 1, fol. 4v (detail). © Bodleian Libraries, University of Oxford — 153

Fig. 5.14: BL MS Harley 3866, fol. 168v, Missal. © The British Library — 154

Fig. 5.15a: BL MS Additional 25588, fol. 138v (detail). © The British Library — 155

Fig. 5.15b (inset): BL MS Additional 57534, fol. 125r (detail). © The British Library — 155

Fig. 5.16a: BL MS Additional 34114, fol. 106r (detail). © The British Library — 156

Fig. 5.16b: BL MS Cotton Claudius E.viii, fol. 21r (detail).
© The British Library ... 156

Fig. 5.16c: Cambridge, Trinity College, MS B.11.7, fol. 4v (detail). By permission of the Master and Fellows of Trinity College, Cambridge ... 156

Fig. 5.17a: Oxford, Bodleian Library, MS Hatton 1, fol. 148v (detail).
© Bodleian Libraries, University of Oxford ... 157

Fig. 5.17b: BL MS Additional 57534, fol. 18v (detail). © The British Library ... 157

Table 5.1: The division of illuminator hands in BL MS Cotton Claudius E.viii, *Flores historiarum* and the *Chronicle* of Adam Murimuth ... 131

Table 5.2: The division of illuminator hands in BL MS Arundel 74, Bede's *Ecclesiastica historia* (fols 1–99), *Epistola Cuthberti de Obitu Bedae*, etc. ... 133

Table 5.3: The distribution of labour among border artists of the Despenser-Hatton group identified in more than one manuscript ... 137

The editors, contributors and publisher are grateful to all the institutions and persons listed for permission to reproduce the materials in which they hold copyright. Every effort has been made to trace the copyright holders; apologies are offered for any omission, and the publisher will be pleased to add any necessary acknowledgement in subsequent editions.

Abbreviations

AND	*Anglo-Norman Dictionary* (AND2 Online Edition) <https://anglo-norman.net>
BL	British Library, London
BnF	Bibliothèque nationale de France, Paris
BodL	Bodleian Library, Oxford
CCCC	Corpus Christi College, Cambridge
CCCM	Corpus Christianorum Continuatio Mediaeualis
CUL	Cambridge University Library
DOE	*Dictionary of Old English*: A to I Online <https://doe.utoronto.ca>
DOML	Dumbarton Oaks Medieval Library
DRBO	Douay-Rheims Bible Online <https://www.drbo.org>
EETS	Early English Text Society (e.s. – Extra Series; o.s. – Original Series; s.s. – Supplementary Series)
LALME	*A Linguistic Atlas of Late Mediaeval English*, ed. Angus McIntosh, M. L. Samuels and Michael Benskin, with Margaret Laing and Keith Williamson, 4 vols (Aberdeen, 1986)
MED	*Middle English Dictionary* <https://quod.lib.umich.edu/m/middle-english-dictionary/dictionary>
MGH	Monumenta Germaniae Historica
NML	*New Medieval Literatures*
ODNB	*Oxford Dictionary of National Biography* (Oxford, 2004) <https://www.oxforddnb.com/>
OED	*Oxford English Dictionary* (Oxford, 2024) <https://www.oed.com/>
RS	Rolls Series

1

Ælfred Grammaticus[1]

Megan Renz Perry

An early medieval schoolboy used a stylus to sketch a crude image of his teacher in the margin of the *Regula pastoralis* he or his peers had annotated for sense.[2] Frustrated students carved slashes in the margins of another copy from present-day western Germany, marking the ends of long Latin periods.[3] Teachers from northeastern France erased errant student notes and doodles in yet other copies, while leaving the more useful ones for subsequent readers.[4] And a scribe in a Welsh schoolroom untangled the *Regula pastoralis* with a developed system of symbolic marks, the same one grammarians used to construe the complex syntax of Latin *auctores* like Arator and Iuvencus.[5] Meanwhile, King Alfred of

---

1 Sincerest thanks to the following individuals for their support and dialogue in this project throughout its development: Shu-han Luo, Kevin Hoffman, Rosalie Stoner and Emily Thornbury. Thanks, as well, to the anonymous reviewers, whose insights greatly improved this piece.
2 Vienna, Österreichische Nationalbibliothek, MS 949, fols. 76v, 77v, with scattered glosses throughout: Bernhard Bischoff and Birgit Ebersperger, *Katalog der festländischen Handschriften des neunten Jahrhunderts*, 4 vols, (Wiesbaden, 2004), no. 7179. Unless otherwise noted, I examined *Regula pastoralis* manuscripts in person.
3 Berlin, Staatsbibliothek, MS theo. lat. fol. 362, fols 87v, 96v: Bischoff and Ebersperger, *Katalog*, no. 461.
4 Troyes, Médiathèque Jacques-Chirac, MS 247, fols 154–241; Laon, Bibliothèque Municipale, MS 187; Paris, Bibliothèque nationale de France, MS lat. 2262, fols 15–143: Bischoff and Ebersperger, *Katalog*, nos 6248, 2088 and 4151, respectively.
5 London, British Library, MS Harley 5228, fol. 140. On construe marks see Fred C. Robinson, 'Syntactical Glosses in Latin Manuscripts of Anglo-Saxon Provenance', *Speculum* 48 (1973), 443–75. Lowe observes the presence of these marks in the Harley *RP* Fragment: Kathryn A. Lowe, 'Worcester and Wales: Copies of the *Regula Pastoralis* in the Early Middle Ages', in *Vernacular Manuscript Culture 1000–1500*, ed. Erik Kwakkel (Leiden, 2018), 25–50 (27).

Wessex, likely through a scribe recorder, bemoaned the fallen state of contemporary Latinity.[6] He proposed a solution that featured the translation of this same text into the vernacular, and the education of eligible youths.[7] Accounts of the Alfredian *Pastoral Care* have resisted framing the translation as consonant with Latin education – not unreasonably[8] – but the proximity of these classroom copies of the *RP* to the clerics that supported the Alfredian intellectual programme allows us to do so no longer. Archbishop Plegmund and his Mercian companions, Asser of St David's, John the Old Saxon, and Grimbald of Saint-Bertin, named either in the 'Prose Preface' to the *Pastoral Care* or in Asser's *Vita Alfredi*, represent some of the same locales – Wales, northeastern Francia and the Old Saxon language region – from which classroom copies of the *RP* emerge.[9] The experience of Latin education that formed the Wessex coterie must be the next question: what precisely did *cunnan arædan*

---

6   Henry Sweet, ed., *King Alfred's West-Saxon Version of Gregory's* Pastoral Care, 2 vols, EETS o.s. 45, 46 (London, 1871–2), 3 (Hatton MS): 'Swæ clæne hio wæs oðfeallenu […] ðæt swiðe feawa wæron […] ðe hiora ðeninga cuðen understondan on Englisc, oððe furðum an ærendgewrit of Lædene on Englisc areccean' ('So entirely had learning declined […] that very few […] knew how to understand their services in English […] or knew how to translate a letter from Latin to English'). Hereafter, *PC*. Cf., *King Alfred's Old English Translation of Pope Gregory the Great's* Regula Pastoralis *and its Cultural Context: A study and partial edition according to all surviving manuscripts based on Cambridge, Corpus Christi College 12*, ed. Carolin Schreiber (Frankfurt am Main, 2003), 192: cited where available (hereafter, Schreiber). I have also gratefully consulted R. D. Fulk's edition and translation based on Hatton 20: *The Old English Pastoral Care*, ed./trans. R. D. Fulk (Cambridge MA, 2021). All translations of the *Regula pastoralis*, the Old English *Pastoral Care* and its 'Prose Preface' are my own, as are all others unless noted otherwise.
7   *PC* 7; Schreiber, 192.
8   Such resistance may stem from the suboptimal state of ninth-century Latinity in England (Mercia perhaps excepted), as Christine Rauer suggests in 'Early Mercian Text Production: Authors, Dialects, and Reputations', *Amsterdamer Beiträge zur älteren Germanistik* 77.3–4 (2017), 541–58; or from an agonistic picture of Latin as the authoritative language against which the Alfredian translation programme rebelled: for example, Robert Stanton, *The Culture of Translation in Anglo-Saxon England* (Cambridge, 2002), 55–100.
9   *PC* 7; John Asser, *The Life of Alfred*, in *Alfred the Great: Asser's Life of King Alfred and Other Contemporary Sources*, ed./trans. Simon Keynes and Michael Lapidge (New York, 1983), 67–112 (77). See also Daniel Anlezark, 'The Old English Pastoral Care: Date, Readership, and Authorship', in *The Age of Alfred: Rethinking English Literary Culture c.850–950*, ed. Francis Leneghan and Amy

('to know how to read') mean to these men, and what relation had this experiential meaning to their aims in translating certain Latin books into English?[10]

Much excellent work on the Alfredian prose corpus has focused on the early medieval ideal of Solomonic wisdom as *philosophia* or *sapientia*, and its political and cultural importance to the realm.[11] The connection I propose between Latin learning, *grammatica*, and the Alfredian translation programme does not challenge such an ideal. Rather, it engages a simultaneous, even subsidiary, way of relating to learned content that rested less on the didactic content of the books than on the spiritual and moral efficacy of reading itself. This approach defers questions of historically contingent identity formation,[12] foregrounding instead the earnest conviction of early medieval grammarians that habits of language learning and literary interpretation generated moral excellence in its practitioners.[13] Like an increasing number of scholars, then, I explore Latinate grammatical education as a pillar of the Alfredian translation enterprise.[14]

Faulkner (Turnhout, 2024), 300–40 (313–14). Sincerest thanks to Prof. Anlezark for sharing this essay with me in advance of its publication.

10   On educational formation see Irena Dumitrescu, *The Experience of Education in Anglo-Saxon Literature* (Cambridge, 2018).

11   See Nicole Guenther Discenza, 'Wealth and Wisdom: Symbolic Capital and the Ruler in the Transformational Program of Alfred the Great', *Exemplaria* 13 (2001), 433–67; Francis Leneghan, 'Royal Wisdom and the Alfredian Context of Cynewulf and Cyneheard', *Anglo-Saxon England* 39 (2011), 71–104; Amy Faulkner, 'Royal Authority in the Biblical Quotations of the Old English Pastoral Care', *Neophilologus* 102 (2018), 125–40.

12   Several important studies have allied the processes of acquiring literacy in Latin, English, or both, with the construction of personal and group identities: Wendy Scase, *Visible English: Graphic Culture, Scribal Practice, and Identity, c. 700–c.1550* (Turnhout, 2022); Emily V. Thornbury and Rebecca Stephenson, eds, *Latinity and Identity in Anglo-Saxon Literature* (Toronto, 2016); Rebecca Stephenson, *The Politics of Language: Byrhtferth, Aelfric, and the Multilingual Identity of the Benedictine Reform* (Toronto, 2015).

13   Vivien Law, *Grammar and Grammarians in the Early Middle Ages* (London, 1997), 240; see also Law, *Wisdom, Authority, and Grammar in the Seventh Century: Decoding Virgilius Maro Grammaticus* (Cambridge, 1995).

14   Martin Irvine reads the Alfredian educational initiative as self-consciously grammatical: *The Making of Textual Culture: 'Grammatica' and Literary Theory, 350–1100* (Cambridge, 1994), 415–20. On specific Alfredian texts and their relation to aspects of *grammatica* see Rosalind Love, 'Latin Commentaries on Boethius's Consolation of Philosophy', in *A Companion to Alfred the Great*,

The Old English *Pastoral Care* retooled a Latin grammatical *auctor* in vogue in the ninth century for vernacular instruction. Three types of evidence strengthen this claim. First, several people at Alfred's court practised *grammatica* in various local flavours. Second, a syntactically glossed fragment of the *Regula pastoralis* from ninth-century Wales speaks to the text's use in an instructional context, familiar to at least one member of the Alfredian intellectual community. The wider manuscript record suggests that more than one knew the *RP* in this context. Finally, I suggest that there is supporting evidence from within the Old English translation itself: in its 'Prose Preface' (hereafter, 'Preface'), additions of the modal verbs *magan* and *cunnan* evince not only an awareness of, but an assent to, the moral and intellectual work of grammar practice. This essay argues that the translation of the *Pastoral Care* into Old English constituted the institutional endorsement of Latin grammatical practice in late ninth-century Wessex.

Grammatica as Practice

The intellectual milieu of the Alfredian revival was thoroughly familiar with grammar as literary and hermeneutic practice. The texts through which the Alfredian intellectual circle accessed Latin learning represent a reasonably self-consistent practice of *grammatica* in northwestern Europe distinguished both by its pursuits – namely, literacy and hermeneutic skill – and by its self-conscious work of moral formation. Martin Irvine and Vivien Law have greatly enriched our knowledge about this first dimension, the skill set and technologies proper to grammatical learning.[15] Law's work distinguishes between the varied sociolinguistic settings of Latin language learning and their ability to generate slightly different kinds of grammar text: the elementary parsing grammar, for example, represented an insular innovation.[16] Similarly, she points to the

---

ed. Nicole Guenther Discenza and Paul E. Szarmach (Leiden, 2015), 82–110; Leslie Lockett, 'Towards an Understanding of the Lost Exemplar of Augustine's *Soliloquia* Consulted by the Translator of the *Old English Soliloquies*', *The Journal of Medieval Latin* 32 (2022), 89 n.34; Patrick P. O'Neill, 'The Sources', in *King Alfred's Old English Prose Translation of the First Fifty Psalms* (Cambridge MA, 2001), 31–40.

15   Irvine, *Making of Textual Culture*; Vivien Law, *History of Linguistic Thought in the Early Middle Ages* (Philadelphia PA, 1993); Law, *Grammar and Grammarians*.

16   Law, *Grammar and Grammarians*, 53–90; 129–34.

difference in the reception of Donatus-derived grammar texts from those based on the more theoretical works of Priscian; and to the revival of dialectic in Carolingian circles of the late ninth and early tenth centuries: both factors contributed to the variety of local grammar traditions.[17] The *compilatio* was the essential technology of Carolingian grammatical instruction, and to subsequent English grammatical instruction. Such manuscripts consisted of *artes*, that is, practical grammar handbooks describing the parts of speech and each of their features, and copies of the *auctores* with which one practised one's interpretative skill.[18]

Even taking into account local variations in grammatical instruction, grammatical practice in northwestern Europe was generally coherent between about 750 and 950.[19] Up to the eleventh century, grammar was a hermeneutic skill; in the most common early medieval definition of this art, it governed and guarded the meaning – *intellectum* – of authoritative or canonical texts, those of the *auctores*, and trained in the discernment of this meaning from texts.[20] As such, it encompassed exegetical practice in this period.[21] The artificiality that Latinity accrued in the course of becoming a less living, though not yet dead, language supported the establishment of *grammatica*: grammatical Latinity consisted in the progressive acquisition of a complex and multilayered intellectual discipline.[22] Learning Latin entailed engaging the *auctores* in hermeneutics, the art of judgement and interpretation that produced oral and written commentary. As Irvine observed of grammatical semiotics, commentary – that is, a particular instance of textual interpretation – can never comprehend the totality of the text's meaning, but 'promises and postpones this totality through dissemination in a limitless chain of

---

17 Ibid., 134–44.
18 Patrizia Lendinara, 'Instructional Manuscripts in England: The Tenth- and Eleventh-Century Codices and The Early Norman Ones', in *Form and Content of Instruction in Anglo-Saxon England in the Light of Contemporary Manuscript Evidence*, ed. Loredana Lazzari and Maria A. D'Aronco (Turnhout, 2007), 59–113. See the handlist of *compilationes* in Irvine, *Making of Textual Culture*, 393–404.
19 See Rita Copeland and Ineke Sluiter, 'Introduction', in *Medieval Grammar and Rhetoric: Language Arts and Literary Theory, AD 300–1475*, ed. Copeland and Sluiter (Oxford, 2009), 62–71; Irvine, *Making of Textual Culture*, esp. 63–8.
20 Irvine, *Making of Textual Culture*, xiii, 1–22.
21 Irvine, *Making of Textual Culture*, 244–71.
22 Carin Ruff, 'Latin as an Acquired Language', in *The Oxford Handbook of Medieval Latin Literature*, ed. Ralph J. Hexter and David Townsend (Oxford, 2012), 46–62.

interpretations in supplementary texts'.[23] The eighth-century West Saxon grammarian Wynfrith–Boniface constructed poetry on the model of the scriptures, habituating the reader to the sort of attention that would have produced such overflowing meanings.[24] His Mercian contemporary Tatwine began his own version of a Donatan parsing grammar with an example of a syntactically complete sentence: 'the fear of the Lord is the beginning of wisdom, right understanding the beginning in all good works'.[25] 'Observe how', the grammarian directed, 'the whole meaning of this sentence is explained by the noun and one verb, with the participle and pronoun being added on so as to fill up the understanding'.[26] Tatwine read the second of the two phrases as a gloss on the first, where 'timor domini [est] initium sapientiae' is sufficiently complete, and 'omnibus facientibus eum' an ornamental addition, supplementing, though not in a superfluous way, what already sufficed.[27]

Grammarians believed that excellence in their craft coincided to a significant degree with moral excellence.[28] This morally earnest vision of grammar practice had its roots in the earliest instantiations of grammatical discourse and extended persistently into the early Middle Ages: the Hellenistic grammarian Diomedes offered the etymology that *ars* ('art') comes from *arete* ('excellence' or 'virtue'); picked up by Isidore, this proliferated through the early medieval West by way of the *Etymologiae*.[29] Donatus and his inheritors used *prudenter* alongside *docte* as an example of the *simplex* adverb, where *indocte* and *imprudente*

23   Irvine, *Making of Textual Culture*, 271.
24   Emily V. Thornbury, 'Boniface as Poet and Teacher', in *A Companion to Boniface*, ed. Michel Aaij and Shannon Godlove (Leiden, 2020), 99–122 (108–9).
25   Tatwine, *Ars grammatica, in Tatuini opera omnia*, ed. Maria De Marco (Turnhout, 1968), 3–93 (Preface, lines 6–8: 'initium sapientiae timor domini – intellectus bonus omnibus facientibus eum').
26   Tatwine, *Ars Grammatica*, Preface, lines 9–12: 'Ecce totus contextus sententiae huius nomine explicatur et uerbo uno, participio et pronomine adiecto ac [sic] implendum intellectum.'
27   In using 'ornamental' in this way, I draw upon Emily V. Thornbury, 'The Ornament of Virginity', in *Feminist Approaches to Early Medieval English Studies*, ed. Robin Norris et al. (Amsterdam, 2022), 171–95 (183).
28   Thornbury, 'Boniface', 99–122. Copeland and Sluiter, 'General Introduction', in *Medieval Grammar and Rhetoric*, 1–60 (52–60).
29   Isidore, *Etymologiae*, I.i.2, trans. in Copeland and Sluiter, *Medieval Grammar and Rhetoric*, 235: '*Ars* ["art"] has got its name because it consists of *artis* ["strict"] instructions and rules. Others say that this word is derived from the Greek *apo tês aretês*, i.e., from virtue, the name they used for knowledge.'

were complex adverbs.[30] Isidore articulated prudence as a distinctly literate virtue; Alcuin in the late eighth century correlated prudence with *sapientia* ('wisdom') among the illiterate and opposed it to *ignavia* ('laziness').[31] More evocatively, Boniface's preface to Sigibert framed the gift of the grammar compilation as the response from a man of some *sagacitas* ('wisdom') to the request of a *prudens* ('morally wise or prudent person').[32] In an interpretation of his own acrostic poem, the diamond shape with cruciform IESUS CHRISTUS in the middle, he wrote: 'Et singula quaeque ueteris ac noui testamenti decreta tunc te canonice intellexisse scias, cum in meditullio christum crucifixum destruentem malignae cupiditatis aedificium et construentem benignae caritatis templum spiritalibus oculis contemplando contueri potueris.' ('Know that you have rightly understood each pronouncement of the Old and New Testament when in the very centre of your being you can gaze with your spiritual eyes upon Christ crucified destroying the building of evil desire and erecting the temple of benevolent affection.')[33] The grammarian aimed to form the reader's powers of

30   Aelius Donatus, *Ars minor*, in *Grammatici Latini*, ed. Heinrich Keil, vol. IV (Leipzig, 1864), 355–66 (363, line 5): 'Quae? Simplex et conposita, simplex, ut docte prudenter, conposita, ut indocte inprudenter.' ('What [are the *figura*]? *Simplex*, like *learnedly* and *prudently*, and composite, like *unlearnedly* and *imprudently*'). Cf. Boniface (Wynfreth), *Ars grammatica*, ed. George John Gebauer and Bengt Løfstedt (Turnhout, 1980), 1564b: 'Figurae aduerbiis accidunt duae: sunt enim simplicia aduerbia, ut *docte prudenter*; conposita, ut *indocte inprudenter*.' ('There are two possible *figura* for adverbs: there are simple adverbs, such as *learnedly* and *prudently*; and composite adverbs, such as *ignorantly* and *imprudently*.') See also Tatwine, *Ars grammatica*, 4, line 110; and the grammars of Clemens the Scott and Aemelius Asper. This reading takes inspiration from Dumitrescu's analysis of Ælfric's *Grammar* in *The Experience of Education*, 60–89 (esp. 66–9).
31   Alcuin, 'Epistula 2', ed. Dümmler. MGH Epp. 4 (Leipzig, 1895), 484–90 (486, line 31: 'Nonne indoctos et inlitteratos non solum ad Deum pervenisse, verum hic multas virtutes fecisse cognovimus? Respondetur: "Simplicitatem cum ignavia vocari stultitiam, simplicitatem vero cum prudentia vocari sapientiam."' ('Go ahead, you say, "Don't we know that the unlearned and illiterate have not only come to God, but have indeed possessed many virtues?" It is responded: "Simplicity attended by laziness is called stupidity, but simplicity attended by prudence is called wisdom."')
32   Boniface, *Praefatio ad Sigibertum*, in Law, *Grammar and Grammarians*, 170–3 (170, line 1).
33   Boniface, *Praefatio ad Sigibertum*, 172, lines 97–110; trans. Law, *Grammar and Grammarians*, 174.

discernment, and encouraged humility as an extension of appropriate discernment.[34] This formation was indirectly pursued via the discipline of close reading ornate poetry in a grammatically complex language, although grammarians' penchants for moral riddles indicates that they could also indulge in the directly morally didactic.[35]

What, then, has grammatical practice to do with the Alfredian *Pastoral Care*? In a recent reassessment of the evidence on the authorship, dating and purpose of the *Pastoral Care* translation, Daniel Anlezark frames the goal of the Alfredian translation project as Latin instruction for the episcopacy (and persons who could be recruited to it) in response to a recognised need for a revitalised English Church hierarchy.[36] Taking this as a point of departure, I will suggest that the Latin education envisioned for the clergy, and suitable for the reform of the English episcopacy, was inextricable from the practice of Latin grammar. The circle of learned clerics engaged in the Alfredian education project could access grammatical materials, and the notation on these texts shows that their local communities were engaged in close reading. Moreover, as Emily Thornbury has shown, expertise in the literary arts was strongly associated with the attainment of ecclesiastical office in centuries prior and in learned continental circles.[37] A consideration of the men of Alfred's circle who aided his translation project, and those, indeed, to whose presence in the schoolroom Asser's *Vita Alfredi* attests, gives a picture of Wessex *grammatica*. First and foremost, these men taught the language arts of Latin literacy and hermeneutics; we have some means of reconstructing grammatical practice for at least Archbishop Plegmund, Bishop Werferth, Werwulf and Athelstan – those associated with Mercia – for Asser of St David's, later Bishop of Sherborne, and for Grimbald of Saint-Bertin.[38]

---

34 Grammarians like Aldhelm and Tatwine stressed the virtue of humility and characterised the poor reader as arrogant or inflated.
35 See, for example, 'Boniface's Riddles on the Virtues and Vices', in *The Old English and Anglo-Latin Riddle Tradition*, ed. Andy Orchard (Cambridge MA, 2021), 183–221.
36 See Anlezark, 'Old English Pastoral Care', 300–40.
37 Emily V. Thornbury, *Becoming a Poet in Anglo-Saxon England* (Cambridge, 2014), 64–5.
38 On the Mercian contingent, see Anlezark, 'The Old English Pastoral Care', 307–8; Rauer, 'Early Mercian Text Production', 541–58. John the Old Saxon's educational must remain obscure; the acrostics once attributed to him have been called into question, and the minimal information Asser gives would

Continental grammar of the late and post-Carolingian period varied somewhat in accord with local practice, but the Auxerre school and its connections with Laon and Reims seem to have had particular influence on Wessex intellectual culture. Grimbald, a monk of Saint-Bertin, may have taken with him continental *compilationes* of Donatus-inspired *artes* and the *auctores* when Archbishop Fulk of Reims dispatched him to Wessex.[39] The prolific grammarian Remigius of Auxerre, active in the last quarter of the ninth century, wrote pedagogical commentaries on the basic grammatical texts – the *Disticha Catonis*, Martianus Capella, and Donatus's *Ars Minor* – as well as on the *auctores* and books of scripture.[40] These commentaries would circulate widely alongside the *artes* and *auctores*; Saint-Bertin possessed copies in the late ninth century, as did England in the mid-tenth century.[41] Remigius' glosses, moreover, represent merely the most widely dispersed witnesses to the robust ninth-century intellectual centre at Auxerre, one of whose early lights was Murethach, one of the *scotti peregrini*.[42] A more specific connection between Wessex and Auxerre should not surprise us: Rosalind Love has

---

point to grammatical training in the expansive region inhabited by speakers of 'Old-Saxon' dialects: Robert Gallagher, 'Latin Acrostic Poetry in Anglo-Saxon England: Reassessing the Contribution of John the Old Saxon', *Medium Ævum* 86 (2017), 249–74.

39   Paris, BnF MS lat. 7560 offers an example of the kind of grammatical compilation common to the continent in the mid-ninth century, including excerpts of Charisius and the *artes* of Boniface and Phocas alongside Priscian's *De nomine, pronomine, et verbo*. See Irvine, *Making of Textual Culture*, 401, no. 68.

40   See Copeland and Sluiter, 'Glosses on Priscian by Remigius and his Followers (ninth and tenth centuries)', in *Medieval Grammar and Rhetoric*, 299–310.

41   From late ninth-century Reims came a copy of the Remigian gloss on Martianus Capella witnessed in London, BL MS Royal 15.1.xxxiii, known to have been at Worcester in the mid-tenth century: see Helmut Gneuss and Michael Lapidge, *Anglo-Saxon Manuscripts: A Bibliographical Handlist of Manuscripts and Manuscript Fragments Written or Owned in England up to 1100* (Toronto, 2014), 490. Remigian glosses on Sedulius were also known and copied at Worcester in the mid-tenth century: London, BL MS Lat. theo. c.4 (Gneuss and Lapidge, *Handlist*, 652). A ninth-century manuscript associated with Saint-Amand contains, along with Phocas's *Ars*, Remigius's commentary on Virgil's *Eclogues*: Valenciennes BM MS 394 (377) (Irvine, *Making of Textual Culture*, 403, no. 100).

42   Law identifies this school's innovative production of meta-commentaries on grammar texts following a lost Irish model: Law, *Grammar and Grammarians*, 144–6. See John Marenbon, *From the Circle of Alcuin to the School of Auxerre: Logic, Theology and Philosophy in the Early Middle Ages* (London, 1981), 120–2.

highlighted the importance of this school in the transmission of glosses to the *Consolation of Philosophy*.[43] As David Pratt notes, Grimbald and Remigius likely did not overlap during Remigius' tenure at Reims, but Hucbald of Saint-Bertin, another student of Remigius' teacher, Heiric of Auxerre, may have crossed paths with Grimbald in Saint-Bertin *c.*885.[44] Moreover, Auxerre's intellectual connections to Reims – Fulk's see, which dispatched Grimbald to Wessex – and to Laon have been reliably established for this period.[45]

As for the teacher credited with Alfred's own Latin education, Bishop Asser's access to the grammatical *artes* and *auctores* bespeaks grammatical training in parsing and hermeneutics in the Welsh tradition.[46] We know from Asser of St David's Latin compositions that he knew the central texts: Virgil's *Aeneid*, Sedulius' *Carmen Paschale* and Cassiodorus' *Expositio Psalmorum*.[47] The syntactically glossed copy of the *Regula pastoralis* from ninth-century Wales will occupy us presently. Asser's association of four Mercians with the Alfredian translation initiative invites more questions about the status of Mercian grammatical practice than can be answered with the present manuscript record.[48] Robert Gallagher and Francesca Tinti's study of Worcester charters reveals that documentary culture of Werferth's episcopacy, concurrent with the Alfredian revival, allowed for the alternation of

---

43   Love, 'Latin Commentaries', 96–8.
44   Pratt, *Political Thought*, 161–2.
45   Pratt, *Political Thought*, 235. See *L'École Carolingienne d'Auxerre de Murethach à Remi, 830–908*, ed. Dominique Iogna-Prat, Colette Jeudy and Guy Lobrichon (Paris, 1991).
46   Examples of Welsh grammar compilations from the mid-ninth century include Columbia, University of Missouri Library, Frag. Man. 2, which contains Priscian's *De nomine, pronomine, et verbo*, the least theoretical of Priscianic grammar materials, as well as the *Institutiones*, Bede's *De orthographia*, and another grammatical excerpt attributed to Jerome; it originated in Wales in the ninth century and moved to Winchester before the mid-tenth century: Gneuss and Lapidge, *Handlist*, 809.9. CCCC MS 153 contains another ninth-century Welsh copy of Martianus Capella's account of *grammatica* in Book II. This manuscript, too, made its way to England before or during the tenth century: Gneuss and Lapidge, *Handlist*, 48.
47   Michael Lapidge, 'Appendix E: Latin Books Cited by the Principal Anglo-Saxon Authors', in Lapidge, *The Anglo-Saxon Library* (Oxford, 2008), 174–274 (238–9).
48   Christine Rauer has made a strong case for further scholarly enquiry: 'Early Mercian Text Production', 551–4.

Latin and vernacular, speaking to relatively widespread Latin acquisition among scribes in Worcestershire.[49] Such Latin style might plausibly be associated with BL MS Royal 5.F.iii, a copy of Aldhelm's *Prosa de virginitate*, one of two manuscripts locatable to late ninth-century Worcester.[50] This manuscript bears scattered construe marks on folios 4v, 6r and 7v, witnessing the text's use in Latin instruction.[51] A complete account of Mercian grammar awaits a thorough catalogue of manuscripts connected to other ninth-century Mercian centres of learning such as Hereford, Lichfield, and Leicester.

So far, I have made the following claims: first, that the well-attested conviction that grammar formed individual moral judgement as a side effect of its main goods – Latin literacy and capacious hermeneutic skill – spanned local variants of grammatical practice; and second, that several people at Alfred's court practised *grammatica*, either the various Carolingian flavours or the more idiosyncratic versions found in Wales and (probably) Mercia and Worcestershire. I will now present evidence that the *Regula pastoralis* functioned as a text suitable for the formative work of Latin learning and hermeneutics.

London, British Library, MS Harley 5228, fol. 140: A Syntactically Glossed Fragment of the Regula pastoralis

The thesis that the Alfredian *Pastoral Care* took inspiration from Latin grammatical practice is supported by the evidence of a ninth-century Welsh copy of the *Regula pastoralis* glossed syntactically in an instructional context. BL MS Harley 5228, fol. 140 is a ninth-century fragment

---

49 Robert Gallagher and Francesca Tinti, 'Latin, Old English and Documentary Practice at Worcester from Wærferth to Oswald', *Anglo-Saxon England* 46 (2017), 271–325 (278–98). See also Ben Snook, 'When Aldhelm Met the Vikings: Advanced Latinity in Ninth-Century Mercian Charters', *Mediaevistik* 26 (2013), 111–48.

50 Gallagher and Tinti, 'Documentary Practice', 295; Scott Gwara, 'Introduction', in *Aldhelmi Malmesbiriensis Prosa de virginitate: cum Glosa Latina atque Anglosaxonica* (Turnhout, 2001), 102. Gwara discerned several late ninth-century scribes and attributed the gloss to a separate hand in the late tenth or early eleventh century. I consulted this manuscript in digital facsimile.

51 That they exhibit the same fading patterns as the main text suggests that they belong to the scribe or a near contemporary, rather than to the subsequent glossator who added Old English ink glosses to 2v and 3r.

of the *Regula pastoralis*, a flyleaf at the end of a twelfth-century medical miscellany written in Worcester.[52] Kathryn Lowe, following the major handlists, has attributed this back flyleaf – what I will call the Harley *RP* Fragment – to ninth-century Wales.[53] The Harley *RP* Fragment originated as the innermost *bifolium* of a quire; the bottom third of the first folio and a small portion of single columns on each side of the second folio remain.[54] The bifolium from which the fragment was excised recorded a continuous section of *Regula pastoralis* I.10–I.12.[55] A pre-twelfth-century binding process – indeed, its use in the Worcester miscellany likely perpetuated an earlier use of the fragment as binding material – damaged the front of the bifolium between lines 2 and 3 of fols 1r and 2v. The Harley *RP* Fragment contains lexical, syntactical and interpretive glosses, all of which predate this first use of the fragment as binding material.[56] The form and signifying function of these glosses reveal that the fragment represents a classbook localisable to the western part of the British Isles.[57] Table 1.1 abstracts the outlay of gloss content and function; the subsequent discussion will move from left to right across it:

---

52 See the digital facsimile of Harley 5228: <https://www.bl.uk/manuscripts/FullDisplay.aspx?ref=Harley_MS_5228> (accessed July 2023). A print facsimile is available in Lowe, 'Worcester and Wales', Plate 4.

53 Gneuss and Lapidge, *Handlist*, 439.6; Michael Lapidge, *The Anglo-Saxon Library* (Oxford, 2008), 306. Lowe observed Celtic abbreviations in the main text: 'Worcester and Wales', 27.

54 For this reason, I renumbered folios based on its original codicological environment and refer to fols 1r–v and 2r–v, columns a and b. Fols 2v (a small part of column b remains) and 1r, columns a and b equate to fol. 140r in its current numeration; Fols 1va–b and 2ra (similarly partial) comprise fol. 140v.

55 Gregory I, *Regula pastoralis*, ed. Bruno Judic, Floribert Rommel and Charles Morel, 2 vols, *Sources Chrétiennes* 382 (Paris, 1992), I.10–I.12. Hereafter, *RP*. Prior description has not noted that fol. 2vb witnesses a part of the twelfth chapter.

56 I adopt Gernot Wieland's categorisation of Latin glosses on slightly later instructional manuscripts: Gernot R. Wieland, *The Latin Glosses on Arator and Prudentius in Cambridge University Library, MS Gg.5.35* (Toronto, 1983).

57 'Classbook' is helpfully defined by Patrizia Lendinara, 'Instructional Manuscripts in England'.

Table 1.1   Outlay of the Harley *RP* gloss programme.

	Signifying Function			
Form	Lexical Glosses	Syntax Construal	Literal interpretation	Allegorical interpretation[58]
Symbolic Gloss (ink)		X	X	
Glosses with Lexemes (ink)	X		X	X

Michael Lapidge has cautioned against taking lexical glosses on manuscripts as evidence for classroom use, on the grounds that scribes often transmitted paratextual lexemes from common or standard glosses in standard copying practice.[59] In the Harley *RP* fragment, words optionally introduced by *.i.* (*id est*) supplied synonyms for unfamiliar words, such as *.i. putatur* ('is thought') above *creditur* ('is believed'), and *servi* ('slaves') beneath *subditis* ('subordinates').[60] *Ubi* adjacent to *quo* allayed the frustration of the beginning Latin student with one of the language's q- words.[61] With advanced imaging, more than these five lexical glosses may become discernible. Andreas Nievergelt's editions show that two ninth-century copies of the *Regula pastoralis* produced in Freising, and one produced in Tegernsee, have many shared Old High German and Latin *interpretamenta*, recorded with ink, pencil and drypoint stylus.[62] The consistencies suggest the gradual development of a standard gloss, rather than many discrete instances of classroom use.[63] None of these texts shows significant symbolic glossing, however, and none of the *interpretamenta* in the Harley *RP* Fragment matches those of

---

58   For this more developed practice of the Cambridge Juvencus glosses, see discussion in Chapter 5 of Wieland, *The Latin Glosses*.
59   Michael Lapidge, 'The Study of Latin Texts in Late Anglo-Saxon England [I] – The Evidence of Latin Glosses', in *Latin and the Vernacular Languages in Early Medieval Britain*, ed. Nicholas Brooks (Leicester, 1982), 99–127. See also Gernot R. Wieland, 'The Glossed Manuscript: Classbook or Library Book?', *Anglo-Saxon England* 14 (1985), 153–73.
60   Harley *RP* Fragment, fol.1ra, lines 11 and 19; *adhibemus* is glossed by *adiuvamus* at fol. 1vb line 2 and *adprehendit* by *videt* at 1vb, line 12.
61   Harley *RP* Fragment, fol. 1rb, line 8.
62   Andreas Nievergelt, *Althochdeutsche Glossen zur* Regula Pastoralis: *Clm 6277, Clm 18550a* (Berlin, 2024).
63   Ibid., 559–73.

the Freising and Tegernsee copies.[64] This contrast uniquely foregrounds the Welsh copy and allays concern about this programme's witnessing a standard gloss.

The Harley *RP* Fragment's syntax glosses construe the skeletal structure of each sentence, and even beyond this, reveal how discourse markers, the connective tissue of Latin prose, arranged smaller parts into larger thoughts. Moreover, symbolic and lexemic items aided in basic literal interpretation. Lexical items supplied words elided or even written earlier in the sentence to help construe meaning, such as where *bonum* ('good') is added above *hoc* ('this') to remind the reader that the deictic refers to *bono* in the line prior.[65] Similarly, *bonis operibus* glosses *ab his*.[66] Forms of *Deus* in oblique cases make explicit what the Latin implies: for example, the glossator explains *iram* ('wrath') with the gloss *dei* ('of God').[67] These glosses look like lexical glosses, but they clarify sense. In addition, at least twenty-three sets of symbolic construe marks consist of combinations of dots, strokes, commas and hooks connecting sentence elements. They appear in sets of two, three or four in keeping with their function of associating elements to help construe the meaning.[68] In the Harley *RP* Fragment, the first in a pair or set sits below the word it designates, and the other(s) above, creating a bracketing effect.

The symbolic gloss programme can be localised to historically Celtic-language speaking regional scriptoria by comparing its form and signifying content to other contemporary manuscripts. Table 1.2 presents a comparison between Harley's syntactical gloss symbols and those of seven other grammatical manuscripts, datable to between *c*.850 and *c*.950 and localisable within northwestern Europe.[69] The extensively

---

64 Ibid., 89–91, 537.
65 Harley *RP* Fragment, fol. 1va, line 7.
66 Ibid., fol. 1va, line 1.
67 Ibid., fol. 1ra, line 11.
68 Robinson, 'Syntactical Glosses', 443–75. See also Michael Korhammer, 'Mittelalterliche Konstruktionshilfen und Altenglische Worstellung', *Scriptorium* 34 (1980), 18–58.
69 Each of the manuscripts uses the technology of construe marks in similar ways; the dots and symbols are neither accretive nor sequential, but connective. See Robinson, 'Syntactical Glosses'. In choosing these manuscripts and identifying the symbols I rely on John F. Petruccione, 'Checklist of Manuscripts Containing Syntax Markers', *Constructionis Signa for Scholars*, <constructionissigna.com/manuscripts> (accessed 24 October 2024). Except for the Harley

glossed copy of Priscian's *Institutiones*, St Gall, Stifstbibliothek, MS 904 ('St Gall Priscian') written c.845, travelled from the western part of the British Isles to St Gall.[70] The symbolic construal programme in the *Ars Amatoria* preserved in 'Dunstan's Classbook', Oxford, Bodleian Library, MS Auct. F. 4.32 (IV), stems from ninth-century Wales, and the scribe himself added the syntax markers.[71] Another of the classbook's components, a copy of Eutyches's *Ars de verbo*, originated in a ninth-century continental context and was subsequently glossed in Old Breton.[72] Bern, Burgerbibliothek, MS C. 219 D is a late ninth or early tenth-century copy of the *Categoriae decem* from Wales or southwestern England.[73] Paris, Bibliothèque nationale de France, MS lat. 16700, fols 56r–96r, is a late ninth-century copy of Aldhelm's *Carmen de virginitate* from the continent,[74] while London, British Library, MS Royal 5.F.iii is a copy of the *Prosa de Virginitate* of ninth-century Worcester provenance.[75] Finally, St Gall, Stiftsbibliothek, MS 844, a glossed continental copy of Boethius's *Consolation*, represents the southeastern-most locale, but also one with a historical connection to Hiberno-Latin learning.[76]

RP Fragment, I examined the construal programmes in digital facsimile or in published editions.

70   Whether it was originally composed in Ireland or by an Irish traveller moving through southeastern Wales, it bears some 3,000 construe marks and glosses (Old Irish and Latin) in at least five different ninth-century hands: see Rijcklof Hofman, 'The Irish Tradition of Priscian', in *Manuscripts and Tradition of Grammatical Texts from Antiquity to the Renaissance*, ed. Mario de Nonno, Paolo de Paolis and Louis Holtz, 2 vols (Cassino, 2000), 1:257–87 (260–2).

71   Paul Russell, *Reading Ovid in Medieval Wales* (Columbus OH, 2017); Robinson, 'Syntactical Glosses', 468.

72   Gneuss and Lapidge, *Handlist*, 538.

73   Marenbon, *From the Circle of Alcuin to the School of Auxerre*, 178. This late antique paraphrase of Aristotle's *Categories* was popular in the Auxerre school as a site of metaphysical reflection. Marenbon showed the glossator on the Bern manuscript to be inclined less towards philosophy than his Carolingian contemporaries. The passage glossed for syntax concerns semiotics, and could have been regarded as grammatical.

74   Bischoff and Ebersperger, *Katalog*, no. 4984.

75   Gneuss and Lapidge, *Handlist*, 462.

76   Love notes that this likely transmitted some of the same glosses from an earlier manuscript: 'Latin Commentaries', 88.

Table 1.2 Relative similarity of construe markers in contemporary grammatical manuscripts.

Harley Fragment Construe Symbol		Bern, Burgerbibl., C.219 D, Wales or southwest England, s. ix–x; Themistius, Categoriae Decem	St Gall, Stifts. 904; Bangor or Nendrum? c.845; Priscian, Institutiones	Oxford, Bodleian, Auct. F 4.32 (IV; fols 37–47); Wales, s.ix; Ovid, Ars Amatoria	Oxford, Bodleian, Auct. F 4.32 (I; fols 1–9); Brittany, s.ix; Eutyches, Ars de Verbo	Paris, BNF, Latin 16700, fols 56r–96r; northwest France s. ix[2]; Aldhelm, Carmen de Virginitate	St Gall, Stifts. 844; St. Gall, s.ix; Boethius, De Consolatione Philosophiae	London, BL, Royal 5.F.iii; Worcester; s.ix; Aldhelm, Prosa de Virginitate
.	single dot	X		X				
..	double dot	X	X	X	X	X	X	X
∴	dot triangle		X			X		
.,	dot–comma	X	X	X	X		X	
,.	comma–dot							
,,	double comma		X					
,.,	dot–comma–dot							
·)	dot–hook	X		X		X		
)·	hook–dot						X	
·)·	dot–hook–dot							

.-	dot-stroke	X	X	X	X	X	X
..-	double-dot-stroke	X	X				
:	colon	X	X	X	X	X	X
.:-	colon-stroke[77]		X		X		X
|:	perpendicular-line-colon						
: —	colon over/under stroke		X	X			
.:							
÷	dot(s) over/under tilda		X				
a,b	alphabetical sequence[78]		X		X		
	Features shared with Harley	8	10	7	5	6	5	3
	Additional Symbols	1	≥ 979	2	2	1	1	1
	Jaccard Similarity[80]	42.1%	≤ 40.1%	35%	31.6%	31.6%	26%	15.8%

77 The Harley *RP* Fragment shows two instances of *positurae*, which, according to Parkes, indicated in insular contexts the end of a paragraph and that the thought would be continued: Malcolm B. Parkes, *Pause and Effect: An Introduction to the History of Punctuation in the West* (London, 1992), 305. Their classification here as construe marks as opposed to punctuation is plausible, if not certain.

78 Harley *RP* Fragment, fol. 1rB, lines 17–18, where *ergo* on 17 is marked with a *b* and *exprimitur* is marked with *a*.

79 Additional symbols: stroke over triple comma, semicolon, oblique-stroke–dot, dot over supine hook, double commas over stroke, hook, triple-dot–dash, double slanted lines, double-dot–comma, *et altera*.

80 Calculation, where α is the manuscript in each column: Jaccard Similarity (α) = (features shared by Harley and α) / (total unique construe marks found in either Harley or α).

Assessed in this wider context, the construe marks added to the *Regula pastoralis* in the syntax gloss are closest to those shared by grammar instruction in Celtic-language speaking regions. Despite the high percentage of similarity between the two, the great variety of additional symbols in the St Gall Priscian absent from the Harley's *RP* fragment suggests that the St Gall Priscian constituted an upper limit of grammatical sophistication in a mid-ninth-century milieu. The Welsh portion of Dunstan's classbook that arrived at Glastonbury in the mid-tenth century shows considerable similarity with the symbolic repertoire of the Harley *RP* Fragment, but the manuscript with the closest construal schema is the Bern *Categoriae Decem*. Even so, a few unique symbols in the Harley fragment took their inspiration from other construe marks and *distinctiones*: we see the requirements of classroom teaching spurring adaptation and innovation from the other signs on the page.[81]

Even if a grammatical tradition local to the western regions of the British Isles in the ninth century undergirds Harley's symbolic repertoire, the signifying values of symbols in each manuscript reflect the diverse preoccupations of grammarians. I present the Harley *RP* Fragment's syntactical designations below in tabular form (Table 1.3), alongside the three manuscripts with the closest symbolic schemata:

Table 1.3   Syntactical emphases in the Harley *RP* Fragment in context.

Symbolic Gloss Function in the Harley *RP* Fragment	Bern C 219 (D)	St Gall Priscian[82]	Dunstan's Classbook IV[83]
adjective/noun–noun agreement		X	X
preposition–object	X	X	
relative pronoun–antecedent	X	X	
relative pronoun–verb of relative clause	X	X	

81   For example, the perpendicular-line–colon, and the variations on the hook-dot and double-dot–comma, are not attested in these other manuscripts.

82   I relied on the digital edition of the St Gall Priscian's gloss programme: Rijcklof Hofman, Pádraic Moran and Bernhard Bauer, *St Gall Priscian Glosses*, version 2.1 (2023) <http://www.stgallpriscian.ie/> (accessed 24 October 2024).

83   Edition of the text and gloss published in Russell, *Reading Ovid in Medieval Wales*, 16–88 (121–2).

other subordinating conjunction–(direct object)–verb of subordinate clause	X	X		X
interrogative pronoun/adjective–(conjunction)–main verb	X	X		
main verb–connective conjunction			X	
main verb–subordinating conjunction			X	
sequence (denoted with letters or accumulating dots)			X	

The construal programme of Dunstan's Classbook (IV), which shares with the Harley *RP* Fragment a high number of symbolic markers, uses them most often to denote nominal agreement.[84] Every one of the symbolic functions attested in the Harley *RP* Fragment can be seen in the St Gall Priscian, but the latter notes a plethora of syntax features in addition that did not interest the Harley glossator. The similarity between the two speaks to local grammatical practice in Celtic-speaking regions in the ninth century, with sophistication and versatility that grammatical practitioners and teachers, such as Asser of St David's, could use to great effect. The final comparand, the Bern *Categoriae Decem*, shows a significant similitude. Both use triplex and quadruplex sets of symbols to mark the constituent parts of subordinate clauses and feature a strong inclination towards untangling hypotaxis over the acquisition of lexis. As with form, the signifying content of these construe marks demonstrates grammatical preoccupations perpetuated through local classroom practices in the western parts of the British Isles.

The Harley's *RP* Fragment's glosses are not ordered towards producing an authoritative reference copy, but towards syntax and sense (literal and moral) interpretation.[85] This can be demonstrated by examining a representative passage from the fragment. The Harley glossator added seven sets of construe marks indicating both syntactic and hermeneutic

---

84 Bodleian Auct. F 4.32 (IV), fols 37r–v. See also BNF lat. 16700's glosses on Aldhelm's *Carmen de virginitate*. Latin poetry relied less on hypotaxis and more on apposition than Latin prose.
85 Row 2, Cols 2–4 in Table 1.1 above.

connections to the following passage, which presents an unintuitive moral interpretation of cataracts from the dictates on clerical purity in Leviticus 21:

> Albuginem vero habet in oculo, qui veritatis lucem videre non sinitur · qui arrogantia sapientiae seu justitiae caecatur · Pupilla namque oculi nigra[86] videt ∴ albuginem tolerans nil videt, quia videlicet sensus humanae cogitationis si stultum se seu peccatorem intelligit, cognitionem intimae claritatis adprehendit ∵ Si autem candorem sibi justitiae seu sapientiae tribuit · a luce se supernae cognitionis excludit ∵ et ex eo claritatem veri luminis nequaquam penetrat quo se apud se per arrogantiam exaltat. (Harley *RP* Fragment, fol. 1vb, lines 7–16)

> Now, a white speck has he in his eye who is not permitted to see the light of truth because he is blinded by the arrogance of wisdom or righteousness. For the pupil of the eye, when black, sees, but when it bears a white speck, sees nothing, evidently because human intellection, if it understands him to be a fool and a sinner, apprehends the thinking of the inmost light. If, on the other hand, it attributes to him the clarity of righteousness or wisdom, it excludes him from the light of higher understanding; and from that state, that state in which he exalts himself in his own presence through arrogance, he never penetrates the clarity of the true light.[87]

In a hermeneutic (that is, interpretative) connection rather than a syntactic one, dot–hook–dots connect *albuginem* to *candorem* five lines down.[88] This associates the whiteness, here, meaning purity, of justice or wisdom ('candor iustitiae seu sapientiae') with *albugo*, the cloudy white covering the eye: the arrogant man attributes purity and clarity to himself, putting a white spot on his own eye metaphorically. The next three sets of symbols demarcate the subordinating conjunction, subject and predicate (including direct object) of subordinate clauses.[89] *Autem*

---

86 The sideways colon underneath a tilda distinguishes *nigra* in a way that was clearer to contemporary readers than to me; this may point to the marginal lexical gloss *.i. sana*, ('healthy').
87 Harley *RP* Fragment, fol. 1rb, lines 3–17.
88 Ibid., fol. 1vb, lines 7 and 12.
89 Two colons join *qui* to *cecatur*; *quia* and *adprehendit* are joined by division signs above the first and below the second; single dots join the subordinating conjunction *si*, the verb with implied subject *intellegit*, and the direct object, *se*. Ibid., fol. 1vb, lines 3 and 6, 8 and 12, 9 and 10.

and *stultum* lack matched symbols; these signal that two alternative conditions followed the repeated *si*.[90] Single dots mark *si* and *tribuit*, delimiting the essential parts of the subordinate if-clause of the sentence by its conjunction, subject (implied), and verb.[91] Finally dot–comma–dots distinguish the pair *eo* and *quo*, evincing the glossator's command of syntax.[92]

Construe symbols associated concepts to aid in interpretation. So too does the scribe employ verbal glosses towards hermeneutic ends. Occasionally, they add moral analogy, such as where '.i. dei' glosses *iudicis*, making a metaphorical jump between the judge in the Gregorian exemplum and the divine judge.[93] *Incurvatus* ('curved inwards') '.i. ad peccatum' ('that is, toward sin') draws out the (Augustinian) metaphor with explicitly moral language.[94] Above 'si autem candorem sibi iustitiae seu sapientae tribuit', the gloss, 'id est, per arrogantiam' ('that is, through arrogance') anticipates the more explicit moral meaning given later in the passage: 'quo se apud se per arrogantiam exaltat'.[95] *Dei* glosses *solis* as well, interpreting it as the genitive of *sol* and drawing out a metaphorical connection between the sun and divine light.[96] The glossator's interpretive marks complement and highlight the hermeneutic work that Gregory does in the *Regula pastoralis* itself, instructing in the practice of reading and interpretation.[97]

---

90   Ibid., fol. 1vb, lines 9 and 12.
91   Ibid., fol. 1vb, lines 12 and 13.
92   Ibid., fol. 1vb, lines 15 and 16. The deictic *id* refers generally to the condition described at the beginning, the state of being unable to see because of arrogance, rather than to a specific neuter noun. *Quo* agrees with *eo*: 'and from that state […] that state in which he exalts himself'.
93   Ibid., fol. 1ra, line 17.
94   Ibid., fol. 1va, line 13. Cf. Lowe, 'Worcester and Wales', 27, n.43, who reads this gloss as *adreccatum*, from *arigo*, while expressing some uncertainty.
95   Harley *RP* Fragment, fol. 1vb, lines 16–17.
96   Ibid., fol. 1va, line 4: 'Gibbus vero est quem terrenae solitudinis pondus deprimit, ne unquam ad superna respiciat, sed solis his quae in infimis calcantur intendat' ('The hunchbacked man is he whom the weight of earthly care bows down, such that he cannot look towards higher things, but extends towards only those things which are trodden upon in the depths'). The glossator may have taken *solis* with the clause preceding *sed*, creating 'such that he cannot look toward the higher things of the sun (i.e., of God)'. Alternatively, the gloss I have read as .i. dei might be .i. dam, adding little more sense than the *dei* reading.
97   Other more extensive glosses on the two columns subjected to significant

The system of symbolic construe marks employed in the Harley *RP* Fragment sufficed for the close-reading work of the Latin classroom. Symbols layered on a single word showed different kinds of connectivity and agreement, at any level from nominal agreement to the structural concord between sentences that discourse markers provided. So too, they foregrounded the hermeneutic potential of the Latin text by connecting text and supporting quotation. The glossator refrained from marking adjacent parallel sentence structures.[98] He favoured simple syntax symbols, the single dot and the double dot. He designated similar elements inconsistently or used the same symbols for syntactical glossing as for interpretive glosses, those that helped the reader see the Gregorian exegesis at play.[99] The tendencies towards simplicity and economy evince limited concern for the perfect production of a record in a dynamic classroom setting. The practice of grammar in service of proliferating interpretation apparently superseded the desire to preserve an authoritative reference text.[100] Overall, the gloss reveals the priorities of its readership; namely, the careful disentangling of complex syntax and the pursuit of capacious meaning within those sentences. It shows that a Welsh grammar teacher, whose monastic institution had some connection to Worcester, knew the *Regula pastoralis* in part as a Latin textbook. Lexis and syntax glosses on northern French *Regula pastoralis* manuscripts from the ninth century suggest that Grimbald of St Bertin recognised a similar usage.[101] John (for whose identity we have only

---

cropping (Harley *RP* Fragment, fols 2ra and 2vb) may show similar interpretive patterns, but the fragment's present state precludes discernment.

98   For example, since the relative clause 'qui [...] nescit' was marked, he omits to mark 'qui [...] ignorat', preferring to note the indirect question 'utrum [...] sit placatus' embedded within it: Harley *RP* Fragment, fol. 1ra, lines 6–9.

99   For example, the postpositive *veros* working in parallel as discourse markers on three adjacent folios are marked with a dot triangle, a colon and nothing at all.

100 Cf. Lowe, 'Worcester and Wales', 16. Lowe, following Richard Clement's theory of two recensions of the *Regula pastoralis*, the earlier of which was favoured in pre-conquest England, suggests that the current dearth of insular *RP* copies stems from such a corrective instinct: first recension copies were destroyed in favour of the 'corrected' versions.

101 Troyes, MS 247 fols 154–241; Laon, Bibliothèque Municipale, MS 187: Bischoff and Ebersperger, *Katalog*, nos 6248 and 2088. Sankt Florian, Chorherrenstiftsbibliothek, MS BAC III.222.B, fols 2–123, originated in early ninth-century Saint-Amand; though glossed in the late ninth century, whether it was appended to Alcuin's treatise on *grammatica* and a glossary before or after

reported association with the Old Saxon language region) may have learned his Latin with this book as well, judging from preliminary assays of *Regula pastoralis* manuscripts from this region.[102] The Gregory who scorned metacism and barbarism, 'lest the [scriptures] be subject to the rules of Donatus', would have found it ironic for his *Regula pastoralis* to have been used centuries later as an instructional text in *grammatica*.[103] But so it seems that it was, in at least one, and probably more, local contexts that would shape the Alfredian educational initiative.

The Reflex of Grammatica in the Pastoral Care

In the last quarter of the ninth century, multiple contributors rendered the *Regula pastoralis* into Old English.[104] Philological evidence from within the Old English *Pastoral Care* and its 'Preface' strengthens a characterisation of the *Pastoral Care* translation team as *grammatici* both familiar with grammatical practice and aware of the *Regula pastoralis* as a text of Latin education.

In the course of the translation, these men faced choices about the best way to render the Latin text; since 'modal' verbs are more common in Old English than Latin, and since their semantic fields in each language were not coextensive, programmatic verb choices offer insight into the attitudes of the translators.[105] Where 'can' in present-day English encompasses in academic and colloquial use 'may', 'am able to' and 'know how to', a different Old English verb, respectively, *motan*, *magan*

---

its move from Saint-Amand to Salzburg will determine the extent to which it can be connected to Grimbald: Bischoff and Ebersperger, *Katalog*, no. 5466.
102 Halberstadt, Domschatz, MS 468 (*olim* 59), fol. 265; Berlin, Theo. lat. fol. 362: Bischoff and Ebersperger, *Katalog*, nos 5466 and 461.
103 Gregory's preface to the *Moralia* objects to classical Latinity and the rules of grammarians concerning *metaplasm*: 'ut uerba caelestis oraculi restringam sub regulis Donati'. Gregory I, *Moralia in Job*, ed. Marc Adriaen (Turnhout, 1979), 5, lines 217–22.
104 Anlezark, 'The Old English Pastoral Care', argues that the text was written by multiple persons, probably not including Alfred himself, or at least not in the way that either the verse or prose prefaces describe; he proposes that authorship changed around the Old English chapter 53, and between chapters 35 and 37.
105 On the terminology of 'modal auxiliaries', see Bruce Mitchell, *Old English Syntax* (Oxford, 1985), 990.

and *cunnan*, conveyed each of these ideas.[106] Their usage in the *Pastoral Care* and its 'Preface', a document without a Latin corollary, shows the influence of grammatical practices and assumptions on the Alfredian translation programme.

Cunnan and *magan* in the Old English *Pastoral Care* possess stable parallels in the Latin source – *scire* and *posse* or *valere*, respectively[107] – that speak to a semantic distinction in the minds of translators between ways of being in relation to a verbal idea, respectively, 'knowing how to' and 'being able to'.[108] Yet their appearances in the Old English *Pastoral Care* far outnumber instances of these Latin corollaries.[109] Such additions reflect translation decisions that categorised the relationship between subject and verbal idea (the infinitive complement) as pertaining either to acquired skill or to a general sense of ability.[110] Interference from the historical grammatical practice explains many additions of *magan* and *cunnan* in the Old English *Pastoral Care*. Additions of *magan* mimic the exegetical positionality of Auxerre grammarians, while additions of *cunnan* in the *Pastoral Care* function as a verbal calque on *ars*. Such claims, based on such common words and philological evidence from a translation whose Latin exemplar remains elusive, stand on plausibility rather than proof.[111] Other changes to the text, especially in *Pastoral*

---

106 Mitchell, 1011–18. See *DOE*, s.v. 'cunnan'. The semantic boundaries between *cunnan*, *magan* and *motan* in various Old English dialects remained in flux over the course of the Old English period.

107 *PC*. *Magan*, when it directly translates a modal verb (25 per cent of the some-350 instances) renders the Latin modals *posse* and *valere*, or *nequire* in the negative. *Cunnan* tends to render *scire* and *noscere*.

108 A few *loci* include a doubled translation, using both *cunnan* and *magan* in apposition or conjunction, sharing a verbal complement.

109 In two-thirds of instances in which *cunnan* functions as modal, no comparable Latin modal appears in the source text. In these, *cunnan* translates indicative finite verbs or the occasional infinitive. Out of the 200 additions of *magan* not spurred by a comparable verbal construction, 40 per cent render a Latin purpose clause, clause of fearing, or other dependent clauses with a subjunctive verb.

110 This reading assumes that additions in a translation do not result only from differing syntactic affordances of each language, but can reflect some third factor, a pressure authorial or discursive, on the translation.

111 Schreiber has called into question Clement's strict demarcation between a continental recension and an insular one, suggesting that some of the *PC*'s variants could well be explained by Frankish copies: Carolin Schreiber, 'The

Care, 48 heighten the likelihood that additions around themes of literacy and interpretation speak to the influence of grammarians.

The interpreters of the Auxerre school, which had connections to northeastern Francia, rather liked the Latin auxiliary verb *posse*. Heiric of Auxerre, one of Remigius's teachers, utilised the phrase *possumus intellegere* ('we can understand') for his exegetical practice: this phrase alone appears twenty-eight times in his commentary on the minor prophets.[112] So too, the phrase frequently characterises the grammatical work of Heiric's forerunners at Auxerre, the exegete Haimo and the Hiberno-Latin grammarian Murethach.[113] The Old English *Pastoral Care* translators preferred this same first-person positionality and modal verb of ability when they linked scriptural passages to interpretation. Thirteen times in the text, *we magon* ('we are able to') in concert with a perception verb follows a passage of scripture to render impersonal interpretative phrases: '[Scripture passage] By these words, we can understand [Gregorian interpretation].' 'Notandum valde est' [*RP* III.2, line 25] ('it must surely be known') inspired the first-person plural 'be ðæm we magon suiðe swutule oncnawan' [*PC* 26.181, line 16] ('by these words we can clearly understand').[114] Similar periphrastic forms indicating necessity at four other junctures became *we magon* plus a perception verb.[115] Sometimes, a passive voice verb invited the shift into

---

Latin Text Underlying King Alfred's Translation', in *King Alfred's Old English Translation*, 26–35.

112 Heiric's homilies exhibit a similar pattern in exegetical moments, of which I count nine instances, such as this one: 'Allegorice per hos septem fratres possumus intellegere omnes reprobos' ('Allegorically, through these seven brothers, we can understand all of the reprobate'): Heiric d'Auxerre, *Homiliae per Circulum Anni*, ed. R Quadri. CCCM 116, 116A, 116B (Turnhout, 1992), 39, line 34. Heiric d'Auxerre, *Commentarii in Prophetas Minores e Schola Autissiodorensi*, ed. Roger Gryson. CCCM 135G (Turnhout, 2020).

113 Haymon d'Auxerre, *Adnotatio libri Hiezechielis imperfecta*, ed. Roger Gryson. CCCM 135E (Turnhout, 2015), 37.371, line 189: 'Vel "pactum sempiternum" possumus intellegere euangelium, cui alia non succedet iam lex, sicuti legi Moysi successit euangelium, quod habent sancti in perpetuum', and twenty-two other instances. Alternative infinitives like *referre* or *dicere* are similarly common for Haimo and the whole school, including Murethach. See also Haymon d'Auxerre, *Haymonis Autissiodorensis 'Commentarii in Prophetas Minores e Schola Autissiodorensi'*, ed. Roger Gryson. CCCM 135:VIII (Turnhout, 2021).

114 Schreiber, 273.

115 *PC* 26.181, line 18: '& eac we magon oncnawan ðæt', Schreiber, 273. ('And we

first-person plural, as where 'Be ðæm we magon ongietan' [*PC* 45.343, line 12] ('by this we can see') translated *ostenditur* [*RP* III.21, line 92].[116] At other loci, the translator added a first-person plural syntactic frame which subordinated the rest of the translated sentence. For example, 'Hwæt we *magon geðencean* gif' [*PC* 49.377, line 17] ('We can consider that') retains the Latin in a subordinate clause.[117] At these locations the Old English translators amplified the grammatical features of the Latin *Regula pastoralis* – its allegorical interpretations – and more closely aligned the translation with continental hermeneutic practice.

When adding modal verbs, the translators preferred *cunnan* ('know how to') to *magan* ('be able to') in contexts concerning reading and interpretation. Of the thirty-four instances where *cunnan* functions as a modal in the *Pastoral Care*, a Latin modal anticipates only a third.[118] Of the other two-thirds, where the author adds a modal *cunnan*, 80 per cent take verbs of perception, understanding, discernment, or teaching. The translation persists in shading *tocnawan* ('to discern') and *gesceadan* ('to distinguish') with *cunnan*, rather than *magan*.[119] Other

---

can also understand that'). Cf. *RP* III.2, line 25, 'quia impendenda est' ('because there must be a devoting to'); *PC* 43.315, line 15, 'Be ðæm we magon geðencean hu' ('by these words we can understand how') renders *RP* III.19, line 86, 'qua in re pensandum est' ('in which thing it must be considered'). Similarly, at *PC* 44.329, line 9 'Be ðæm we magon geðencean hu micles wites' ('about this, we can consider how') renders *RP* III.20, line 110 'hinc ergo colligendum est', ('hence, it should be inferred that'). At *PC* 46.349, line 14 'Of ðissum bebode we magon geðencean' ('Concerning this command we can consider') renders 'ex qua scilicet pensandum est' ('from which, clearly, this must be thought') of *RP* III.22, line 50.

116 Similarly, at *PC* 49.385, line 32, 'Ðæt we magon sweotolor ongietan' ('We can clearly see that') Schreiber, 339, translates *RP* III.25, line 14 'quod citius ostenditur' ('which is clearly shown'). Likewise, at *PC* 50.387, line 31, 'Be ðæm wordum we mægon gehieran ðæt' ('By which words we can hear that') renders *RP* III.26, lines 25–7 'quibus verbis perpenditur, quod' ('by which words it is assessed that'). See Schreiber, 343.

117 *RP* III.25, line 14, 'si [...] medicinalis [...] cerneret'. Cf. *PC* 49.377, line 7, 'hwelc god læce bið ðe wel cann wunda sniðan' ('if a good doctor who knows how to cut a wound'). Similarly, the translator adds 'be ðissum magon ongietan' as a framing clause for what otherwise translates the Latin closely. *PC* 49.377, line 9: 'ða lareowas hwelces wites hi wyrðe bioð ðonne hie lætað ða sawla acwellan for hungre hira worda & hie nyllað hie fedan mid ðæm hlafe ðære giefe ðe hie onfengon.' Cf. *RP* III.25, line 428.

118 As noted above, the Latin source has *(ne)scire* or *noscere*.

119 As at *PC* 13.77 line 22; 20.149, line 16; and 28.195, line 5.

established practices and professions, to the extent that they appear in the *Pastoral Care*, also feature *cunnan* additions.[120] In many instances, *cunnan* functions as a verbal auxiliary calque on *ars*, and when paired with verbs of perception, understanding and discernment, effectively translates the hidden assumptions and presuppositions about reading and interpreting that the *ars grammatica* commanded. For example, in the first chapter, *cunnan genawan* ('know how to comprehend') and *cunnon ongitan* [*PC* 1.25, line 19] ('know how to understand') appear as a double gloss on *praecepta cognoverunt* [*RP* I.1, line 6] ('understand the precepts').[121] In a passage advising that the *reccere* ('teacher') exercise moral discernment, *cunne wel toscadan* [*PC* 20.149, lines 16–17] ('that he know how discern') heightens the sense of expertise implicit in discernment: the *RP*'s *discernat* [*RP* II.9, line 10] appears not as *tosceade*, but with modal colour implying skill or craft.[122]

In *PC* 48 translators added five iterations of *cunnan* to the verb *ongietan*, each time rendering the finite verb *intellegunt*.[123] Instead of a finite version of *ongietan*, which could and often did mean 'understand' on its own, we have *cunnan ongietan*, involving an apparent duplication or redundancy.[124] The chapter's titular categories, those who *(non) recte intellegunt* ('do (not) correctly understand') transformed in Old English into those who 'do (not) know the art of interpreting the holy law' or 'are (not) practitioners of the art of interpretation'.

---

120 Such as where the teacher's work is compared to that of a doctor, and the modal used for the doctor's art is *cunnan*.
121 *PC* 1.25, line 19: '& ðeah ða woroldlecan læcas scomaþ ðæt hi onginnen ða wunda lacnian ðe hi gesion ne magon, & huru gif hi nouðer gecnawan ne cunnan ne ða medtrymnesse ne eac ða wyrta ðe ðærwið sculon. & hwilon ne scomað ða ðe ðæs modes læceas beon scoldon, ðeah ðe hi nana wuht ongitan ne cunnon ðara gæstlecena beboda, ðæt hie him onteoð ðæt hie sien heortan læcas.' (*RP* 'et tamen saepe qui [...] praecepta cognoverunt, cordis'.)
122 *PC* 20.149, lines 16–17: 'Forðæm is micel niedðearf ðæt se reccere ða ðeawas & ða unðeawas cunne wel toscadan, ðylæs se hneawa & se gitsigenda fægnige ðæs ðætte menn wenen ðæt he sie gehealdsum on ðæm ðe he healdan scyle oððe dælan.' Schreiber, 239.
123 In the *titulus* and first lines of *PC* 48, the same modal–auxiliary phrase *cunnan ongietan* persistently renders the finite verb *intellegunt*. See *RP* III.21, lines 1–3; *PC* 48.365.5–6.
124 See Benjamin A. Saltzman, 'The Mind, Perception and the Reflexivity of Forgetting in Alfred's *Pastoral Care*', *Anglo-Saxon England* 42 (2013), 147–82 (157 n.35).

With this persistence two other major changes co-occur in the translation. This chapter, *RP* III.23, characterises two modes of encounter with the scriptural *auctores*. As most of the other chapters in this third book of the *RP* do, it pairs together 'opposite' things, where both require remedy or advice: the Latin chapter extends a binary between poor reading as prideful and arrogant heresy, and good reading problematised by pride, a failure to apply the text toward one's own life.[125] As R. D. Fulk observes, the titulus and first sentence misconstrue the second category of persons in Gregory's Latin.[126] The *RP*'s second category of poor readers, the skilled but proud, presented a problem to a framework in which there remained a question of whether the disciplines of literacy could help but produce humility in their practitioners. When the translators encountered the *titulus* that opposed the grammatically unlearned with the grammatically skilled but proud, they solved the resulting cognitive dissonance by changing the title altogether, replacing the learned but proud interpreter – a questionable category if *grammatica* supposedly created humility – with the learned interpreter problematic in his failure to profess his interpretation.[127] Reading on, they engaged again with the figure of the proud interpreter, and, there, they did not offer significant changes to that picture. The heading, however, stands as witness to the earnest and optimistic instincts of the *grammatici* involved in translation.

Persistent changes to Gregorian exegesis of a passage from Amos further support a grammatical picture of the morally formed reader and the vitality of interpretative work. In Gregory's moral reading of 'secuerunt praegnantes Galaad ad dilatandum terminum suum' (*RP* III.24, lines 22–3: 'they ripped open the pregnant women of Gilead

---

125 *RP* III.21, lines 1–3: 'quod aliter ammonendi sunt qui sacrae legis verba non recte intellegunt atque aliter qui recte quidem intellegunt sed haec humiliter non loquuntur' ('that those who do not properly understand the sacred law should be guided in one fashion, and in another those who correctly understand, but do not speak humbly').
126 R. D. Fulk, 'Notes to the Translation', in *The Old English Pastoral Care* (Cambridge MA, 2021), 555–79 (573).
127 'On oðre wisan sint to manigenne ða ðe ða halgan æ *ryhtlice ongietan ne cunnon*; on oðre ða ðe hie *ryhtlice ongietan cunnon*, & ðeah for eaðmodnesse swigiað ðæt hie hie ne bodiað' [*PC* 48.365.5–6, my italics] ('In one manner those who *do not know how* to understand the holy laws correctly should be advised; in another those who, although *they know how* to interpret them correctly, out of humility remain silent, not professing it').

and desired thereby to extend their borders'), heresy stands at the forefront of the stylistically compressed exegesis. Gregory typologically equated the violence to which gravid bodies were subjected with the violence that heretical thinkers enacted.[128] In the Old English *Pastoral Care*, translators pressed into the typological equivalency between reader and pregnant woman and between her child and the interpretation, thereby shifting the focus. The Old English version develops the metaphor between the reader of scripture and the gravid soul, with the interpretation of text existing in growth and fragility within her.[129] It figures the practice of reading as capacious, growing, and subject to time and process within a person's lifetime; the translator furnished understanding with a life of its own, comparing it metaphorically to an unborn child (*unborenan bearn*).[130] The typological reading of the violent

---

128 *RP* III.24, lines 28–34: 'Praegnantes autem vocantur animae, quae intellectum verbi ex divino amore concipiunt, si ad perfectum tempus veniant, conceptam intelligentiam operis ostensione pariturae [...] *Secuerunt ergo praegnantes Galaad ad dilatandum terminum suum*, quia nimirum haeretici mentes fidelium quae jam aliquid de veritatis intellectu conceperant perversa praedicatione perimunt, et scientiae sibi nomen extendunt. Parvulorum corda jam de verbi conceptione gravida, erroris gladio scindunt, et, quasi doctrinae sibi opinionem faciunt' ('The souls who desire out of divine love to understand a word are called pregnant if they come to full term, about to birth in patent deeds the understanding conceived [...] *They cut open the pregnant ones of Gilead to enlarge their limit*, because heretics destroy through perverse preaching the minds of too many faithful – which had just conceived something of the understanding of truth – and extend the name of knowledge to themselves. They tear open with sword of error the hearts of little ones pregnant with the conception of the word and make for themselves an opinion as if it were one of doctrine').
129 *PC* 48.367, lines 9–12; Schreiber, 315: 'Ðonne getacniað ða geeacniendan wif ða saule ðe ða gebodu angietað, & hie mid godcundlicre lufan underfoð: gif ðæt underfangne andgit to ryhtre tide bið forðbroht, ðonne bið hit mid ðy ðurhtogenan weorce gedon, swelce hit sie geboren' ('Then the pregnant women signify the souls who recognise the commands, and they bear them with divine love: if that beginning understanding is brought forth at the right time, then will it be completed through righteous works, as if it were born').
130 *PC* 48.367, lines 14–22; Schreiber, 315: 'Ac ðonne mon snið ða bearneacnan wif on Galað hira mearce mid to rymanne, ðonne ða gedwolmenn mid wore lare ofslead ðæt mod geleaffullra monna, ðonne ðonne hit furðum ryht andgiet underfangen hæfð, & him hwæthwugu sio soðfæsðnes on geeacnod bið, ær ðæm ðe hit fullboren sie, & willað mid ðy gedon ðæt hie mon hlige wisdomes, mid ðy ðe hie ofsniðen mid ðy seaxe hefiglices gedwolan ða unborenan bearn, ðe ðonne furðum beoð mid wordum geeacnode on geleaffullra mode' ('But one rips open

offenders, called *gedwolmen*, also shifts in translation. Heretics, a clear category in sixth century Christianity, undergirded the Latin text. While in the prose of Ælfric of Eynsham less than a century later, *gedwolmenn* referred to theological heretics, in Alfredian prose *gedwolmaen* encompassed even poor reading.[131] The passage's description of these figures' murdering fragile understanding with 'wrong teaching' and 'violent error' reflects a grammarian's earnest convictions about the guardianship of texts by way of grammatically correct reading and its attendant moral formation. Amid the imagery of gestation and maternity for the reading mind, which presupposes the vitality of textual interpretation, excessive anxiety about singular 'orthodox' reading sits uncomfortably. Alongside church doctrine and the authority of tradition stood the Lady Grammatica, guarding the meaning and interpretation of texts. Boniface's acrostic poem captured the play between these two guardians, where grammar and tradition worked together as boundaries around the *artem interpretationis*: the reader tested everything against and within the walls of common belief.[132] Conversely, interpretive as much as doctrinal error threatened, imperilled even, the assembled church.[133]

Even an attenuated reception of the Anglo-Latin grammatical tradition inflected the *Hierdeboc*: its translators adopted the rhetorical positionality of continental grammarians, preferred *cunnan* in metadiscussions of interpretation, and intensified the Latin source's image of the vitality of interpretation. So too, the author of the 'Preface' employed modals on his favourite theme of language education, differentiating between *cunnan* ('to know how to') and *magan* ('to be able to'). *Cunnan*

---

the pregnant women of Gilead when men-in-error with wrong teaching slay the mind of believers when it has just received right understanding and the truth has been only somewhat conceived in it, before it might be fully developed; and they desire with that deed that wisdom be attributed to them when they murder with the knife of violent error the unborn children, who were then just conceived with words in the mind of believers').

131 *DOE, s.v.* 'gedwolmann' (accessed October 2023).

132 Boniface, *Praefatio ad Sigibertum*, lines 102–6: '*omnia probate: quod bonum est, tenete*, ad tutissimum catholicae fidei circulum sensus tui litteris occurentibus dirigas et extra moenia huius circuli mentis inconstantia vagare non praesumas, ne forte vulnerantes te tulerint pallium tuum custodes murorum' ('"Try all things and hold fast to what is good": As you read, direct your mind to the secure circle of the Catholic faith and do not presume to let your mind stray outside the fortifications of this circle lest the guardians of the walls take away your robe and wound you': trans. Law, *Grammar and Grammarians*, 175).

133 See Thornbury, 'Boniface', 116.

governs translation, reading, and the metaphorical pursuit of the paths of wise forebears: 'So entirely had learning declined [...] that very few [...] *knew how to* understand their services in English [...] or *knew how to* translate a letter from Latin to English'; 'the path of [sages of old] *can* be seen, but we *do not know* how to follow them'; 'many *knew how to* read English writing' (my italics).[134] In the two famous sentences that describe the translation initiative and 'Alfred's' methods therein, the vernacular constitutes the language 'we are *capable of* recognising' (my italics) and the translation initiative that which 'we will *be able to* accomplish' (my italics), both with *magan*.[135] The youths eligible will be set to learning 'as long as they *cannot be* otherwise useful, until they *know how to* read English writing' (my italics), with *magan* and *cunnan*, respectively.[136] Of the alternative modes of capacity with which one could shade Old English verbs, in this author's idiom, *cunnan* governed literacy. The practices that preoccupied the 'Preface' author – reading, interpreting, translating and (metaphorically) following the paths of the *wiotan* – he shaded with the 'know-how' modal. In so doing, he evoked contemporary visions of *grammatica* as the liberal art that governed Latin literacy and interpretation and signalled the Alfredian investment in it.

* * *

Within the grammatical tradition, *cunnan arædan*, knowing how to read – or, as I translate it, knowing the art of interpretation – went much deeper than intelligibility of the literal meanings of language.[137] Situating the Alfredian translation programme within the early

---

134 *PC*: 'Swæ clæne hio wæs oðfeallenu [...] ðæt swiðe feawa wæron [...] ðe hiora ðeninga cuðen understondan on Englisc, oððe furðum an ærendgewrit of Lædene on Englisc areccean' (3); 'Her mon mæg giet gesion hiora swæð, ac we him ne cunnon æfterspyrigean' (5); 'ðeah monige cuðon Englisc gewrit arædan' (7). The 'Preface' author's reference to 'wiotan' (referent of the demonstrative *hiora* in the quotation), which some have interpreted as a reference to the Canterbury school, strikes me as a recollection of the subsequent generations of grammarians, Aldhelm, Tatwine, Boniface and Alcuin.
135 *PC* 7: 'on ðæt geðiode [...] ðe we ealle gecnawan mægen'; 'gedon swæ we swiðe eaðe magon mid Godes fultume'. Schreiber, 192.
136 *PC* 7: 'eall sio giogud [...] sien to liornunga oðfæste, ða hwile ðe hie to nanre oðerre note ne mægen, oð ðone first ðe hie wel cunnen Englisc gewrit arædan.' ('The youths [...] are to be set to learning while they are able to be of no other use, until they know how to read English writing.') Schreiber, 192.
137 *PC*, Pr.Pref 7, line 13.

medieval grammatical tradition illuminates the modal verb choices in the 'Preface' of the *Pastoral Care* to shade reading, understanding, and learning from the *wiotan* of old with *cunnan*; beyond that, it specifies as the goal of the Alfredian revival the conveyance of hermeneutic or interpretative judgement, conceived of as moral potency. The glossed Harley *RP* Fragment provides the concrete evidence for this contextualisation. Moreover, the Old English *Pastoral Care* as a translation amplified grammatical priorities present in the Latin *Regula pastoralis*, and aligned the Latin text's vision of language and hermeneutics more intimately with the goals and modalities of grammar education. The *Pastoral Care* habituated the reader of Old English to encountering the canonical texts, ultimately the *auctores* of scripture in which the *Regula pastoralis* was rich, and to reading them with attention to the text's rich depths. At a social level, the perpetuation of grammatical practice involved, purportedly, the extension of moral categories; grammarians taught ethics to individuals and generations. At stake in the continuation of grammatical practice among the English episcopacy of the late ninth century lay not only a set of intellectual skills, but the moral wisdom that would shape ecclesiastical and political life.[138] Assuredly, the Old English *Pastoral Care* is pastoral, but it inscribed the pastor's role as that of an early medieval grammarian. The *lareow*, insofar as he taught language and hermeneutics, taught ethics, specifically the moral wisdom of prudence and humility, the virtues that made men *wiotan*. The *Hierdeboc*'s pastoral care resides, then, in the pastoral practice of teaching the language arts; the choice to render it into English and distribute it to the English episcopacy represents Alfred's and the Wessex monarchy's endorsement of Lady Grammatica's formative work.

138 This conclusion supports Discenza's observations of the semantic slippage between virtue and skill in the Alfredian usage of *cræft*: Nicole Guenther Discenza, 'Power, Skill and Virtue in the Old English Boethius', *Anglo-Saxon England* 26 (1997), 81–108.

2

Wicked Wolves, Culpable Sheep: Animal Lessons in Medieval British Fables

Linnet Heald

The lessons imparted by animal fables, it is usually supposed, pertain to human society, above all else – the diverse range of creatures depicted is there to entertain and to edify, and they are not the true subject. Jacques Derrida, notably, deemed fables 'a discourse of man, on man, indeed on the animality of man, but for and in man'.[1] Susan Crane has claimed, along the same lines, 'From an animal studies perspective, the trouble with fable is above all that the form invites little thought on creatures other than human [...] In the fables' move from narrative to apologue, the beasts of narrative are useful in that they illuminate human ways, but they are of no interest beyond that usefulness'.[2] It is easy to argue that fables, despite all the animal characters, don't say much *about* animals. Not only do fables unapologetically anthropomorphise, particularly in portraying animals who talk, but fable authors and literary critics alike, from antiquity to the present, have maintained that imparting a figurative interpretation of the animal actors for human instruction is the deeper purpose of fables.

Nonetheless, fables propagate messages about the other denizens of the more-than-human world that we inhabit, as well as about ourselves; they have more to say about animals than the fact that we may anthropomorphise them and use them as metaphors,[3] and are a rich

---

[1] Jacques Derrida, *The Animal that therefore I Am*, ed. Marie-Louise Mallet, trans. David Wills (New York, 2008), 37.
[2] Susan Crane, *Animal Encounters: Contacts and Concepts in Medieval Britain* (Philadelphia PA, 2012), 43.
[3] B. E. Perry argues that 'fables are essentially metaphors': 'Fable', in *Proverbia in Fabula: Essays on the Relationship of the Proverb and the Fable*, ed. Pack Carnes (Bern, 1988 [first publ. in *Studium Generale*, 12 (1959), 17–37]), 65–116 (109 n. 28). Psychologists Paul E. Jose, Catherine A. D'Anna and Dana Balsink

yet overlooked source for understanding human perceptions of other species and our relationships with them. My starting premise is that fable animals can be read *as* animals, not just as symbols or human stand-ins; there is a persistent animality in even anthropomorphic and metaphoric animals. The animality of fable animals becomes most apparent when they share narratives with human characters. Fable animals may be ascribed speech, but this doesn't fundamentally change the status quo of violence in interspecies relationships; it is humans' violent domination of animals, above all, that is 'central to distinguishing humans from animals and indeed to creating the opposing categories of human and animal', as Karl Steel argues.[4] In fables, talking deer and hares are still hunted, talking dogs are still chained and beaten, talking horses still ridden and whipped, and talking sheep still sheared and slaughtered. However, fables imagine animals speaking from 'the subject position of their species'.[5] Fables imagine what animals would say to us, or about us, if they could.

Take, for instance, the fable of 'The Wolf and the Kid' (Perry Index 261).[6] This tale reiterates anthropocentric values surrounding the slaughter of domesticated 'livestock' animals – namely, the notion that when humans kill animals, this is both different from when other species do it, and better than when other species do it. 'The Wolf and the Kid' features the two titular animals in familiar roles: the kid (in some versions, a lamb) flees; the wolf pursues. When his prey eludes him, the wolf attempts to lure the kid out with words, claiming that if he does not return to the fields, humans will kill him as a sacrifice to their gods, as they kill many others. The kid does not dispute the likelihood

---

Krieg have similarly argued that 'fables are metaphoric in the sense that the fable's narrative, which typically involves talking animals, is nonliteral in that it conveys a message (i.e., a moral) about human moral behavior, and this moral is perceived as self-relevant by listeners or readers': Jose et al., 'Development of the Comprehension and Appreciation of Fables', *Genetic, Social, and General Psychology Monographs* 131.1 (2005), 5–37 (7).

4   Karl Steel, *How to Make a Human: Animals and Violence in the Middle Ages* (Columbus OH, 2011), 14.

5   Frank Palmeri, 'The Autocritique of Fables', in *Humans and Other Animals in Eighteenth-Century British Culture: Representation, Hybridity, Ethics*, ed. Frank Palmeri (Burlington VT, 2006), 83–100 (84).

6   Perry Index numbering is derived from B. E. Perry, *Aesopica: A series of texts relating to Aesop or ascribed to him or closely connected with the literary tradition that bears his name* (Urbana IL, 1952).

of such a fate. Rather, he replies that he would rather be sacrificed than be devoured by the wolf. The moral echoes this sentiment; Avianus's version of the fable, written *c*.400 CE, asserts that, if one is caught between two unfortunate alternatives, 'it is advantageous to achieve a distinguished death' ('expedit insignem promeruisse necem').[7] This fable, then, suggests that animals are better off sacrificed by humans than slain by non-human predators, *and that the victims themselves would see it that way*. Though 'The Wolf and the Kid' is not meant as an indictment of animal slaughter, and in fact conveys humans' self-serving judgements about this being better than predation, the fable also acknowledges a truth that can be obscured by the sheer volume of fables about rapacious wolves, wily foxes, tyrannical lions, etc.: humans too are deadly.

Below, as a further exploration of fables' tendency to treat non-human predation differently from human slaughter, I consider medieval fables about sheep, as well as the reality of medieval sheep husbandry behind the fables' analogies. The fable of 'The Wolf and the Lamb', I argue, is representative of how the fable corpus tends to construe predation as ill-intentioned, unjust and evil. The fable of 'The Butcher and the Sheep', by contrast, is one of only a handful of fables that alludes to humans' slaughter of 'livestock'. But although 'The Butcher and the Sheep' depicts a human as a prolific and even cruel killer, the ultimate reproach in this fable lies with the slaughtered sheep themselves. The sheep's passivity before human violence does not make them innocent victims, as they so often are elsewhere (within the fable genre itself, as well as in sermons and Scripture). Rather, their passivity renders them culpable in their own demise – a reassuring story to tell about innocuous beings who are routinely slaughtered for human ends, and one of many conscience-easing yet untenable narratives surrounding animal exploitation.

In-depth analysis of what occurs within particular fables on the literal level, as this article offers, is in a sense contrarian; that is, not how these stories were 'meant' to be read by even elementary readers.[8] I am,

---

7   *Minor Latin Poets, Vol. 2*, ed. Arnold Mackay Duff and John Wright Duff (Cambridge MA, 2006), 746, line 16. All translations in this article are my own.
8   As Rita Copeland observes, 'Ancient and medieval theories of education identify the literal sense with elementary teaching, with the preliminary stage of reading and acquisition of literacy (and for the Middle Ages, latinity), and thus with childhood itself': *Pedagogy, Intellectuals, and Dissent in the Later Middle Ages: Lollardy and Ideas of Learning* (Cambridge, 2004), 53.

then, reading fables 'against the grain', as Crane suggested one must to make these texts amenable to animal studies.[9] My approach, though, despite a focus on the literal level of fables, is not to sieve out moments of 'real' animality in these texts, by seeking glimpses of animals who seem to be neither anthropomorphic nor construed in morals as representing humans – although those moments do surely exist in a variety of medieval works[10] and are a valuable corrective to notions that, in the Middle Ages, animals *qua* animals were mostly absent from the page. When it comes to fables, disregarding the anthropomorphising elements, particularly animal speech, or the moralising elements, would disregard what fable is and what it does. Speech and animality are both integral to fable animals, and the genre is both moralising and didactic, encouraging one to draw lessons from fictional scenarios involving other species.

Frank Palmeri has argued that certain fables, albeit 'a minority in most collections', are 'autocritical': that is, from within the fable form itself, they critique the genre's tendency to make animals 'invisible' via interpretation.[11] Palmeri analyses several fables by eighteenth-century authors such as Jean de La Fontaine, John Gay, and Jonathan Swift, claiming that in some cases the fable animals stand for their own species, not for humans. Notably, these are fables in which the animals criticise humans' mistreatment of them. I too analyse fable animals as standing for their own species, and agree that human-animal fables bring the animality of fable animals to the forefront. However, I do not argue that only in a select minority of cases can fable animals be read as animals. Even allegorical or metaphorical animals retain some animality, because of the way that analogy functions in our cognition.

While animal-standpoint critics have advocated that we seek those texts where animals are not 'displaced metaphors for the human',[12] even in such works, the literal referents – the animals – have an enduring presence. To discount that presence because those narratives can be (and indeed, were *supposed* to be) read non-literally is premature. An animal

9   Crane, *Animal Encounters*, 48.
10 As Lisa J. Kiser has discussed with respect to Chaucer, for example: 'The Animals That Therefore They Were: Some Chaucerian Animal/Human Relationships', *Studies in the Age of Chaucer* 34 (2012), 311–17.
11 Palmeri, 'The Autocritique of Fables', 83.
12 John Simons, *Animal Rights and the Politics of Literary Representation* (Basingstoke, 2002), 6, quoted in Josephine Donovan, *The Aesthetics of Care: On the Literary Treatment of Animals* (New York, 2016), 101.

analogy encodes what the author imagines to be the salient features of that animal as it is understood in their culture: characteristics of body and/or behaviour, and ways of interacting with other species and/or environment. Though these features may, of course, diverge from what we would now consider natural history, the animal analogy's success still rests upon readers finding that analogy recognisable or plausible, based on a mélange of what they have witnessed, heard and read. Such analogies therefore involve thinking and talking about animals, even if the purpose of doing so is ostensibly to elucidate something about humans. When, for example, Robert Henryson draws a parallel between a sheep being fleeced against his will and the exploitation of tenant farmers in his rendition of 'The Sheep and the Dog', the aim may be to elicit readers' sympathy for the tenant farmers. In constructing this fable and this analogy, however, the author must speak of the sheep, delineate his circumstances, and suggest that he, too, is pitiable. The fact that animal fables prompt one to reflect on humans and human society does not retroactively erase the animals in them. Fables may be anthropocentric, but so is all literature, inevitably – even texts which seek to undermine anthropocentrism.

My aim, then, is to expand the purview of animal studies to regard metaphoric and anthropomorphic animals – what one might call the 'animal unreal', to play on Carolynn Van Dyke's phrase – beyond critiquing these as anthropocentric distortions. Attending to the 'animal real' entails acknowledging literary animals who are *not* only 'metaphoric or anthropomorphic',[13] as well as acknowledging the 'extratextual reality' of other species' (and our own) embodied existence.[14] I acknowledge this reality here as well. The fable analyses that follow would be of less import, were it not for the real animals who have lived and died, whose circumstances lie behind the analogies that fables establish. Attention to the 'animal unreal' entails recognising, in addition to the lived reality of animals behind animal analogies, the abiding animality even in anthropomorphic constructs and metaphors.

The cultural prominence of the fable genre was arguably at its height in the Middle Ages, when fable collections were both key to Latin pedagogy for children and the basis of sophisticated literary adaptations for adults. As such, if one recognises the animality of fable animals,

---

13 Carolynn Van Dyke, 'Introduction: *In Hir Corages*', in *Rethinking Chaucerian Beasts*, ed. Carolynn Van Dyke (New York, 2012), 1–10 (5).
14 Van Dyke, 'Introduction: *In Hir Corages*', 6.

fables are potentially fertile sources regarding how humans viewed other species, and interspecies relationships, in this period. The versions of the two sheep fables that I discuss below are either from collections that were much circulated in the Middle Ages, or those that display the craft of a particular well-known author, or both. My five sources for the two abovementioned sheep fables are the *Novus Aesopus* of Alexander Neckam (1157–1217), in Latin verse; the 'elegiac *Romulus*', a popular Latin verse collection from the late twelfth century, sometimes ascribed to 'Walter the Englishman'; the *Fables* attributed to Marie de France, in Old French verse, thought to have been composed in the 1180s; William Caxton's *Aesop*, in late Middle English prose (1483–4); and Robert Henryson's *Morall Fabillis*, in Middle Scots verse, c.1500. While these collections were written in several languages and span several centuries, they share a connection to Britain: the Anglo-Norman Marie, the English Neckam and Caxton, the Scottish Henryson, and possibly the author of the elegiac *Romulus* as well, if the attribution to 'Walter the Englishman' is not spurious.

Sheep in Medieval Britain

Sheep are humans' commodities in vast numbers, bred and raised so that their bodies can be exploited, and killed when their deaths are expedient. The same was true in the Middle Ages; this is the reality behind authors' sheep analogies, in the fables that this article discusses. Sheep first arrived in Britain during the Neolithic period, around 6,000 years ago.[15] In 1086, the Domesday Book recorded more than 1 million sheep in English demesne flocks,[16] with the total number of sheep in England at the time being perhaps 7.5 million, thereby outnumbering humans two to one.[17] By the early fourteenth century the sheep population had likely risen to over 12 million.[18] Large estates or monasteries might own

---

15 Terry O'Connor, 'Introduction: The British Fauna in a Changing World', in *Extinctions and Invasions: A Social History of British Fauna*, ed. Terry O'Connor and Naomi Sykes (Oxford, 2010), 1–9 (4).
16 Aleksander Pluskowski, *Wolves and the Wilderness in the Middle Ages* (Woodbridge, 2006), 79.
17 Derek Hurst, *Sheep in the Cotswolds: The Medieval Wool Trade* (Stroud, 2005), 51.
18 Susan Rose, *The Wealth of England: The Medieval Wool Trade and Its Political Importance 1100–1600* (Oxford, 2018), 37.

thousands of animals, while large flocks could contain several hundred sheep. While some peasants might have had 'sizeable flocks', others had 'only a handful of sheep'.[19] Flocks were often divided, with wethers, ewes and younger female sheep kept separately; the wool of wethers was considered more valuable than that of ewes or younger animals.[20] This division is reflected in 'The Butcher and the Sheep', in which the doomed flock is sometimes specified to be composed of wethers.

While pigs were raised in the Middle Ages almost solely to be slaughtered for meat, sheep were exploited for other purposes as well, particularly wool and dairy products.[21] Sheep were also of use for their dung, leading to the practice of 'fold-coursing' in some regions, where flocks were enclosed in hurdles and regularly moved over open fields and fallow land during the autumn and winter, so that their manure would enhance the soil.[22] However, though sheep milk and dung were of importance in agrarian economies, it was wool production that was the 'prime object of sheep farming' in England from the twelfth to the eighteenth century.[23] Much has been written about the socio-economic history of wool in England, which I will not recapitulate here;[24] my focus is on the animals themselves and the extent of their exploitation by humans.

The significance of wool in English history has sometimes occasioned scholars to downplay the slaughter and 'post-mortem usage'[25] of sheep for meat and skin and other products, which were extensive, in keeping with the prodigious number of animals. This extensiveness is evidenced by faunal assemblages that date to the peak period of wool production in England, between the late twelfth and mid-fourteenth centuries, in most of which sheep outnumber cattle.[26] Both young and old sheep were

19 David Stone, 'The Productivity and Management of Sheep in Late Medieval England', *The Agricultural History Review* 51 (2003), 1–22 (21).
20 Rose, *The Wealth of England*, 20–1.
21 U. Albarella, 'Pig Husbandry and Pork Consumption in Medieval England', in *Food in Medieval England: Diet and Nutrition*, ed. C. M. Woolgar, D. Serjeantson and T. Waldron (Oxford, 2006), 71–87 (72).
22 Rose, *The Wealth of England*, 26.
23 M. L. Ryder, *Sheep and Man* (London, 2007 [first publ. 1983]), 447.
24 A seminal, comprehensive account is T. H. Lloyd, *The English Wool Trade in the Middle Ages* (Cambridge, 1977). Notable as well is the foundational work of Eileen Power, *The Wool Trade in English Medieval History* (Oxford, 1941).
25 Pluskowski, *Wolves and the Wilderness*, 80.
26 N. J. Sykes, 'From Cu and Sceap to Beffe and Motton', in *Food in Medieval*

slaughtered and eaten, with a greater tendency towards the slaughtering and consumption of young animals near sites of production.[27]

Archaeological and documentary evidence indicates the presence of meat markets and specialised meat sellers in English towns from the mid-tenth century. These same urban markets may have provided pre-cut joints of meat to high-status buyers in locales outside the city, from the late eleventh century onwards.[28] The sheep and cattle eaten by townsfolk were herded into town from rural regions and slaughtered in or near the meat market or butcher's shop. 'Vivid imaginations are unnecessary to picture the effects of these procedures on the street', notes David R. Carr;[29] the later Middle Ages saw a spate of governmental attempts to regulate urban butchers, prohibiting the slaughter of animals and the disposal of offal within cities.[30] Due to the economics of wool production, most sheep were kept alive until they had produced at least two crops of wool,[31] being culled when their teeth were too worn to allow them to eat.[32] The slaughter of an entire flock of wethers in 'The Butcher and the Sheep' perhaps suggests a scenario in which a group of similarly aged animals were considered past their prime and dispatched.

In addition to sheep's medieval status as commodities and producers of commodities (wool, milk, meat, skin, manure, etc.), they were also potent symbols; there are more than 700 references to sheep and lambs throughout the Bible. Lambs, particularly, were symbols for Christ, representing the innocent sacrificed, and lambs also represented 'the faithful, the righteous, and the sinless throughout biblical and patristic texts'.[33] There are, as well, several hundred references in the Bible to shepherds, pastures, enclosures and predators of sheep; the motif of Christ as the 'Good Shepherd', based on passages such as John 10,

---

England: Diet and Nutrition, ed. C. M. Woolgar, D. Serjeantson and T. Waldron (Oxford, 2006), 56–71 (58).

27 J. M. Bond and T. P. O'Connor, *Bones from Medieval Deposits at 16–22 Coppergate and Other Sites in York* (York, 1999), 416.

28 Sykes, 'From Cu and Sceap to Beffe and Motton', 69.

29 David R. Carr, 'Controlling the Butchers in Late Medieval English Towns', *The Historian* 70 (2008), 450–61 (452).

30 See Carole Rawcliffe, *Urban Bodies: Communal Health in Late Medieval English Towns and Cities* (Woodbridge, 2013), 147–53.

31 Pluskowski, *Wolves and the Wilderness*, 80.

32 Ryder, *Sheep and Man*, 448.

33 Lisa J. Kiser, 'Silencing the Lambs: Economics, Ethics, and Animal Life in Medieval Franciscan Hagiography', *Modern Philology* 108 (2011), 323–42 (324).

Luke 15, and 1 Peter 2, was a regular presence in medieval sermons.[34] Shepherding served in the Middle Ages not only as an actual occupation, but also as a prominent metaphor for the protective and sustaining roles of both Christ and clergy.

Fables, too, represent shepherds as protectors of sheep. Repeatedly, fables insist that human stewardship of sheep is normal, natural and necessary,[35] through the ubiquity of tales about predatory non-humans ravaging vulnerable flocks, with shepherds as well-meaning intercessors. Shepherds may even stand as protectors in contradistinction to other humans. For example, in the fable of 'The Shepherd and the Butcher' (Perry Index 465), a shepherd and a butcher vie for possession of a stray lamb. The lamb weighs in upon hearing their respective occupations, stating that he would prefer to go with the shepherd. Of course, in the greater scheme of things, lambs are bound for the butcher eventually. The partitioning of humans' occupational roles – keeper and killer – permits the fiction that a shepherd is 'safer' for sheep than a butcher; this safety is only temporary.

Nonetheless, when it comes to sheep in literature, it is the wolf that surely springs to mind as nemesis before the butcher; the two animals are often paired. Fables, as well as sermons and Scripture, all played a role in the propagation of the wolf and sheep as a conceptual duo. But if the wolf seems like the sheep's natural antagonist, this owes more to the pervasiveness of this perceived relationship in human culture than it does to the actual prevalence of wolf predation on sheep. Aleksander Pluskowski observes, 'Clearly the relationship between the wolf and sheep/lamb was a popular and widely recognised metaphor in medieval Christian society, but its source and proliferation had little to do with livestock management and economics in medieval Britain'.[36] Indeed, in Britain, wolves were extirpated over the centuries – much earlier than in a number of regions on the Eurasian continent – and they were locally extinct from England by the end of the Middle Ages,[37] finally vanishing

---

34 Daniel Nodes, 'Theology before Church Polity: A Fourteenth-Century Guide for Mendicant Preachers on the Good Shepherd', *Medieval Sermon Studies* 64 (2020), 66–76 (66).
35 In Melanie Joy's analysis, these 'Three N's of Justification' underlie carnism, the 'violent ideology' behind killing certain animals for meat, and in fact behind 'all exploitative systems': *Why We Love Dogs, Eat Pigs, and Wear Cows: An Introduction to Carnism* (San Francisco CA, 2010), 33; 97.
36 Pluskowski, *Wolves and the Wilderness*, 83.
37 Ibid., 7.

from Scotland by the late seventeenth century.[38] Wolves loomed far larger as literary figures and symbols than as actual competitors against humans for resources.

Though medieval fables, sermons and Scripture may have represented the wolf as a predominant danger to sheep, medieval agricultural treatises, such as the late thirteenth-century *Seneschaucy*, suggest otherwise. The *Seneschaucy* identifies dog attacks and disease as the most pressing concerns faced by shepherds.[39] Sheep might also drown, or be injured by a flockmate, or be lost or stolen, the treatise relates;[40] the risk of predation by wild animals, such as wolves, foxes or birds, goes unmentioned. Another book on shepherding, the late fourteenth-century French *Le Bon Berger*, does make occasional mention of predation by wild animals. For example, newborn lambs might be attacked by ravens, kites or crows.[41] Wolves, too, are mentioned a handful of times, though rather vaguely. Yet the presence of predators in this work is quite outweighed by the author's extensive, practical discussion of various sheep maladies and how to treat them, which takes up eighteen of thirty-nine chapters. 'Whereas losses from disease today probably lie between 2 per cent and 5 per cent, 30 per cent losses were usual during the Middle Ages', says M. L. Ryder, 'and they often rose to between 50 per cent and 70 per cent'.[42]

Really, humans were and are the biggest killers of sheep other than pathogens. More than half a billion sheep are now slaughtered annually across the globe.[43] Slaughter aside, many lambs do not survive more than a few days, for various reasons. Data from the past few decades show lamb mortality rates as relatively stable, at around 15 per cent, with up to half of these deaths occurring on the day of birth. Common causes of death are birth injuries, starvation or hypothermia due to poor ewe-lamb bond, and infectious disease. The impact of predation and other causes

---

38   Garry Marvin, *Wolf* (London, 2012), 82.
39   Dorothea Oschinsky, *Walter of Henley and Other Treatises on Estate Management and Accounting* (Oxford, 1971), 287.
40   Oschinsky, *Walter of Henley*, 273.
41   *The Medieval Shepherd: Jean de Brie's Le Bon Berger (1379)*, ed./trans Carleton W. Carroll and Lois Hawley Wilson (Tempe AZ, 2012), 111.
42   Ryder, *Sheep and Man*, 448.
43   karol orzechowski, 'Global Animal Slaughter Statistics & Charts', *Faunalytics* <https://faunalytics.org/global-animal-slaughter-statistics-and-charts/> (accessed 25 October 2024).

on lamb mortality is 'relatively minor',[44] although the frequency of predation varies from country to country, 'depending on predator abundance'.[45] Sheep farmers may nonetheless *perceive* predation as a significant problem, more so than it is in reality. For example, farmers overestimated predation as a cause of lamb mortality at three times the rate of published data, in a recent Australian study.[46] Another such study observed that surveyed farmers tended to attribute lamb loss to factors that they could not control (such as predators and weather), rather than factors in which their husbandry played a strong role (such as birth weight and disease transmission); farmers even blamed predators for newborn lamb mortality when ewes gave birth indoors.[47]

Perhaps, then, sheep farmers disproportionately place blame on predators for their losses because it is less distressing to blame what one does not control. But why is it that works such as medieval fables placed such emphasis on the figure of the rapacious wolf, while populations of real wolves drastically diminished? Garry Marvin suggests that wolves have been 'persecuted because they were perceived to be evil-intentioned, criminal animals'.[48] The notion of wolves as 'criminal' may derive from the cultural status of domesticated 'livestock'. As these animals are both living beings and human property, predation of 'livestock' has been construed as not just killing, but as theft, too.[49] Marvin further argues that humans *need* to ascribe ill-intention to wolves 'because humans need an image for their own wickedness and wrongdoing'.[50] The wolf is a convenient figure to represent the 'predatory' nature of human greed,

---

44 C. M. Dwyer, J. Conington, F. Corbiere, I. H. Holmøy, K. Muri, R. Nowak, J. Rooke, J. Vipond and J. M. Gautier, 'Invited Review: Improving Neonatal Survival in Small Ruminants: Science into Practice', *Animal* 10 (2016), 449–59 (450).
45 C. M. Dwyer, 'The Welfare of the Neonatal Lamb', *Small Ruminant Research* 76 (2008), 31–41 (37).
46 Kayla Kopp, Marta Hernandez-Jover, Susan Robertson, Angel Abuelo and Michael Friend, 'A Survey of New South Wales Sheep Producer Practices and Perceptions on Lamb Mortality and Ewe Supplementation', *Animals* 10 (2020), 1586.
47 Dwayne Shiels, Jason Loughrey, Cathy M. Dwyer, Kevin Hanrahan, John F. Mee and Timothy W. J. Keady, 'A Survey of Farm Management Practices Relating to the Risk Factors, Prevalence, and Causes of Lamb Mortality in Ireland', *Animals* 12 (2022), 30 (13 of 14).
48 Marvin, *Wolf*, 46.
49 Ibid., 36.
50 Ibid., 45.

among other things – the sort of inveterate malefactor that others ought to beware of. Perhaps it was not only a dubious perception of wolves as significant competitors for human property, but an increasing lack of experience with the real animal, that allowed this myth to flourish.

Wolf-and-Sheep Fables

Fable animals are not simply ciphers who systematically signify the same thing from one narrative to another; fables are richer and more diverse than that. Jill Mann, in fact, calls the fable of 'The Wolf and the Lamb' 'misleading' with respect to the way that the genre tends to construct meaning from animals; after all, 'it is easy to call the wolf "cruel" and the lamb "innocent" (as does the fable itself)', but numerous fables do not offer such straightforward and consistent animal symbolism. At times, argues Mann, there may be 'physical justifications' for the use of a given animal in a story (for example, in 'The Frog and the Mouse', there has to be an animal who can swim, and in 'The Wolf and the Crane' or 'The Fox and the Stork', there has to be an animal with a long beak), but 'even such physical justifications […] are for the most part lacking', as evidenced by the fact that characters sometimes change species in different versions of the same fable. 'It is the individual narrative that fixes the "character" of an animal, but it fixes it only for the duration of that particular fable', claims Mann.[51]

I would generally agree, but with two qualifications: first, some animals in the fable genre tend to be more variable in their meaning than others. Frogs, for example, are relatively multivalent.[52] But, second, common fable animals' meanings shift with some predictability, depending on who the other actors in the narrative are. As Maurizio Bettini proposes, there is an 'ecology of animal symbols'. Bettini, building on James Gibson and colleagues' concept of 'affordances' in ecological psychology, argues that animals have 'metaphorical

---

51 Jill Mann, *From Aesop to Reynard: Beast Literature in Medieval Britain* (Oxford, 2009), 30–1.
52 Frogs in fables may represent, say, duplicitousness and self-sabotage ('The Mouse and the Frog'), excessive ambition ('The Frog that Burst and the Ox'), cowardice ('The Hares and the Frogs') or ingratitude ('The Frogs Asking for a King').

affordances' for humans.[53] An object has 'affordances' (possibilities for action and interaction which it 'affords' to animate beings, based on its physical characteristics), and 'we as humans engage in a metaphorical project that depends on turning animals into symbols, basing specific beliefs on the animals' affordances'.[54] Animals' perceived characteristics shape (but do not entirely predict or determine) the meanings we make of them. Extending Bettini's argument, I would add that stories about different species interacting with one another exhibit a further shaping of those animals' metaphorical affordances, as not only individual species' perceived characteristics, but perceived interspecies relationships, come into play.

Wolves and sheep, when they share a fable, tend to conform to expected predator-prey dynamics (expected in literature, at least, which is often not an accurate representation of real animal behaviour). There are at least forty fables in which sheep are attacked or threatened by wolves, whereas there is one fable portraying the converse: in 'The Misfortune of the Wolf' (Perry Index 699), two rams trick and then assail a wolf. Their trick, however, is only enabled by the wolf's anticipation that he will be able to devour one of them, as he so often does elsewhere in the genre. When paired in fables with sheep, then, the wolf is represented as rapacious and violent, often as deceptive, too; he is the perpetrator of violence, or the would-be perpetrator. The sheep in these fables, meanwhile, is typically vulnerable, at times simple or naïve – the object of sympathy, or suggested reader identification, or both.

To somewhat quantify these claims about the fable corpus, and the frequency with which predation and slaughter are represented: non-human predators such as the wolf are conspicuous as fable characters, even as real wolf populations have dwindled over the centuries. Francisco Rodríguez Adrados, in his very extensive, though 'not exhaustive', inventory of the Graeco-Latin fable tradition,[55] lists 131 separate fables under the index heading of 'Wolf' (by comparison, there are 133 separate fables under the 'Fox' heading, and ninety-three under the 'Lion' heading). Examining this inventory, I count forty

---

53 Maurizio Bettini, *Women and Weasels: Mythologies of Birth in Ancient Greece and Rome*, trans. Emlyn Eisenach (Chicago IL, 2013), 125–30, citing James J. Gibson, *The Ecological Approach to Visual Perception* (Boston MA, 1979).
54 Bettini, *Women and Weasels*, 127.
55 Francisco Rodríguez Adrados, *History of the Graeco-Latin Fable*, trans. Leslie A. Ray, 3 vols (Leiden, 1999–2003), 3:1033.

distinct fables in which wolves are portrayed as attacking or menacing sheep,[56] as well as another fifteen fables in which wolves attack or threaten another domesticated animal, such as an ox, a pig, an ass or even a dog. By contrast, 'The Butcher and the Sheep' is one of only a handful of fables to even allude to, let alone depict, humans' slaughter of 'livestock'.[57] Although in reality most 'livestock' are killed by humans (or by disease, particularly in the Middle Ages), the fable corpus repeatedly portrays predation as the key threat facing domesticated animals; 'The Wolf and the Lamb' encapsulates this tendency.

'The Wolf and the Lamb' is, in a number of ways, an emblematic fable. It opens the first book of the first extant literary fable collection, that of Phaedrus in the first century CE, and it immediately establishes the usual pattern of fable analogy, in which the behaviours of non-human animals are compared to human characteristics and social dynamics. 'The Wolf

---

56 These fables are as follows (titles and abbreviations follow Adrados's inventory): 'The Advice of the Fox' (S. 88); 'The Bear and the Wolf' (M. 459); 'The Deer and the Sheep' (M. 116); 'The Dog, the Wolf and the Miserly Master' (M. 98); 'The Dog, the Wolf and the Ram' (M. 97); 'The Evil Hog' (M. 471); 'The Five Lambs, their Tutors, and the Wolf' (S. 8); 'The Head of the Household, the Sheep and the Wolf' (M. 340b); 'The Hunter and the Wolves' (not-H. 123); 'The Lion and the Farmer 2' (H. 149); 'The Misfortune of the Wolf' (M. 245); 'The Peasant and the Wolves' (M. 409); 'The Ram and the Wolf' (M. 40); 'The Sheep that Complained about the Wolf' (M. 331); 'The Sheep, the Deer and the Wolf' (not-H. 241); 'The Sheep, the Dog and the Wolf' (not-H. 240, M. 329); 'The Shepherd and the Wolf' 1 (H. 276); 'The Shepherd and the Wolf 2' (M. 337); 'The Shepherd and the Wolves' (H. 225); 'The Shepherd that Fed a Wolf' (not-H. 249); 'The Shepherd who Joked' (H. 226); 'The Wether, the He-Goat, and the Wolf' (S. 331); 'The Wolf and the Dog 2' (not-H. 195); 'The Wolf and the Lamb 1' (H. 160, M. 247); 'The Wolf and the Lamb 2' (M. 168, M. 254B); 'The Wolf and the Ram' (M. 248); 'The Wolf and the Raven who Settled on the Ram' (M. 251); 'The Wolf and the Sheep 1' (H. 164); 'The Wolf and the Sheep 2' (H. 166); 'The Wolf and the Sheep Kissing' (M. 261); 'The Wolf and the Shepherd 1' (H. 165); 'The Wolf and the Shepherd 2' (M. 260); 'The Wolf that Dressed in a Sheepskin' (not-H. 188, M. 361); 'The Wolf who Became a Monk' (M. 257); 'The Wolf who Learned how to Read' (M. 246); 'The Wolf, the Shepherd and the Pursuer' (M. 262); 'The Wolf's Ears' (S. 43); 'The Wolves and the Dogs Reconciled' (not-H. 185); 'The Wolves and the Sheep' (H. 158, M. 330); and 'The Wolves and the Shepherds' (not-H. 194).

57 These fables include, in addition to 'The Butcher and the Sheep', which this article discusses at length, 'The Farmer and the Dogs' (Perry Index 52); 'The Shepherd and the Butcher' (Perry Index 465); 'The Peasant and the Bull' (Perry Index 582); and 'The Pig and His Owner' (Perry Index 583).

and the Lamb' appears in many medieval fable collections, including my five sources mentioned above, as well as in Odo of Cheriton's *Parabolae* and other prose and verse compendia in the *Romulus* tradition. As mentioned above, 'The Wolf and the Lamb' can be seen as part of a strong cultural and literary trend (also manifest in sermons and Scripture) in which wolves stand for wickedness, violence and deceit, and sheep (especially lambs) stand for innocence, victimhood and truth. This is particularly the case when these two animals are paired together; one might call these their 'mutual metaphorical affordances'.

The plot of 'The Wolf and the Lamb' is that the two animals happen to drink from the same stream, with the lamb being downstream of the wolf. The wolf accuses the lamb of muddying his drinking water – which, the lamb points out, is not possible. The wolf, undeterred, proceeds to levy other impossible and unjust accusations, which vary from telling to telling, for which the lamb has sensible and truthful rejoinders. But of course, the wolf had intended to attack the lamb all along, regardless of what he might say, and the fable ends with his doing just that.

The earliest version of this fable, Phaedrus's, refers to the wolf as a 'robber, urged on by his wicked gullet' ('fauce improba latro incitatus'),[58] and medieval versions are similarly unsparing in their judgements. Alexander Neckam's version characterises the wolf as cruel or violent ('sevus', line 14), as well as deceitful ('dolosus', lines 2 and 15).[59] His moral reiterates the comparison between predation and both deception and injustice, suggesting as well that the lamb represents those who are truthful, righteous and innocent: 'Let the honest learn from this to always avoid the deceitful, who hurt the just and oppress the harmless' ('Hinc discat simplex semper vitare dolosum, qui iustos dampnat innocuosque premit', lines 15–16). The elegiac *Romulus* version similarly casts predation in terms of harm to the innocent, and is somewhat more explicit in likening predation to social injustice among humans. Playing on forms of the word *noceo*, 'to harm', the moral concludes, 'Thus the harmful harm the harmless, and invent reasons to harm. These wolves rule everywhere in the city' ('Sic nocet innocuo nocuus, causamque nocendi / invenit. Hii regnant qualibet urbe lupi').[60] The moral of 'The

---

58 *Babrius and Phaedrus*, ed. Ben Edwin Perry (Cambridge MA, 1965), 190, lines 3–4.
59 *Alessandro Neckam: Novus Aesopus*, ed. Giovanni Garbugino (Genoa, 1987), 74. All citations of Neckam from this edition.
60 *L'Esopus attribuito a Gualtiero Anglico*, ed. Paola Busdraghi (Genoa, 2005),

Wolf and the Lamb' in Marie's *Fables* is more specific still, both in its mention of particular human vocations, and in its graphic language for the wolf's dismemberment of his prey:

> Issi funt li riche seignur,
> li vescunte e li jugeür
> de ceus qu'il unt en leur justise;
> faus' acheisuns par coveitise
> treovent asez pur eus cunfundre:
> suvent les funt a pleit somundre;
> la char lur tolent e la pel,
> si cum li lus fist a l'aignel.[61]

(The rich lords do thus, the sheriffs and the judges, with those who are in their power; they invent enough false accusations out of greed to destroy them: they often summon them to trial; they take away the flesh and the skin, just like the wolf did to the lamb.)

However, it is Robert Henryson's version – by far the longest, at 161 lines – that opines most profusely on the parallels between the wolf's predation and humans' legal and financial exploitation of their vulnerable inferiors, particularly in the moral. The narrative had set up the typical contrast between the wicked wolf and the pathetic, virtuous lamb, as they are introduced by the streamside: 'The volfis thocht wes all on wickitnes; / The selie lamb wes meik and innocent' ('The wolf's mind was entirely on wickedness, the poor lamb was meek and innocent').[62] After the usual sequence of the lamb's disregarded defences, followed by his bloody death, the moral opens by declaring, 'The pure pepill this lamb may signifie / As maill men, merchandis, and all lauboureris' (lines 2707–8: 'This lamb may represent poor people, such as tenant-farmers, merchants, and all workers'), whereas 'The wolf betakinnis fals extortioneris / And oppressouris of pure men, as we se, / Be violence, or craft in suteltie' (lines 2711–13: 'The wolf signifies dishonest extortioners and oppressors of poor men, as we see, by violence, or skill in craftiness'). Henryson then states that 'Thre kind of wolfis in this warld now rings'

48, lines 15–16.
61 *Les Fables: édition critique accompagnée d'une introduction, d'une traduction, des notes et d'un glossaire*, ed. Charles Brucker, 2nd edn (Paris, 1998), 54, lines 31–8. All citations of Marie's Fables from this edition.
62 *The Poems of Robert Henryson*, ed. Denton Fox (Oxford, 1981), 97, lines 2624–5. All citations of Henryson from this edition.

(line 2714: 'three kinds of wolves now reign in this world'): namely, those who make untrue allegations and accept bribes, ruining poor men; rich men who seize their poor tenants' leased property, even if it causes them to starve; and lords who harass hard-working renters on their land for payment, leaving them barely able to eke out a living.

Another fable in Henryson's collection, 'The Sheep and the Dog' (Perry Index 478; versions appear in the other medieval collections that I discuss as well), tells of a sheep who loses a lawsuit, in a court stacked with various species of predators and headed by a wolf judge. The crooked machinations of the animal court result in the sheep having to sell his own wool to pay a non-existent debt – a more anthropomorphic setting than the streamside, and a far more elaborate means of attack than a bite to the throat. Still, this fable is a further instance of the genre portraying predation by non-human animals as motivated by enmity, and as comparable to human corruption. This sort of enmity is not ascribed to a human killer, in the fable of 'The Butcher and the Sheep', in which a man systematically slaughters an entire flock. Rather, this fable relocates the responsibility for violence to its recipients, and it is the victim sheep themselves who deserve their fate.

'The Butcher and the Sheep': 'They let themselves be taken'

Unlike the many fables in which wolves attack sheep, the fable of 'The Butcher and the Sheep' (Perry Index 575) casts a human as the killer, and the sheep as his less-than-innocent victims. This fable tells of a flock of sheep who are dragged off and killed, one by one, by a human. The last sheep who remains reflects on his and his companions' inaction in the face of this, declaring that they were mistaken to have not resisted the man and escaped slaughter. In a way this affords the sheep – animals stereotyped as docile and obedient – the possibility of noncompliance, even though this remains unrealised. Yet in another way, this fable casts the sheep not as blameless, but as responsible for their own deaths.

Other fables about humans slaughtering livestock may portray slaughter as a consequence for an animal's misbehaviour, which fits unremarkably within a wider fable context of characters who die as a result of their own vices or poor judgement. For example, in the Caxton's *Aesop* version of 'The Peasant and the Bull' (Perry Index 582), a man successfully curbs the rebellious antics of a bull by threatening to send him to the butcher.[63] Avianus also tells the fable of 'The Pig and His Owner' (Perry Index 583), in which a pig's repeated forays into the grain fields culminate in his being caught, killed and eaten.[64]

'The Butcher and the Sheep' presents a more complicated scenario, however, with respect to the relationship between characters' errors and their deaths; what all the versions have in common, though, is that the fault ultimately lies with the unresisting sheep. In this fable, the slaughter of an entire flock of sheep is not *instigated* by anything that the sheep have done or failed to do. Rather, the killing begins with a human acting in an occupational role or satisfying his own inclinations. A human, that is, who treats sheep as they are often really treated, killing them for the acquisition of meat and other products, for reasons that are entirely noncontingent upon the animals' personal merits or lack thereof. The three medieval versions of 'The Butcher and the Sheep' discussed below do not, at the outset, blame the victim. However, the flock's continual inaction becomes the crucial mistake that readers are prompted to take heed of.

The fable's chain of events commences when a man drags off a single member of the flock and dispatches him. There is a considerable amount of variation among versions and indeed manuscript recensions of this fable when it comes to the term used to denote the character who slaughters the sheep. In the versions that I examine, the killer is either a butcher (Neckam and Caxton) or a thief (Marie). Which of these categories he seems to occupy has implications within the narrative in terms of how the sheep respond to his actions, and whether they interpret what happens to them to be just or to be wrong.

Manuscripts of Marie's *Fables* are particularly varied regarding this character.[65] Harriet Spiegel, noting the variety of words introducing him

---

63 *Caxton's Aesop: Edited with an Introduction and Notes*, ed. R. T. Lenaghan (Cambridge MA, 1967), 188. All citations of Caxton's *Aesop* from this edition.
64 *Minor Latin Poets, Vol. 2*, ed. Duff and Duff, 728.
65 One important witness, London, British Library, MS Harley 978, calls the man 'bucher' ('butcher', also 'executioner'; see *AND, s.v.* 'bocher', (1). Another manuscript calls him a 'shepherd' ('berker'), while another calls him a 'thief' ('lerre'). The greatest number of manuscripts in fact refer to him as some variation of 'bres' (a 'scoundrel' or 'fool'). Even the character's species is not stable. Two other witnesses call him a 'man' ('home'), yet one calls him a 'goat' ('chevres'), and three manuscripts actually call him a 'wolf' ('leus'). For these variants and the manuscripts in which they appear, see Marie de France, *Fables*, ed. Harriet Spiegel (Toronto, 1987), 271. Complicating things further are the

in the third line, says, 'The word seems to have posed problems for the scribes'.[66] In any case, this character, in Marie's fable, is depicted more like a thief than a butcher (or a shepherd, or a non-human animal such as a wolf, etc. The character is elsewhere referred to as 'this man', 'cest humme').[67] His gradual slaughter of the flock is an illicit and opportunistic one, and the sense of his activities as illicit, and indeed wrong, is reflected throughout the poem. The man and his wife (who is mentioned in only one line, and who is not present in any other versions) enter a pasture in order to walk about or amuse themselves ('par mi le champ esbaniër', line 4). They come across the flock of sheep by chance. When the man observes that they are unguarded ('sanz garde', line 5), he kills one of them and carries him away, and returns every day to kill yet another sheep. His actions are not the systematic performance of a socially sanctioned occupation, as it would be if he were a butcher tasked to kill a group of livestock. Unlike the meek or apathetic animals in the other two versions I discuss, where the man is called a butcher, Marie's sheep are said to grow very angry ('Les berbiz mut s'en curucerent', line 9) – a 'just anger', moreover ('dreit' ire', line 12). The last remaining sheep refers to his killer as 'cest humme, ki a grant tort / nus a tuz pris e traiz a mort' (lines 23–4: 'this man, who very wrongfully has taken us all and put us to death').

That the slaughter enrages the sheep, and that the final victim deems the killer a wrongdoer, sharply separates Marie's version from the two others I consider, that of Alexander Neckam and that in Caxton's *Aesop*. In these versions, the last survivor claims that what has been done to the unresisting sheep is just, because they should have helped one another but did not. The flock's continual lack of resistance eventually, even retroactively, justifies the fate of its constituents. Addressing the man who is about to kill him, Neckam's sheep says:

Iure gregem totum laniasti, seve lanista;
ad mortem merito nunc quoque ducor ego:
nam, dum de medio gregis unumquemque trahebas,
si te quisque suis cornibus appeteret,

---

fables' titles, which in some manuscripts are French, in others Latin. The Latin title for some manuscripts, 'De fure et ove', deems him a thief; see *Die Fabeln der Marie de France*, ed. Karl Warnke, Biblioteca Normannica 6 (Halle, 1898), 112.
66   Spiegel, ed., *Fables*, 271.
67   *Les Fables*, ed. Brucker, 114, line 23.

salvus grex et ego nunc essem, tuque perisses;
nunc quam non tulimus, iure caremus ope.[68]

(You justly butchered the whole flock, cruel butcher;[69] now I too am led deservedly to death: for, when you were taking us out of the flock one by one, if anyone had attacked you with his horns, the flock and I would be safe now, and you would have died; now we justly lack the help that we didn't give.)

The sheep's strenuous insistence on the justice of this slaughter, in his repetition of the word 'iure' ('justly', lines 7 and 12) and in the word 'merito' ('deservedly', line 8), is perhaps somewhat counterpointed by the man's appellation of 'cruel butcher' ('seve lanista', line 7). The phrase could be seen as a condemnation, but on the other hand, if we accept the sheep's assessment of events as just, then what the flock deserves for not coming to one another's aid is not simply death, but a *cruel* death.

The last wether in the Caxton's *Aesop* version delivers a similar though more concise assessment of his fate, saying to the butcher, 'Iustly I am worthy to be take / by cause I haue not holpen my felawes'.[70] While Neckam's sheep emphasised the fact that *any one* of the sheep ('quisque', line 10), himself included, could have resisted at some point, Caxton's sheep seems to feel a specific and personal culpability. Yet in both versions, the sheep's final speech to the butcher ultimately functions to sanction what has been done to the flock. The lone surviving sheep, while dismayed, acknowledges his own fault to the very person about to kill him, asserting that he deserves his impending death.

'The Butcher and the Sheep', as in so many other fables, portrays the animal characters as talking, both to one another and to a human. Through their conference, in the Marie and Caxton versions, the flock make their ill-fated decision to remain passive. But in these versions, the points at which the animals do *not* speak are crucial. Their silence is not due to linguistic incapacity, and is also not one of the occasional times in fable where the animals do not use language because their doing so is unnecessary for the plot. Rather, these versions emphasise that the animals choose not to *speak up* for themselves, which is an indication of

---

68 *Alessandro Neckam Novus Aesopus*, ed. Garbugino, 116, lines 7–12.
69 I accept Garbugino's reading of 'lanio', 'butcher', for Neckam's 'lanista'. Garbugino, ed., *Alessandro Neckam Novus Aesopus*, 117.
70 *Caxton's Aesop*, ed. Lenaghan, 126.

their lack of resistance; this non-resistance leads to their death. Marie's version recounts:

> Les berbiz mut s'en curucerent:
> entre eus distrent e cunseilerent
> que ne se veulent pas defendre;
> par dreit' ire se laissent prendre,
> ne ja ne se desturnerunt,
> ne pur murir mot ne dirrunt. (lines 9–14)

(The sheep grew very angry. They talked amongst themselves and decided in council that they did not wish to defend themselves. With just anger they would let themselves be taken, and would never protect themselves, nor say a word, even though they died.)

While Marie's sheep take counsel after several sheep have already been picked off, the sheep in the Caxton's *Aesop* version react to the *initial appearance* of the butcher with a marked lack of speech, and it is in this silence that the man proceeds to seize and kill the first victim: 'And after as the whethers sawe hym / none of them sayd one word / And the bocher toke the fyrst that he fonde'. Their silence is not framed as a collective decision reached through conferral; they seem meeker than the outraged, self-martyring sheep in Marie's version.

But in both those versions, to 'not say a word' is a sort of *pars pro toto* expression for the sheep's utter lack of resistance. That is, we might conceive of attempts at resistance or self-preservation as occurring through speech as well as other, more forceful actions (that is, physical confrontation, as Neckam's final sheep suggests). For the sheep not to raise so much as a verbal objection to injustices committed against them constitutes the utmost in passivity. The choice to be silent is essentially framed as the choice to acquiesce to death – the deaths of members of one's community, and eventually one's own death as well. One implication of their pointedly 'not saying a word' is that they *could* have spoken up. What they might have said, however, remains unarticulated and unknown.

Would their words have made any difference? Jeremy Lefkowitz has argued that there is a 'futility' to animal speech in fables.[71] Regarding

---

71 Jeremy Lefkowitz, 'Aesop and Animal Fable', in *The Oxford Handbook of Animals in Classical Thought and Life*, ed. Gordon Lindsay Campbell (Oxford, 2014), 1–23 (11).

the fable of 'The Wolf and the Lamb', in which the lamb shoots down the wolf's spurious accusations but is devoured nonetheless, he claims, '[T]he only message one can draw from the fable is that words and just causes are irrelevant'.[72] Jill Mann also argues, regarding this fable, that 'it is the *irrelevance* of the verbal exchange to the development of the action that is the very point of its inclusion' (original italics).[73] Lefkowitz analyses a second wolf and sheep fable as well (Perry Index 159), which features a wolf who has 'eaten his fill'. This wolf, by contrast, releases the sheep after the sheep makes three truthful statements, as requested. Lefkowitz argues that the wolf's lack of hunger is key to the outcome, and that the fable 'suggests that animal *speech* is effective only when *animal instincts* have been taken out of the equation' (original italics).[74] Mann comes to a similar conclusion about speech and instinct with respect to the fable of 'The Lion and the Mouse' (Perry Index 150): 'Rhetoric is effective only when it is supported by natural instinct'.[75] In 'The Wolf and the Lamb', the sheep's arguments were in vain. Meanwhile, in Marie's and Caxton's versions of 'The Butcher and the Sheep', speech among the sheep – conferral – is seemingly the vehicle for their downfall; this supports Mann's argument that fables tend to teach the 'mistrust of words'.[76] But words are untrustworthy for entirely different reasons, in these two fables. In one, the lamb's truthful verbal defences are heard, but disregarded, by a malicious non-human predator intent on killing. In the other, misguided counsel within an animal community promotes an unwise passivity, which not only allows for, but finally justifies, the actions of a human, who seems to be equally intent on killing.

Literary sheep and lambs are often portrayed as innocent victims. They are innocents when attacked by vicious non-human predators such as wolves, as in a number of fables, and innocents when slaughtered by humans *outside* of fable, as in Biblical metaphors, including Isaiah 53:7 and John 1:29 and 1:36. The sheep in 'The Butcher and the Sheep', however, do not begin the fable as innocent victims, but nor are they wrongdoers. The slaughter seems to begin irrespective of the sheep's virtues or failings, in order to satisfy human ends (that is, to procure products from the sheep's dead bodies). Unlike the 'livestock' animals

---

72 Lefkowitz, 'Aesop and Animal Fable', 12.
73 Mann, *From Aesop to Reynard*, 40.
74 Lefkowitz, 'Aesop and Animal Fable', 12.
75 Mann, *From Aesop to Reynard*, 280.
76 Mann, *From Aesop to Reynard*, 96.

in fables such as 'The Peasant and the Bull' or 'The Pig and His Owner', these sheep's deaths commence without a sense that the animals are being judged and punished. It is only as events unfold that the sheep become culpable for their own inaction.

It is striking that so many wolf-and-sheep fables, such as 'The Wolf and the Lamb' (and 'The Dog and the Sheep', and others) portray sheep as unable to adequately defend themselves, verbally *or* physically, try though they might. Yet, in one of the few fables that involves *human* violence against sheep, the animals are apparently capable of resisting – with deadly force even, in Neckam's version – and they opt not to. They opt to submit, viewing their own deaths as a just, even if unwanted, outcome. This is a useful fantasy for humans to entertain regarding their 'livestock'.

Conclusion

'The Wolf and the Lamb' and 'The Butcher and the Sheep' are part of a larger corpus that both evidences and reinscribes anthropocentric beliefs about animal husbandry, through its repeated portrayal of non-human predators as malign towards domesticated animals, as well as its portrayal of slaughtered animals as to blame for their fates. Wolf-and-sheep fables, of which 'The Wolf and the Lamb' is a prime example, tend to suggest that there is something inimical, and immoral, about non-human predators' behaviour towards their prey. Fable readers are repeatedly impelled to assume that there would be ill will from non-human predator species such as wolves towards the animals they kill and eat, while comparable malevolence is not necessarily ascribed to the human character in a fable where he slaughters animals.

In 'The Butcher and the Sheep', human violence against a group of animals is the key event. Yet the sheep's inaction, and their self-blame, both authorises their deaths and de-emphasises the responsibility borne by the butcher, who wordlessly executes his occupational role. Arguably, by assigning the animal characters the capacity to consider one another's welfare and then having them fall short, the fable puts them in a more precarious position, morally speaking, than the typical literary sheep who has done no wrong. The fable of 'The Butcher and the Sheep', particularly in the Neckam and Caxton versions, casts the slaughter as – eventually – just.

One possible reading of all this is that the sheep in 'The Butcher and the Sheep' can be moral agents precisely because they are not functioning in the text as animals. Elizaveta Strakhov argues along these lines: despite fables' attention to the suffering and death of animal characters, 'the animal fable, to my mind, resists the posthumanist approach'.[77] Strakhov makes particular reference to a fable (Perry Index 52) in which a farmer's dogs flee the man, reasoning that they may be his next victims, after they witness him slaughter and eat first his sheep, then his goats, then his oxen. Building on Karl Steel's argument that, according to human-constructed categories, 'an animal is human when it can be murdered',[78] Strakhov interprets the dogs' 'claim [that] their death would be a homicide' as indicating the extent to which this fable is 'fundamentally discursively treating animals as humans'.[79] This is indeed one way – and, in a sense, a traditional way – to read 'The Farmer and His Dogs', and fable in general: the animal characters, particularly when they speak, are not to be understood as animals.

Yet, if the non-animal status of fable animals is evidenced through those moments when they articulate their own subjectivity and the value of their own lives, this forecloses interpretive possibilities. Humans have often insisted, after all, that killing actual animals does not constitute murder, and that actual animals are objects and not subjects. But what does one do, then, with the fact that, through fables, humans imagine *literary animals* who appear to regard *themselves* as subjects? One could say that in the act of imagining animal subjectivity and giving animals voice, one ceases to imagine animals, but that is an analytical dead end, and a premature erasure of fable animals' animality. Alternatively, one could say that humans can and do think of fable animals perceiving themselves as subjects, as beings with other than instrumental value, as beings who can be murdered – even as humans, both within the fable world and in real life, regard them otherwise.

Fables with humans and animals interacting provide a sort of schism between hegemonic-human and imagined-animal discourse surrounding the very same events; these 'unreal' creatures offer glimpses into a counterfactual world where animals speak up about what humans

---

[77] Elizaveta Strakhov, 'Political Animals: Form and the Animal Fable in Langland's Rodent Parliament and Chaucer's Nun's Priest's Tale', *The Yearbook of Langland Studies* 32 (2018), 289–313 (297).
[78] Karl Steel, *How to Make a Human* (Columbus OH, 2011), 15.
[79] Strakhov, 'Political Animals', 297.

do to them. To return to 'The Butcher and the Sheep': it is the sheep's voices that we hear, not the butcher's; his take on events is absent. It is unclear whether he hears or cares about the last sheep's final words. Perhaps from the butcher's point of view, he is simply doing his job (or from the thief's point of view, he is simply availing himself of an unguarded resource). To this silent human, the slaughter may have seemed unremarkable and amoral; such deadly violence towards another species, after all, is the status quo for how humans treat their 'livestock'. By contrast, from the perspectives of the sheep in this fable, the slaughter is cruel, or their own fault, or both – but it is profoundly laden with moral significance. One can compare this slaughter by humans in 'The Butcher and the Sheep', which is rationalised by its very victims, to the portrayal of interspecies killing in 'The Wolf and the Lamb', and so many other fables, in which for one (non-human) species to kill another indicates the killer's enmity and evil.

Isaiah 53:7 reads, 'He was offered because it was his own will, and he opened not his mouth: he shall be led as a sheep to the slaughter, and shall be dumb as a lamb before his shearer, and he shall not open his mouth'.[80] In this passage, then, the victim is slaughtered because he wishes it, and his silence evinces his willingness and innocence. That the sheep in 'The Butcher and the Sheep' do not open their mouths in their own defence, however, is neither a sign that they actually wish to be killed, nor is it construed as virtuous; it is a mistake that is admonished. In a genre where animal speech is endemic, these animals' silence is not an attempt at naturalism (that is, representing real sheep's inability to verbally object to being slaughtered). It is both a significant choice and a grave error, which renders the sheep complicit in their own murder, rather than quintessential righteous victims.

It could be argued that the patent fictionality of fables undermines the idea of *real* animals as murderable – that the counterfactual nature of the genre means that authors, and readers, are not taking the prospect of non-human perspectives seriously. Yet, the fables examined above, as well as many others not mentioned, display authors' readiness to imagine how vulnerable animals might regard their own circumstances – what they would say about it, if they could – with the aim of imparting genuine ethical and philosophical lessons to readers. Readers, meanwhile, are compelled to imagine how the last survivor of a flock would react to his companions' violent deaths, or whether a doomed

---

80 Isaiah 53:7, DRBO.

young goat would prefer the priest's knife or the wolf's teeth. Reading these characters as speaking *animals*, and not just memorable stand-ins for exclusively human concerns, invites closer examination of the messages that fables promulgate about other species, whose existence is intertwined with ours.

3

Medieval Networks of Memory: Writing the Mortuary Roll in Thirteenth-Century Britain

Elaine Treharne and Mateusz Fafinski[1]

Two mortuary rolls compiled between 1215 and 1230, to commemorate senior religious women, allow scholars access to a world of quotidian scribal endeavours that is normally occluded by standard palaeographical and book historical studies.[2] Between them, the mortuary rolls contain almost 500 examples of handwriting from different religious houses around Britain. They constitute an exceptional resource for analysis of letterforms and scribal practices such as punctuation, abbreviation and correction; and they illustrate what preference and capability there was in the religious houses visited for particular forms of script, like *textura* (also labelled 'text hand', *littera textualis* or 'Gothic') and particular levels of formality in writing.[3] This scribal evidence comes at a time when

---

1   Our research is facilitated by Medieval Networks of Memory – a digital project hosted and funded by Stanford Text Technologies; and Treharne benefitted from a Stanford Clayman Institute for Gender Studies Fellowship, 2021–2. We are grateful to the two anonymous readers of this essay; their criticisms and comments have been immensely helpful.
2   Both mortuary rolls have been available for some time in the invaluable volumes of A. G. Watson, *Catalogue of Dated and Datable Manuscripts, c. 700–1600, in the Department of Manuscripts, the British Library* (Cambridge, 1979); and P. R. Robinson, *Dated and Datable Manuscripts, c. 737–1600 in Cambridge Libraries*, 2 vols (Cambridge, 1988), I. 90.
3   On nomenclature, see, among others, G. I. Lieftinck, *Manuscrits Datés Conservés dans Les Pays-Bas, Volume I: Texte* (Amsterdam, 1964); N. R. Ker, 'Preface', *Medieval Manuscripts in British Libraries, Volume 1: London* (Oxford, 1969), x; and M. B. Parkes, *English Cursive Book Hands, 1250–1500* (Oxford, 1969), xiii. For an overview of the specific documentary features emergent in the course of the twelfth century, see Teresa Webber, 'L'écriture des documents

new features in documentary hands were developing; and when what one might call 'scribal presence' was more prevalent socioculturally than it had been previously.

London, British Library, Egerton MS 2849, Parts 1 and 2, is a mortuary roll with 122 entries from religious houses, who each wrote an individual *titulus* to commemorate Prioress Lucy de Vere of Castle Hedingham, in Essex, who died in 1225.[4] To acknowledge Lucy's death, the new prioress, Agnes, sent a messenger – possibly a lay brother – out to other religious houses in the south of England to request that they enter a short memorial (the *titulus*) for Lucy. The roll was created over a span of time, presumably within a few years of Lucy's death. The slightly earlier mortuary roll of Prioress Amphelisa of Lillechurch, who died sometime between 1208 and 1214, is Cambridge, St John's College, MS N. 31; it is extensive and contains 378 scribal entries. Both rolls are in good condition overall: Egerton 2849 is 7-foot long; while St John's N. 31 is 37-foot long, and contains entries on the front of the membrane as well as on the dorse at membranes 2, 3 and 18.[5]

---

en Angleterre au XIIe siècle', *Bibliothèque de l'École des chartes* 165.1 (2007), 139–65. Scholars stress the variability in terms used for labelling scripts in this period and variability in the hands of individual scribes in the late twelfth to the fifteenth centuries; on this see, *inter alia*, Albert Derolez, *The Palaeography of Gothic Manuscript Books: From the Twelfth to the Early Sixteenth Century* (Cambridge, 2003), 14–17.

4   On Lucy de Vere, an aristocratic woman, and the de Vere family, see Sally Thompson, *Women Religious: The Founding of English Nunneries after the Norman Conquest* (Oxford, 1991), 11, 180. An indispensable online resource for British women's religious history is the *Monastic Matrix*, directed by Professor Alison Beach at the University of St Andrews: <https://arts.st-andrews.ac.uk/monasticmatrix/monasticon/browse> (accessed 25 October 2024).

5   Both rolls are included in the remarkable volumes of medieval mortuary rolls published in 2005 by Jean Dufour, *Recueil des Rouleaux des Morts (VIIIe siècle-vers 1536)*, 4 vols (Paris, 2005). The rolls of Lucy and Amphelisa are in volume 2 (1181–1399). In Dufour's listing, St John's N. 31 is item 172 and Egerton 2849 is item 178. Dufour transcribes every *titulus* or commemorative record, and he provides maps and a list of the type of religious house represented by every *titulus* entry. This scholarship is foundational and deeply significant, and in our own project, we have worked in detail with Dufour as we created our curated database, re-transcribing every entry with additional information on the foundation of each religious establishment, and focusing on the palaeographical features that each entry offers in the light of its place and moment of historical production. We accessed the rolls themselves and worked with images formerly hosted at the London, British Library Digitised Manuscripts website, where

Foundation dates of institutions help in providing the possible *termini* for the production of the rolls. St John's N. 31 must be dated after 1210, as St Sepulchre and St Helen, the present-day St Helen's in Bishopsgate, London, was founded for Benedictine nuns in c.1210;[6] and it is probably to be dated after 1219, as Snelshall Priory in Buckinghamshire, which has an entry in the roll, seems not to have been functional between 1207 and c.1219.[7] Egerton 2849 *may* have been completed prior to 1230; Lacock Abbey, founded in 1229/30, is not represented.[8]

Part I was, <http://www.bl.uk/manuscripts/FullDisplay.aspx?ref=Egerton_MS_2849/1> (accessed October 2022) and Part II was <http://www.bl.uk/manuscripts/FullDisplay.aspx?ref=Egerton_MS_2849/2> (accessed October 2022); and at the Illuminated Manuscripts Catalogue at the British Library website: <https://www.bl.uk/catalogues/illuminatedmanuscripts/record.asp?MSID=6342&CollID=28&NStart=2849> (accessed October 2022). Here, we cite links to the British Library as they existed before the cyberattack on the Library in October 2023. We consider these links (even if defunct at the time of publication) to be the record of our research practice, necessary to document the archival path we took. On the methodological rationale behind this decision, see Mateusz Fafinski, 'Facsimile Narratives: Researching the Past in the Age of Digital Reproduction', *Digital Scholarship in the Humanities* 37.1 (April 2022), 94–108.

6   Establishing the precise date of foundation is somewhat tricky. The founding charter has been edited by Gibbs and she gives as the possible date of the document 'c.1202–1216', conservatively representing the whole span of Alardus de Burnham's tenure as the dean of St Pauls: see Marion Gibbs, *Early Charters of the Cathedral Church of St. Paul, London* (London, 1939), no. 235 (185–6). Earlier antiquarian literature agreed on a slightly later date, with Cox, Newcourt and Dugdale giving c.1212: see John Edmund Cox, *The Annals of St. Helen's, Bishopsgate, London* (London, 1876), 6; Richard Newcourt, *Repertorium Ecclesiasticum Parochiale Londinense: Comprising All London and Middlesex, with the Parts of Hertfordshire and Buckinghamshire to the Said Diocese Belonging* (London, 1708), 364; William Dugdale, *Monasticon Anglicanum, a History of the Abbies and Other Monasteries, Hospitals, Frieries and Cathedral and Collegiate Churches in England and Wales, Also of All Such Scotch, Irish and French Monasteries Connected with Religious Houses in England. Translated from Latin,* ed. John Caley, Henry Ellis and Bulkeley Bandinel, 6 vols (London, 1817 [1693]), IV. 551.

7   See *British History Online, A County History of Buckinghamshire*, I, <https://www.british-history.ac.uk/vch/bucks/vol1/pp352-353> (accessed 25 October 2024).

8   For the foundation date of 1229, see William Lisle Bowles and John Gough Nichols, *Annals and Antiquities of Lacock Abbey, in the County of Wilts* (London, 1835), 180–6; for the founding charter see viii–ix. The cartulary of Lacock is

Breviators, circulating to collect *tituli*, could be acting on behalf of more than one institution at a time and would visit the relevant religious institutions, expecting hospitality from each one as the day's work was completed.[9] The 378 houses appearing on the Amphelisa Roll may represent networks of prayer and commemoration rather than straightforward geographical proximity.[10] Several clusters of monasteries entered into the rolls in sequence probably reflect confraternal relationships between houses. Confraternal communities included both men and women, who were admitted to prayer communities. This explains the presence of laypersons in a handful of *tituli*, such as the entry for the Augustinian house, Holy Trinity, Hastings, in St John's N. 31, which mentions both men and women. These would have been canons and nuns of this and affiliated houses, but the entry differentiates between the priest John, the canon Firmin, and the 'domestics' of the monastery, who were surely laypeople; namely, Guy, Wilhelm, Margaret, Elisabeth, Mathilde, Helewidis and Clementia.[11]

Both rolls circulated between c.1220 and c.1230, providing detailed, contemporary testimony to hundreds of individual scribal hands at a critical time in the development of Latin and English writing.[12] Sixty-three of the entire set of *tituli* are inscribed by the same religious houses,

---

preserved in two volumes as London, British Library, Additional MS 88973 and Additional MS 88974. The chronicle of the abbey was badly damaged in the Cotton fire of 1731, but an early modern copy exists as London, British Library, Harley MS 5019. Of course, the lack of representation of a particular abbey or priory does not affect the supposed date of the respective roll. Many religious institutions were not part of the cycle of visits.

9   *The Obituary Roll of William of Ebchester*, ed. James Raine, Surtees Society (London, 1856), xvii, explains that 'the names for this Roll-Carrier varied in the records from *Breviator*, to *Brevigerulus, Rolliger, Rotuli Portitor*, and *Brevium Portitor*'. Raine is describing fourteenth-century practices for licensing a breviator.

10   See Robert Bartlett, *England under the Norman and Angevin Kings, 1075–1225* (Oxford, 2000), 601.

11   This may then also be the case in the *tituli* for St Martin, Battle, and St Pancras, Lewes, in Egerton 2849, and Shouldham Priory in St John's N. 31. On membership of lay people in monastic prayer confraternities, see Sarah Hamilton, *Church and People in the Medieval West, 900–1200* (London, 2015), 247. On laypersons' positions in mortuary rolls on the continent, see Hugh Feiss, 'Necrologies and Mortuary Rolls', in *Women and Gender in Medieval Europe: An Encyclopedia*, ed. Margaret C. Schauss (London, 2006), 607.

12   For which see, most recently, Matthew Aiello, 'English Vernacular Script

while a handful of entries that represent two houses are written by the same scribe within the same roll. Otherwise, the sheer scale of contemporary palaeographical detail is impressive, measurable and analysable using quantification tools and automated processes. From hundreds of scribal entries in these rolls, too, we may have dozens of examples of women's hands or certainly hands from women's religious institutions. The rolls thus represent an important witness to the emergence and use of both formal and less formal forms of handwriting, and the role that women could have played in the development of script at this time.[13] This rich record of entries allows for a dynamic reappraisal of earlier thirteenth-century religious and social networks and community commemoration. Fresh research on the rolls adds to the considerable scholarship of Alison Beach, Lynda Rollason and Jean Dufour, among others.[14] Our research on the rolls' signatories explores how Benedictine, Cistercian, Augustinian, Gilbertine, Premonstratensian, military and clerical orders sought to represent their respects to these women, and confirms the lengths to which the individual houses went to ensure that senior female religious were positively commemorated.

Our investigation of the data – the hands, the language, the composition, the space, the ink and the localisation of the *tituli* in the rolls – operates on the following assumptions: that religious houses, unless a shared scribe is demonstrable, wrote their own entries; that some of the scribes whose hands we evaluate were not what contemporary palaeographers would call *professional* scribes;[15] that there is a degree of emulation

---

in the Thirteenth Century (c.1175–c.1325)', *New Medieval Literatures* 21 (2021), 28–77.

13 See comments in M. B. Parkes, *Their Hands Before Our Eyes: A Closer Look at Scribes. The Lyell Lectures Delivered in the University of Oxford 1999* (London, 2016), 80–1.

14 Alison Beach, *Women as Scribes: Book Production and Monastic Reform in Twelfth-Century Bavaria* (Cambridge, 2004); Lynda Rollason, 'Medieval Mortuary Rolls: Prayers for the Dead and Travel in Medieval England', *Northern History* 48.2 (2011), 187–223; and Dufour, *Recueil des Rouleaux des Morts*.

15 On criteria for assessing medieval writing, and on training, see Malcolm Parkes, 'Handwriting in English Books', in *The Cambridge History of the Book, Volume 2, 1100–1400*, ed. Nigel J. Morgan and R. M. Thompson (Cambridge, 2008), 110–35: he states that 'professional' scribes were 'scribes, like parish priests, scholars and laymen who were accustomed to write in the course of pursuing their professions' (120–1). For Parkes these are scribes 'other' than 'itinerant craftsmen […] commercial scribes (including part-timers, like lay clerks and secular clergy – especially chaplains) who worked in major centres, such as

occasionally evinced by particular writers suggesting close aesthetic and cultural links between some houses or clusters of houses; that script is deployed in some cases as a visual witness to the house's aspirations or desire to be read in a particular way – an individuation device; that the rolls were carried by the breviator to the houses themselves over a period of time, which might have been as short as some months in the case, particularly, of the Egerton Roll; that each roll was compiled and sewn during the journey in an accretive process, but that the precise order of *tituli* does not equate to an obvious or straightforward geographical route;[16] and that it is at least possible that within the women's houses female scribes could have completed the *titulus*, as we discuss below. Finally, we offer here a further and more in-depth corrective to Michael Clanchy's discussion about the deployment of rolls in the high Middle Ages, in which he implies that rolls were avoided – except in centralised bureaucracy – because of the association of the form with Jewish religious practices.[17] The mortuary rolls of Lucy and Amphelisa (as well as others throughout the period) demonstrate that this is not the case, and that the technology proved resilient and useful for the recording of prayers like those *tituli* that we read and analyse here.

London, Oxford, Cambridge and Salisbury, and produced books to order'. See also Elaine Treharne, 'Writing the Book: Cambridge University Library, Ii. 1. 33', in *Producing and Using English Manuscripts in the Post-Conquest Period*, ed. Elaine Treharne, Orietta Da Rold and Mary Swan, special issue, *New Medieval Literatures* 13 (2011), 303–12, and references therein. Professional scribes might be thought of as those who have produced multiple examples of writing, have received scribal training, and for whom writing and copying texts was a primary, and perhaps remunerated, occupation. See Linne R. Mooney, 'Identifying English Scribes Who Had a Hand in More Than One Manuscript', in *New Directions in Later Medieval Manuscript Studies: Papers from the 1998 Harvard Conference*, ed. Derek Pearsall (York, 2000), 131–41; and G. W. S. Barrow, *The Acts of William I, 1165–1214, Regesta Regum Scottorum*, II (Edinburgh, 1971).
16 Note that the manuscript space does not directly reflect the landscape.
17 M. T. Clanchy, *From Memory to Written Record*, 3rd edn (Oxford, 2013), 140–1. For an overview of the portability argument for the use of rolls, see Pamela Robinson, 'The Format of Books: Books, Booklets and Rolls', in *Cambridge History of the Book in Britain*, ed. Morgan and Thompson, 39–54, esp. 46.

Form of the Manuscript Rolls

The basic form of these membrane rolls is described in detail by Dufour in his multi-volume edition of all medieval mortuary rolls. Both rolls under investigation here begin with elaborate panegyric statements about the deaths of their subjects. In the case of Egerton 2849, an accomplished set of illustrations of the prioress opens the roll, followed by the *tituli* entered by each house visited.

Throughout the rolls, a typical *titulus* might run as follows (with modern editorial intervention):

> T[itulus] ecclesie Sancti Augustini Cantuariensis. Anima donne Lucie, priorisse de Hengham, et a[nimae] o[mnium] f[idelium] d[efunctorum], per m[isericordiam] D[ei], r[equiescant in pace]. Amen. Concedimus ei commune beneficium ecclesie nostre. Oravimus p[ro] v[estris], orate p[ro] n[obis].
>
> (*Titulus* of the church of St Augustine of Canterbury. May the soul of Lucy, prioress of Hedingham, and all the souls of the faithful departed, through the mercy of God, rest in peace. Amen. We grant this for the benefit of our church. We pray for you; pray for us.)

Each house visited wrote a similar *titulus* in essence – an entry that largely formulaically prayed for the soul of the deceased and respectfully asked for prayers in return. There is variation in the form and the details that are included, but most echo the Canterbury, St Augustine's example. Each of the *tituli* reflected in our data is recorded with a full edition of each entry and an accompanying image presented online.[18] In addition to the questions noted above that such rolls inspire, they also reveal a great deal about the varieties of religious houses in around 1215–30; the kinds of scribes and resources that the houses were likely to have had available to them at a point where they were asked to inscribe these commemorations; how these forms of communication functioned; and the esteem in which senior aristocratic nuns like Lucy and Amphelisa were held.

As Neil Ker commented in his *English Manuscripts in the Century after the Conquest*, in a discussion of the utility of a medieval mortuary roll, it 'contains so many specimens of hand-writing of one year, 1122,

---

18   *Medieval Networks of Memory* <https://medievalnetworks.github.io/mnm/> (accessed 25 October 2024).

that it can show how far English script had then developed and to what extent features characteristic of or common in the mid-century were already to be found in English script'.[19] That is to say, the sheer range of a roll's examples of writing provides an exemplary view of palaeographical characteristics at a given moment. This is only strengthened by the major characteristic connected with the form of a roll; namely, that it is geared towards presentation and performance,[20] and that it retains the potential to grow over time.[21] It becomes a space of experimental demonstration of script and scribal capability. In addition, the contemporaneity and on-the-spot nature of many of the entries in this, and other such rolls, pre-empts scribal characteristics seen later in the century, especially in *textura* and more formal modes of textual production (and notably, all the images that Ker shows in *English Manuscripts* are of *textura* or semicurrent hands; nothing cursive is illustrated in his discussion).

Tricky textual objects like the mortuary rolls can be examined for the exceptional range of information they yield about religious institutions in the British high Middle Ages. The rolls permit a snapshot of the breadth of writing at a supraregional scale within a short period, and this breadth can be described, categorised and quantified. Shared scribal entries, where the same hand writes for more than one house, suggest close relationships between specific houses within regions and locales. It seems reasonable to assume that such double entries may reflect the kind of relationships that were previously only traceable for large monasteries: shared devotions, familiar links or similar liturgical interests.[22] It may also be that such shared entries emerged from the unavailability of a willing monk or nun to complete a *titulus*, and thus a need to rely

---

19   Neil Ker, *English Manuscripts in the Century After the Norman Conquest* (Oxford, 1960), 35. His case study was the *Rouleau Mortuaire* in Paris, Musee des Archives Nationales 138.
20   Jack Hartnell, 'The Continous Page', in Jack Hartnell, ed., *Continuous Page: Scrolls and Scrolling from Papyrus to Hypertext* (London, 2020), 11, <https://courtauld.ac.uk/research/courtauld-books-online/continuouspage>   (accessed September 2024).
21   Thomas Forrest Kelly, *The Roll of the Scroll: An Illustrated Introduction to Scrolls in the Middle Ages* (New York, 2019), 41–74.
22   The possibility of tracing and evaluating such links through palaeography is very tempting. We know that they existed in macro scale; see the example of Farfa and Cluny in the eleventh century described in S. Boynton, *Shaping a Monastic Identity: Liturgy and History at the Imperial Abbey of Farfa, 1000–1125* (New York, 2006), 106–43.

on an affiliated monastery. Individual scribal efforts can potentially be assigned to women writers inscribing *tituli* for their respective houses, and it is possible that characteristics of potential hands of women can be diagnosed and found elsewhere.[23] Each of these areas of research encourages present-day scholars to look again at inherited categories of script, of the designation of 'scribe' and of conceptions of what constitutes a 'scriptorium'. These categories, as they have been inherited by contemporary scholars, are problematic;[24] *why* they are troubling is effectively demonstrated by the rolls themselves. Below, therefore, we examine three principal foci: model scripts and associations with gender; so-called 'grade', where the rolls demonstrate the coexistence of normally demarcated formalities and types of writing, and where 'grade' may indicate the scribe's desire for prestige in his or her work; and aspects of textual production that permit palaeographers to consider scribes' ages, regional location, training and writing responsibilities. Features normally seen as testimony to specific dating show instead that different generations of scribe coexist, and that it might be possible to suggest specific elements of script intimating the age and training of a particular scribe. This does not mean that features and the morphology of script lose all diagnostic criteria for dating. We must account instead for the changing curve of features over time. Particular executions of features (for example, a willingness to adapt one's handwriting to recent trends beyond the period of training) can still reveal information about chronology. They are simply not *absolute* and *finite* for a particular hand – or particular house. Some hands reflect updated trends in writing that suggest access to ongoing scribal training – a facet of the writing environment that distinguishes the 'professional' scribe from the 'non-professional'. Finally, it is also important to consider the space that the writers occupy in the rolls, as it might reflect the social order of institution and scribe represented. This suggests a new way of thinking

---

23 As outlined by Elaine Treharne in '"Miserere, Meidens": Abbesses and Nuns', in *Women and Medieval Literary Culture: From the Early Middle Ages to the Fifteenth Century*, ed. Corinne Saunders and Diane Watt (Cambridge, 2023), 27–49.
24 On script, see Elaine M. Treharne, 'The Good, the Bad, and the Ugly: Old English Manuscripts and their Physical Description', in *The Genesis of Books: Studies in the Scribal Culture of Medieval England in Honour of A. N. Doane*, ed. Matthew T. Hussey and John D. Niles (Turnhout, 2011), 261–83; on what constitutes a 'scriptorium', see Rodney M. Thomson, *Books and Learning in Twelfth-Century England: The Ending of 'Alter Orbis'* (Walkern, 2006), 23.

about scribal practice: that the individual expression of a script is chronological, resource and training-dependent, and centred on specific places and resources.

On Script and Grade

While acknowledging the famous advertisement sheet widely discussed by scholars in support of the modern concept of 'grade' in palaeography, it is important to note that neither that late medieval advertiser, Johannes vam Hagen, nor other commentators and practitioners in the premodern period seem to hierarchise scripts into the aesthetic categories now deployed in contemporary palaeographical studies.[25] While some have problematised the very concept of 'grade' seen through the modern gaze, they have also seen grades as at least partly recognised by medieval scribes.[26] This is not immediately obvious. Particularly troubling is the discussion of grade as connected to aesthetic quality rather than simply prestigious effect, and both authors here would dispute the usefulness of value judgement based on aesthetics.[27] 'Grade' is to be understood as a means of measuring scripts according to adherence to a model that exists conceptually and in relation to the type of book written in a particular script (liturgical books written in a formal *textura*, for example). But measuring against an imaginary aesthetic model may make scholars miss diverse periods of experimentation, such as those in the later twelfth and first half of the thirteenth centuries.[28] The assumption that individual scribes always had a model in mind and worked *towards* that model-script is questionable in all circumstances. As scribes' initial training underwent various influences and changes,

25   Johannes vam Hagen advertised his scripts in what is now Berlin, Staatsbibliothek, MS Lat. fol. 384. That sheet of scripts has no title, so its overall function seems to be principally illustrative. See Derolez, *Palaeography of Gothic Manuscript Books*, 17–20, plate 17; a good example of accepting the notion of hierarchy as related to quality can be found in Parkes, *English Cursive Book Hands*, xiii; see also Parkes, *Their Hands Before Our Eyes*, 108–25.
26   Peter Stokes, 'The Problem of Grade in Post-Conquest Vernacular Minuscule', in *Producing and Using English Manuscripts*, ed. Treharne, Da Rold and Swan, 23–47 (26).
27   See Derolez, *Palaeography of Gothic Manuscript Books*, 25; Treharne, 'The Good, Bad, and the Ugly'.
28   Aiello, 'English Vernacular Script', 35.

even if such changes were subtle, adherence to a *single* model script would diminish. A better mental image might be of the writer moving away from the model scripts that they have acquainted themselves with during their training – sometimes in a barely noticeable way.

The mortuary rolls under scrutiny here themselves present a wide variety of examples of acceptable writing, many of which do not adhere to a specific or easily labelled model. These are the writings of patently well-trained scribes, as well as those who can only be considered non-professional scribes; that is, those for whom writing was not their main business or responsibility. These basically trained, or relatively unpractised scribes, had nothing to move away from, as it were; they orbited the world of contemporary scripts. They seem to have engaged either in emulation of others' hands as best as they could; or their writing betrays their earlier and often elementary training. Still, it is possible to see on occasion how they integrated features from the newest writing trends into their stints with varying degrees of competency. In the entry for Egglestone Abbey from St John N. 31 (see Fig. 3.1), a poor, isolated and struggling Premonstratensian house, we can see this in practice. The scribe writes in a small hand and the entry is slightly wavy and unruled. The script betrays features common much earlier than the 1210s or 1220s, like the **d**+ high **e** ligature, but also elements that are clearly more contemporary, such as a crossed Tironian *nota*. There are minor spelling mistakes ('Battiste', 'eclesie'), too. It is the hand of someone who may have been trained a couple of decades earlier, who writes in a consistent script but seems to be not very practised.

This is not an isolated example in the rolls. The scribe of St Andrews, Northampton (Northampton Priory) in St John's N. 31 might also have been an older monk, as the letters are somewhat shaky, and several features (including the **d**+ high **e** ligature) are rather old-fashioned. Yet, other elements are very contemporary; there are, for example, singular attempts at newer features like a single, looped **d**. In addition, while

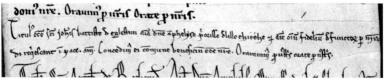

Fig. 3.1 Cambridge, St John's College, MS N. 31, entry for Egglestone Abbey.

the entry is not ruled, the writing is practised, regular and straight. Similarly, in Egerton 2849, entries like that of Stoke-by-Clare Priory or Horkesley Priory cannot easily be placed on a 'grade' scale, rendering such value qualification impractical. To describe these diverse 'takes' on script qualitatively, superimposing hierarchies of grade, is to reinforce aesthetic value judgements on what constitute genuinely representative scribal efforts.

While divisions between *textura* (or 'book' hands) and *documentaria* ('documentary' hands) were known and used widely in this period, this was a division of type and not of aesthetics. Scribes most often wrote their version of a script that was appropriate to the form of the textual object: the adaptability of mode of writing to the task in hand. These forms do not, and did not, have to correspond to our ideas of what constitutes a 'document' or a 'book'. Scribes, as a group, can be considered to encompass many different people with varying degrees of skill, training and practice. There were those who wrote with the most consistent and intentional expertise, fully trained in script(s) and then-contemporary expectations of calligraphic skill; those who were clearly practised scribes with consistency and regularity and an up-to-date script; those who were competent and must have been trained to a demonstrably sufficient level of practice, but who do not show evidence of newer trends; and those who are less practised, whose writing is irregular graphically and linearly, and who must have had only 'basic training'. For these last writers, engagement in regular writing seems not to have been available, possible or, perhaps, desirable. Each of these scribal endeavours might most helpfully be described on their own terms without the need to assign praise or derogation to the effort.

A Spotlight on Blended Script

Several entries in both rolls exhibit scripts that would be described as 'hybrid' according to some palaeographical nomenclature. This terminology is problematic, even though it emerged at least partly in response to value-laden terms that dominate the literature of the early twentieth century. In this earlier scholarship, scribal hands that are in-between scripts, such as forms of cursive that do not fit a presupposed model, have been described, for example, as a 'bad country hand' where 'letters are carelessly formed and very angular, and the writing is altogether irregular'.[29] The use of 'hybrid' is an improvement on 'bad' or 'irregular', but it means different things in different contexts. Even though in the 1950s Cencetti criticised arbitrary systems that can 'never adapt the whole concrete, rich, multifaceted and polytonal reality',[30] the widespread adoption of script categories has led to the proliferation of value judgements in the analysis of hands. Parkes, speaking of a mid-fourteenth century manuscript, described an example of a script with mixed features as a 'half-hearted attempt to produce Anglicana *Formata*, mainly by adding feet to the minims'.[31] More recently, Michelle Brown evaluated hybridity as the 'contamination of scripts', where 'bastard' is a 'mixed script' and 'hybrida' is 'basically a *textualis* with a few cursive letter-forms'.[32] This implies that a hybrid script is an imperfect, debased version of an existing, purer model. Derolez insists on Latin terms that are intended to be neutral by virtue of their Latin nomenclature, but cause major confusion (*hybrida* is not a hybrid script as such in his qualification).[33] Lieftinck speaks of 'hybridization' and *hybrida* is for him essentially a script between two other forms – tellingly the plate used to show it is from a 'laboratory example', a specimen book.[34] For Bischoff the issue of hybridisation of scripts is, in essence, marginal; '*bastarda* scripts' of the thirteenth century 'combine peculiarities of two genres of script'.[35] As a counterbalance to this, Aiello makes a forceful case for

29 C. Johnson and H. Jenkinson, *English Court Hand, AD 1066–1500*, 2 vols (Oxford, 1916), I. 213.
30 Giorgio Cencetti, *Lineamenti di storia della scrittura latina* (Bologna, 1956), 479: 'non potranno mai adeguarsi alla concreta, ricca, multicorde e multitonale realtà'.
31 M. B. Parkes, *English Cursive Book Hands: 1250–1500*, 2nd edn (London, 1979), i.
32 Michelle P. Brown, *A Guide to Western Historical Scripts from Antiquity to 1600* (Toronto, 1990), 81.
33 Derolez, *Palaeography of Gothic Manuscript Books*; and Derolez, 'The Nomenclature of Gothic Scripts', in *The Oxford Handbook of Latin Palaeography*, ed. Frank T. Coulson and Robert Gary Babcock (Oxford, 2020), 301–20.
34 Gerard Lieftinck, 'Pour une nomenclature de l'écriture livresque de la période dite gothique', in *Nomenclature Des Écritures Livresques Du IXe Au XVIe Siècle* (1. Colloque International de Paléographie Latine. Paris, 28–30 Avril 1953), ed. Bernhard Bischoff, Gerard Lieftinck and Giulio Battelli (Paris, 1954), 15–34, at 18 and 26.
35 Bernhard Bischoff, *Latin Palaeography: Antiquity and the Middle Ages*, trans. Dáibhí Ó Cróinín and David Ganz (Cambridge, 1990), 142. Bischoff did not regard the existence of 'transitional' scripts as problematic for the use

departing from 'hybrid' as a descriptor; he questions whether or not scribes were actually working with any of the scripts in mind. He shows that most manuscripts in the thirteenth century have been written in a 'fluid and multivalent' way, with a flow of features from *Textualis* to *Anglicana*, and he thus proposes 'medial script' as a better term.[36]

If most manuscripts are 'fluid', to talk about 'hybrid' is certainly misleading, but so, one might argue, is 'medial'. This denotes a state in between, a type of transitional hand, and transitionality itself suggests an end point – perhaps even a consciousness of evolving from one thing to another. Instead, a preferable term might be 'blended' script: a script that unselfconsciously incorporates elements simultaneously from both book and documentary hands, but essentially remains a separate model, capable of being analysed in its own right.[37] Entries like that of Southwark Priory in Cambridge, St John's College, MS. N. 31, are written in a small Gothic *textura*, but include elements that are extraneous to speed alone and would be more common in documentary hands; the looped **d**, for example, or the curved descender of **p**, the loop of the terminal of high **s**, and the elaborate hook on the final minim strokes, show that while this blended script was flexible, it was deliberate and consistent.

The scribes of these mortuary rolls, as we suggested, do not seem to be working *towards* a model script. The evidence shows that a medieval scribe did not have a model in mind which they sought to (re)produce. Blended script implies that there are options for the *ductus* and specific morphological features from which the scribe could choose, but that there was no hierarchy of model scripts in mind here. 'Blended' seems preferable to 'hybrid', with its pejorative connotations; or 'medial' with the sense of being in-between. Blended script suggests a scribe's

---

of precise terminology: see 'Nomenclature des écritures livresques du IXe au XIIIe siècle', in *Nomenclature des Écritures Livresques du IXe Au XVIe Siècle*, ed. Bernhard Bischoff, Gerard Isaac Lieftinck and Giulio Battelli (Paris, 1954), 1–14 (13).

36   Aiello, 'English Vernacular Script', 43.

37   This might be read in conjunction with Marc H. Smith's arguments about the nature of cursive Gothic scripts, and the notion of 'mutation' in documentary scripts: Smith, 'Les "gothiques documentaires": un carrefour dans l'histoire de l'ecriture latine', *Archiv für Diplomatik* 50, issue JG (December 2004), 417–66. See also E. Poulle, 'La cursive gothique à la chancellerie de Philippe Auguste', in *La France de Philippe Auguste. Le temps des mutations*, ed. R.-H. Bautier (Paris, 1980), 455–67.

WRITING THE MORTUARY ROLL IN THIRTEENTH-CENTURY BRITAIN   73

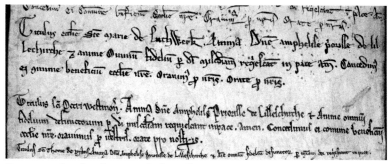

Fig. 3.2   Cambridge, St John's College, MS N. 31, entries for Southwark Priory and Westminster Abbey.

deliberate and thoughtful choice of features from a spectrum of possibilities to create a new form. Blended scripts are not 'in-between'; rather, they are fully made by the individual through their own preferences, rather than from a script that is institutionally imposed. It is an idioscript – a phenomenon that Derolez highlights explicitly when he advocates for the importance of the 'impact of individual hands' while acknowledging the 'fluidity of the boundaries between one type of script and another'.[38] That blended scripts *are* fluid and subject to change through time accurately represents the manifestation of multiple hands in these mortuary rolls, and in other non-book environments. The acceptance of blended scripts as an analytical category has far-reaching consequences, then, not only for the development of scripts but also for the institutional arrangements of book and document production. The change from hybrid to blended is intended to be more than a matter of nomenclature; it highlights the ability to employ individually formed scripts across the categories of manuscript production. The prevalence of entries in a blended script in mortuary rolls, a form encouraging presentation and giving space for houses with little to no preserved chirographic production, underlines how it may have been a dominant form in a certain stratum of the monastic landscape. Blended script also cannot be considered inferior in terms of training, education or milieu. If anything, it attests to the ability to form a comprehensive script individually and in an environment with limited resources. Blended hands could be precise, deliberate and sustained.

38   Derolez, *Palaeography of Gothic Manuscript Books*, 15.

The entry for Westminster Abbey in St John's N. 31 (see Fig. 3.2 above) is interesting in this regard. It is a blended script with, at its basis, a Gothic *textura*, but containing distinctive and visually impactful elements usually connected with documentary hand: for example, embellishments on 'uestris' and 'nobis'; the elongated ascenders and descenders; and the looped terminals of high **s**. Again, these are not haphazard elements; they represent a typical set of components. These features could be upheld by the individual scribe if they so wished, and were not dictated simply by convenience or the intended type of the document. They were discretionary but not arbitrary. Another good example is the elaborate and precise hand of St John the Baptist in Chester, which also appears on St John's N. 31: while its *ductus* is that of a Gothic *textura rotunda*, it employs several 'documentary' features, such as ladder ascenders and other decorative features.

A fascinating pair of entries for the Cistercian foundation of Furness Abbey in St John's, N. 31, provide noteworthy evidence for the use of blended hands (see Fig. 3.3 below). For these entries, while the membrane was ruled, the ruling was not followed. The first example maintains linear straightness, but the second does not. The two hands are different manifestations of a similar semi-current blended script, the first being more decorative and presentational in style than the second. The first entry is written in a very contemporary script, which is on trend with its looped high ascenders, its oversized bow of **a**, and its barred initials. The second entry, with its **d+** high **e** ligature, long **r**, round-backed **d**, and uncrossed nota, is a hand that belongs palaeographically to the later twelfth century and is probably that of an older scribe, since some shakiness can also be detected. This scribe, possibly trained some decades prior to the date of the roll, may have been a more senior colleague in age to the person who wrote the first entry immediately above it. These two entries, nonetheless, were completed by two individual colleagues at the same monastic community at Furness.[39]

39 It must be said there is a possibility that the second entry for 'Furness' could be a mistake made by a scribe entering for a house other than Furness but copying the preceding entry. According to Dufour, *Recueil des Rouleaux des Morts*, the sequence of the monastic houses at this geographical point should be Furness to Bolton Abbey, an Augustinian foundation. However, the roll instead has Furness entered twice, followed by Kirkstall Abbey (also Cistercian). But it is not possible to ascertain which house could be intended by the second Furness, if that entry's location-name is a mistake. A few other houses copy preceding entries and miswrite their house's name, but correct it immediately.

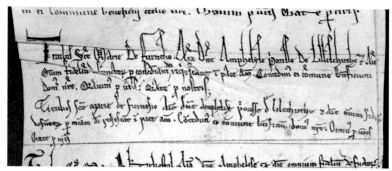

Fig. 3.3   Cambridge, St John's College, MS N. 31, two successive entries for Furness Abbey.

What could have motivated a double successive entry? It seems unlikely that the older scribe would be a scribe-in-training copying a more proficient scribe's entry, so perhaps the second entry is something of a social indicator: the second scribe has some personal or rank reason for entering a second *titulus*. It is a second 'signature', a second set of condolences insisted upon by this older scribe.

From this pair of examples, it no longer seems obvious that the house would have selected their 'best' writer, for here are two using different, but related, forms of blended script. If there was no careful selection of writer, was the decision of who acted as scribe a spontaneous and pragmatic one, dependent not on the standard of writer, but on their availability and/or capability? If the second scribe at Furness was senior in age and position, did his writing of a second entry have a *social* or institutional rationale, and who, in practice, made these decisions? If, as we noted, blended hands present more starkly features that may be older or tend to incorporate newer trends not for institutional but individual reasons, that also makes them crucial for creating dating criteria.

This selection of entries illustrating the blended hand demonstrates effectively that these scribes did not stray from a *textura* or documentary hand, nor did they work their way towards one or another model. They blended forms of both models to create a different script, based on their training and preference and adapted for the specific context of the mortuary roll, which can be considered neither 'book' nor 'document'. It is noteworthy given these observations that most hands in London, British Library, Egerton MS 2849 and Cambridge, St John's College, MS N. 31 are written in a form of blended script. This in turn begs the question of how, when and where scribes were trained. This is an issue that is important to address as more medieval manuscripts and documents are made available digitally for scrutiny by scholars, widening the materials available for study well beyond those described in the standard palaeographical textbooks and articles to this point, and demonstrating that the categories by which we learn do not always match the visible efforts of the scribes themselves.

Gender and Script

Standard palaeographical textbooks describe medieval manuscript production as if the medieval scribe was by default a monk, canon or other male clerical figure. Occasionally there is an emphasis on the production of books by nunneries, more so in scholarship on continental manuscript studies.[40] In researching the mortuary rolls, one of the most important considerations is that of gender and textual production.[41] Not only are the rolls commemorations of senior women, who clearly held

---

40 See, for example, Hartmut Hoffmann, 'Das Skriptorium von Essen in ottonischer und frühsalischer Zeit', in *Kunst im Zeitalter der Kaiserin Theophanu. Akten des Internationalen Colloquiums veranstaltet vom Schnütgen-Museum Köln 13.–15. Juni 1991*, ed. Anton von Euw and Peter Schreiner (Köln, 1993), 113–53.

41 There has long been an interest in medieval female scribal activity, though a general, sustained overview has yet to be developed. Pioneering studies include Bernhard Bischoff, 'Die Kölner Nonnenhandschriften und das Skriptorium von Chelles', *Mittelalterliche Studien* 1 (1966), 16–34; Rosamond McKitterick, 'Nuns' Scriptoria in England and Francia in the Eighth Century', *Francia* 19.1 (1992), 1–35; Alison I. Beach, *Women as Scribes: Book Production and Monastic Reform in Twelfth-Century Bavaria* (Cambridge, 2004); Veronica O'Mara, 'The Late Medieval English Nun and her Scribal Activity: A Complicated Quest', in *Nuns' Literacies in Medieval Europe: The Hull Dialogue*, ed. Virginia Blanton, Veronica O'Mara and Patricia Stoop (Turnhout, 2013), 69–93; Laura Light, *Women and the Book in the Middle Ages and the Renaissance* (New York, 2015); and H. Lähnemann, 'The Materiality of Medieval Manuscripts', *Oxford German Studies* 45.2 (2016), 121–41. See also Diane Watt, *Women, Writing and Religion in England and Beyond, 650–1100* (London, 2020). The articles in *Women and Medieval Literary Culture*, ed. Saunders and Watt, offer a broader perspective on the involvement of women in book production. The most recent exploration of scribal and reading agency in manuscripts is Eike Grossmann, 'Introduction: Issues in the Study of Female Agency in Manuscript Cultures', in *Female Agency in Manuscript Cultures* (Berlin, 2024), 1–18.

high status and belonged to institutions with the resources to pay for and oversee these collections of condolences, but also there are many entries that testify to the possibility of women's handwriting: women scribes entering *tituli* on behalf of their houses. James Raine supposes that the *tituli* were entered by members of the respective institution; probably, he suggests, the Precentor.[42] If this were the case, then almost *all* the entries from the dozens of women's houses would be physically inscribed by women. Scholars must allow this possibility: if the *titulus* is from a female house, then we might consider it to be written by a female scribe, perhaps the precentrix, until proven otherwise. Moreover, if the house is female and the *titulus* represents that house, it is 'women's script' (sanctioned by women religious), no matter who wrote it. It cannot be assumed, as often seems to be the unspoken presumption, that women's houses only contained a single person (a man – the chaplain, the nun's priest) who could write.

Three entries of the many from nunneries can be highlighted to demonstrate issues that arise when working with an eye to the gender of scribes. In the first example, from Barking (see Fig. 3.4), the unassailable evidence is of a house that can provide competent, trained scribes to write the entries into the two rolls in the decade that separates them. Barking was a royal institution founded in the seventh century by Bishop Erkenwald, and one of the wealthiest and most prestigious establishments throughout its history. Its nuns were renowned for their learning, and books are known both to have been commissioned by abbesses and written for them as dedicatees.[43] In the decade when the two mortuary rolls made their way around religious houses, Barking's scribes offer two distinct forms of script. In St John's College, MS N. 31, the six-line entry takes up a commanding position on its membrane by virtue of the length of the *titulus*, which particularises the prayers that this house will offer for Amphelisa during daily masses and annually. The entry is written in a fairly formal, semi-cursive hand that is part 'small' hand, as Parkes might label it,[44] and part documentary hand, on unruled lines with a scattering of contemporary palaeographical features; for example, the **d** with the beginning of a loop; single-barred

---

42 Raine, *Obituary Roll of William of Ebchester*, xxviii.
43 Elaine Treharne, '"Miserere Meidens": Abbesses and Nuns'; and Jennifer N. Brown and Donna Alfano Bussell, eds, *Barking Abbey and Medieval Literary Culture: Authorship and Authority in a Female Community* (York, 2012).
44 Parkes, 'Handwriting in English Books'.

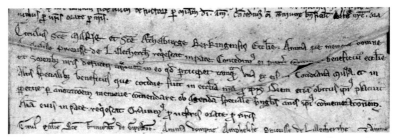

Fig. 3.4 Cambridge, St John's College, MS N. 31, entry for Barking Abbey.

initials (**T**, **E** and **C**); the tail of **g**, which loops around itself; and **a**, which often has an exaggerated bow. Ascenders are spurred, as are many of the tops of the graphs, like **c**, **q** and **s**. This latter feature is rather unusual in the roll.

> Titulus Sancte MARIE et Sancte Æthelburge Berkingensis Ecclesie. Anima pie memorie domne Amphelise, priorisse de Lillecherch', requiescant in pace. Concedimus ei, preter commune beneficium ecclesie, ut sororibus nostris defunctis associetur in eo quod participet tamquam una ex eis in cotidiana missa, et in aliis specialibus beneficiis, que cotidie fiunt in ecclesia nostra pro ipsis. Diem etiam obitus ipsius placuit perpetue per annotationem memorie commendare, ob agendam specialem singulis annis ipsius commemorationem. Anima eius in pace requiescat. Oravimus pro vestris, orate pro nostris.

> (*Titulus* of Saint Mary and Saint Æthelburh's Church in Barking. May the soul and the pious memory of Lady Amphelisa, prioress of Lillechurch, rest in peace. We grant her, beyond the general benefit of the church, an association with our deceased sisters in that she participates as one of them in the daily mass and in other special benefits that are daily performed in our church for them. It pleases us to commemorate in perpetuity the day of her death through a note of memory in order to observe a special commemoration of her each year. May her soul rest in peace. We have prayed for you, pray for us.)

Notably, the hand of this entry uses Old English Æ in the patron saint's name, and capitalises 'Marie', a feature that is found in later twelfth-century manuscripts (such as London, British Library, Cotton MS Claudius B. ix, fol. 183r/a/15). The hand is probably of a scribe who acquired her expertise towards the end of the twelfth century but was in a position to maintain an eye on current trends. A more general sense of intellectual engagement is also hinted at by the phrase 'Diem etiam obitus ipsius placuit perpetue per annotationem memorie commendare ob agendam specialem singulis annis ipsius commemorationem' ('It pleases us to commemorate in perpetuity the day of her death through a note of memory in order to observe a special commemoration of her each year'). This bespeaks a broader, book-aware community concerned with information transmission and the recording of knowledge; presumably Amphelisa's name was entered as an annotation into a *liber vitae*, service book or confraternity list after this *titulus* was written in St John's N. 31. This may have been done immediately, or a slip of vellum might have been passed on for this purpose. This single individuating sentence thus adds to the overall scene of this dynamic textual community at Barking in the first decades of the thirteenth century.

In contrast to the small, blended hand of this Barking scribe in the Amphelisa Roll and to the personalised response to Amphelisa's death and ongoing commemoration, the Egerton Roll a decade later provides evidence of a different Barking Abbey writer. Again, this is probably a woman religious of Barking, but one who provides a very typical and formulaic response to the commemoration of Lucy, Prioress of Hedingham:

> Titulus Sancte Marie et Sancte ætelburge uirginis Berkingensis ecclesie. Anima Domne Lucie, Priorisse de Heengeham, et anime omnium fidelium defunctorum, per dei misericordiam, resquiescant in pace Amen. Concedimus ei commune beneficium Ecclesie nostre. Orauimus pro uestris, orate pro nobis.[45]

> (*Titulus* of Saint Mary and Saint Æthelburh's Church in Barking. May the soul of Lady Lucy, prioress of Hedingham and the souls of all the faithful departed, through the mercy of God, rest in peace, Amen. We grant her the common benefit of our Church. We have prayed for you, pray for us.)

This three-line *titulus* is written in black ink on very widely spaced lines in a *textura* that, despite its relatively formality (it contains upright **d** as well as round-backed **d** and there are multiple pen lifts between letters), engages in decorative elements of script that belong more typically to

---

[45] See the image of the *titulus* under 'Barking' (east London; no. 16) on the Egerton Roll map, <https://medievalnetworks.github.io/mnm/map/map_egerton.html> (accessed 25 October 2024).

documentary hands. Thus, the ascender of every high **s** is decorated with a double-celled flag; the **A**, **C**, **E**, **D**, **M**, **O** and **P** are all decorated with horizontal bars; and the Tironian *nota* in the first line is crossed twice. The two-line-high enlarged **T** of *Titulus* is decorated with a swirl, as one might find in bookhand, though. It is a competent and contemporary script with biting of the **a+r** of 'Marie', an elaborate **or** ligature, and attention to the regularity of the minims and precision. Like the earlier Barking scribe, this one also uses Old English ash in 'ætelburge', which, slight evidence though it may be, does attest to a sensitivity to earlier English forms of the saint's name. Both entries for Barking indicate a writing environment in which competent and contemporary scripts could flourish, and in which book production methods (such as annotations, ruling and bookhand) are clearly known and deployed for writing out even this short *titulus* text.

Such is also the case at numerous other women's religious institutions included in the two rolls. Stamford and Flamstead Benedictine nunneries exemplify capable *textura* in St John's N. 31. In both cases the scribes rule for their entry, writing 'above top line', indicating an earlier thirteenth-century habit of *mise-en-page*. In the Egerton Roll, at folio 6r, the entry for Nunnaminster, Winchester, is an exemplary manifestation of a formal *textura*, though the breviator appears to have rolled up the membrane too quickly, since the last line is smudged. Writing 'above top line', the hand may be one with experience of writing liturgical books, since it demonstrates a slight decorative wave in the downstroke of minims evident in service books in the first decades of the thirteenth century. The names of the titular saints – 'MARIE' and 'EDBURGE' – are written in Rustic Capitals, the wavy Tironian *nota* is crossed, and two nested **V**s create a distinctive form of **W**.

A few entries beneath that of Nunnaminster are the tituli of Wilton and Shaftesbury, both ancient and elite Benedictine nunneries. Their entries are written in hands that exemplify absolutely on-trend characteristics of textura blended with the less formal but decorative qualities of documentary hands (in the embellished ascenders, swooping descenders, and semi-cursivity in the Shaftesbury hand). In St John's N. 31, there are several expert contemporary hands, including that of Westwood Benedictine Nunnery (see Fig. 3.5 below), which might be one of the most notable hands among the many examples: a Gothic *textura* prescissa.

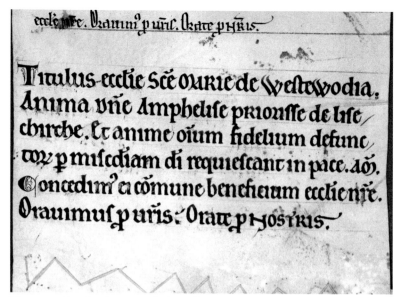

Fig. 3.5 Cambridge, St John's College, MS N. 31, entry for Westwood Benedictine Priory, Worcestershire.

The scribe of this *titulus* rules and writes 'below top line', which is an important indicator of date and of knowledge of the newest trends.[46] The six-line entry announces itself in its dominant presence on the membrane, the black ink confirming the determination of the scribe to have their entry seen. The T of 'Titulus' is decorated; the arches of the minim strokes are precise in their *ductus*; the terminals of downstrokes float evenly just above the ruled line. It is a masterly exposition of the script. And yet, Westwood is not a particularly well-known religious institution, scarcely featuring on the landscape of women's houses. Near Droitwich in Worcestershire, the priory was founded in the reign of Henry II by the de Say family as a daughter house of Fontevrault.[47] While initially there were only six nuns, the institution grew to about eighteen

---

46 N. R. Ker, 'From "Above Top Line" to "Below Top Line": A Change in Scribal Practice', in Ker, *Books, Collectors and Libraries: Studies in the Medieval Heritage*, ed. Andrew G. Watson (London, 1985), 71–4.

47 For this, as for all religious institutions in this period, see *British History Online*: <https://www.british-history.ac.uk/vch/worcs/vol2/pp148-151> (accessed 25 October 2022).

nuns later in the medieval period. The house was favoured by women from noble families, and as such, one might speculate that literacy levels were high in the priory, and certainly the nuns' entry into the Amphelisa Roll suggests a well-trained scribe with a good knowledge of contemporary liturgical book production methods.

Not all *tituli* written to represent women's houses in the two rolls indicate a high level of scribal expertise. The majority, in fact, can be seen to illustrate quite the opposite. Rather than casting value judgements on the quality or calligraphic finesse of the exemplified hands, though, it is preferable simply to note the kinds of treatment given to the copying of the respective *titulus* in order to determine what conclusions one can draw from these scribal stints. A couple of examples will suffice here to illustrate the kinds of issues that emerge. In the case of Wroxall Priory, a Benedictine nunnery in Warwickshire founded in the first half of the twelfth century, it can be surmised from extant fabric that the house was never particularly large or wealthy (sustaining perhaps ten nuns?). The entry for the priory in St John's, N. 31, is a quite remarkable, very large, non-current but informal *textura* (see Fig. 3.6). It is unpractised, as can be seen from the forms of **d**, which are round-backed, but almost indistinguishable from Caroline **a**; old-fashioned in its *ductus*, with no serifs or embellishments but using the contemporary straight macron and Caroline **r**; and struggling to spell ('qondam' for 'quondam'; 'oniu[m]' for 'omniu[m]'), to stay straight and to manage the quill.[48] There is no ruling to guide the five lines of the entry, which contains smudges, squeezed-in letters to complete words at the line-ends, and very notably (and helpfully) condolences for the wrong subject. Instead of commemorating Amphelisa, prioress of Lillechurch, the scribe names 'Hen[ricus] qondam prioris Colecestre' (Prior Henry of St Botolph's, Colchester, who died in 1205 or 1206).[49] The characteristics of this distinctive hand suggest a scribe who was trained in the later decades of the twelfth

---

48 On unpractised hands see Elaine Treharne, '"Terrible Letters": Bad Handwriting and its Implications, 1020–1220', *SELIM* 28 (2023), 79–96; and on the gap between literary activity and the ability to write in a script designated for books, see Benjamin Pohl, '*Abbas qui et scriptor?* The Handwriting of Robert of Torigni and His Scribal Activity as Abbot of Mont-Saint-Michel (1154–1186)', *Traditio* 69 (2014), 45–86.

49 Note that the same mistaken subject is named in the Boxgrove Priory entry of the same roll – a curious coincidence worth exploring further. Dufour suggested that Henry's mortuary roll circulated at the same time (*Recueil des Rouleaux des Morts*, 2.104), but this seems unlikely over a decade after his death.

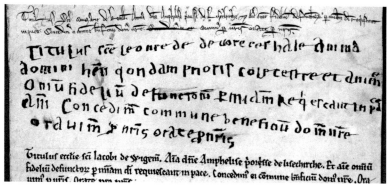

Fig. 3.6 Cambridge, St John's College, MS N. 31, entry for Wroxhall Priory.

century (perhaps even by 1180) and who was not used to writing a great deal. This scribe possesses an advanced pragmatic literacy, perhaps; that is to say, the ability to do the most necessary writing tasks. One question must be whether, on the day when the roll arrived for signing, this writer was Wroxall's most senior literate figure and, possibly, proficient scribe. It is worth pointing out the implication (in any case) that the institution was satisfied to be represented by this sizeable hand, which was apparently not considered embarrassing, underwhelming or insufficient in any way. It is good enough; and it takes up its fill of five bold, wonky lines on this membrane, sandwiched between the expert cursive hand of Kenilworth and the proficient *textura* of Wigmore Abbey (which itself is written on a ruled space 'below top line').

Just three miles from Wroxall in the low Warwickshire countryside near Kenilworth is another nunnery, a twelfth-century Cistercian foundation called Pinley. In St John's, N. 31, this entry (see Fig. 3.7 below) is two after that of Wroxall, even though the houses were such a short distance away from each other. Both could have been visited in one morning; neither was wealthy or well-endowed; neither saw the generation of an urban environment around them. Pinley is an institution where the scribe was sufficiently competent to write legibly in a contemporary hand, using the 'small' script that blends *textura* (written on unruled membrane) with a cursivity more common to documents. It is an unembellished script, written thinly, unevenly, self-consciously and a little shakily. But the main text is error-free (though the scribe has had to begin the *Titulus* twice). It uses contemporary punctuation and

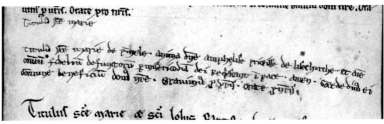

Fig. 3.7 Cambridge, St John's College, MS N. 31, entry for Pinley Priory.

abbreviation markers (straight macrons, dashed **i**, and a barred initial **O** in 'Orauim*us*'); and seeks balance and an eye to calligraphic detail in the extended last limb of **n** and **m** and **h**. Without seeking to romanticise this hand, what is clear is the thoughtful effort to present a *titulus* that is tidy and timely. Pinley might have been a small and modest house, but the stint, while sloping and irregularly spaced, is legible and certainly undertaken by a scribe who knew what she was doing.

The question of gender and script is a promising line of enquiry using this and other rolls, and further 'everyday' kinds of documentation and correspondence. While the same varieties of types of script and competencies apply as principal concerns to all the houses represented in the rolls, there is much more to be discovered about the display of practisedness among the scribes. If, as one might reasonably surmise, religious women did not always have access to the same levels of training or the same quantity of writing experience as monks and canons, our evidence, if generously understood, suggests that there were numerous capable women scribes, and that those who might be considered less capable were nonetheless willing to act (and accepted) as scribes. Their hands, while not as calligraphic or, at times, up to date as most of the male scribes', nevertheless attest to a rich, dynamic, and common environment for women's literacy in the earlier thirteenth century. We can only appreciate their scribal production if we allow a place for their hands in palaeography, and a place without aesthetic value judgement. Both the script and the religious networks formed between the women's houses are rich areas for more detailed exploration.

Scriptscape

What we see on the substrate – the scripts and the hands – occupied and still occupies a physical landscape space. The entries for houses in the county of Lincolnshire offer a fundamentally significant example of this. The Witham Valley, running from Lincoln to Boston, was one of the densest monastic landscapes in medieval England.[50] The breviator of St John's, N. 31, visited all seven monasteries: Kirkstead, Stixwould, Tupholme, Bardney, Stainfield, Oxney (Barlings), and Bullington on the east side of the River Witham. These seven houses existed in proximity, at a total distance of under 13 miles. This monastic geography was greatly influenced by key factors such as the fertile soil of the valley (especially in comparison with surrounding countryside) and the importance of the river as a trading tract; the chain of monasteries was situated just at the edge of the fens, on the bank of the river. These physical factors seem to have had curious palaeographical consequences that suggest potential links between institutions in terms of scribal training, intellectual exchange, and conversation. As a diocese, Lincolnshire has a high concentration of scribal features that are much rarer than in other regions represented on the roll. Barred initials (capitals with decorative parallel bars) are particularly widespread. In the Witham Valley, only Steinfield and Stixwould, the female houses, do not have this feature, which might relate to a more conservative training of their scribes.[51] While the scripts differ, the features seem to reflect a common geography and relationships that are closer between the male-only houses than between the male and female houses.[52] The social space of parchment – highly gendered, populated by male and female houses, intersectional in its very construction – interacts with the socio-topographical landscape of England in the early thirteenth century. The space of the roll reflects, to an extent, the gender relationships of the monasteries visited. Of the institutions represented in St John's, N. 31, 16.77 per cent are female, and, in a spatial parallel, they take 18.77 per cent of the roll's space.

50   Paul Everson and David A. Stocker, 'The Witham Valley: a landscape with monasteries?', *Church Archaeology* 13 (2009), 1–15.
51   The Gilbertine house, Bullington Priory, was the only double house in the Valley.
52   Here, it should be noted that Dufour probably misidentified 'Oxenay' in the Barlings entry; it is not Oxney Priory but Barlings Abbey, a Premonstratensian house, that was sometimes called 'Oxenay' in the documents, representing an 'island' in the fens. See further, <http://epns.nottingham.ac.uk/browse/Lincolnshire/Barlings/53286846b47fc40b93000f7d-Barlings> (accessed 26 October 2024). This case of mistaken identity helps consolidate the order of visits in the Amphelisa Roll, and is a reminder that the rolls can only be fully understood in relationship with the landscape itself.

The ownership of landscape is also reflected in palaeographical features. We lack complete information about the houses' economic status, but some of the larger houses tend to use documentary scripts, which would indicate an active administration in the institution, connected with the need to manage property. The well-resourced royal abbey of Waltham is a good example, with its extensive possessions and role as a major pilgrimage site; its high status is visually represented by the strongly contemporary and well-executed documentary hand of its *titulus* in the St John's College, N. 31, roll. In this sense we can see the rolls as metaphorically akin to a daguerreotype of the landscape and the inner logistics of the roll.

We can also observe these relationships in reverse. While parchment space is not a great leveller, it does allow participation to agents that might otherwise be considered to be marginal. Small monasteries with perhaps only five or six nuns, like St Sepulchre's in Canterbury, take up a similar amount of space to the larger institutions. In cases like St Leonard's in Wroxall, mentioned above, the larger space taken up is due to the irregularity of a non-professional hand, where the *ductus* requires generous spacing. The collaborative endeavour of the mortuary roll represents a different demonstration of the way social space was envisaged. You may have possessed few worldly goods – and represent fewer souls – but your *titulus* could still occupy a significant part of the membrane.[53] The rolls are then also an impressive expression of diversity, and clear proof of the participation of non-professional, but literate, monks and nuns within medieval commemorative culture – regardless of, and sometimes even in contrast with, their position in social and economic space. Each scribal effort – irrespective of whether it is that of an expert or less expert hand – is given similar space, subverting the category of aesthetic judgement.

Monasteries that the breviator was tasked or chose to visit were selected based on their role and position in the ecclesiastical landscape. However, the entries also reflect the anchoring of the monasteries in the society around them. Some institutions, like Battle Abbey as represented in Egerton 2849, give us a glimpse of the sheer variety of scripts that were exercised in the one house. This entry is written by three hands,

---

[53] See also, for example, the entry for Esholt, a relatively small and impoverished house of Cistercian nuns in Yorkshire. For more on this institution, see Henry Esmond Bell, 'Esholt Priory', *Yorkshire Archaeological Journal* 33 (1936), 4–33.

the first two blended, the third one a *textura* hand. While the first hand produces the *titulus*, the other two add names of people – probably benefactors – for whom they are asking for prayers. The second hand gives us 'Willelmus, Willelmus, Herbertus, Durandus, Petrus, Ricardus, Robertus, Radulfus, Robertus, Ema, Emma, Ricardus' and the third one 'Maria, [erased name], Dionisia, Johannes'. Such collaboration shows not only the connection of the monastery itself with these people, but also the monks' own status and role within the roll's social space, as different hands seem to be responsible for different people.

As well as detecting relationships within the rolls, filiations according to houses, forms of training, and levels of practice can be evaluated. Clearly some scribes' hands are more conservative; some represent fashions pertinent to the moment; and some are evidently dependent on training from some decades earlier. Such findings speak to any number of crucial intellectual and cultural aspects of scribal practice: that many writers were not 'professional', and neither did they update their hands. These scribes, even those who are unpractised, may have been the only person available to inscribe a competent *titulus* when the Breviator came knocking. The rolls are monuments to condolence, but through them, it is possible to determine how sometimes even the smallest of houses, numbering just a few nuns or monks, have been sure to write a *titulus*, sometimes confidently and sometimes with significant effort. For some of them these *tituli* are the only surviving textual witnesses to the residents of those institutions. We see hands that are clearly not what palaeographers would call 'trained' or professional: ones that are struggling to keep to their allotted space, but that still participate in the commemorative practice. They all converge in a scriptscape that exists not only on the membrane of the rolls, but also from the landscape that produced it.

Conclusion

These diverse hands and scripts, concentrated in both rolls within a relatively short span of space and time, allow us to observe a remarkable variety of features, several of which are demonstrably earlier than palaeographers would generally date them, and many of which are not easily assigned to the categories of script typically taught in modern manuscript studies. Received assumptions about dating scribal features and mapping the transmission of scripts can begin to be reappraised. It is clear, for example, that in real and everyday scribal practices scripts that combine features from *textura* and documentary hand were able to exist independently as idioscripts. These can usefully be thought of as 'blended', incorporating features from different scripts, but remaining individuated, identifiable and influential.

The entries of the rolls encourage new questions and new hypotheses: are terms like 'grade' applicable or useful? How was the 'professionalisation' of scribes anchored within the thirteenth-century reality of the regions and institutions of England, Wales and Scotland?[54] Far from being 'ugly' or 'bad', these hands represent the diversity of writing practice present in Britain in the earlier thirteenth century, as Gothic scripts and their documentary equivalents, plus blended scripts, evolved. Increased administration throughout the country, and a large developing bureaucracy, meant the development of all kinds of pragmatic writing sometimes exigently performed. The writers' hands on display in this roll run the gamut of script-type and execution. Rather than strictly categorising or labelling the qualitative aspects of handwriting of this period, it might be more beneficial to focus on asking what script in its practice reveals about religious institutions and their textual production. It would be useful to assess which institutions had members trained in book hands and charter hands, and how this relates to the economic standing and social connections of these houses. Some houses clearly had no professional scribes and could not (or did not want to) hire one to compose their respective *titulus*.

At the same time the rolls prompt us to think about the role of women in textual production. It is likely that further research can reveal particular features for diagnosing women's hands. Not all entries from female institutions will necessarily be written by a woman's hand, but undoubtedly some are, and it should be noted that this evidence provides leverage for reconceiving the broader world of manuscript and documentary production.

---

54 Scholars of later fourteenth and fifteenth-century London are currently engaging with the question of professional scribes: see, most recently, the contributions to the special issue of *Speculum* 99 (2024), 663–804, 'Essay Cluster: Communities of Practice: New Methodological Approaches to Adam Pinkhurst and Chaucer's Earliest Scribes', by Kathryn Kerby-Fulton, Simon Horobin, Linne R. Mooney, Orietta Da Rold, Theresa O'Byrne, Jeremy J. Smith and Sebastian Sobecki.

And finally, the rolls show us a 'scriptscape'; that is, a rich landscape of relationships, social connections, networks of power and influence within and between the religious establishments that produced the unique social spaces of London, British Library, Egerton MS 2849 and Cambridge, St John's College, MS N. 31. These scriptscapes represent real-world connections with consequences for the study of medieval palaeography itself. The physical presence of the monasteries, and the very material circumstances of the hands that we witness, influenced scribal choices on display in the rolls. This evidence has important repercussions for the study of medieval handwriting that go far beyond discussion of the scribes of the rolls themselves, involving some of the most fundamental areas of the field: from how script is classified and described; to the involvement of women in textual production; and to the representation of power, place and privilege on the pages of the past.

4

Domestic Politics/Insurrection Politics: Parables of Obedience in the *Mesnagier de Paris* and the Revolts of 1380–3

Michael Sizer

The fundamental problem in studying medieval revolt is the nature of the available sources, which, as Claude Gauvard notes, 'come to us almost exclusively from authorities and [...] give us only the point of view of those holding power and the dominant social classes'.[1] Juridical and narrative sources alike generally frame revolt activity as criminal or outside the proper conduct of political life: as a threat to, or an interruption of, the harmonious society of orders.[2] For this reason, oblique or passing references to revolt in literature or other sorts of texts, in which the marginalising agenda found in most conventional political sources is secondary or absent, can help uncover a new side of these historical phenomena.

It is in this context that I turn to an odd little story in the form of a parable, found in the *Mesnagier de Paris*.[3] This story, which I will call the parable of the Bourgeois Rebel's Wife, comes from the section on wifely obedience in Chapter 6 of the first of three 'distinctions'. Most of this chapter's instruction on a wife's obligation to be obedient is delivered in the form of parables, or exempla, drawn from sources

---

1 Claude Gauvard, 'Révoltes populaires', in *Dictionnaire du Moyen Âge*, ed. Claude Gauvard, Alain de Libera and Michel Zink (Paris, 2002), 1206–9 (1206): 'proviennent presque exclusivement des autorités et qui ne donnent que le point de vue des pouvoirs en place et des couches sociales dominantes.'
2 General methodological and theoretical approaches to this problem are covered in Ranajit Guha, *Elementary Aspects of Peasant Insurgency in Colonial India* (Durham NC, 1999; first publ. 1983), 14–7.
3 *Le Mesnagier de Paris*, ed. Georgina E. Brereton and Janet Ferrier, trans. Karin Ueltschi (Paris, 1994).

both popular and learned: biblical stories, didactic Bible commentaries, conduct books and folklore, as well as the author's personal experience.[4] Unlike the more famous stories in this section of the *Mesnagier* (such as the Griselda tale), this parable has received little direct attention from scholars.[5] The text is as follows:

> In and for all things – good or bad – that you have done, you are free and clear of blame when you say, 'My husband ordered me to do it'. Even if a wrong comes from your constancy to your husband's commands, it is said of a married woman, 'She acted well, since her husband directed her; in so doing she performed her duty'. Thus, at worst, you will not only be excused but also well praised.
>
> On this subject, I will tell you a piteous and astonishing tale, which provokes sympathy. I know a woman from a bourgeois family of distinction who is married to a good man, and they are both decent creatures, an irreproachable couple with two beautiful young children. The woman is blamed for having received the company of a great lord, but, by God, when people speak about it, the other women and men who know the story, and even those who hate the sin, say that the woman should not be held responsible because she was following her husband's orders. This is the situation: they live in one of the greatest cities of this kingdom. The king because of a rebellion of the city's inhabitants imprisoned her husband and several other compatriots. Each day, three or four of these prisoners were beheaded. The woman and the other wives of the prisoners went before the lords each day, in tears, on their knees and with clasped hands, imploring them to have pity and mercy and agree to set their husbands free. One of the lords who was close to the king, a cruel and treacherous tyrant fearing neither God nor His justice, sent a wicked message to the bourgeoise saying that if she agreed to satisfy his lustful desires, he would have her husband set free without fail. She answered nothing to this missive but begged the messenger that, for the love of God, he arrange with those who guarded her husband in prison that she might visit and speak with him. And thus it was done. In the prison cell with her husband, weeping, she reported to him what she saw or could perceive of the others in prison with him and also about the

---

4 Janet Ferrier, 'Seulement pour vous endoctriner: the author's use of exempla in the *Ménagier de Paris*', *Medium Aevum* 48 (1979), 77–89.
5 Léon Mirot's dated but definitive study of these uprisings makes only passing references to the *Mesnagier*, with no significant discussion of the parable; see Mirot, *Les insurrections urbaines au début du règne de Charles VI: 1380–1383: leurs causes, leurs conséquences* (Geneva, 1974; first publ., 1905).

prospect of his deliverance because of the foul request made of her. Her husband bid her do what was necessary for him to escape with his life, whatever it took, and not to spare her body or her honor or any other thing to save him. On this they parted from each other tearfully. Several of the other prisoners were beheaded, but her husband was freed. She is excused for such a grave matter because, supposing that it is true, she has neither sin nor guilt, nor has she committed a crime or bad deed, since her husband had commanded it. On the contrary, she acted wisely to save her husband, as a good wife. At any rate, I now leave this matter that is unpleasant to tell and too serious (cursed be the tyrant who did it!), and I return to my topic, that one must obey one's husband, and I will leave such weighty matters for those of lesser magnitude.[6]

6 *The Good Wife's Guide*, trans. Gina L. Greco and Christine M. Rose (Ithaca NY, 2009), 123–4, with some alterations of my own. *Le Mesnagier de Paris*, 248–50: 'Car en tout et par tout, soit bien soit mal que vous aiez fait, vous estes quictes et délivrés, "Mon mary le m'a commandé". Encores se mal vient par vostre courage, si dit l'en d'une femme mariee: "Elle fist bien, puis que son mary lui commanda; car en ce faisant elle fist son devoir." Et ainsi au pis venir vous en seriez non mie seulement excusé, mais bien louee. / Et a ce propos je vous diray une piteuse merveille, et que je plain bien. Je scay une femme de tresgrant nom en bourgeoisie qui est mariee en une bonne personne, et sont deux bonnes creatures, jennes gens paisibles et qui ont de beaux petis enfans. La femme est blasmee d'avoir receu la compaignie d'un grant seigneur mais, par Dieu, quant l'on en parle, les autres femmes et hommes qui scevent le cas, et mesmement ceulx qui heent ce pechié, dient que la femme n'en doit point estre blasmee, car son mary lui commanda. Le cas est tel, qu'ilz demeurent en une des plus grans citez de ce royaume. Son mary et pluseurs autres bourgoiz furent de par le roy emprisonnez pour une rebellion que le commun avoit faite. Chascun jour l'en en coppoit les testes a iii ou a iiii d'iceulx. Elle et les autres femmes d'iceulx prisonniers estoient chascun jour devers les seigneurs, plourans et agenoillans et les mains jointes requerans que l'en eust pitié et misericorde, et entendesist l'en a la deliverance de leurs mariz. L'un des seigneurs qui estoit entour le roy, comme non cremant Dieu ne sa justice, mais comme cruel et felon tirant, fist dire a icelle bourgoise que s'elle vouloir faire sa voulonté, sans faulte il feroit delivrer son mary. Elle ne respondy riens sur ce, mais dit au messaige que pour l'amour de Dieu il feist par devers ceulx qui gardoient son mary en la prison qu'elle veist son mary et qu'elle parlast a lui, et ainsi fut fait. Car elle fut mise en prison avec son mary et toute plourant lui deist ce qu'elle veoit ou povoit appercevoir des autres, et aussi de l'estat de sa delivrance et la villeinne requeste que l'en lui avoit faicte. Son mary lui commanda que, comment qu'il fust, qu'elle fist tant qu'il eschappast sans mort, et qu'elle n'y espargnast ne son corps, ne son honneur, ne autre chose pour le sauver et rescourre sa vie. A tant se partirent l'un de l'autre tous deux plorans. Pluseurs des autres prisonniers bourgoiz furent decapitez, son mary fut

Like the more frequently studied, fictional parables in the chapter, this tale instructs the young woman on the importance of wifely obedience. The crucial difference is that it is taken (ostensibly) from real life. The tale is set during the repression of the rebellious bourgeois residents of an unnamed city – almost certainly Paris in the aftermath of the Maillotin ('Mallet-Wielders') Revolts of 1380–3, which took place just a decade or so before the publication of the *Mesnagier*. Setting the story during what was, for the author and his audience, a major, even traumatic event from recent memory gives it a powerful immediacy, and furthermore serves as a fascinating commentary on these revolts from the perspective, rarely found in other source material, of a bourgeois observer. Studying the story also presents an opportunity for a deeper understanding of the *Mesnagier*: though scholars have pointed out the conjunction between the text's message on bourgeois conjugal life and its more implicit commentary on public politics, this question has only been approached in broad strokes.[7] The exemplum of the Bourgeois Rebel's Wife allows us a more specific and penetrating review of this question, as its subject matter was, for the author and his audience, a quite unsettled and unsettling political event. Because the *Mesnagier*'s parable weaves gendered power dynamics together with a story concerning political authority, it provides a particularly rich account of the functioning of power at the micro-level and the macro-level, and the relationship between them.

What is most interesting is the disjuncture created by the combination of these two political dynamics: a story about obedience and harmonious relations in the conjugal sphere is set in a situation of

---

delivré. Si l'excuse l'en d'un si grant cas que soupposé ores qu'il soit vray, sy n'y a elle ne pechié ne coulpe, ne ne commist delit ne mauvestié quant son mary lui commanda. Mais fist pour sauver son mary sagement et que bonne femme. Mais toutesvoyes je laisse le cas qui est villain a reconter et trop grant (maudit sois le tirant qui ce fist!) et revien a mon propos que l'en doit obeir a son mary, et laisseray les grans cas et prendray les petis cas d'esbatement.'

7 Glenn Burger discusses the *Mesnagier*'s implications for a new kind of bourgeois subject and argues that this went beyond the area of conjugal/gender relations into the wider political sphere: *Conduct Becoming: Good Wives and Husbands in the Later Middle Ages* (Philadelphia PA, 2018), esp. 22–3, 129–40, 191–7. Lynn Staley comments on the dynamics of class power in the *Mesnagier* in *Languages of Power in the Age of Richard II* (University Park PA, 2005), 275–88. Roberta Krueger comments on the unsettled nature of authority in the text in 'Identity Begins at Home: Female Conduct and the Failure of Counsel in *Le Menagier de Paris*', *Essays in Medieval Studies* 22 (2005), 21–39.

disobedience and disorder in the political sphere. This juxtaposition makes the text distinctively useful for understanding the complex and contested political culture of the revolutionary years of the late fourteenth century, as well as the interconnection between domestic and public politics in medieval bourgeois culture. The parable critiques the tyranny experienced by the text's audience in a specific real-world event, and contrasts the excess of power seen there with the supposed amity of the well-ordered conjugal sphere, an ethic of mutuality that functions as a political commentary even as it reinforces bourgeois patriarchy.

The Mesnagier: Author and Audience

Most scholars agree that the author/narrator was a wealthy Parisian man of bourgeois extraction.[8] Because first-hand accounts of bourgeois life and worldviews are rare in medieval France, this would make the *Mesnagier* a precious and valuable source. Nonetheless, rather than take for granted the social identity of the author and his audience, this section will outline the social setting of the *Mesnagier* and the late medieval Parisian bourgeois world in order to situate the text socially.

Written around 1394 as a guide on household management ostensibly by an older husband to his new, fifteen-year-old wife, the *Mesnagier* is a wide-ranging text that includes, among other things, recipes, instructions on how to direct servants, a treatise on falconry, a poem, and moral instructions on proper wifely behaviour. Its form as a compendium of disparate sources of moral and practical instruction may have been influenced by bourgeois *livres de raison*, which were collections of family documents and didactic materials assembled by a *pater familias* for the benefit of his descendants, and also by the 'Mirror for Princes' genre thriving in the late Middle Ages, as well as Aristotelian and pseudo-Aristotelian texts on household management.[9] The author was not

---

8   On speculations regarding the author's identity, see Greco and Rose, 'Introduction', in *The Good Wife's Guide*, 1–2; Brereton and Ferrier, 'Introduction', in *Le Mesnagier de Paris*, 8–9; and the introduction to Jérôme Pichon, ed., *Le Ménagier de Paris: traité de morale et d'économie domestique*, 2 vols (Paris, 1846), 1:xxv–xxviii. Nicole Crossley-Holland argues that the author was not a bourgeois but rather a knight, Guy de Montigny: *Living and Dining in Medieval Paris: The Household of a Fourteenth-century Knight* (Cardiff, 1996).

9   On bourgeois conduct books as possible influence on the *Mesnagier*, see Ionut Epurescu-Pascovici, 'From Moral Agent to Actant: Conduct in *Le*

unfamiliar with court circles – several references in the text suggest some sort of connection with the household of the Duke of Berry,[10] and at least two of the three extant pre-1500 manuscripts come from the collections of members of the Duke of Burgundy's court[11] – but the narrator's self-fashioning is repeatedly bourgeois, as when he enjoins his wife not to frequent parties or dances of high-ranking lords, because 'that would not be appropriate to your rank or mine'.[12]

This possible association with the court of the Duke of Berry, as well as the book's presence in the libraries of courtiers of the Duke of Burgundy, indicates the fluidity of the 'bourgeois' as a social or cultural category in late medieval France. Contemporary vocabulary for social categories is notoriously confusing.[13] The title 'Bourgeois of Paris', for example, was a legal term denoting specific rights and privileges associated with trade and citizenship rights in the city,[14] but by the late fourteenth century, it could be used generically to refer to an urban citizen.[15] At times, a Bourgeois of Paris or a wealthy merchant could

---

Ménagier de Paris', *Exemplaria* 24.3 (2012), 214–37. For more on these sources, see Katherine Lewis, 'Model Girls? Virgin-Martyrs and the Training of Young Women in Late-Medieval England', in *Young Medieval Women*, ed. Katherine J. Lewis, Noël James Menuge and Kim M. Phillips (New York, 1999), 25–46. On the connection between the *Mesnagier* and 'Mirrors for Princes' and other conduct books, see Roberta Krueger, '*Nouvelles choses*: Social Instability and the Problem of Fashion in the *Livre du Chevalier de la Tour Landry*, the *Ménagier de Paris*, and Christine de Pizan's *Livre des Trois Vertus*', in *Medieval Conduct*, ed. Kathleen Ashley and Robert L. A. Clark (Minneapolis MN, 2001), 49–85. On the connection between the *Mesnagier* and Aristotle and pseudo-Aristotle's texts, see Staley, *Languages of Power*, 275; and Sylvana Vecchio, 'The Good Wife', in *A History of Women in the West: Silences of the Middle Ages (Vol. 2)*, ed. Christiane Klapisch-Zuber (Cambridge MA, 1992), 105–35 (107–9).

10   *Le Mesnagier de Paris*, 182, 430, 540.
11   Greco and Rose, 'Introduction', in *The Good Wife's Guide*, 2–3.
12   *Le Mesnagier de Paris*, 24: 'car ce ne vous est mie convenable ne afferant a vostre estat ne au mien'.
13   Philip Braunstein, 'Pour une histoire des élites urbaines: vocabulaire, réalités et représentations', in *Les Élites Urbaines au Moyen Âge: XVIIème Congrès de la S.H.M.E.S. (Rome, 1996)* (Paris, 1997), 29–38.
14   Joseph Di Corcia, 'Bourg, bourgeois, bourgeois de Paris from the Eleventh to the Eighteenth Century', *Journal of Modern History* 50 (1978), 207–33; Boris Bove, *Dominer la ville: Prévôts des marchands et échevins parisiens de 1260 à 1350* (Paris, 2004), 540.
15   In several fifteenth-century farces the term is stripped of its quasi-juridical meaning, particularly when referring to women 'bourgeoises'; in one instance

be grouped with those beneath him socially, referred to collectively as 'non-nobles' or 'the people';[16] elsewhere, texts were careful to differentiate the 'greater men' from others in the city.[17] In terms of wealth, social affinities and cultural self-styling, the highest of the bourgeois could certainly resemble the aristocracy they admired and sought to emulate, conducting jousts, building great halls, reading romances, and otherwise engaging in conspicuous displays of wealth.[18] The *Mesnagier* itself is strong evidence for this. Indeed, a crucial characteristic of the bourgeois, so relevant to its political history as well, has been its chameleon-like ability to ally with those above and those below in the social scale where it was useful and expedient.[19] Many Bourgeois of Paris were ultimately accepted into the ranks of the nobility, ennobled as a reward

---

the word is even used to describe a city woman's dress: *Recueil de farces inédites du XVème siècle*, ed. Gustave Cohen (Cambridge MA, 1949), 44, 55, 113, 167, 205, 277, 300–1 ('bourgeoises'), and for the dress, 304. By the end of the fourteenth century, Bove estimates that there were only a hundred or so title-holding Bourgeois of Paris; see *Dominer la ville*, 551. This may be a conservative estimate: Le Roux de Lincy provides a list of well over 1,000 'notable bourgeois' from the late fourteenth/early fifteenth centuries, but the list includes several who probably did not carry the title of Bourgeois, repeats a few names, and covers several generations; see *Le Paris de Charles V et de Charles VI: vu par les écrivains contemporains*, ed. Le Roux de Lincy and L. M. Tisserand (Caen, 1992 [1867]), 206–23.

16 Bernard Guenée, *L'Opinion publique à la fin du Moyen Age d'après la 'Chronique de Charles VI' du Religieux de Saint-Denis* (Paris, 2002), 98–101.

17 [Michel Pintoin], *Chronique du Religieux de Saint-Denys contenant le règne de Charles VI de 1380 à 1422*, ed. Bernard Guenée and M. L. Bellaguet, trans. M. L. Bellaguet, 6 vols, 2nd edn (Paris, 1994), 3:340: 'auctoritatis viros urbis Parisiensis'; 5:10, 26, 34, 38, etc.: 'auctoritatis cives'; 5:36, 52, 120, etc.: 'auctoritatis burgenses'. *Journal d'un Bourgeois de Paris, 1405–1449*, ed. Colette Beaune (Paris, 1990), 70: 'greigneurs bourgeois de la ville'; 56, 67, 359–60: 'Les grands'.

18 Bove discusses these aspects of emulation of aristocratic culture in *Dominer la ville*, 537–620. See also Jean Favier, *Le Bourgeois de Paris au Moyen Âge* (Paris, 2012), 415–87. Guillebert De Mets's lengthy description of the sumptuous household of Jaques Duchié shows the wealth and grandeur of an early fifteenth-century bourgeois: *Description de la ville de Paris 1434*, ed./trans. Evelyn Mullally (Turnhout, 2015), 96–9.

19 Beatrix Le Wita, in her ethnographic/historical analysis of modern bourgeois culture, emphasizes its 'middleness' and tendency to assimilate: *French Bourgeois Culture*, trans. J. A. Underwood (Cambridge, 1994; first publ. 1988). See also Sharon Zukin, 'Mimesis in the Origins of Bourgeois Culture', *Theory and Society* 4.3 (1977), 333–58.

for service in royal and ducal courts, and occasionally they established alliances through marriage into aristocratic families.[20] It is with good reason that Guillebert de Mets, describing early fifteenth-century Paris, characterises some wealthy bourgeois as 'little kinglets of grandeur [*petis royetaux de grandeur*]'.[21] At the same time, as his mockery suggests, satirical literature also increasingly differentiated the bourgeois as an object of critique.[22] In all, the bourgeois as a distinct social phenomenon existed somewhat provisionally in the late Middle Ages.[23]

Nonetheless, some scholars have identified characteristics that they believe aligned with a bourgeois identity in the Middle Ages: focused on money and trade, seeking prestige outside a martial or intellectual sphere, emphasising private space apart from a public one, defining selfhood through wealth and action as opposed to inherited status, and focused on social advancement.[24] Burger shows the ways in which conduct literature like the *Mesnagier* both created and reflected a new kind of bourgeois subject empowered through self-restraint and moral virtue in the conjugal sphere.[25] The *Mesnagier* conforms to this outline in several important ways, equating 'acquiring riches' with the knight's quest for honour, though both are then subordinated to spiritual

---

20   On ennoblements, see Bove, *Dominer la ville*, 596–603; Favier, *Le Bourgeois de Paris*, 439–44; Philippe Contamine, *La noblesse au royaume de France de Philippe le Bel à Louis XII: essai de synthèse* (Paris, 1997), 67–8; Lucas Robert, 'Ennoblement in Late Medieval France', *Mediaeval Studies* 39 (1977), 239–60; Edouard Perroy, 'Social Mobility among the French Noblesse in the Later Middle Ages', *Past and Present* 21 (1962), 25–38.
21   De Mets, *Description de la ville*, 96.
22   Jean Alter, *Les origines de la satire anti-bourgeoise en France: Moyen Âge-XVIème siècle* (Geneva, 1966).
23   Although this could be said of the modern context as well: see Alfred Cobban, 'The Vocabulary of Social History', *Political Science Quarterly* 71 (1956), 1–17; Arno Mayer, 'The Lower Middle Class as a Historical Problem', *Journal of Modern History* 47.3 (1975), 409–36.
24   This list of features is distilled from readings from Bove, *Dominer la ville*, 579–623; *A History of Private Life. Vol. II: Revelations of the Medieval World*, ed. Georges Duby, trans. Arthur Goldhammer (Cambridge MA, 1988); Emma Lipton, *Affections of the Mind: The Politics of Sacramental Marriage in Late Medieval English Literature* (Notre Dame IN, 2007), 129–60; Sheila Delany, '*Flore et Jehane*: A Case Study of the Bourgeois Woman in Medieval Life and Letters', *Science and Society* 45.3 (1981), 274–87.
25   Burger, *Conduct Becoming*, esp. 123–40; 193–5.

pursuits;[26] it exalts the domestic space as a refuge from the more tumultuous public zone, promotes personal virtue and sobriety as a means to self-betterment rather than as features of the obligations of an inherent status, and sees social mobility as a fraught but aspirational possibility. The oscillation between private and public highlighted by Burger, between actions of personal virtue and public significance, is also a key factor in the Parable of the Bourgeois Rebel's Wife.[27] The *Mesnagier* is able to exploit this bourgeois subjectivity to fashion commentary on a contentious political issue in the public sphere – the Maillotin Revolt – by framing its discussion of that event as primarily related to personal moral betterment.

The parable is itself an excellent example of the hodgepodge quality and genre-mixing of the *Mesnagier*, as it combines elements of folktale, hagiography, romance, and real-life experience. Yet even as the *Mesnagier* borrows from all these elements of aristocratic, clerical, and popular culture, its self-positioning is outside those realms of the court, church, or workshop and field, as the product of a particular kind of urban subject.[28]

The Maillotin Revolt in Chronicles and Judicial Records

There is little evidence describing the experiences of the participants of the Maillotin revolt; this presents an especially acute problem for analysis of a tale that seems so reliant on the extra-textual knowledge and experience of its 1390s audience, for whom the revolt would have been immediate and powerful in the collective memory. These uprisings of 1380–3 remain some of the most under-studied revolts of the late Middle Ages, in spite of their magnitude.[29] The available sources are

---

26 *Le Mesnagier de Paris*, 120: 'Car ainsi comme le bourgoiz veille pour acquerir richesses a lui et a ses enfans, le chevalier et le noble veille pour acquerre pris et loz ou monde; chascun selon son estat en ce siecle veille pour les choses mondaines acquerre.'
27 Burger, *Conduct Becoming*, 62–74, 112–19, 194–5.
28 This is exemplified nicely when the *Mesnagier*, in distancing himself from the cruel Marquis in the Griselda story, emphasises that 'I am no marquis nor did I take you as a shepherdess' ('je ne suis mie marquis ne ne vous ay prise bergiere'): *Le Mesnagier de Paris*, 232.
29 The standard account remains the excellent but now dated study of Léon Mirot, *Les insurrections*. See also Michel Mollat and Philippe Wolff, *Ongles bleus*,

mostly chronicle accounts and judicial records.[30] The former are by no means monolithic: there is much difference, for example, between courtly 'clerc' Froissart and his wide audience seeking entertaining edification, and the quasi-official royal chronicle of Michel Pintoin, the Monk of Saint-Denis.[31] But these perspectives are still those of outsiders and observers. Criminal records stretch further our range of understanding; in the protestations of implicated bourgeois seeking royal grace in letters of remission can be seen self-serving but nonetheless useful glimpses of the motivations of rebel participants and on-lookers. Together these sources offer indirect access to the parable's setting.

The causes of the uprisings were complex. The rebellious cities expressed anti-fiscal – and particularly anti-taxation – grievances, which they combined with assertions of a defence of 'liberty' and local authority vis-à-vis royal administration.[32] Tactical opportunism also

---

Jacques et Ciompi. Les révolution populaires en Europe aux XIVème et XVème siècles (Paris, 1970), 139–212; Françoise Autrand, *Charles VI: la folie du roi* (Paris, 1980), 75–119; Samuel K. Cohn Jr, *Lust for Liberty: The Politics of Social Revolt in Medieval Europe, 1200–1425* (Cambridge MA, 2006), 99–100.

30 The chronicles referred to for this article are: *Chronique du Religieux de Saint-Denys, vol. 1; Chronique des quatre premiers Valois, 1327–1393*, ed. Siméon Luce (Paris, 1862); Jean Froissart, *Chroniques*, ed. Siméon Luce, Gaston Raynaud and Léon Mirot, 13 vols (Paris, 1869–), vol. 11, ed. Raynaud; *Chronographia Regum Francorum*, ed. Henri Moranvillé, 3 vols (Paris, 1891–7), vol. 3. For criminal records, I used letters of remission found in collection JJ in the Archives Nationales (hereafter AN JJ), and also those described in the notes of Mirot, *Les insurrections*.

31 On the historical approach, patronage, and audiences of Froissart, see *Froissart dans sa forge: actes du colloque réuni à Paris, du 4 au 6 novembre 2004*, ed. Michel Zink (Paris, 2006); Martin Nejedly, *La représentation des pouvoirs et des hiérarchies dans les chroniques de Jean Froissart* (Villeneuve d'Ascq, 2002); Peter Ainsworth, *Jean Froissart and the Fabric of History: Truth, Myth and Fiction in the Chroniques* (Oxford, 1990). For Pintoin, see Bernard Guenée, *Un Roi et son historien: Vingt études sur le règne de Charles VI et la 'Chronique du Religieux de Saint-Denis'* (Paris, 1999); Nicole Grévy-Pons and Ezio Ornato, 'Qui est l'auteur de la Chronique latine de Charles VI dite du Religieux de Saint-Denis?', *Bibliothèque de l'École des Chartes* 134 (1976), 85–102. For a useful study comparing chroniclers' treatments of revolt scenarios, see Marie-Thérèse de Medeiros, *Jacques et chroniqueurs: une étude comparée de récits contemporains relatant la Jacquerie de 1358* (Paris, 1979).

32 *Chronique du Religieux de Saint-Denys*, 1:130: 'libertatem'. A July 1383 pardon letter for valet goldsmith Jehan de Louvres describes a pre-uprising assembly in which Parisians vowed that 'the tax would not go forward so as to preserve the

explains their timing, at the moment of the accession of a new and unproven king, in this case the 1380 coronation of the teenaged Charles VI, whose government was to be administered by his uncles, the Dukes of Anjou, Berry and Burgundy, during the king's minority. Anger was expressed at these intermediaries, deemed corrupt or repressive, that lay between the idealised king and his loyal subjects, criticism exacerbated by these ministers' abrogation of Charles V's deathbed pledge to annul special taxation. Momentum and influence played a part: rebel cities were inspired by revolts in other communities, both within the kingdom and without.[33] The revolts did not take the form of sustained violence throughout their three-year duration, but instead consisted of episodes of rioting in between negotiations and periods of tenuous reconciliation. The Parisian rebels were sometimes called the Maillez or Maillotins (Mallet-wielders), as one of the major riots in the uprising featured Parisians using these unusual (and non-chivalric) weapons to gain control of the city in 1382.

The *Mesnagier*'s evocation of the corrupt judge's 'tyranny' was a loaded term, connected to a deep tradition of complaints of tyranny in late medieval political discourse, as well as the grievances of the Parisians in the Maillotins Revolt.[34] Immoderate taxation, the use of

---

liberties and freedoms that we (the king) had previously granted to our city of Paris' ('l'imposition ne couroit point afin de garder les libertés et franchises que octroyées et données avions a Nostre ville de Paris'): AN JJ 123 #235, 239.

33 Pintoin makes connections between the revolts in Paris and those in Flanders and England, and also relates that revolts in other cities within the realm were inspired by Paris: *Chronique du Religieux de Saint-Denys*, 1:130–4. For a discussion of these revolts as related, see *Il Tumulto dei Ciompi: un momento di storia fiorentina ed Europea*, ed. Istituto nazionale di studi sul Rinascimento. Atti di convegni 13 (Florence, 1981).

34 References to tyranny in medieval political texts are numerous and varied. A French example roughly contemporary with the *Mesnagier* comes from philosopher Nicolas Oresme, who translated and glossed Aristotle's *Politics* in the 1370s: 'whomever governs for his own profit against that of the common good, whether one or several persons, can be called a tyrant', in *Le Livre de Politiques d'Aristote*, ed. Albert Douglas Menut. Transactions of the American Philosophical Society n.s. 60.6 (Philadelphia PA, 1970), 112. Other useful discussions can be found in John of Salisbury, *Policraticus*, ed./trans. Cary J. Nederman (Cambridge, 1992), 28; Aquinas, *On Kingship, to the King of Cyprus*, trans. Gerald B. Phelan, rev. I. Th. Eschmann (Toronto, 1949, 1982), 13–8; Giles de Rome, *Li Livres du Gouvernement des Rois*, ed. Samuel Paul Molenaer (New York, 1899), 17, 99, 312–4, 322–5; Christine de Pisan, *The 'Livre de la Paix' of Christine de Pisan*:

corrupt subordinates and the abuse of a population's women were all seen as features of the tyrant, defined as the king who rules in his own interest rather than that of the Common Good. Royal subordinates were often seen as the agents of tyranny – the king was to blame for allowing flatterers and corrupt officials to manipulate him.[35] Parallel to the tyrant judge's crimes in the parable, Philippe de Mézières, a moralising cleric who was a contemporary of the *Mesnagier* author, writes in his *Songe du Vieil Pélerin* that one of the features of tyranny is forcefully disrespecting the marriage of subjects, an affront to their 'liberty and freedom', and also later declares that a king must preserve merchants' 'bodies and goods from all violence'.[36] Though they were often vague about the means by which a tyrant should be removed from power, it was clear that the tyrant should be deposed.[37] Aquinas argued that only those with 'public authority' should be charged with this, a sentiment echoed by Nicolas Oresme and Christine de Pisan, and though they stop short of sanctioning violent rebellion, they do note that popular rebellion is a natural and predictable outcome of a community subjected to tyranny.[38]

Bourgeois of Paris played variable roles in these uprisings. Wary of the commons' radicalism and anti-wealth sentiments, of which some of

---

A Critical Edition, ed. Charity Cannon Willard (The Hague, 1958), 121–3; Diego Quaglioni, ed., *Politica e diritto nel Trecento italiano: il 'De Tyranno' di Bartolo da Sassoferrato (1314-1357)* (Florence, 1983). See also Oscar Jászi and John D. Lewis, *Against the Tyrant: The Tradition and Theory of Tyrannicide* (Glencoe IL, 1957), 3–41.

35 Oresme, *Le Livre de Politiques*, 175.

36 Philippe de Mézières, *Le Songe du Vieil Pelerin*, ed. G. W. Coopland, 2 vols (Cambridge, 1969), 2:347, 422; cf. Christine de Pisan, *Livre de Paix*, 123; Giles de Rome, *Li Livres du Gouvernement des Rois*, 317, 322.

37 Aquinas, *On Kingship*, 26–7; Oresme, *Le Livre de Politiques*, 152; Ptolemy of Lucca, *On the Government of Rulers: De regimine principum*, ed./trans. James M. Blythe (Philadelphia PA, 1997), 74–6, 90; Giovanni Boccaccio, *De Casibus Virorum Illustrium*, cited in Jászi and Lewis, *Against the Tyrant*, 39.

38 Aquinas, *On Kingship*, 47–8; Oresme, *Le Livre de Politiques*, 152, 204; Christine de Pisan, *Livre de Paix*, 143–4. This belief is articulated in political theory texts, but it is also a common belief as articulated in chronicles. The prophecy of Franciscan Jean de Roquetaillade, as described in the *Chronique dite de Jean de Venette*, ed./trans. Colette Beaune (Paris, 2011), 140, foretold that tyranny will come, and thus 'many powerful men and nobles will fall, and will be cruelly killed by the commons, and detached from their dignities'. Another example in chronicle literature comes from the *Journal d'un Bourgeois de Paris*, 126.

their number were often the targets, many Parisian bourgeois led efforts at reconciliation with the Crown, while at the same time they organised resistance and maintained an anti-taxation stance in the city, not seeing this as a contradiction.[39] Nor were all bourgeois on the same side of the conflict: those involved in royal administration or the apparatus of tax collection could be pitted against those outside those structures, and sometimes individuals switched between the two.[40]

The Crown's repression of the revolts combined tactical and ritualised measures that reinforced royal power and the king's absolute authority over his subjects. In January 1383, in a manner pre-arranged with the Paris Bourgeoisie who had conceded defeat, the king entered Paris at the head of an armed force. To show that reconciliation was premature, the king dismissed a delegation of Bourgeois who had come with an offering of gifts, and with his army proceeded to smash the city gates off their hinges, march to Notre Dame for a *Te Deum* service, and then on to the Louvre. A brutal occupation of the city followed. Much as the *Mesnagier* parable describes, there were summary arrests of Bourgeois of Paris, three hundred according to the Monk of Saint-Denis.[41] The Crown would eventually establish special commissions to investigate and identify more specifically those deserving of punishment, but in this initial phase of the repression justice was sweeping and general, and bourgeois who had not participated in the violence were sometimes

---

39 One remission letter describes how members of the bourgeoisie organised 'the men of the commons with other inhabitants' in a tavern: AN JJ 146 #71, 72. A November 1383 remission letter for goldsmith Adam Pélerin illustrates bourgeois ambivalence, stating that 'notable men' were buying mallets not to revolt but to 'resist the evil will of those whom the uprising first excited': Louis-Claude Douët-d'Arcq, *Choix de pièces inédites relatives au règne de Charles VI*, 2 vols (Paris, 1863), 1:49–50.

40 A June 1383 remission letter for Guillaume Herice, a Parisian wine-seller, encapsulates this duality. The letter describes how Herice reluctantly armed himself and marched with the rebel militias on the orders of his neighbourhood militia captain, but also 'was in great peril at the times of the Mallet-wielders' since he held several tax farms in the city: AN JJ 122 #361, 343. An April 1383 pardon letter for Jehan du Moustier, a Parisian harness-maker, describes how he participated in the anti-Jewish riots that were part of an early phase of the revolt, but that when the Mallet-wielders roamed the streets, 'for fear of death, because he had been participant of some of the tax-collecting [compaingnon d'aucunes impositions], this compelled him to hide with some good and notable merchants': AN JJ 122 #233, 234–5.

41 *Chronique du Religieux de Saint-Denys*, 1:236.

punished for having failed to contain the lower classes, or as examples to others. The citizens of Paris responded by signalling their subjection to the king's will through gestures of submission and appeals for mercy, including the pleas of the wives of the bourgeois described in the parable. The ritualised pathos of the women's displays of submission and mourning, enhanced by the *Mesnagier*'s use of words such as 'piteous' to describe the tale, is also part of the description of this event in the chronicle literature. The *Chronique des Premiers Quatre Valois* mentions that the bourgeois prisoners' wives were 'all dressed in black', and Pintoin describes how 'the wives having imprisoned husbands, with disheveled clothes [...], unmade hair, stretching their hands to the king, with continuous tears and laments, begged forgiveness'.[42] These were larger-scale and more public forms of petitioning the king for mercy than those commonly found in pardon letters, where the kin – often including wives – of the accused were usually the agents of the supplication on their kin or husband's behalf for royal remission.[43] Wives were supplicants in several of the pardon letters for those implicated in the Mallet-wielders' Revolt.[44]

Many of these appeals were in vain, as the Crown's withholding of mercy reinforced the idea that justice was entirely the king's prerogative. In all, around forty bourgeois were executed,[45] and the severity of this response is commented upon in most of the narrative sources. Pintoin reports that the Duchess of Orléans and the University of Paris both spoke on behalf of the bourgeois arrested in the aftermath of the uprising. The University's orator 'gave multiple examples that the ill-advised fervor of one unthinking assembly [of the common people] should not result in the harm of good men'.[46] Most shocking for Parisians was the arrest

---

42 *Chronique des quatre premiers Valois*, 309: 'toutes vestues de noir'; *Chronique du Religieux de Saint-Denys*, 1:246: 'mulieres maritos incarceratos habentes, in sordidis vestimentis, [...] crinibus resolutis, tensis ad regem manibus, cum ingeminatis lacrimis et querelis veniam poposcerunt.'
43 Claude Gauvard, *Condamner à mort au Moyen âge. Pratiques de la peine capitale en France XIIIème–XVème siècle* (Paris, 2019), 179. See also the discussion of Helen Lacey in the context of English pardons in *The Royal Pardon: Access to Mercy in Fourteenth-century England* (York, 2009), 26–43.
44 See, for example, AN JJ 122 #334, 320; JJ 123 #101, 109; JJ 123 #159, 167-8; JJ 124 #130, 158.
45 Mirot discusses the varying figures given for the number of bourgeois executed: *Les insurrections*, 188.
46 *Chronique du Religieux de Saint-Denys*, 1:240: 'ostendens multis exemplis

and execution of Jean des Marets, a seventy-year-old lawyer of the King who had been the somewhat reluctant mouthpiece of the Parisians in negotiations with the Crown from the outset of the revolt, but who had also been instrumental in 'often moderat[ing] the fury of the popular classes' during the uprising.[47] His execution scene is recounted in the Chronicle of the Monk of Saint-Denis, Froissart, and the *Chronique des Premiers Quatre Valois*. Froissart writes that on his way to the scaffold Jean des Marets called out for those who had condemned him to show themselves and explain the charges against him, and also that the king would not condemn him 'if he had a man's age and understanding'.[48] The *Chronique des Premiers Quatre Valois* reports that he was ignorant of his charges as he was led to the scaffold,[49] and Froissart writes that the 'greater part [of the people] wept for him' as he was executed.[50]

While by design they rhetorically condemn the uprising, pardon letters also sometimes reveal everyday Parisians' fear of the post-revolt repression, and their opinion of its harshness. A 'poor valet' Jehan de Poitiers explained that he fled Paris 'seeing that Our [the king's] Provost of Paris and men-at-arms from Our household were going night and day seizing many from the said town [Paris] and bringing them as prisoners to the Châtelet, some of whom were hastily executed' and so he escaped 'for fear that he might be seized in spite of the fact that he had done no wrong'.[51] Jehan le Grant, who was denounced by a fellow Paris merchant executed in the post-revolt repression, departed the city 'for fear that [the Revolt Commission] would try him without hearing from him his good reasons and excuses'.[52] Richart l'Anglois, a 'poor valet' metal-worker, describes how the Provost of Paris sent sergeants to his house and interviewed his neighbours to evaluate his claim that he could not afford a 10 franc fine levied against him, and Jehan le Gay complains

---

calorem inconsultum unius concionis indiscrete non debere redundare in prejudicium infinitorum melius affectorum.'
47   Ibid., I:244: 'furorem popularem sepe moderatus fuerat.'
48   Froissart, *Chroniques*, 11:81: 'se il avoit eage et cognisanche d'omme.'
49   *Chronique des quatre premiers Valois*, 310.
50   Froissart, Chroniques, 11:81: 'la grigneur partie ploroit pour lui.'
51   AN JJ 123 #146, 156–7: 'veant que Nostre Prevost de Paris et gens d'armes de Nostre hostel aloient de nuit et de jour prandre plusieurs d'icelle ville et mener prisonniers en Nostre dit Chastellet dont les aucuns l'en fist hastives executions'; 'pour paeur qu'il eust d'estre pris sans que toutesfois qu'il eust en riens mespris.'
52   AN JJ 123 #120, 130–1: 'pour doubte que l'on ne precedast contre luy sans le oyr en ses bonnes raisons et deffenses.'

that he was 'vexed and troubled without cause' when arrested and his goods confiscated unfairly by royal officials after the revolt.[53] Jehan le Sauvage, a resident not of Paris but of the Gâtinois region, is pardoned due to his age (about seventy) and 'simplicity' in May 1383 for having uttered several indiscreet political comments, including his declaration on hearing of the executions in Paris that 'it was very hideous, and the same with regards to the said [Jehan] des Marès, and that in the future ill could come of it'.[54] These hints of bitterness at the summary repression of the city's inhabitants are given fuller voice in the Parable, as will be discussed below.

The restoration of the rebel community into the king's good graces finally took place on 1 March 1383. Once again bourgeois and bourgeoises 'without hats', in a further display of submission, came before the king and the ruling Dukes of Berry and Burgundy, and amnesty was declared. The municipal government and the militia were abolished, a fact bitterly recalled by Parisians for a generation – they would not be fully restored until 1409 – and the trades were placed under the supervision of the Provost of Paris, the king's main representative in the city.[55] The city was heavily fined, and the taxes that had been at the heart of the conflict were restored.

The *Mesnagier*'s narrator claims that the event the parable describes actually happened. However, while the chronicle literature and judicial records corroborate in broad strokes the feelings of bitterness felt by the Parisian bourgeois in these days of repression, beyond the *Mesnagier* there is no mention of a confrontation with such a lecherous and tyrannical royal agent. Nonetheless, if there was a real-life basis for the tyrannical 'great lord' in the parable text, a plausible candidate is Olivier de Clisson.[56] De Clisson, who was royal constable in 1383, played a central

---

53 AN JJ 124 #82, 102-3; AN JJ 124 #327, 374-6 (375): 'vexé et travaillié sans cause.'

54 AN JJ 122 #286, 277: 'c'estoit grant hideur, et mesmement du dis des Marés et que ou temps avenir s'en pourroit ensuir mal.'

55 The 1383 Ordinance outlawing the trades is printed in *Métiers et Corporations de la ville de Paris Tome 1: 14e-18e siècle Ordonnances générales, métiers de l'alimentation*, ed. René de Lespinasse (Paris, 1886), 50-2; Gustave Fagniez describes how 'visitors' (inspectors) of the trades that formerly been elected by the tradesmen were appointed by the Provost of Paris after 1383: *Etudes sur l'industrie et la classe industrielle à Paris au XIIIème et au XIVème siècles* (New York, 1970), 122.

56 For Olivier de Clisson's life and his role in the Marmosets, see John Bell

role in the early days of the repression of the Parisians: along with the Lord d'Albret he was entrusted with judging Parisians' culpability and punishment in February 1383, just prior to Jean des Marets's execution. The *Chronographia* says that these two lords called many Paris bourgeois before them and declared, 'You have forfeited your body and your goods; say what you prefer, either justice or mercy'.[57] The choice of 'justice' meant punishment of the body; the choice of 'mercy' meant payment of money or goods, and the *Chronographia* and Froissart each report that the Parisians paid massive amounts to avoid punishment.[58] The bourgeois wife's surrender of her body might be seen to stand between a punishment of the body and the 'mercy' of a payment, suggesting a parallel in de Clisson's reported speech and the *Mesnagier*'s language. Furthermore, Olivier de Clisson, as a core ally of the Marmoset faction recently displaced as power holders in the royal court in 1394, would be a more palatable – even attractive – target for an accusation or smear for a supporter of the Duke of Berry, as the *Mesnagier*'s author may well have been. De Clisson would elsewhere be accused of tyranny: a later text, the *Songe Véritable*, a satirical polemical poem dated to 1406 by its nineteenth-century editor Henri Moranvillé, names de Clisson along with other Marmosets in a list of historical tyrants laid low by Fortune's Wheel.[59] Interestingly, the manuscript containing the *Songe Véritable* also includes the moralising poem 'Adresse de Povreté et Richesse', which is found in manuscripts of the *Mesnagier*, indirectly suggesting that the texts shared a common cultural milieu and political sentiment.

Jérôme Pichon, who edited one of the earliest modern editions of the *Mesnagier* in 1846, also speculates on the possible identity of the bourgeois prisoner referred to in the parable.[60] Using letters of remission, he identifies three bourgeois with young wives – Châtelet notary Jehan Filleul, draper Colin Brun, and Parlement *procureur* Giles Labat – who received pardons following the revolt. Filleul would seem to be the best candidate, as he receives the most inexplicable pardon

---

Henneman, *Olivier de Clisson and Political Society in France Under Charles V and Charles VI* (Philadelphia PA, 1996).
57 *Chronographia*, 3:50: 'Vos corpora et bona vestra forfecistis; videte quid eligitis, aut justiciam aut misericordiam.'
58 Ibid.; Froissart, *Chroniques*, 11:81.
59 Henri Moranvillé, ed., 'Le Songe Véritable: pamphlet politique d'un Parisien du XVème siècle', *Mémoires de la Société de l'histoire de Paris et de l'Ile-de-France* 17 (1890), 217–437 (272).
60 Pichon, *Le Ménagier de Paris*, note 136–7.

despite seemingly deep implication in the revolt. Although identified as a ringleader by Pintoin, and in spite of the fact that his letter of remission states that he advised his comrade draper Aubert de Dampierre to incite the city to riot in order to forestall his arrest, Filleul received a full royal pardon in August 1383.[61] The pardon letter mentions Filleul's 'young wife' as having interceded on his behalf, although as stated earlier such intercessions were customary. Pichon acknowledges that his efforts to identify the bourgeois in question are speculative, but it is clear that Parisian bourgeois implicated in the revolt engaged in intense negotiations for pardons in the uprising's aftermath.

In all it is difficult to say for certain whether the Parable of the Bourgeois Rebel's Wife related to a real episode, and how closely it did so, and what outside information in the form or rumour, innuendo or fact the *Mesnagier*'s audience would have brought to their reading of the text. Whatever the relationship of factual event to the parable plot, the story draws its energy from powerful resentments and political tensions that can be detected in other sources. The events described in the parable would therefore seem plausible to its audience: its relationship to reality renders tangible and immediate the text's abstract moral message, and gives more weight to the other, clearly fictionalised, parables within this section and throughout the *Mesnagier*.

Conjugal Obedience Amid Political Disobedience

Notwithstanding its violent context, the parable presents itself as a political commentary second, and as instruction on the relationship of husband and wife first. Given the parable's concern with criticism of authorities in the political realm, it would seem an odd choice to deliver a message of obedience in the conjugal realm. How and why the parable advances an ethic of conjugal obedience in this framework of wider political disorder will be the topic of this final section of the essay.

It is central to the parable's meaning that the *Mesnagier* author chose to graft a morality tale of wifely obedience to a fraught political situation of his own experience, differentiating it in crucial ways from other obedience exempla within the text. The open, unresolved real-world context of the parable contrasts with – and serves as a crucial gloss on – the other exempla drawn from religious/didactic literature within

---

61 AN JJ 123 #83, 47.

this section on wifely obedience in the *Mesnagier* that, though similar in theme, have more 'closed' meanings and resolved moral lessons.

The parable's plot is also common in didactic and hagiographic literature, but these stories – some of which are even found within the *Mesnagier* itself – prioritise the importance of a woman preserving her chastity at all costs, and thus present a different moral outcome on which the parable serves as a sort of commentary. The section of the *Mesnagier* that focuses on female chastity, which comes before that on wifely obedience, presents several cases drawn from hagiographic and other moral literature where women choose death over enduring the shame of rape. The *Mesnagier*'s versions of the biblical tale of Susanna (Daniel 13), and the Roman tale of the rape of Lucretia, which present positive examples of women preferring death to the dishonour of rape, and the negative example drawn from Cerxes's 'Jeu des Echées' of the Duchess Raymonde, who follows her lust and is executed because of it, seemingly advance an absolute ethic of preserving female sexual virtue. The *Mesnagier* even declares at the outset of this chapter that 'neither wealth, nor beauty, nor intelligence, nor noble lineage, nor any other excellence can ever erase a reputation for vice, particularly in a woman, if she has committed it once, or even been suspected of it'.[62] Other common stories from fourteenth-century hagiographic literature reinforce this message. The highly popular *Legende Dorée* of Jacques de Voragine presents several different scenarios similar to the *Mesnagier* parable, where Christian virgins are confronted by cruel 'tyrant' judges – as with the parable, these authority figures are most often not the Emperor himself but some representative subordinate – who seek to marry or rape them.[63] When tested in this way, the saintly women resist so that their honour, chastity, and holiness are preserved, though they are often martyred as a result.

Even in these tales celebrating absolute chastity, the punishment of the tyrannical judge, by means of a popular uprising and/or a higher authority, is critical to many of these hagiographies as well as some of

62 *Le Mesnagier de Paris*, 130: 'Ne richesse, ne beauté, ne sens, ne hault lignaige, ne nul autre bien ne peut jamaiz effacer la renommee de vice contraire, se en femme especialment il est une foiz commis, voire seulement suspeçonné.' He reiterates this at 150.
63 The saints' lives of Lucie, Agnes, Agatha, Cecilia, and Catherine of Alexandria offer the best analogs; see Jacques de Voragine, *La Légende dorée*, ed. Alain Boureau (Paris, 2004), 37–40, 139–43, 205–10, 954–61 and 975–85, respectively.

the folkloric tales. The cruel judge's comeuppance is delivered in the case of Saint Lucie's tormentor Paschas by Caesar himself, and in the case of Saint Agatha's 'tyrant' oppressor, Governor Quintien, by the combination of an earthquake and 'the sedition of the people'.[64] The *Mesnagier*'s lengthy treatment in the chapter on Chastity of the rape of Lucretia by Sixtus, the son of the tyrant Tarquin, also pointedly ends with Tarquin's removal from power through a popular rebellion. The *Mesnagier* mostly borrows the version of this tale found in Cerxes, but in order to emphasise the connection between lechery and the tyrant's downfall, the *Mesnagier* author comments (citing the *Romance of the Rose* as a gloss) that this ended the practice of monarchy in Rome.[65] These chastity stories function on the tension between a public challenge to the inner holiness of the saintly woman, mirrored in reverse by the inner corruption of the authority figure contrasting with his outer, public honour and authority. The moments of retribution at the close of these tales are when the tension between the saintly woman's private and public status is resolved, and the stories' characters receive the public, worldly status that corresponds with their inner goodness or evil. The earthly mechanism for this punishment is often the loss of their political power at the hands of a popular uprising, a feature that we are to keep in mind for the Parable of the Bourgeois Rebel's Wife.

How do we square the existence of these strong messages advancing chastity in the *Mesnagier* text, borrowed from this hagiographic literature, with the more ambiguous moral message regarding this virtue in the Parable of the Bourgeois Rebel's Wife? One interpretation is that we need not resolve these seeming conflicts: as Epurescu-Pascovici argues, the *Mesnagier* is a compendium of didactic stories whose goal is to instil a discipline of self-improvement rather than articulate a coherent plan of moral action.[66] Other areas in the *Mesnagier*'s commentary on chastity reveal a measured stance, allowing for women's virtue to be contextualised by circumstances. Whereas the saints' lives of virgins advance absolute physical chastity above all, the *Mesnagier* cites patristic authorities Saints Augustine and Gregory in including faithful but sexually active wives as spiritually chaste.[67] This more moderate form of women's sexual morality corresponds to a late medieval trend in

---

64 Ibid., 'tyran' (207) and 'sedition du peuple' (209).
65 *The Good Wife's Guide*, 90–2.
66 Epurescu-Pascovici, 'From Moral Agent to Actant', 223.
67 *Le Mesnagier de Paris*, 130–2. On this expansion of the concept of chastity

didactic literature towards more pragmatic material, that could relate to the needs and experiences of married women.[68] In the *Mesnagier*, this updated and more nuanced material coexists with the earlier, more absolute moral stance of the earlier hagiographic tradition.

If chastity is de-centred within the moral landscape of the *Mesnagier* by the qualifying commentary that comes from these tales of obedience, what then of obedience itself? Though fundamental for the good wife's virtue, even obedience is not a one-sided absolute, though it appears to be at first. The *Mesnagier* defines wifely obedience earlier in the chapter: 'in any situation, under any terms, in any place or season, you must perform without objecting all his orders whatever they may be.'[69] It is not enough that wives' obedience be reliable, it must also be unquestioning: they are enjoined not to 'gloss or dissect' their husbands' commands, and if they do so out loud and in public, 'they show themselves to be uppity and sovereign [*maistresses et dames*], and they bring blame to themselves and great villainy to their husbands'.[70] Other exempla in the chapter describe instances where husbands play games to test their wives' degree of acquiescence to their demands, where anything less than automatic and immediate compliance leaves 'a stain of disobedience a long time afterwards on the husband's heart'.[71] What the *Mesnagier* seeks, according to Christine Rose, is for the wife to internalise this discipline.[72] If bourgeois resistance to unjust authority functions as an important dynamic of the parable, this does not mean that such disobedience should extend to the wife against her husband.

---

see Ruth Mazo Karras, *Sexuality in Medieval Europe: Doing Unto Others* (New York, 2005), 53.

68   On the existence of this marriage literature, see Carolyn Collette, *Performing Polity: Women and Agency in the Anglo-French Tradition, 1385–1620* (Turnhout, 2006), 41.

69   *Le Mesnagier de Paris*, 242: 'en tous cas, en tous termes, en tous lieux et en toutes saisons vous accomplissez sanz redargucion tous ses commandemens quelxconques.'

70   Ibid., 244: 'gloser et esplucher'; 'elles se demonstrent comme maistresses et dames, et a elles mesmes feroient grant blasme, et grant vilenie a leurs mariz'.

71   Ibid., 246: 'la tache de la desobeissance demeure longtemps aprez dedans le cuer du mary.'

72   Christine M. Rose, 'What Every Goodwoman Wants: The Parameters of Desire in *Le Ménagier de Paris*/The Goodman of Paris', *Studia Anglica Posnaniensia* 38 (2002), 393–410.

Several male anxieties animate this drive for control. One of these, which is at the core of the *Mesnagier* as a whole since its premise is that of an older husband instructing his youthful wife, is the husband's anxiety of dying and leaving a widow. Widowhood was an ambiguous status for women: though generally it signalled a decrease in social status, it could also allow for unique autonomy, since widows possessed legal rights and agency that wives and dependent daughters did not.[73] Furthermore, any remarriage could imperil the dead husband's legacy, a matter of concern for bourgeois husbands who placed a great deal of importance on establishing their family's name and passing down their wealth.[74] The parable assumes that the fear of the husband's death – and thus the wife's widowhood – is a shared anxiety, and that the wife's priority is to prevent this even at the cost of her honour. The parable does not provide any window into the wife's state of mind when she is presented with the tyrant judge's offer – 'she answered nothing to this missive' – aside from her tears, and so it does not allow us seriously to entertain the (potentially preferable) alternative decision to reject the lord's offer and allow her husband to die. The bourgeoise's apparent lack of consideration of this alternative in the parable narrative is not just a reflection of her dutifulness in having her husband make the choice for her; it also closes off the option of a partially willed widowhood.

Another masculine anxiety manifest in the text is that over women's 'soft power'.[75] The *Mesnagier* states that though excluded from 'external

---

73   See Judith Bennett, 'Public Power and Authority in the Medieval English Countryside', in *Women and Power in the Middle Ages*, ed. Mary C. Erler and Maryanne Kowaleski (Athens GA, 1988), 22–4 of 18–36; and *Widowhood in Medieval and Early Modern Europe*, ed. Sandra Cavallo and Lyndan Warner (Harlow, 1999).

74   Recall the *Mesnagier*'s comment, cited above, that 'to acquire riches for himself and his children' is equivalent to the knight's search for prowess on the battlefield: *The Good Wife's Guide*, 82. Roberta Gilchrist comments that the difference in spousal age meant that husbands would often pre-decease their wives, and estimates that about one-third of medieval widows remarried: *Medieval Life: Archaeology and the Life Course* (Woodbridge, 2012), 129. On widow inheritance and remarriage, see also *Widowhood in Medieval and Early Modern Europe*, ed. Cavallo and Warner; Jean Favier, *Le Bourgeois de Paris*, 117–18; and Richard C. Famiglietti, *Tales of the Marriage Bed from Medieval France (1300–1500)* (Providence RI, 1992), 47.

75   See discussion in Collette, *Performing Polity*, 47–56. As Collette notes, 'soft' power refers to the unofficial power and influence wielded by women in private.

matters',[76] the wife is expected to run an efficient and comfortable household and serve as counsel for the husband. Through these means women could have significant influence. The promise of this 'soft power' is illustrated in the *Mesnagier*'s Story of Melibée, in which Prudence, the clear-thinking wife, attempts to soothe her husband's anger and prevent rash acts of vengeance through calm, persuasive words delivered at their home.[77] However, this power can also be negative: elsewhere the *Mesnagier* warns against wives who try to gain 'authority, command, and lordship' through caresses, deception and ruses.[78] In the political realm, this soft power manifested itself in the important role of the 'mediatrix', in which women, paradoxically powerful because of their social weakness, interceded between opposing factions to create peace.[79] In the Parable of the Bourgeois Rebel's Wife, the decisive potency of the woman's persuasive powers as a mediatrix is acknowledged, but these abilities are being controlled by the husband. Her sexuality is but a resource to be marshalled in the husband's political struggle.

The husband's ability to dictate his wife's use of her body recalls the theological and canon law concept of the Conjugal Debt, which held that the wife was required to give her body to the husband for sexual use when asked, but was not guilty of the sin of lust for having done so.[80] Here the husband is claiming his wife's body – in this patriarchal economy a significant source of her soft power – not for his own sexual enjoyment but rather as a sort of currency with which he can buy his freedom, and she is not morally accountable for her payment of the debt to her husband. The exchange described in the parable functions similarly to that of the pledge in debt imprisonment, which, as Julie Claustre has described, had grown in its frequency and was increasingly administered in the Paris region by the Provost of Paris, the king's representative in the fourteenth century.[81] Olivier de Clisson's language

---

76 *Le Mesnagier de Paris*, 302: 'des choses de dehors.'
77 Ibid., 326–400.
78 Ibid., 306: 'auctorité, commandement et seigneurie.'
79 Nicolas Offenstadt, *Faire la paix au moyen âge: discours et gestes de paix pendant la guerre de Cent Ans* (Paris, 2007), 107–27. Tracy Adams describes the cultural role of the mediatrix in her study of Queen Isabeau of Bavaria: *The Life and Afterlife of Isabeau of Bavaria* (Baltimore MD, 2010), 73–88.
80 Elizabeth M. Makowski, 'The Conjugal Debt and Medieval Canon Law', in *Equally in God's Image: Women in the Middle Ages*, ed. Julia Bolton Holloway, Joan Bechtold and Constance S. Wright (New York, 1990), 129–43.
81 Julie Claustre, *Dans les geôles du roi. L'emprisonnement pour dette à Paris à*

cited above – 'You have forfeited your body and your goods' – employs the same language of debt prison contracts, in which debtors pledge themselves 'body and goods' to their creditor.[82] The parable itself does not use this language, but in other ways the arrangement between the tyrant lord and the imprisoned bourgeois resembles a business deal, settled by the exchange of letters and with the wife's body as property to be used as a bargaining chip. Elsewhere in the *Mesnagier*, wives are depicted as playing the role of go-between in business dealings.[83] In all, just as the system of debt imprisonment allowed for a debtor's body to be collateral for a loan, the wife in the parable was both body and goods, ensuring the bourgeois husband's security. In the logic of the *Mesnagier*, then, this makes her a sort of ultimate mediatrix, and thus the ultimate wife, fully mobilised with her soft power as the husband's own resource, projected outwards to smooth over conflicts that the husband encounters as part of his public dealings.

Another theme developed throughout the *Mesnagier* and reinforced by this parable is the primacy of the husband's sovereignty. An earlier parable in the text illustrates the proper form of this sovereignty through a negative example. It describes a quarrelling couple who attempt to resolve their differences in understanding by writing down the wife's 'rights, point by point, with all of the obligations she owed her husband' on a piece of paper.[84] One day when the husband falls into a river, she looks at her paper, sees nothing about helping her husband out of water, and leaves him there. The husband almost dies, but a lord comes and rescues him; when that lord hears the explanation, he finds the woman and burns her to death for her pride.[85] In the *Mesnagier*'s analysis, the failure of the husband to 'have instructed her carefully' was the root of this problem.[86] Rather than rules or even moral codes to determine action in the marriage, the form of sovereignty of the husband over the wife sought by the *Mesnagier* is akin to what early twentieth-century

---

la fin du Moyen Âge (Paris, 2007).
82 'Vos corpora et bona vestra forfecistis', *Chronographia* 3:50.
83 In another parable of (dis)obedience, a wife is entrusted with her husband's debtor's IOU letter, which, thinking it insignificant in spite of her husband's order to keep it secure, she carelessly throws in the fire: *The Good Wife's Guide*, 122.
84 *Le Mesnagier de Paris*, 234: 'ses droiz tous esclarciz par poins, et les obeissances et services.'
85 *The Good Wife's Guide*, 119–20.
86 *Le Mesnagier de Paris*, 234: 'ne l'avoit pas dotrinee doulcement.'

political philosopher Carl Schmitt defined as the sovereignty of the Exception. For Schmitt, the sovereign is 'he who decides upon the exception', he who is above the law.[87] The *Mesnagier*, using the Virgin Mary as its exemplar, expresses a concept of wifely practice that stresses obedience over rules or rights, saying, 'by God, it is not always advisable to say to one's lord, "I will not do it. It isn't right." More good comes from obeying'.[88] Other examples from the text show a husband's pardon 'erasing' the sin of adultery on an unfaithful wife's deathbed, and another where the husband defuses (accurate) rumours about his wife's infidelities by spreading a story that instead of running off with a lover she was on a pilgrimage.[89] As with these examples, the Parable of the Bourgeois Rebel's Wife is the embodiment of this principle in the conjugal sphere: even the law of female chastity, one of the most sacred laws in Christian life, is overturned by the husband's fiat, the decision of the exception.[90]

Although the exemplum revolves around the axis of the husband-wife negotiation of authority and obedience, the charged politics of the story's backdrop, taking place in the aftermath of a revolt, and with the tyrannical lord presenting a second axis around which authority and obedience must be negotiated, means that the smaller household power dynamic and the larger political power dynamic are implicitly intended for comparison. Such a comparison is set up in other passages in the text, as well as in other medieval writings, and it was common to see the household as a microcosm of larger political society.[91] The Griselda story is structured on the comparison between the husband's management of

87 Giorgio Agamben, *State of Exception*, trans. Kevin Attell (Chicago IL, 2005). Schmitt's theory was originally expressed in Carl Schmitt, *Political Theology: Four Chapters on the Concept of Sovereignty*, trans. George Schwab (Chicago IL, 1985).
88 *The Good Wife's Guide*, 120.
89 Ibid., 145–6.
90 As the text states, 'She is excused for such a grave matter because [...] she has neither sin nor guilt, nor has she committed a crime or bad deed, since her husband had commanded it': *The Good Wife's Guide*, 124. Silvana Vecchio writes of the wife's abdication of moral responsibility created by the extreme ethic of obedience in the *Mesnagier*: 'The Good Wife', 112.
91 Oresme's fourteenth-century translation of Aristotle's *Politics* begins with the idea that the household is the building-block of the larger political society: *Le Livre de Politiques*, 46. See also Felicity Riddy, 'Looking Closely: Authority and Intimacy in the Late Medieval Urban Home', in *Gendering the Master Narrative: Women and Power in the Middle Ages*, ed. Mary C. Erler and Maryanne Kowaleski (Ithaca NY, 2003), 212–28.

his realm and his rule over his wife, and Griselda declares her husband the Marquis to be 'sovereign over me and our children'.[92] The *Mesnagier* draws the analogy between the husband's authority and that of a prince: once married the wife 'is a subject to her husband as she is to lords' and the husband 'must be and is sovereign'.[93]

At first glance, the parable would seem to be drawing a clean analogy between the lord's sovereignty and that of the husband. Both, after all, operate according to fiat, both seemingly display the sovereignty of the Exception. Such a parallel seems to be at work in the *Mesnagier*'s version of the Griselda tale, where the Marquis Gaultier's sovereignty over Griselda is both that of a prince over a peasant and of a husband over a wife. But the palpable unease about the Marquis's exercise of his power over Griselda, manifested in the 'murmurs' of his people within the tale as well as in the *Mesnagier*'s commentary on the story's 'excessive [...] cruelty', is given more shape and depth in the Parable of the Bourgeois Rebel's Wife.[94] Unlike the Griselda tale, in the parable the sovereignty of husband and the sovereignty of political authority are separated from one another and placed in opposition. And unlike the husband's absolute power, which is described earlier in the chapter as sanctioned by God as shown in scripture (the *Mesnagier* cites Genesis, Paul's letter to the Ephesians, and Saint Jerome),[95] the tyrant lord here 'fear[s] neither God nor his Justice' and is 'cursed'. So, while both the husband and the lord have a form of sovereignty over the wife in this tale, a distinction exists between the two.

As the author explains to his wife and his audience, the Griselda story is not 'true', but this one is.[96] Burger's analysis of the different versions of the Griselda story explains how the variations in the tale revolve in large part around the question of the affective bond versus the virtue of Griselda's steadfastness.[97] The *Mesnagier*'s version of the Griselda story, especially when glossed by the parable, reinforces the bourgeois ethic of the mutuality of the husband-wife relationship even within a context of

---

92 *The Good Wife's Guide*, 112.
93 *Le Mesnagier de Paris*, 188: 'femmes soient subgectes a leurs maris comme a seigneurs'; 190: 'doit-il et estre souverain'.
94 *The Good Wife's Guide*, 115 and 119, respectively.
95 Ibid., 188–90.
96 The *Mesnagier* says of the Griselda story, in assuring his wife that he would never behave like Walter, 'I don't believe it was ever true': *The Good Wife's Guide*, 119.
97 Burger, *Conduct Becoming*, 141–90.

sovereignty and obedience. The parable's moral thus heightens the stakes of those expressions of class-conscious difference the *Mesnagier* delivers earlier in the text, as when he warns his wife not to 'frequent parties or dances of high-ranking lords' or 'consort [...] with courtiers', or when he reminds her that he is 'no Marquis' like Walter.[98] As such, it relativises the extreme morality on chastity found in some of these other sources, and makes tangible both the stakes and the rewards of wifely obedience in the bourgeois sphere of the *Mesnagier*'s milieu. This parable represents the victory – though partial and deferred – of conjugal virtue residing in the domestic space over public aristocratic status and power.[99]

The *Mesnagier*'s comments immediately after the Parable bring home the primacy of mutual love within the domestic sphere: 'In God's name, I believe that when two good, virtuous people are married, all other loves outside of each other are remote and forgotten'.[100] This is a clear, idealised articulation of love in the domestic, bourgeois style, a sanctuary not only of virtue but a sort of collective, resistant strength that comes from this virtue, in a brutal world. The promotion of a domestic, private sphere as important and distinct from the public world has been associated with bourgeois culture.[101] If didactic tales celebrating the virtue of chastity above all resolve with the punishment of the lecherous tyrant judge, thus squaring public and private virtue, the Parable does not do this: the wife is still 'blamed' by some in public, and the corrupt judge is unpunished. Within the domestic, private space, her virtue is secure, but this remains as yet unharmonised in the post-revolt Paris public social world.

This disjunction gives the Parable its power. Burger articulates how late medieval conduct literature emphasises the mutuality of the affective conjugal bond, thereby giving the wife more agency within marriage, reflecting the growing influence of women in social life and as audience for this literature.[102] As with other aspects of moral agency in the *Mesnagier*, the wife is not merely to follow slavishly and

---

98   Ibid., 49, 94, 118.
99   Ferrier also connects the Parable with a bourgeois promotion of the domestic space: 'Seulement pour vous endoctriner', 84.
100 *The Good Wife's Guide*, 124.
101 For discussions of private virtue and mutual marriage as a feature of bourgeois marriage, see Lipton, *Affections of the Mind*, 139–40; 150–2. For a more general discussion, see *A History of Private Life Vol. III: Passions of the Renaissance*, ed. Roger Chartier, trans. Arthur Goldhammer (Cambridge MA, 1989).
102 Burger, *Conduct Becoming*, 15–25, 125–8.

mindlessly the dictates of her husband, but is to model an obedience within marriage that is strengthened and animated by mutual love. Burger notes briefly that this ethic of mutual amity had its parallels in the political realm, but it is worth emphasising this further, because it is at the heart of the political message of the Parable of the Bourgeois Rebel's Wife.[103] Lydwine Scordia extensively analyses the ubiquitous evocations of mutual love between ruler and subject in late medieval French discourse on taxation.[104] Without amity and consent, taxation was a tyrannical violation. She cites the early fourteenth-century 'Mirror for Princes', *Le Mirouer Exemplaire*, as one of her examples:

> When the prince is loved by his people, they pay his debts with great joy and obey his commands and help him when it is necessary. And they are prepared to expose themselves and their goods when they see that he has need of them. And it is a treasure for a prince [...] to acquire and hold the love of his subjects.[105]

Aquinas defines the tyrant as he who rules by fear as opposed to love, and Christine de Pisan connects the ruler's defence of justice with his ability to hold 'the bourgeois in love [...] and the people in peace'.[106] This ethic of amity and mutuality as the necessary bond between ruler and subject was not merely found in the works of political philosophers, but was also regularly featured in royal decrees, treaties and chroniclers' descriptions of the ideal ruler.[107] The Parable highlights the contrast between the

---

103 Ibid., 22–3.
104 Lydwine Scordia, 'Le Roi doit vivre du sien': La théorie de l'impôt en France, (XIIIe–XVe siècles) (Paris, 2005), 151–3, 339–41, 363–98.
105 Scordia, *'Le Roi doit vivre du sien'*, 380: 'Quant le prince est ayme de son peuple, ilz luy paient ses debtes a grant ioye et obeissent a ses commandemens et luy aydeet quant il en necessite. Et sont appareillez pour exposer soy et leurs biens quant ilz voyent quile en a necessite. Et cest ung tresor a prince [...] que lamour des ses subiectz acuerir et tenir.'
106 Aquinas, *On Kingship*, 46; Christine de Pisan, *Livre de Paix*, 69. See also Giles de Rome, *Li Livres du Gouvernement des Rois*, 98–101.
107 *Ordonnances des roys de France de la troisième race*, ed. Denis-François Secousse, 21 vols (Paris, 1723–1849), 9:668: 'Our well-loved bourgeois [of Paris]' ('nostre bien amez bourgois'); 10:69: the 'great reverence, love and loyalty that they [Parisians] naturally have for Us, who are their sovereign and lawful lord' ('grant reverence, amour & loyauté qu'ils ont naturellement à Nous qui sommes leur souverain & droiturier Seigneur'). Nicolas Offenstadt notes recurring references to 'love' in peace treaties: *Faire la paix au moyen âge*, 185–91. Froissart

amity in the harmonious but hierarchised bourgeois conjugal sphere, with the fractious tyrannical exercise of power of the king's subordinates in the aftermath of the Maillotin Revolt. Though obedience to royal power and acceptance of the king's requests for taxation are expected, these only come when there is mutual love and respect between ruler and subject, an ethic that had been violated in these early, rebellious years of Charles VI's rule.

The lack of resolution of the tale leaves this as an unsettled, still active political concern. As stated before, the abuse of justice represented by the tyrannical lord's action is never truly resolved as it is in other tales, where comparable injustices are mended, usually with the comeuppance of the cruel judge, often in the form of divine or collective punishment, or at the hands of the king, God's representative on earth. The system of justice within the parable, however, is not a closed one: it is palpably marked by the absence of the king. It is he, not the lord, who has the authority to close the system and resolve injustices as he does in other versions of the tale, but in the aftermath of the Maillotins Revolt, he is not there. As noted above, the chronicle accounts of Paris bourgeois leader Jean des Marets's harsh execution during the post-Maillotin Revolt repression described the condemned as he walked to the scaffold amid the Parisian crowd, deploring the absence of royal justice. The implicit comparison between the lord and the husband shows that the lord does not have, as the husband does, the full sovereignty of the Exception, and in fact that the proper comparison point is between the husband and the (absent) king. The husband's absolute sovereignty over his wife reflects proper mastery over his household; the lord's sovereignty, when it displays the same authoritarianism, is tyrannical. Implicitly, it is the king's duty to get his household in order, to have it governed by the same moral probity that empowers the bourgeois marriage of the parable's couple.

The text self-consciously cuts itself off abruptly from discussing 'this matter that is unpleasant to tell and too serious' and declares that

---

frequently contrasts loyalty from fear with that derived from love, and his ideal ruler the Count of Foix is said to have had the love of his subjects: Froissart, *Chroniques* in Besançon, Bibliothèque municipale, MS 864–5, fol. 184r–v (Book 1); fol. 193v (Book 2), in *The Online Froissart*, version 1.5, ed. Peter Ainsworth and Godfried Croenen (Sheffield, 2013) <http://www.dhi.ac.uk/onlinefroissart> (accessed 26 October 2024); Froissart, *Chroniques: Livres III et IV*, ed. Peter Ainsworth and Alberto Varvaro (Paris, 2004), 371, 564.

it 'will leave such weighty matters for those of lesser magnitude', and therefore does not articulate a clear pathway to delivering justice to the cruel judge as we see in the other stories. But given the late medieval discourse on tyranny, this abrupt ending suggests a deferral of justice rather than a compromise of it. If the text does not openly spell out the form that revenge on the tyrannical judge would take, this is merely because the text is agnostic about the punishment that comes ultimately from God, but that should be delivered (hopefully) through the just king. Philippe de Mézières is clear that the just king must, even in cases regarding the great barons of royal blood 'that might feel in any way like tyranny' renounce their rulings 'by your royal mouth publicly'.[108] Given the propensity of the Parisian population to revolt, which provides the backdrop of the tale, the menace of rebellion would have been at the forefront of the audience's mind, and would serve as a potential consequence if the king does not take action to purge his court of unjust courtiers. By naming the unjust judge a 'tyrant', the parable is labelling him as requiring punishment, and thus if the king does not purge him, then the community may have to do so. The open-endedness of the parable veils a threat rather than advocates a concession.

The fourteenth-century audience of the *Mesnagier* had been witnesses to, if not participants in, one of the most tumultuous uprisings in the kingdom's history just ten years prior to the text's publication. Not only had the revolt left the Parisian population beaten, resentful and traumatised; the political questions that had inspired the revolt – on the right of the Crown to tax without legitimate consent, on the scope of local rights and privileges, and on how the popular and merchant classes would participate in political society – had not been resolved by the young king Charles VI and his court. Some of this uncertainty came from the Parisian bourgeoisie's ongoing process of renegotiating the relationship of ruler and subject, one in which their private domestic space was autonomous and distinct from public power. This domestic space was animated by the moral probity of the well-ordered and prosperous household. More than merely to justify a claim to autonomy, though, the amity of the married couple within the domestic space could serve as a model for the proper, just relationship of ruler and ruled: just as the wife's obedience was forged (theoretically, ideally and in the eyes of the husband) by love and moral instruction, so too could the subject be

---

108 De Mézières, *Songe du Vieil Pelerin*, 2:323: 'qui sentiront aucunement de tyrannie [...] par ta bouche royalle publiquement.'

obedient, so long as the king's household was equally well-ordered and just, and his orders driven by respect and love. The consequence of a failure to realise this well-ordered royal household could be rebellion, as it had been in 1380.

5

Bishop Henry Despenser and Manuscript Production in Late Medieval Norwich

HOLLY JAMES-MADDOCKS AND R. F. YEAGER

Three illuminated manuscripts now in the British Library were once the property of Henry Despenser, who served as bishop of Norwich from 1370 to 1406. That they were made for him during his long episcopacy is evident from his distinctive heraldic devices displayed prominently in each: quarterly first and fourth, *argent*; second and third, *gules fretty or*; a *bend sable* overall; a *bordure argent* of bishop's mitres *or*. These manuscripts are: London, British Library MS Additional 34114 (*olim* Spalding), containing five poems, all in Anglo-French (a version of the *Chanson d'Antioche*, the *Roman d'Éneas*, the *Roman de Thèbes*, *Le Songe Vert* – a dream-vision – and a 170-line segment of the *Ordène de Chevalerie*, attributed to Hue de Tabarie); BL MS Arundel 74, a copy of Bede's *Historia Ecclesiastica*; and BL MS Cotton Claudius E.viii, a compendium of works bound together by Robert Cotton in the seventeenth century.[1] The main texts of this last, a *Flores Historiarum* with the *Continuatio chronicarum* of Adam Murimuth brought to 1340, belonged unequivocally to Despenser.[2] Previous scholars (with different degrees

---

1   On Cotton's practice of reconstituting manuscripts to suit his own tastes, see in particular James P. Carley and Colin G. C. Tite, 'Sir Robert Cotton as Collector of Manuscripts and the Question of Dismemberment: British Library MSS Royal 13 D.I and Cotton Otho D.VIII', *The Library* 6th ser. 14 (1992), 94–9.
2   The full contents of the manuscript, using contemporary numbering, all likely belonging to Despenser, are: *De fundatoribus ecclesiarum per Angliam* (fol. 5r); prophecies (fols 5v, 27r–v); description of Rome (fols 10r–11r); a brief list of weights and measures (fol. 12r); *De uiris illustribus quo tempore scripserunt* (fols 13v–14r); *Expositio vocabulorum*, a list of legal terms translated from Old English (fol. 14v); brief notes on coronation and a dispute of King John, liberties of Yarmouth from Domesday Book, descriptions of Rome and of England (fols 15r–17v), index to *Flores historiarum* (fols 18r–26v); brief list of the priors

of certainty) have assigned the production of these books to Norwich based on the evidence of their provenance – criteria that are ultimately insufficient for establishing *origin*. We hope here to build a more rigorous case for the bishop's commission of all three books – not in London or even Oxford, but locally – in the city of Norwich itself, and we will do this by analysing the two main artists involved, together with a larger grouping of contemporary illuminated manuscripts uniform in both style and provenance. Our investigation will have four parts: the first, to consider the man, Henry Despenser, as a reader and collector of fine books; the second, to make the case for a 'Despenser Master' and several associates through careful examination of the bishop's three surviving books; the third, to engage in stylistic comparison with *other* manuscripts of established Norfolk provenance; and finally, to establish more firmly the feasibility of Norwich's place as a locus for manuscript production during the years of Despenser's episcopacy.

The 'Fighting Bishop'

Henry Despenser, if he comes to mind at all, is not often thought of with a book in his hand, but rather a sword. The life of the historical bishop is commonly reduced to two events, both martial, one much praised at the time, the other much reviled. The earlier is of course his vigorous response to the revolt of 1381, in particular at the so-called 'Battle of North Walsham', wherein a small but well-armed group led by Despenser defeated a larger force of rebels, capturing and summarily executing its leader, and thereby effectively ending the uprising in East Anglia.[3] The latter occurred two years later, when Despenser commanded a disastrous 'crusade' in Flanders, ostensibly against the French followers of the anti-Pope Clement VII, but quickly sidetracked to benefit the English wool trade, of which Norwich, not incidentally, was an important centre. The failure brought impeachment and condemnation by parliament,

---

of Norwich Cathedral Priory (fol. 26v); *Flores historiarum*, AD 1–1307 (fols 27v–240r); Adam Murimuth, *Chronicon*, AD 1303–40 (fols 242r–253v); ecclesiastical lists (fols 268r–272v).

3   For details see R. G. Davies, 'Despenser, Henry (d. 1406)', *ODNB*; and further Richard Allington-Smith, *Henry Despenser, the Fighting Bishop* (Dereham, 2003). The justice of Despenser's impeachment is somewhat disputable. Nigel Saul argues that 'the bishop had been made the scapegoat for the errors and omissions of others': *Richard II* (New Haven CT, 1997), 107.

the loss of his temporalities for over two years, and a royal demand for return of sums advanced by the crown, amounting to £37,475 7s. 6d., finally repaid eight years later.[4]

To some degree, the characteristics that led to both results – courage on one battlefield and imprudence on the other – could be thought of as family legacies. The fifth son of a Marcher lord, and the grandson of Hugh Despenser the younger, favourite of Edward II, Henry followed his elder brother Edward, Lord Despenser (made Knight of the Garter in 1361 and Constable of the English army in France in 1373) into Italy, initially as part of the wedding party accompanying Lionel Plantagenet, and subsequently to fight for Urban V against Bernabò Visconti. Henry Despenser's performance in the attack on Milan was instrumental in garnering his appointment to the suddenly vacant bishopric of Norwich in 1370. As it had been for many years, doubtless a word from his brother was helpful too – probably sweetened by a financial 'loan' to the pope. As a fifth son, with little hope of acceding to the lordship, Henry had been destined for the church. In furtherance of this, Edward had garnered for his brother first a canonry with expectation of a prebend in Salisbury Cathedral in 1354 when Henry was ten or twelve years old; in 1361 a papal dispensation set aside his youth to allow him to take up a rectory in Leicestershire, although his ordination (as a sub-deacon) came a year later. Neither impeded his military life in Italy. At the time of his appointment to the see of Norwich, Henry had added an archdeaconry at Llandaff (not far from family estates), a canonry in Lincoln cathedral, and a rectory in Cambridgeshire to his benefices.[5]

These experiences are important for understanding the bishop, and the book collector, that Despenser eventually became. Clearly, he learned to fight in Italy, but seemingly no less was he blind to the visual culture around him. Some of what he saw may have influenced the so-called 'Despenser Retable', given to the Cathedral Church of the Holy Trinity in Norwich, c.1382, perhaps by Despenser.[6] Italian influ-

4   And drew, as well, a vehement rebuke from John Wyclif: see *De cruciate sive contra bella clericorum* (1382). The repayment remained an issue until 1391, when the matter was resolved by the Exchequer. See Édouard Perroy, *L'Angleterre et le Grand Schisme d'Occident: Étude sur la politique religieuse de Angleterre sous Richard II, 1378–1399* (Paris, 1933), 186; Margaret Aston, 'The Impeachment of Bishop Despenser', *Bulletin of the Institute of Historical Research* 38 (1965), 127–48 (129–31).
5   See Davies, 'Despenser, Henry'; Allington-Smith, *Henry Despenser*, 7–8.
6   The question of the donors of the Retable and their purposes is unresolved,

ences, as well as German, French, and Bohemian, have been claimed to explain its richness and figure styles.[7] It may – or may not – have been produced locally.[8] Certainly, however, the chancel ceiling of St Giles hospital with 250 painted panels showing the arms of Anne of Bohemia was local work, and ordered by Despenser to greet Richard II and his queen during their visit to Norwich in 1383.[9] More centrally, as part of his training for his predetermined ecclesiastical career, the future bishop studied civil law at Oxford, earning a bachelor's degree before 1361; by 1370, he was a licentiate.[10] Thoughtfully considered, then, Despenser would seem a man a good deal more complex than Thomas Walsingham's disparaging characterisation of him as 'vir nec literis nec discretione preditus, juvenis effrenis et insolens' ('a man neither lettered nor gifted with discretion, an unbridled and insolent youth').[11]

Such a Despenser, a reader with an eye for aesthetic effect, accords well with the high quality of the three volumes that once belonged to him. These are very fine books indeed. Additional 34114 has 237 folia, measuring 360x260mm; Arundel 74 is 106 folia, measuring 345x240mm; Cotton Claudius E.viii is massive, containing 267 folia, and measuring 415x280mm. High-grade parchment is the norm in all (Additional 34114

---

and likely to remain so, given that the evidence depends upon the border of heraldic devices, much of which was cut away during the Reformation. See David J. King, 'The Panel Paintings and Stained Glass', in *Norwich Cathedral: Church, City, and Diocese 1096–1996*, ed. Ian Atherton et al. (London, 1996), 410–30, and his caveat at 412.

7   Nikolaus Pevsner cites Italian Trecento in the colours and the treatment of draperies, and compares the 'facial types' to the work of 'Master Bertram in Hamburg': *The Buildings of England: North-East Norfolk and Norwich* (Harmondsworth, 1962), 221–2 (222).

8   See King, 'Panel Paintings', 410–13.

9   Specifically, the ceiling panels derive from the arms of the Holy Roman Empire, borne by Anne's father, Charles IV of Luxembourg, Holy Roman Emperor and King of Bohemia, whose personal arms showed a *gules lion rampant argent, queue fourchée in saltire, armed langued and crowned or*, often placed at the centre of the eagle's breast once Charles became Emperor. Anne's personal arms showed the eagle in the first and fourth quarters, the lion in the second and third.

10 A. B. Emden, *A Biographical Register of the University of Oxford to A.D. 1500*, 3 vols (Oxford, 1957–9), III:2169–70. Davies, 'Despenser, Henry'; Allington-Smith, *Henry Despenser*, 8.

11 See Thomas Walsingham, *Chronicon Angliae*, ed. E. Maunde Thompson. RS 64 (London, 1874), 258.

being exceptional in quality), gold leaf is abundantly in evidence, and – as will be discussed in the next section – some of the illuminating artists exhibit significant skill in rendering border designs that include both stylised and naturalistic motifs. The contents, too, are potentially revealing, and further undermine Walsingham's dyspeptic assessment of the bishop. Historical texts such as Bede's *Historia Ecclesiastica*, the *Flores Historiarum*, and Murimuth's *Continuatio*, all relatively common in ecclesiastical libraries, are nonetheless far from easy reads.[12] On the other hand, the five Anglo-French poems collected in Additional 34114 – *Chanson d'Antioche, Roman d'Énéas, Roman de Thèbes, Le Songe Vert* and the segment of Hue de Tabarie's *Ordène de Chevalerie* – while lighter fare and suggestive of literary tastes unsurprising for a man of Despenser's martial background, are yet works that, for full enjoyment, require a reader's thoughtful engagement.[13] Moreover, it is clear that the bishop's bookish tastes, and possibly his mathematical ability, were no secret. At least one manuscript is known to have been composed as a gift for Despenser, *Tractatus de ludo philosophorum*, by the monk John Lavenham, probably in hope of preferment. It demonstrates the pleasures of rithmomachia, a game requiring no little calculative skill.[14]

Could such books as these have been produced in the Norwich of Despenser's time? From an economic point of view, the answer doubtless should be 'yes', but with several caveats. The period of Despenser's tenure corresponds to a temporary dip in Norwich's wealth. The medieval history of Norwich is in effect a tale of two cities. Prior to the great plague of 1348–50, Norwich ranked with Bristol, Lincoln and York among England's leading provincial towns, based on extant tax records,

---

12 On the presence of historical texts in monastic libraries generally, and in Norwich cathedral in particular, see Barbara Dodwell, 'The Muniments and the Library', in *Norwich Cathedral*, ed. Atherton, 336–7.

13 A differently slanted view of Despenser's interest in these poems has been taken by Christopher Baswell, who finds indications of 'part of a complex pattern [...] of asserting aristocratic ideology': 'Aeneas in 1381', *New Medieval Literatures* 5 (2002), 8–58 (42).

14 A copy of Lavenham's *Tractatus* – not an autograph – survives in Princeton NJ, Princeton University Library, MS Garrett 95, fols 47r–54r. In a brief dedicatory letter, Lavenham identifies 'domino Henrico Norwiciensis episcopo' as the intended benefactor. For transcription and discussion of Lavenham's gift, see Don C. Skemer, 'From the Fighting Bishop to the Wizard Earl: A Medieval Book as Text and Object', in *The Medieval Book as Object, Idea and Symbol*, ed. Julian Luxford (Donington, 2021), 272–91.

its wealth sustained by a diversified industry and significant domestic and cross-channel trade.[15] By the end of the century, in contrast, the population had more than halved, with a significant percentage of urban poor, its diminished prosperity by then heavily dependent on woollen cloth, especially the manufacture of worsteds, and by an extensive herring fishery.[16] This is not to assert that Norwich was impoverished during Despenser's episcopacy, but the drop in its fortunes is visible today in its notable religious buildings, from the thirteenth century, when Norwich flourished initially, and – predominantly – from the first half of the fifteenth century, when the city's fortunes swelled again.[17]

Whatever most citizens' conditions were at any time, however, the bishops themselves did rather better. Based upon the assessment of the *Valor Ecclesiasticus* of 1535 – admittedly a good deal after our period – the bishop of Norwich 'was probably the wealthiest magnate in Norfolk'.[18] Coming closer to home, it is likely corroborative that Richard II, always with a shrewd eye for sources of income, saw fit to punish Despenser for the disastrous failure of the Flanders Crusade in 1383 by confiscating his temporalities for two years. Except perhaps during those two years (1383–5), it would seem that the bishop could easily have afforded fine books if he so chose.

The question then would be, were conditions such in Norwich as to encourage him to commission books locally, rather than in – say – London?

Despenser's Books: Origin versus Provenance

In the exhibition catalogue *Medieval Art in East Anglia*, Andrew Martindale makes the rather striking point that only one book from the period *c*.1360–1430 can be assigned unequivocally to Norfolk: a book with a colophon. The rest 'are merely connected with East Anglia, either via a liturgical text or heraldically'. Evidence for a book's intended use does not tell us where it was made. In other words, evidence for

---

15   See Elizabeth Rutledge, 'Economic Life', in *Medieval Norwich*, ed. Carole Rawcliffe and Richard Wilson (London, 2004), 157–88 (hereafter *Medieval Norwich*).
16   See Penelope Dunn, 'Trade', in *Medieval Norwich*, 213–34.
17   See Jonathan Finch, 'The Churches', in *Medieval Norwich*, 48–72 (60).
18   Christopher Harper-Bill and Carole Rawcliffe, 'The Religious Houses', in *Medieval Norwich*, 73–120 (80–1).

provenance is not evidence for origin, even if it is sometimes indicative of it, making the business of localising the production of manuscripts notoriously difficult. The illuminated borderwork in Despenser's library is assigned by Martindale to 'Norwich?' with fair warning: it 'may have been produced by local citizens; equally it may all have been ordered in London, or it may have been produced in Norwich by London people'.[19] The problem is intractable unless we can establish a grouping of manuscripts 'characterized both by uniform style and identical provenance', which suggest by their association that they 'were probably made in the place they were intended to be used'.[20] Establishing such a grouping on the basis of shared style, and assessing the quality of its evidence for Norwich origin, is the main aim of this essay.

In the case of Despenser's extant library, the first important connection between two of the books – uniform in style and provenance – was established by Christopher Baswell (with the assistance of Lucy Freeman Sandler). Their identification of the same illuminator in Additional 34114 and in parts of Cotton Claudius E.viii is an important starting point, in view of the coincident heraldic evidence. Baswell turned to Sandler's and Scott's catalogues of Gothic illuminated manuscripts for comparative material and concluded that the Despenser volumes were 'clearly in the Norwich style [...] Bishop Despenser employed a Norwich atelier, then, to decorate at least these two manuscripts of secular texts for him'.[21] Two relevant entries in these catalogues – a psalter (Holkham Hall MS 26) and a missal (Bodleian Library, MS Hatton 1) – certainly share with the Despenser group a comparable repertory of decorative motifs. That similarity notwithstanding, however, no other work by the 'Hatton Missal Artist' has been identified until now, while the manuscripts attributable to the 'Holkham Psalter Artist' (primarily Latin service books and secular history) suggest that he was a peripatetic lay

---

19   *Medieval Art in East Anglia 1300–1520*, ed. P. Lasko and N. J. Morgan (London, 1974), 29, and cat. nos 41 and 42. For the difficulties in establishing origin see Teresa Webber, 'Where Were Books Made and Kept?', in *The Cambridge Companion to Medieval British Manuscripts*, ed. Elaine Treharne and Orietta Da Rold (Cambridge, 2020), 214–33.
20   Lucy Freeman Sandler, *A Survey of Manuscripts Illuminated in the British Isles: Gothic Manuscripts 1275–1385*, 2 vols (London, 1986), I:50.
21   Baswell, 'Aeneas in 1381', 45, with reference to Sandler, *Gothic Manuscripts*, no. 143 (Psalter for Ramsey Abbey); and Kathleen L. Scott, *A Survey of Manuscripts Illuminated in the British Isles: Later Gothic Manuscripts 1390–1490*, 2 vols (London, 1996), no. 5 (Missal, Diocese of Norwich).

professional on a 'monastic circuit'.[22] Thus in spite of their shared style with Despenser's books, the mixed provenance evidence is (as it stands) insufficient for establishing origin. Baswell has opened an important topic, one that warrants closer investigation precisely because we know so little about non-metropolitan book production in the later medieval period.[23] In what follows it will be shown for the first time that the production of Despenser's three surviving books involved six artists, and that several more manuscripts containing evidence for Norwich provenance can be associated with the Despenser group through aspects such as style and collaboration. One of these newly related books involved both the main Despenser artist and the Hatton Missal Artist, suggesting that it was a shared urban location that formed the basis of their comparable styles. Although caution is necessary when dealing with the combined evidence of stylistic attribution and intended use, cumulatively such indications strengthen the likelihood that Norwich was the place of production.

Beginning with the division of artists' hands in Despenser's three manuscripts, the most straightforward case is the compilation of Anglo-French poems in Additional 34114. One illuminator carried out the full programme of work: a clasp border to open the crusade poem (fol. 1v), a three-quarter border for each of the openings of *Eneas* (fol. 106r) and *Thèbes* (fol. 164r), and a three-line illuminated initial 'A' for the start of the dream vision, *Le Songe vert* (fol. 227r). Only *Eneas* contains any additional visual punctuation, or demarcation of text with illumination: the four-line gold initial 'T' that begins a description of

22   Lynda Dennison, 'The Significance of Ornamental Penwork in Illuminated and Decorated Manuscripts of the Second-Half of the Fourteenth Century', in *Tributes to Kathleen L. Scott: English Medieval Manuscripts: Readers, Makers and Illuminators*, ed. Marlene Villalobos Hennessy (London, 2009), 31–64 (33). The career of the Holkham Psalter Artist is dealt with in greater detail in Lynda Dennison, 'Monastic or Secular? The Artist of the Ramsey Psalter, now at Holkham Hall, Norfolk', in *Monasteries and Society in Medieval Britain: Proceedings of the 1994 Harlaxton Symposium*, ed. Benjamin Thompson (Stamford, 1999), 223–61. The relevant aspects of this artist's career will be discussed briefly below.

23   For a recent exception, see Lynda Dennison's case for Oxford as an important centre for manuscript production in the fourteenth century: 'The Dating and Origin of Cambridge, Corpus Christi College, MS 180: Adam Easton's copy of Richard FitzRalph's *De Pauperie Salvatoris*', in *Cardinal Adam Easton (c. 1330–1397): Monk, Scholar, Theologian, Diplomat*, ed. M. Wendling (Amsterdam, 2020), 65–99.

the city of Troy on folio 113r.[24] The large format of Additional 34114, its fine-grade parchment, and the discipline with which the scribe maintains an elegant *textura rotunda* throughout, is matched by the bold scale of finely executed decorative motifs. The three folios with three-sided borders feature large, decorated initials of modelled foliage on gold ground; the initial finials extend into profile-serrated leaves with interstices of golden triangles which, in turn, form thin, rectilinear extensions (a bar-frame of gold alternating with blue or rose). The golden triangles give the impression of scalloped edges to the bar-frame, with added interest provided by the semi-circular notches 'cut' into the frame, the quatrefoils 'pinned' to it (fol. 1v), or by the gold balls that hedge both bar-frame and initials (Figure 5.1). These borders terminate in gently curling sprigs of conventional foliate forms (kidney- and heart-shaped leaves, three-pointed leaves, daisy buds and flowers), punctuated by short sprigs tipped with gold balls and black squiggles. Some foliate nodules at corner points and mid-points provide the occasion for lion masks, heraldic devices or for the emergence of the winged dragon, in profile, 'biting on' to further foliage, stem or letter form (as in Fig. 5.1). These features are all typical of the late fourteenth century, especially the use of dragons or grotesques (cf. Figs 5.5 and 5.8), which virtually disappear from English borders by around 1400.[25]

This artist, whom we have designated the 'Despenser Master', also provided some of the more substantial decoration in Cotton Claudius E.viii, as Baswell and Sandler recognised.[26] It is extensively illuminated and required the collaboration of another three artists for its completion (Table 5.1). The Despenser Master's work features on nearly every folio in the second to sixth quires, and comprises bar-borders (in various designs), a new instance of an elaborate trellis border not seen in Additional 34114, and champ initials in gold with fine white reserve-work on rose/blue grounds, characteristic of this man's work. The sheer volume of illumination in Cotton Claudius E.viii compared with Additional 34114 extends the range of motifs expected in the artist's

---

24   Line 859 in *Eneas: Roman du XIIe siècle*, ed. J.-J. Salverda de Grave, 2 vols (Paris, 1929, rept. 1983, 1985), I:27.
25   Kathleen L. Scott, *Dated & Datable English Manuscript Borders c. 1395–1499* (London, 2002), 13.
26   Our own examination of Cotton agrees exactly with Baswell and Sandler's partial account of the artists' stints (given for selected folios up to folio 115): 'Aeneas in 1381', 45 n. 111.

repertoire (holly, kite, triangular, lobe-and-tongue leaves, an illusionistic form of deeply-folded leaf), as well as the variety with which a single motif might be executed, such as the use of balls (normally gold) in colour with white decorative highlighting (cf. Figs 5.1–5.3). Artist C of Cotton, the third hand in the manuscript and quite possibly the 'junior assistant' of Baswell and Sandler's terminology, is here designated the 'Despenser Assistant' (Figs 5.4–5.7). He is the only artist other than the Despenser Master to feature in two of the volumes in Despenser's library.[27] Both Master and Assistant use the same range of colours and motifs, although the palette is less vivid in the Assistant's usage, and the motifs are differently executed. The conventional foliate forms, for example, are the same as those described for the Despenser Master but slightly larger and cruder in the Despenser Assistant's handling, with less care taken in the use of white for decorative highlighting. Even small details of penwork are coincident in design if not in execution. The black penwork vines that end in a single motif, for example, intersect at right angles with the 'main' pen-vine, often overlapping, and accompanied by short slashes (cf. Figs 5.3 and 5.4). As with every coincident factor, the Despenser Master's handling is crisper, more detailed, and often elaborated: single or double slashes intersect the vine, for example, in addition to the more occasional black dots (Fig. 5.3).[28] Clear difference is also evident in the artists' treatment of the 'squiggle' on gold balls: the assistant's approach is to 'stack' flattened lines in between the ball and the squiggle. The Despenser Assistant replicates the Master's grotesques and masks (Fig. 5.5), but he also differs significantly from him in his use of naturalistic figural forms, flora and fauna: acorns and oak leaves, roses, peapods and birds, including the owl and spoonbill(?) on folio 137v (Fig. 5.6). In view of the question of origin, the important point about the occurrence of both drolleries and realistic representations is that they 'are not typical of late 14th or early 15th-century border decoration in London shops [...] the presence of these motifs probably indicates a continuing regional tradition'.[29]

---

27 See Table 3 below.
28 Another instance of elaboration occurs in their different treatment of gold grounds: in the trellis border (fol. 27v) the Despenser Master's gold is punched with lines of dots in various patterns, executed freehand.
29 Scott, *Later Gothic Manuscripts*, II:34.

Table 5.1 The division of illuminator hands in BL MS Cotton Claudius E.viii, *Flores historiarum* and the *Chronicle* of Adam Murimuth.

Quire / fols[30]	Decoration type	Illuminator	Comments
1 / 5–12v	Full trellis border with Despenser arms (5r); champ initials	Artist A	This quire only
2–6 / 13–51v	Full trellis border (27v); full bar-border with central bar (43r); variety of three-sided and single-bar borders; champ initials	Artist B (**Despenser Master**)	
7–8 / 52–67v		Artist C (**Despenser Assistant**)	
9 / 68–75v	Full bar-border with central bar (71v); champ initials	Artist D and Artist C	Artist D on fols 68r–v and 75r–v (i.e., the outer bifolium)
10 / 76–83v	Borders, various (76r–v, 77r, etc); champ initials	Artist D and Artist C	Artist D on fols 76r–v, 83r–v, and 79r–80v (i.e., the outer and inner bifolia)
11 / 84–91v	Champ initials	Artist C	
12 / 92–99v	Champ initials	Artist D and Artist C	Working on the same bifolia
13 / 100–107v	Champ initials	Artist C	
14–19 / 108–153v	Borders; champ initials	Artist D and Artist C	Pattern: border pages by Artist C and initials divided between D and C Working on the same bifolia except in quire 17
20–34 / 154–270v[31]	Borders (161v, 163r, 205v, 225r, 239v); champ initials	Artist C	

30 The manuscript has two sets of modern foliation, one of which (cited here) counts flyleaves, and is located in the lower-right corner of the leaf.
31 Quire 35, the final quire at fol. 271, contains no illumination. It comprises a single

Artist D of Cotton provides eight bar-frame borders in quire 10 and shares in the provision of champ initials between quires 9 and 19 with Artist C (Despenser Assistant). Cotton Artist D is difficult to distinguish from Artist B (Despenser Master), although direct comparison of the champ initials at the end of quire 6 (fol. 51v) and the start of quire 9 (fol. 68r) shows a decline in quality, particularly in the absence of the fine white reserve-work replaced with simpler, cruder highlighting both on motifs and groundwork of initials. Near the end of Artist D's stint in quires 18 and 19, motifs are increasingly oversized, an inconsistency in handling that is difficult to attribute to the Despenser Master (Artist B). The impression, certainly, is of another 'junior assistant', quite possibly in training. In conjunction with the similarities in style between artists B, C and D, the mode of collaboration between artists C and D strongly indicates that they worked in close proximity. Before the bifolia were assembled into quires (presumably), the two artists often worked on the same bifolia (quires 12, 14–16, 18–19) and more occasionally on separate bifolia (quires 9, 10, 17). This indicates that artists C and D, at least, who appear to have been the two main assistants of the Despenser Master, could feasibly have worked within the same environment (whether monastic or secular). Cotton Artist A's biting dragons, lion masks and foliate forms indicate a shared stylistic milieu, and yet his independent work in the first quire (the preface to *Flores historiarum*) gives no clue as to whether he worked in the same physical space as any of the other artists. Nevertheless, whatever the precise organisation of the illuminators involved, the iconographic scheme is coherent. The first quire's opening trellis border is replete with crowns and bishop's mitres in alternating roundels, and an initial occupied by the Despenser arms. Thereafter the arms recur within initials that begin descriptions of key moments in royal English history, especially coronations, thus continuing the visual associations of the first folio.[32] Although neither of the books discussed so far contains miniatures, we should not doubt that they are high-grade productions: sixteen decorated initials are infilled with the Despenser arms in Cotton, thereby providing the main

---

bifolium followed by three flyleaves, with the first flyleaf foliated as fol. 273. For a description of the manuscript, see *Flores historiarum*, 3 vols. RS 95, ed. H. R. Luard (London, 1890), I:xxiv–xxvi.

32   In Additional 34114 Despenser's arms are associated with 'majestic events in imperial history' (Baswell's observation, 'Aeneas in 1381', 45–6), while in Cotton they are tied to major events in royal English history.

focal point of the illumination (and obviating the need for historiated initials).[33] No other work by Cotton artists A or D has been found; nevertheless, we suggest that Cotton Artist C (Despenser Assistant) is identifiable in parts of another Despenser-owned book, reinforcing the idea that Cotton artists B, C, and D were located in the same area for at least the time that Despenser's books were in production.

Table 5.2 The division of illuminator hands in BL MS Arundel 74, Bede's *Ecclesiastica historia* (fols 1–99), *Epistola Cuthberti de Obitu Bedae*, etc.

Quire / fols	Decoration type	Illuminator	Comments
1 / 1–8v	Full bar border with historiated initial (2v); three-sided border (1r); champ initials	Artist A **(Despenser Assistant)**	
2 / 9–16v	Champ initials	Artist B	This quire only
3 / 17–24v	Champ initials, incl. one 7-line 'h' with Despenser arms (21r)	Artist C and Artist A	Artist A on fols 20v–21r (i.e., the inner bifolium only)
4 / 25–32v	Champ initials	Artist A	
5 / 33–40v	Champ initials	Artist C and Artist A	Artist A on fols 36r–v, 37r (i.e. the inner bifolium only)
6–9 / 41–72v	Champ initials	Artist A	
10 / 73–80v	Champ initials	Artist C and Artist A	Artist A on fols 75v, 78r–v (i.e., the third bifolium only)
11 / 81–88v	Champ initials	Artist C	
12–13 / 89–106v (quire 13 at fol. 97)	Champ initials	Artist A	

33 On fols 5r, 27v, 43r, 71v, 113r, 115v, 120r, 127r, 130v, 135v, 137v, 140r, 142r, 161v, 225r and 239v. The same pattern is evident in Additional 34114 (fols 106r, 164r) with the exception of fol. 1r, where the arms are incorporated within the lower mid-point of the bar-frame.

The third and final manuscript known to have been owned by Bishop Despenser is Arundel 74, a copy of Bede's *Ecclesiastical History*. As illustrated in Table 5.2, no part of it was decorated by the Despenser Master, and Artist A appears to have been the Despenser Assistant (Fig. 5.7). This manuscript is less lavish in most respects than the other two books, with a programme of illumination comprising two border pages in quire 1 and champ initials throughout. The occurrence of an unfinished historiated initial of a man (Bede?) at his writing desk is unexpected in more ways than one, given that historical chronicles were seldom illustrated at all.[34] Quite possibly the patron had a special affection for the work of this foremost medieval historian of British and Saxon history, although apparently not enough to situate the figure of authority (fol. 2v) before the placement of the Despenser arms (fol. 1r). The Despenser Assistant provided the main aspects of the illumination in Arundel, including the only two occurrences of the Despenser arms within the book (fols 1r, 21r). Artists B and C of Arundel 74 do not occur in either of Despenser's other books, adding to the impression that there was a plentiful supply of artists in the vicinity of the Despenser Master and Despenser Assistant. It is not clear that Artist C of Arundel 74 worked in the same physical space as Artist A. Even though his hand appears together with the Despenser Assistant's in quires 3, 5 and 10, he consistently worked on what were almost certainly separable bifolia at that stage in the manuscript's making – a task requiring vicinity, albeit not necessarily proximity. All of this points to sustained activity in one locality, a factor that *can* confirm a single area of production for Despenser's library; what it *cannot* confirm, at this stage, is that it was produced in a 'Norwich atelier'.[35] Baswell's suggested reading of Additional 34114's legendary texts 'as a myth book of the Despensers' is certainly compelling, and a Norwich origin would help to reinforce his idea that it 'was produced at Bishop Despenser's direct commission, and that it hence reflects his interests and, in its decoration, his familial ambitions'.[36] Confirming this hypothesis, however, will require new identification of some (ideally all) of the artists in other books – books not related to Despenser – in order to compile 'the relatively richer evidence of groups of manuscripts of a given date with the same provenance'.[37]

34 Scott, *Later Gothic Manuscripts*, I:36, and I:71 n. 26.
35 Baswell, 'Aeneas in 1381', 45.
36 Baswell, 'Aeneas in 1381', 44.
37 Webber, 'Where Were Books Made and Kept?', 221.

Beyond Despenser's Books: Related Manuscripts

A selective search of manuscript catalogues for items with East Anglian provenance, as well as of bibliographic listings relating to Norfolk specifically, has enabled us to identify manuscripts illuminated in the period *c.*1380–1400.[38] So far, the Despenser Master can be identified in the calendar (fols 1r–6v) of the Sarum Hours in Cambridge, Trinity College, MS B.11.7, which contains the synodal feasts of Norwich (Fig. 5.2).[39] The continuator of the original programme of borderwork from fols 7r–217r is the Hatton Missal Artist, whose work is currently known only in Hatton 1 – a missal with a Norwich calendar and other masses and non-Sarum feasts of Norwich designated in the sanctoral (cf. Figs 5.8–5.9, 5.11–5.12).[40] Two further manuscripts contain illumination that is in part attributable to the Hatton Missal Artist – a missal ('Wellis') and a processional – and their borderwork may be compared with Hatton 1 in Figs 5.10–5.13. A smaller-format missal ('Bedingfield') contains illuminated borders that are clearly related in style to Hatton Missal Artist's,

---

38 N. R. Ker, 'Medieval Manuscripts from Norwich Cathedral Priory', *Transactions of the Cambridge Bibliographical Society* 1 (1949), 1–28; Richard Beadle, 'Prolegomena to a literary geography of later medieval Norfolk', in *Regionalism in Late Medieval Manuscripts and Texts*, ed. Felicity Riddy (Cambridge, 1991), 89–108 (Beadle's list supplements that given in *LALME*); *Medieval Art in East Anglia*, ed. Lasko and Morgan; Sandler, *Gothic Manuscripts*; Scott, *Later Gothic Manuscripts*; the BL's *Catalogue of Illuminated Manuscripts* <https://www.bl.uk/catalogues/illuminatedmanuscripts/welcome.htm> (accessed June 2023); and notes taken by James-Maddocks during the preparation of the section on Trinity College, Cambridge, in Ann E. Nichols and Holly James-Maddocks, *An Index of Images in English Manuscripts: Cambridge II* (London, 2022).

39 Felix (8 March), Translation of Edmund (29 April), Dominic (5 August), Thomas of Hereford (2 October) and Francis (4 October). See Nicholas Rogers, 'The Artist of Trinity B.11.7 and his Patrons', in *England in the Fifteenth Century*, ed. Nicholas Rogers (Stamford, 1994), 170–86 (172); and M. R. James, *The Western Manuscripts in the Library of Trinity College, Cambridge*, 4 vols (Cambridge, 1900), I:342–6. The manuscript is fully digitised: 'B.11.7', *The Wren Digital Library* <https://mss-cat.trin.cam.ac.uk/Manuscript/B.11.7> (accessed 27 October 2024).

40 *Medieval Art in East Anglia*, 31. See also Scott, *Later Gothic Manuscripts*, no. 5. In comparing the images supplied here of Hatton 1 and Trinity B.11.7 (for example, Figs 5.8 and 5.9), it is worth noting the markedly different dimensions of the original folios (Hatton at 440x300mm and Trinity at 270x180mm), and the consequent impact upon the proportions of the motifs in reproduction.

although the green wash on vine tendrils is characteristic of post-1400 production and thus points to a younger contemporary or follower of his style (Fig. 5.14). The distribution of labour is as follows:[41]

1. BL MS Additional 25588, 'Wellis' Missal. Hatton Missal Artist as Artist B on folio 109v only, with two assistants, the second of whom (Artist C) commences on folio 112v;

2. BL MS Additional 57534, Processional of St Giles's Hospital, Norwich. Hatton Missal Artist as Artist A of the borderwork, with one assistant (Artist B) for the champ initials; and

3. *Related*: BL MS Harley 3866, 'Bedingfield' Missal (one illuminator working in the style of the Hatton Missal Artist).

The processional in Additional 57534 (Fig. 5.13a) is substantially smaller in format than the missals in Hatton 1 and Additional 25588, and thus the clearest indication that this seemingly cruder work can be attributed to the same 'Hatton Missal Artist' comes from comparison with the minor decoration in Hatton 1 such as the champ initials or demi-vinets (cf. Fig. 5.13b).[42] Remarkably, both the Wellis Missal and St Giles Processional contain illuminated initials by the same collaborator, here referred to as the 'Wellis Missal Assistant' (Figs 5.15a and 5.15b). Table 5.3 summarises the evidence for overlapping work across the wider group. This collaborative characteristic, as well as the evidence for provenance in all the books newly related to the Despenser-Hatton group, will be considered further below.

---

41 Basic catalogue entries can be accessed on the British Library's (BL) *Catalogue of Illuminated Manuscripts* <https://www.bl.uk/catalogues/illuminatedmanuscripts/welcome.htm> (for MSS Additional 25588 and Harley 3866); and on the BL's *Catalogue: Archives and Manuscripts* <https://searcharchives.bl.uk/> (accessed June 2023) (MS Additional 57534).

42 Page dimensions for the Hatton group are as follows: Hatton 1 (missal), 440x300mm; Additional 25588 (missal), 380x250mm; Harley 3866 (missal), 280x185mm; Trinity B.11.7 (hours), 270x180mm; Additional 57534 (processional), 210x140mm.

Table 5.3 The distribution of labour among border artists of the Despenser-Hatton group identified in more than one manuscript.

Despenser Master	Despenser Assistant	Hatton Missal Artist	Wellis Missal Assistant
Additional 34114*			
Cotton Claud.E.viii* (Artist B)	Cotton Claud.E.viii (Artist C)		
TCC B.11.7 * (calendar)		TCC B.11.7 (original borderwork from fol. 7r)	
	Arundel 74 (Artist A)		
		Hatton 1#	
		Additional 25588 (Artist B)	Additional 25588 (Artist C)
		Additional 57534# (Artist A)	Additional 57534 (Artist B)

(The symbols * and # mark the recurrence of the same styles of pen-flourishing)

The Hours of the Virgin in Trinity B.11.7 – the book to which both the Despenser Master and Hatton Missal Artist contributed – is the complex product of an aggregation of labour, arising from at least two phases of production. The first campaign, conducted in the late fourteenth century, saw the completion of the calendar in its entirety, as well as most of the decorated borders throughout the rest of the book (Figs 5.2 and 5.9).[43] Following the calendar, the illustrative programme appears to have been left unfinished until the blanks were filled during the second campaign, although (as Michael Orr observed) some of the miniatures and historiated initials were repainted.[44] Indeed, erasures and adjustments to the borderwork in this section were made to accommodate the new illustrations' frames, often accompanied by rubbed

43   The exceptions are the borders on fols 20r, 21r–v, and 45r–v, which are early fifteenth century in style. These folios also contain the patronal figures identified by Nicholas Rogers (discussed below, n. 46).
44   Michael Orr, 'Illustration as Preface and Postscript in the Hours of the Virgin of Trinity College MS B.11.7', *Gesta* 34.2 (1995), 162–76 (163).

areas of text.[45] The illuminations of the second campaign, which include depictions of the book's new owners, can be assigned more firmly to c.1413–22.[46] The important point for the present discussion is that all of the illumination in the calendar (roundel miniatures and borders) and most of the borders in the hours appear to have been completed earlier, during the late fourteenth century, meaning that work by the Despenser Master and Hatton Missal Artist was probably contemporaneous.[47] The calendar's roundel miniatures, depicting the Occupations of the Months and Zodiacal signs, are set within three-sided borders illuminated by the Despenser Master (fols 1r–6v). Iconographically the Occupations constitute a relatively rare subject, as Scott has noted, and one would need to look to 'very lavish manuscripts' such as the Sherborne Missal or the Hours of Elizabeth the Queen for comparable calendars.[48]

45   Rubbed or erased borderwork is visible on fols 20v, 29v (motifs on the inside of the border frame), 22v (gutter), 29r (top R corner), etc. Most of the band-borders infilled with gold filigree have been adjusted to match the patterned surfaces within the miniatures and frames, for example, fols 23v, 25r, 28r, 41v, 53v (for an original band-border, cf. fol. 19v). Other adjustments include the monochrome roundels set within borders on fols 7r and 13r where, in each case, the same pigment was used for the monochrome curled acanthus of the new historiated initial. Occasional outlining in green has been added to border-frames in both the calendar (fol. 1r) and hours (fol. 13r), further indicating that the later illuminating shop inherited both sections together. It was not necessarily the case, of course, that the calendar and hours were originally intended for each other.
46   Rogers has identified the owners of two mottoes which occur in some of the miniatures as those of Sir John Cornwall, Baron Fanhope (d.1443), and his wife Elizabeth, Henry IV's sister (d.1425). The miniature of the young, unbearded king kneeling at a prie-dieu (fol. 31v) is interpreted as Henry V: see 'The Artist of Trinity B.11.7', 173–5.
47   Scott's suggestion that the borders may be an attempt to imitate the late fourteenth-century decoration of the calendar would not explain the alterations made to some borders after fol. 7r, or why this imitation-principle was not employed on fols 21 or 45 (cf. *Later Gothic Manuscripts*, II:153) (fol. 20r is, conversely, an attempt to imitate fol. 27r). We share the view of both Orr and Rogers that the illumination of the calendar and hours was contemporary, and while Rogers' 1410s dating is conceivable for the hours-illustrations, as well as the borders on fols 20, 21 and 45, it is too late for the careers of the Despenser Master and Hatton Missal Artist (Orr, 'Illustration as Preface and Postscript', 162–3; cf. Rogers, 'The Artist of Trinity B.11.7', 176).
48   Scott, *Later Gothic Manuscripts*, II:153. No other work has been identified by the illustrator of the roundels.

Whether or not the roundels themselves are the work of the Despenser Master or a separate 'miniaturist', what is clear is that he participated in some of the highest-grade productions of his day – a factor worth emphasising if we are indeed dealing with a non-metropolitan illuminator. The calendar contains the synodal feasts of Norwich, as noted, and 'a certain East Anglian flavour' continues in the text decorated by the Hatton Missal Artist, with the inclusion of St Edmund and St Etheldreda in the *memoriae* at Lauds.[49] Since the Trinity Hours constitutes newly identified work by both the Despenser Master and Hatton Missal Artist, the localisation of one illuminator is clearly of potential relevance to the other. Books attributed to the Hatton Missal Artist, therefore, help us to develop further the theory that they were Norwich-based book producers.

The cataloguer of Hatton 1 for *Medieval Art in East Anglia* remarked upon the similarity of its borders to those in Despenser's *Flores Historiarum* – a stylistic correspondence that is now explicable in light of the identification of both artists in Trinity B.11.7.[50] Comparison with Cotton Claudius E.viii reveals that the Hatton Missal Artist employed the extended repertoire of the Despenser Assistant, preferring the use of naturalistic foliage and animals in combination with various drolleries (including the distinctive grotesque with the bill of a spoonbill: cf. Figs 5.5–5.6 and 5.8). The interest in realistic motifs is far more developed in Hatton 1, and its borders teem with strawberries and columbines, as well as foxes, dogs, boars, apes, squirrels and one snail – several forming dramatic vignettes that make this 'large and splendid book worthy of comparison with other great missals of the period' (Fig. 5.11).[51] It is clear from comparison of the smallest details – such as the intersecting pen-vines with slashes and dots, or the interest in colour modulated by white (as modelling, filigree or reserve-work) – that the Hatton Missal Artist worked to the same level of refinement as the Despenser Master. Yet there are differences in Hatton 1's borderwork, both in repertoire and in execution, that make it distinguishable from work attributed to the Despenser Master. In repertoire there is the Hatton Artist's frequent use of band-borders in pink/blue with white reserve-work or repeat-pattern (for example, Figs 5.10–5.11); the naturalistic vignettes; and a

---

49   James, *Trinity College*, I:343; and discussed in greater detail in Rogers, 'The Artist of Trinity B.11.7'.
50   Andrew Martindale, in *Medieval Art in East Anglia*, 32.
51   *Medieval Art in East Anglia*, 31.

kidney-triangle (or leaf-triangle) motif in opposing colours (see lower borders of Figs 5.12–5.13a; cf. 5.14). In terms of execution, the Hatton Artist is consistent in 'stacking' semi-circular curves on gold balls (some stacked on three sides of the ball and forming near-foliate lobes); in the curled tendrils in penwork that 'grow' from the bar-frame or vine; and in the propensity to place a gold foliate-form within a grouping of the same form in colour (for example, Fig. 5.10). It is these differences that make the Hatton Missal Artist distinguishable from the Despenser Master and it is these differences found in combination in parts of the Trinity Hours, the Wellis Missal and the St Giles Processional that encourage their attribution to the border artist of Hatton 1 (Figs 5.8–5.13).

Analysis of aspects of minor decoration, such as the pen-flourished initials in manuscripts attributable to the Despenser Master and Hatton Missal Artist, proves relevant to the arguments made for distinguishing between the illuminators. In Additional 34114, for example, the manuscript illuminated solely by the Despenser Master, the initials are occasionally infilled with lion-masks or foliage, and the foliate saw-tooth style is unusually elongated, and interspersed with a spiral coil or a dotted circle, while (in larger initials) tendrils form staves terminating in trefoils or circles (Fig. 5.1). The same style of flourishing recurs in quire 3 of Cotton, coinciding with the Despenser Master's stint, and throughout the calendar in Trinity B.11.7 (Fig. 5.16), stopping short of folio 7r where the Hatton Missal Artist takes over the borderwork (and pen-flourishing ceases altogether).[52] The pen-flourished initials throughout Hatton 1 are broadly similar although executed differently, with less well-defined foliate 'teeth' separated by cross-hatching in ink; further decorative elements may include circles grouped together to form triangles at the initial edges, or double slashes on tendrils which themselves end in kites, faces, trefoils or circles. Pen-flourished initials remarkably similar to those in Hatton 1 occur in the St Giles Processional (Additional 57534), a manuscript largely illuminated by the Hatton Missal Artist (Fig. 5.17).[53] Analysis of the decoration in all

---

52 See Table 3, marked by '*'. The only other pen-flourishing in Cotton is in quire 1 (illuminated by Cotton Artist A) and it is different from that in quire 3. Arundel 74 contains no pen-flourishing.
53 See '#' in Table 3. For completion, the 'Wellis' Missal (MS Add. 25588) contains two different styles of pen-flourishing: the first occurs in quires illuminated by Artist A and the second in quires illuminated by Artist C. The Hatton Missal Artist (Artist B) contributed only the borderwork (and possibly the miniature) on fol. 109v.

of these books has revealed four illuminators so far who worked on multiple volumes (Table 5.3, above). Some of them even appear to have collaborated with the same flourisher more than once, if they did not simply carry out this minor decoration themselves.

The emerging pattern seems to demonstrate a consistency in the availability of hands in one area – an origin point that is strongly indicated by the provenance evidence for Norwich diocese in every single volume. Like the Hatton Missal and Trinity Hours, both of the Wellis and Bedingfield missals contain calendars that include the synodal feasts of Norwich. In addition to this textual connection with East Anglia, both volumes can be linked by ownership to the same area: an early owner of Additional 25588 was Henry Wellis, chaplain in the diocese of Norwich (fols 4v, 250r), and an unnoticed fifteenth-century inscription on folio 10r places the volume in the church at 'Bixley, near Norwich'; similarly, Harley 3866 appears to have been in the hands of the Bedingfield family of Suffolk by the second quarter of the fifteenth century (calendar). A combination of internal evidence and added inscription indicates that the processional in Additional 57534 belonged to St Giles's Hospital in Norwich, and may even have been made for its clerical community.[54] All three manuscripts are thus coherent in their evidence for early provenance and complement the uniformity in styles of illumination found in manuscripts attributed to the Despenser Master, Hatton Missal Artist and their assistants.

The eight books discussed so far support the view of East Anglia and, in particular, Norwich, as a thriving locus for manuscript illumination, as we might expect for one of the major regional centres. The rich illustration of the Hatton Missal Artist's books – a half-page Crucifixion miniature (Additional 25588), eighteen historiated initials (Hatton 1) and nine schematic diagrams of liturgical conduct (Additional 57534) – clearly associates this border artist's with high status work, and the same can now be said of the sumptuous 'occupations' roundels that feature in the Despenser Master's calendar in the Trinity Hours (MS B.11.7). The Despenser Master's connection through the Trinity Hours to the Hatton Missal Artist and, through him, to a wider circle of Norwich-related books, clearly strengthens the case for the local production of Bishop Despenser's surviving library. This has implications for other important

---

54 Aden Kumler, '*Imitatio Rerum*: Sacred Objects in the St Giles's Hospital Processional', *Journal of Medieval and Early Modern Studies* 44 (2014), 469–502 (474–5).

Fig. 5.1   BL MS Additional 34114, fol. 164r, *Roman de Thèbes*. © The British Library. 'Despenser Master'. Three-quarter border with two 'biting' dragons (initial and lower left corner).

Fig. 5.2 Cambridge, Trinity College, MS B.11.7, fol. 6r, Hours. By permission of the Master and Fellows of Trinity College, Cambridge. 'Despenser Master'. The use of balls in colour with white highlighting (roundel edges) recurs in this artist's stint in BL MS Cotton Claudius E.viii on fols 32r and 42v.

Fig. 5.3   BL MS Cotton Claudius E.viii, fol. 43r, *Flores historiarum* (detail). © The British Library. 'Despenser Master'.

Fig. 5.4 BL MS Cotton Claudius E.viii, fol. 71v (detail). © The British Library. 'Despenser Assistant'.

Fig. 5.5   BL MS Cotton Claudius E.viii, fol. 77r (detail). © The British Library. 'Despenser Assistant'. Detail of lion mask (centre) and grotesque with a spoonbill-shaped bill (left).

Fig. 5.6   BL MS Cotton Claudius E.viii, fol. 137v. © The British Library. 'Despenser Assistant'. Realistic figures and naturalistic flora and fauna.

Fig. 5.7 BL MS Arundel 74, fol. 2v, Bede, *Ecclesiastica historia*. © The British Library. 'Despenser Assistant'. Unfinished historiated initial of ?Bede at his writing desk.

Fig. 5.8 Oxford, Bodleian Library, MS Hatton 1, fol. 181v, Missal. © Bodleian Libraries, University of Oxford. 'Hatton Missal Artist'. Note grotesque with spoonbill-shaped bill in the top L corner (cf. Fig. 5.5).

Fig. 5.9 Cambridge, Trinity College, MS B.11.7, fol. 8v. By permission of the Master and Fellows of Trinity College, Cambridge. 'Hatton Missal Artist'.

Fig. 5.10   BL MS Additional 25588, fol. 109v, Missal. © The British Library. 'Hatton Missal Artist'. Gold replaces colour within some motif-clusters: cf. Hatton 1, fols 8v, 20v, etc.

Fig. 5.11   Oxford, Bodleian Library, MS Hatton 1, fol. 120v. © Bodleian Libraries, University of Oxford. 'Hatton Missal Artist'. Vignette (lower border) of ape with crossbow pointed at snail.

Fig. 5.12 Oxford, Bodleian Library, MS Hatton 1, fol. 148v. © Bodleian Libraries, University of Oxford. 'Hatton Missal Artist'.

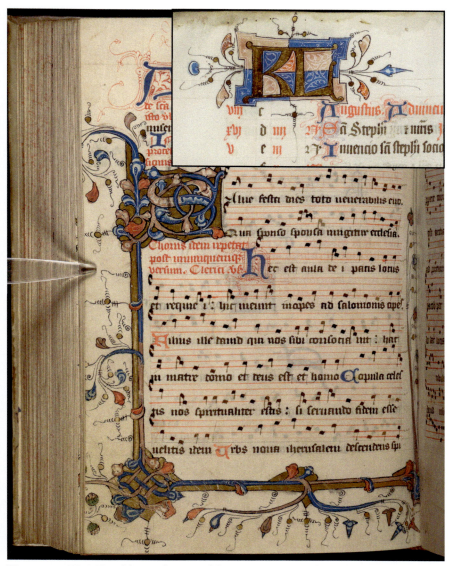

Fig. 5.13a   BL MS Additional 57534, fol. 96v, Processional. © The British Library. The gutter contains a barbed trefoil motif (visible in the LHS border in Fig. 5.10).
Fig. 5.13b (inset)   Oxford, Bodleian Library, Hatton 1, fol. 4v (detail). © Bodleian Libraries, University of Oxford. Both 'Hatton Missal Artist'.

Fig. 5.14   BL MS Harley 3866, fol. 168v, Missal. © The British Library. See fol. 235v for a wingless variation on the 'biting' dragon shown in Fig. 5.1. Related to the style of the 'Hatton Missal Artist'.

Fig. 5.15a BL MS Additional 25588, fol. 138v (detail). © The British Library. Fig. 5.15b (inset) BL MS Additional 57534, fol. 125r (detail). © The British Library. Both 'Wellis Missal Assistant'.

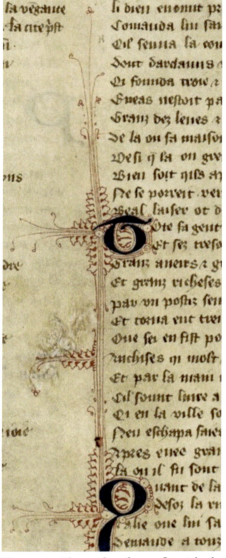

Fig. 5.16 The style of pen-flourished initials associated with the 'Despenser Master' in: Fig. 5.16a BL MS Additional 34114, fol. 106r (detail). © The British Library (throughout); Fig. 5.16b BL MS Cotton Claudius E.viii, fol. 21r (detail). © The British Library (quire 3 only); Fig. 5.16c Cambridge, Trinity College, MS B.11.7, fol. 4v (detail). By permission of the Master and Fellows of Trinity College, Cambridge (quire 1 only).

Fig. 5.17 The style of pen-flourished initials associated with the 'Hatton Missal Artist' in:
Fig. 5.17a Oxford, Bodleian Library, MS Hatton 1, fol. 148v (detail).
© Bodleian Libraries, University of Oxford (throughout);
Fig. 5.17b BL MS Additional 57534, fol. 18v (detail).
© The British Library (throughout).

manuscripts tentatively localised to East Anglia. Early fourteenth-century books assigned 'rather too definitely' to Norwich, according to Doyle, such as the Ormesby and Bromholm psalters, do nevertheless assert an influence in the continued use of narrative vignettes and naturalistic motifs in the later books with identical provenance.[55] A desideratum of future research must be the attempt to track chronological developments in styles of manuscript illumination in multiple regional centres over extended periods of time – creating a meaningfully diagnostic framework for understanding the relationship between use and origin. Until then we cannot be sure, as Webber warns, that any stylistic elements assigned to a given place 'are not to be found in material produced elsewhere'.[56] One such thorny problem in the attempt to localise the Despenser Master is the career of an older contemporary known as the 'Holkham Psalter Artist'. Several scholars have noticed a resemblance between the borderwork in the psalter for Ramsey abbey, now Holkham Hall MS 26, and in the *Flores Historiarum* for Henry Despenser, with its comparable repertory of large-scale foliage, interlace, and lion masks, alongside the 'uniquely characteristic' 'profile dog-headed, web-winged dragons with disc-patterned backbone and the large, pendant lavender columbines' all set within rectilinear borders.[57] The issue that arises with respect to localisation, given their close resemblance in style to the Holkham Psalter Artist, is that the latter was almost certainly itinerant. His known *oeuvre* comprises at least twelve manuscripts, according to Lynda Dennison, which indicate that he was active from c.1360 to c.1395 and that he illuminated books destined for the monastic orders, both Augustinian and Benedictine.[58] The disparity in provenance

---

55 A. I. Doyle, 'English Provincial Book Trade Before Printing', in *Six Centuries of the Provincial Book Trade in Britain*, ed. Peter Isaac (Winchester, 1990), 13–29 (20–1). Sandler, *Gothic Manuscripts*, II:49–52, nos 43 and 44.
56 Webber, 'Where Were Books Made and Kept?', 223.
57 Sandler, *Gothic Manuscripts*, II:166. The same observation is made in Dennison, 'Monastic or Secular?', 229; and in Lynda Dennison and Nicholas Rogers, 'A Medieval Best-Seller: Some Examples of Decorated Copies of Higden's *Polychronicon*', in *The Church and Learning in Later Medieval Society: Essays in Honour of R. B. Dobson*, ed. Caroline Barron and Jenny Stratford (Donington, 2002), 80–99 (90). Columbines feature in the Hatton Missal too, and the general stylistic unity between the Despenser Master and Hatton Missal Artist are now, as argued here, better substantiated by the work they each contributed to the original portions of the Trinity Hours.
58 A synthesis of Dennison's work on this artist is given in 'The Significance

evidence is stark, with one early production made for the Augustinians of Christ Church, Dublin (c.1360–80),[59] while eight later productions (c.1380–95) were destined for a variety of Benedictine communities: two for Ramsey abbey;[60] two for Norwich cathedral priory;[61] and one each for St Augustine's abbey, Canterbury, Christ Church cathedral priory, Canterbury. Abingdon abbey and Reading abbey.[62] Dennison's assessment of this artist's patronage led her to conclude that 'he was a semi-itinerant, secular, illuminator who travelled from one monastic centre to another but had a stable base at one or possibly two such centres, where lay persons and the secular clergy could also order books'. One potential stable base, it seems, was a Benedictine 'centre, or centres, in East Anglia, most likely Ramsey and/or Norwich'.[63] Indeed, the recurrent columbine motif is likely to prove indicative of provenance: Scott's hypothesis that it was 'an identifying badge of the Norwich house' requires further substantiation,[64] while Doyle and Dennison

---

of Ornamental Penwork', 31–64. A more recent, tentative identification of the Holkham artist's hand is the fine border on folio 117r of the Vernon manuscript, plus verse initials in the same gathering: see Dennison, 'The Artistic Origins of the Vernon Manuscript', in *The Making of the Vernon Manuscript: The Production and Contexts of Oxford, Bodleian Library, MS Eng. poet.a.1*, ed. Wendy Scase (Turnhout, 2013), 171–205.

59   The information on the Holkham Psalter Artist's career given in the rest of this paragraph is drawn from Dennison, 'The Significance of Ornamental Penwork', 31–2, 35–6, 42. The 'Derby Psalter' (with undisputed Augustinian destination) is Bodleian Library, MS Rawlinson G. 185.

60   Holkham Hall, MS 26, Psalter; BL, MS Royal 14 C.ix, *Polychronicon*.

61   Bodleian Library, MS Bodley 316, *Polychronicon*; Paris, Bibliothèque nationale de France, MS lat. 4922, *Polychronicon*.

62   Respectively: Cambridge, University Library, MS Ii.2.24, *Polychronicon*; Bodleian Library, MS Rawlinson B. 191, *Polychronicon*; Oxford, Pembroke College, MS 2, John Mirifield, *Breviarium Bartholomei*; and BL, MS Royal 4 C.vi, anon., Commentary on Wisdom.

63   'The Significance of Ornamental Penwork', 32. In Dennison's most recent statement on the Holkham artist's later career, Norwich is hypothesised as the most feasible location for the particular confluence of artistic styles in the Vernon manuscript: see 'Vernon Manuscript', 202–5.

64   Scott, *Later Gothic Manuscripts*, II:34–5, in a discussion of the columbines in Hatton 1 (of Norwich provenance), refers to their presence in other manuscripts probably made for Norwich Cathedral Priory: the *Polychronicon* in both Bodley 316 (with BL, MS Harley 3634, fols 125–96 (1394–97)), and BnF, MS lat. 4922, and the works of Alanus de Insulis et al., in Bodleian Library, MS Canon Misc. 110, cited from Ker, 'Norwich Cathedral Priory', nos 57, 62, 105.

agree on the columbine's primary association with monasticism, and with Benedictines in particular.[65] If the Holkham Psalter Artist's career was facilitated by a monastic network, his clear influence on the styles of both the Despenser Master and Hatton Missal Artist lends support to Dennison's idea that Norwich may have been one of the primary centres in which he settled during the 1380s to 1390s. Certainly, what we can say is that *all* of the manuscripts attributable to the Despenser-Hatton group (Table 5.3, above) show textual connections with the diocese of Norwich, whether liturgical, as in most cases, or heraldic, or even dialectal, as in the case of Despenser's *Flores Historiarum*, whose main scribe switches to Norfolk-English.[66] Coincidence is unlikely. Parallels in the findings of different scholars – such as the convergences in style, provenance and date evident in the careers of the Holkham, Hatton and Despenser artists – cumulatively lead to a better sense of book illumination as a sustained activity in late medieval Norwich. We have few specific indications for the *circumstances* of production (what were the specific roles of the bishop and the priory, for example?), but we can be more confident about *place* of production.

Norwich

The question then would be, were conditions such in Norwich as to encourage Despenser to commission books locally, rather than in – say – London? Stylistically, the answer to that question is a probable 'yes'. This conclusion gains further support for reasons both biographical and contextual. Foremost we should consider proximity: as his Registers show, for ten years after 1385, Despenser scarcely left Norwich, other than brief attendance at parliament and convocations.[67] He was resident in London from May 1397 to February 1398, and may have commissioned books then; but other, more pressing concerns probably occupied him in those months.[68] Thus, the most likely period, and place, for the

65 A. I. Doyle, 'Introduction', in *The Vernon Manuscript: A Facsimile of Bodleian Library, Oxford, MS Eng. poet.a.1* (Cambridge, 1987), 1–16 (9); Dennison, 'The Significance of Ornamental Penwork', 33 n. 14.
66 *LALME*, I:223. The measures of weight given on fol. 12r in the main hand.
67 Despenser's Registers are kept in the Norfolk Record Office, as DN/REG 3/6.
68 Davies, 'Despenser, Henry', opines that Despenser's London stay was in support of Richard II against the Appellants, and to secure Archbishop Arundel's favourable settlement of his dispute with the Norwich priory.

making of these three manuscripts is that decade that the bishop spent in Norwich (c.1385–95). Two pieces of circumstantial evidence would seem to corroborate this assumption. Records from various sources, including sacrist and obedientiary rolls from the Cathedral priory and lists of freemen working in the city, though incomplete in both cases, nonetheless show two distinct periods of book-related activities: broadly 1280–1300 and 1381–96.[69] Neil Ker explained the first as the monks hiring scribes and artisans to replace the manuscripts destroyed during the citizens' riot of 1272; the second, we suggest, was encouraged by Despenser's decade of residence – a supposition that accords well with stylistic elements in the manuscripts.[70]

Secondarily, from 1381 on, the city was again prospering. Fiscally the leading citizenry possessed the wherewithal to have supported a local book trade. And late fourteenth-century Norwich residents, like their bishop, clearly had the tooth for aesthetically fine things, even if the city's best years for such production were on either side of Despenser's episcopacy. Norwich stained glass is a distinctive style that bloomed in the fifteenth century – much of it sadly destroyed during the Reformation – but fragmentary evidence affirms its high quality contemporaneous with Despenser.[71] Sculpture flourished as well in and about Norwich, especially of baptismal fonts; notably also, in the cathedral nave and cloister are the finest and most numerous roof bosses in England. While most of the latter were added during the tenure of Despenser's successor, that they accumulated so quickly after his death suggests both an earlier interest and an already-functioning local community of designers, stoneworkers, and colourists.[72]

---

69 See, in addition to L'Estrange's Freemen's *Calendar*, discussed below (n. 75), data accumulated by M. A. Michael, 'English Illuminators *c.* 1190–1450: A Survey of Documentary Sources', *English Manuscript Studies 1100–1700* 4 (1993), 62–113.
70 See Ker, 'Norwich Cathedral Priory', 8–9.
71 See David J. King, 'Glass Painting', in *Medieval Norwich*, ed. Rawcliffe and Wilson, 121–36, who notes (at 124): 'Glass datable between 1370 and 1390 [...] found near the church of St. Parmentergate [...] demonstrates that the glaziers then documented in the city were working in a style close to that seen elsewhere in glass and manuscript painting'.
72 See in particular M. R. James, *The Sculptured Bosses in the Cloisters of Norwich Cathedral* (Norwich, 1911); and further Martial Rose, 'The Vault Bosses', in *Norwich Cathedral*, ed. Atherton, 363–78. At Norwich there are more than 1,400 bosses; the next largest grouping in England numbers about 250, at St Mary the Virgin Abbey in Tewkesbury. Perhaps not insignificantly,

More closely related and relevant to our present enquiry, nonetheless, is figure painting. Lamentably, Cromwellian iconoclasts were particularly efficient in Norfolk and, like glass, frescoes and painted panels proved especially vulnerable targets. As with Norwich glass, however, enough remains here and there to suggest confidently that the many churches must have been replete with polychrome art.[73] For our purposes, two examples of painted wooden panels offer suggestive comparison: the aforementioned 'Despenser Retable', so named because it, like the manuscripts under consideration, bears his episcopal arms, assuring at least his financial contribution to its production; and an altarpiece assembled from unrelated survivors, several contemporaneous with Despenser and showing the same cosmopolitan style as the Retable.[74] Judging from such examples, the extensive tradition of the arts in Norwich implies that culturally/aesthetically the late fourteenth-century city could easily have accommodated production of fine books. But among these many craftsmen, were there any in fact in the book trade at work there, and if so, who were they?

To the first question we have definitively answered 'yes'. To the second, affirmatives of two kinds can be offered, based on existing documents. Here we need to consider manuscript producers of two types, commercial and clerical. Of the former, one probable pool can be drawn from the *Calendar of the Freemen of Norwich*, with significant entries from 1317 through the early seventeenth century. Less fortunately – but hardly surprising – the records are fullest for Edward III and then from Henry V forward – that is, 1327–77 and 1413–71 – and less so for our period of interest, Richard II and Henry IV (1377–1413).[75] Despite the gaps, however, enough remains to be suggestive. Prior to the arrival

---

five Despensers were patrons of St Mary the Virgin, and Lord Edward, Henry's eldest brother, is buried there in a magnificent chantry chapel. The relationship continued into the 1430s: see Julian M. Luxford, 'The Construction of English Monastic Patronage', in *Patronage, Power, and Agency in Medieval Art*, ed. Colum Hourihane (University Park PA, 2013), 31–53 (esp. 42, 46).

73 '58 parish churches have stood within the medieval city walls of Norwich': see Sandy Heslop et al., *The Medieval Churches of Norwich* <norwichmedieval-churches.org> (accessed 28 October 2024). See David Park and Helen Howard, 'The Medieval Polychromy', in *Norwich Cathedral*, ed. Atherton, 379–409. Especially valuable evidence are obedientiary rolls and sacrists' accounts listing sums paid for materials and to painters, at 401–4.

74 See n. 7 above.

75 See John L'Estrange, *Calendar of the Freemen of Norwich, from 1317 to 1603*

of Henry Despenser in 1370, Norwich would seem to have had active scriveners, 'writers', and proportionately a large number of parchment-makers.[76] Notable too, probably, are those enrolled as 'peyntour' during Edward's reign, since painters sometimes doubled as limners, illuminating manuscripts. Under Richard II the trades apparently continue, in concentrated numbers as noted above. Noteworthy is the cross-reign presence of certain surnames, evidence perhaps of multi-generational 'family' trades: that is, John de Frenge, painter (48 Edward III), and Stephen Frenge, painter (10 and 11 Richard II); Thomas de Ocle, painter (10 and 11 Richard II), and Robert Ocle, painter (9 Henry IV); Peter Brice, scrivener (38 Edward III) and John Brice, scrivener (2 Henry V); Robert de Gunton, 'writer' (?) (23 Edward III), Ralph Gunton, 'writer' (8 Henry IV), and Ralph Gunton, notary and 'writer' (3 Henry V).[77]

(Edward II to Elizabeth Inclusive), ed. Walter Rye (London, 1888); and more recently the charts in Rutledge, 'Economic life', 170–2.

76 The following list (with *Calendar* page numbers in parenthesis, and those working during Richard's reign in **bold**) covers the reigns of Edward III to Henry VI, on the assumption that some practitioners had extended careers: Nicholas Baldok, parchmener 21 & 22 Edw.III (4); William Archer, scrivener 7 Henry V (8); John de Bradewelle, peyntour 48 Edw.III (19); John Brice, scrivener 2 Henry V (20); Peter Brice, scrivener 38 Edw.III (20); **Robert Castell**, scriptor 8 & 9 Rich.II (28); Richard Clerk, text writer 27 & 28 Henry VI (32); William Dene, skrevener 16, 17, 18 Henry VI (42); William Dowty, scrivener 5 Henry VI (45); **John Drable alias Gilbert**, scrivener (?) 18 & 19 Rich.II (45); William de Draitone, scrivener (?) 23 Edw.III (45); John de Frenge, peyntour 48 Edw.III (55); **Stephen Frenge**, peyntour 10 & 11 Rich.II (55); **Edmund Frensshe**, peyntour 10 & 11 Rich.II (55); Master Ralph Gunton, notary and writer 3 Henry V (65); Ralph Gunton, writer 8 Henry IV (65); Robert de Gunton, writer (?) 23 Edw.III (65); Thomas Hamond, screvyner 3 Henry V (67); Richard Herbeger, scrivener 30 Henry VI (71); Thomas de Horning, parchmener 21 & 22 Edw.III (76); Peter Laurence, skryvener 1 Henry VI (85); William Lote, parchmener 3 Henry V (88); William de Lucham, scrivener (?) 1 Edw.III (89); John de Ludham, parchmener (?) 12 Edw.III (89); Roger March, parchmener 24 Henry VI (92); John Marchaunt, parchmener 9 Henry V (92); **John Mathew**, 'le roller' 16 & 17 Rich.II (94); Robert Ocle, peyntor 9 Henry IV (103); **Thomas de Ocle**, peyntor 10 & 11 Rich.II (103); Richard Ode, parchmener 3 Henry V (103); Thomas Percy, 'lomynour' 20 Henry VI (108); John Skrevener, text writer 16, 17, 18 Henry VI (124); **Henry J. Strykere**, parchmyner 4 Rich.II (132); Nicholas Sutton, 'Qwylwright' (penmaker) 5 Henry IV (133); Robert Werkton, scrivener 13 Henry VI (147); William West, 'loumer' 24 Henry VI (148).

77 This Ralph Gunton may in fact be the same person. Our thanks are due to the anonymous reviewer for alerting us to two wills: Thomas Frenge, peyntour,

In these cases, the Frenges, John and Stephen, the Ocles, Thomas and Robert, were all clearly working during Despenser's tenure; and if the families Brice and (de) Gunton carried on such a family enterprise, their presence in the more complete records of Edward III and Henry V that bookend the Despenser years could suggest continual scribal activity by relatives during the less well-documented period. Finally, of some interest, perhaps, is one 'Adam Bookebynder', listed without occupational title in 10 and 11 Richard II, about whom L'Estrange comments that 'it seems probable that most of the early trade names really indicated the occupations of their owners'.[78]

Alternatives to commercial producers also existed, in the form of clerical scribes and limners. These are of several types. Unbeneficed clergy comprise one such, as a possible source-pool for at least some of portions of Despenser's books. During his episcopacy Norwich resembled London in regard to such clergy, albeit on a smaller scale. As Norman Tanner has pointed out:

> two tax assessments from the reign of Richard II show that the city of Norwich contained a substantial number of unbeneficed secular priests by the end of the [fourteenth] century. Thus under the deanery of Norwich, whose boundaries coincided almost exactly with those of the city, forty-five unbeneficed chaplains were listed in one assessment and fifty-two or fifty-three in the other.[79]

Such men found work where they could. For many, of course, that meant the chantries, of which Norwich had an abundance. Nevertheless, few

---

1426–7 (will at Norfolk Record Office, NCR 1/18 r.11), who can be added to L'Estrange's list; and Thomas Oxley (Ocle), citizen of Norwich, 1424 (Norwich County Council, Will Register Hirning, 138), who may be the Thomas de Ocle, peyntour, recorded in 10 & 11 Richard II.

78 L'Estrange, *Calendar*, x. His guess may be correct, yet trade-originated surnames require careful handling. In some cases, such as 'John Skrevener, text writer 16, 17, 18 Henry VI', the name corresponds; but in others, such as Henry Lomynour and William Lomynour, who appear in *Norfolk Official Lists, from the Earliest Period to the Present Day*, ed. Hamon Le Strange (Norwich, 1890), 99, as bailiffs in 1379 and 1381, respectively, were not in fact limners, but cloth merchants. See, for example, on Henry, *The History of Parliament III, The House of Commons 1386–1421*, ed. J. S. Roskell et al. (Stroud, 1992), 605–6. Apparently, this confused M. A. Michael as well: see 'English Illuminators', 90.

79 Norman P. Tanner, *The Church in Late Medieval Norwich, 1370–1532* (Toronto, 1984), 22.

chantry endowments were lucrative, and many weren't funded for the long term, leaving clergy to find other sources of income. To quote Alison McHardy:

> Not all the qualities and skills these men provided were necessarily connected with ministry; their duties might be primarily legal, secretarial, administrative, or advisory, and their ranks included a small number of doctors, astrologers, and entertainers.[80]

These are the 'clerical proletariat' described by Kathryn Kerby-Fulton; and although we have no way of knowing exactly who these men were, undoubtedly to McHardy's list of substitute employments in Norwich could be added scribes and limners.[81] Indeed, the so-called 'Holkham Psalter Artist', discussed above, seems to have been one of that type.

Norwich Cathedral priory could be considered a second possible locus – perhaps a better descriptor than 'source', in this case. Bishop Henry's relations with the priory were complex, to say the least, over more than one issue, beginning in 1386 and continuing past his death in 1406.[82] So considered, the probability that Despenser would obtain manuscripts copied there would seem slight. Yet much evidence exists that, despite the long-running litigation, the bishop and the priory were able to work in tandem, even cordially: obtaining freedom for a serf in 1382, providing water for a Lynn friary, settling a dispute (in the priory's favour) with the Norwich citizenry in 1390. In 1395 Despenser gifted the prior, Alexander Tottington, with one of the episcopal manors valued at £10 annually, apparently uncoerced.[83] Perhaps more telling

---

80 Alison K. McHardy, 'Careers and Disappointments in the Late Medieval Church', *Studies in Church History* 26 (1989), 111–30 (118).
81 See Kathryn Kerby-Fulton, 'The Clerical Proletariat: The Underemployed Scribe and Vocational Crisis', *Journal of the Early Book Society* 17 (2015), 1–34, and more recently Kerby-Fulton, *The Clerical Proletariat and the Resurgence of English Poetry* (Philadelphia PA, 2021).
82 The disputes concerned a host of issues, including disposal of property, discipline of monks, visitation, allotment of certain tithes, and dues from dependent churches. Litigation variously extended to the Crown, three archbishops of Canterbury and two popes, before finally being resolved in 1411. See Tanner, *Church in Late Medieval Norwich*, 158–62; Allington-Smith, *Henry Despenser*, 61–2; and esp. E. H. Carter, *Studies in Norwich Cathedral History* (Norwich, 1935), 37–57.
83 And apparently at some cost to himself: Despenser's failure to obtain the necessary royal permission to reallocate title prompted an official enquiry: see

as signs of episcopal-monastic relations are the generous epitaph the monks accorded him at his tomb before the cathedral altar, recorded by Capgrave, and the inclusion of prayers for Despenser in the mass established for himself by Tottington, once Despenser's fiercest opponent during the litigation, but subsequently his successor.[84] Thus, despite initial appearances, Despenser might seemingly have sought willing scribes and artists in his local monastic community.

Whom he would have found working there, however, is another uncertain matter. Obedientiary rolls show sums advanced to priory monks to purchase books – though they do not indicate to whom the payments were made, whether from workers in the city or from monks in-house.[85] A. I. Doyle has suggested both, observing that:

> There was a widespread practice of individual religious using monetary allowances and gifts for book purchases [...] Not infrequently they employed their funds and friends to provide items direct for the communal collections, sometimes perhaps by meeting the material costs of work actually executed by themselves or their brethren.

He goes on to demonstrate the 'ample evidence that religious houses and their members employed named and unnamed scribes in the fourteenth and fifteenth centuries to write documents and books, both over a period and occasionally'.[86] Examples accumulate of books produced in consort by a variety of hands, commercial and clerical, of different orders, some of whose members were itinerant.[87] Dennison has taken this further, arguing in multiple studies for a pattern of probably lay illuminators who were peripatetic and who worked mostly for monastic patrons.

Calendar of Inquisitions Miscellaneous, Volume VI, 1392–1399 (London, 1963), 41, no. 86.
84 For Capgrave, see *Liber de Illustribus Henricis*, ed. F. C. Hingeston. RS 7 (London, 1858), 174; for Tottington, see Tanner, *Church in Late Medieval Norwich*, 214.
85 To 1317, many of these are non-monastic; subsequent affairs are less clear. See Ker, 'Manuscripts from Norwich Cathedral Priory', 8–9.
86 A. I. Doyle, 'Book Production by the Monastic Orders in England, 1375–1530: Assessing the Evidence', in *Medieval Book Production: Assessing the Evidence*, ed. Linda L. Brownrigg (Los Altos Hills CA, 1990), 1–19 (1–2).
87 One contemporary example is the Sherborne Missal written by the monk John Whas, presumably a member of that Benedictine community, and illuminated by the Dominican John Siferwas. See BL MS Additional 74236, for example, 216, 276 (paginated), where both are pictured in their respective habits.

Norwich Cathedral Priory is often central to Dennison's hypotheses regarding a 'Benedictine monastic circuit' – whether the object of consideration is the decoration of the Vernon manuscript or the later career of the Holkham Psalter Artist.[88] One final example of a book related to this context is that of the Helmingham Breviary discussed by Janet Backhouse, who concluded that it was 'most probably produced in a professional commercial workshop, very likely in Norwich'.[89] Equally viable candidates for those involved in the manufacture of this and other Norwich-provenance books, including Despenser's, certainly include the city's clerical population.

Conclusion

To sum up, then: it is our considered view that the three manuscripts known to have belonged to Henry Despenser, Bishop of Norwich – BL MSS Additional 34114, Arundel 74 and Cotton Claudius E.viii – were commissioned and produced in Norwich between 1380 and 1400, a period that can perhaps be narrowed further to 1385–95, when the bishop was in residence almost exclusively. Conditions in an economically resurgent Norwich were at that time amply supportive of a scribal workshop (or perhaps shops), part of a flourishing community of associated trades: painters of wood, stone and glass, parchmeners, scriveners and sculptors. Nor is it doubtful any longer that Despenser, historically a controversial figure in many respects, possessed the character of a collector of fine books. Clearly he did, and his interest was known to others, at least one of whom sought preferment at his hand with a gift of books.

Details of provenance alone, however, are insufficient to locate origin. While the precise circumstances of production of Despenser's manuscripts continue to remain elusive, much is evident about the hands that rendered them. Stylistic analysis shows that Despenser's

---

88   See Dennison, 'Vernon Manuscript', 203; Dennison, 'Monastic or Secular?', 251–61. For the involvement of monastic orders in book production in fourteenth-century Oxford, including consideration of both the Holkham Psalter Artist's stylistic influence and the patron's (in this case Adam Easton's) connections with Norwich Cathedral Priory, see Dennison, 'Adam Easton's copy', 68–73, 90–3.

89   'The Helmingham Breviary: the Reinstatement of a Norwich Masterpiece', *National Art Collections Fund Review* (1993), 23–5 (25). With thanks to one of the reviewers for bringing this to our attention.

three surviving books involved six artists, one of whom – clearly the most accomplished – we have identified elsewhere for the first time and designated the 'Despenser Master'. He stands out as the lead contributor to two of the bishop's three manuscripts, Additional 34114 and Cotton Claudius E.viii. A second artist, close to the Master in skill but notably drawing on his effects and working, very probably, in close proximity, we have designated the 'Despenser Assistant'. He produced Arundel 74. Significantly, their work can be associated with a larger grouping of important contemporary illuminated manuscripts of established Norfolk provenance that extends beyond the important Hatton Missal and Holkham Psalter. While the 'Holkham Psalter Artist' was probably a peripatetic lay professional on a 'monastic circuit', the joint presence of work by the main Despenser artist and the Hatton Missal Artist in the Trinity Hours suggests that their comparable styles were formed in a shared urban location. That location, where Despenser's three known books were commissioned and produced, can safely be claimed as Norwich. The exact circumstances of these commissions, whether they were manufactured within a secular or monastic environment (or both), remains to be established.

6

Accumulating Easts: Ancient Geographies and Genealogies in John Gower's *Confessio Amantis*[1]

AMANDA J. GERBER

As John Tolan's *Saracens* demonstrates, medieval Latin Christendom expressed varied and ultimately ambivalent attitudes towards the world of Islam.[2] In historical terms, medieval Christians struggled to rationalise the expansion of Muslim control into Asia, Africa and Europe, while maintaining their belief that God's will determined victories.[3] Despite this experience, late medieval Latin Christendom's representations of Islam tended to develop independently from personal encounters.[4]

---

1   I would like to thank James Madison University for providing the financial support and collegial environment that allowed me to write this essay. My thanks also extend to Eve Salisbury and Georgiana Donavin of the Gower Project for inviting me to present the first draft of this paper at the V International Congress of the John Gower Society, 2023, whose attendees offered feedback that helped me refine my approach. I am also indebted to Chris Chism, Candace Barrington, Sylvia Tomasch and Amy Goodwin, whose comments, questions and camaraderie have been invaluable throughout this article's many guises. Furthermore, I am grateful for the thorough and insightful suggestions provided by Laura Ashe and the anonymous readers for *New Medieval Literatures*. Although this essay attests to the generous contributions of numerous scholars, its errors are all my own.
2   John V. Tolan, *Saracens: Islam in the Medieval European Imagination* (New York, 2002), xiii.
3   Ibid., xiv–xv.
4   Tolan claims that Latin Christendom's representations of Islam and Arab peoples became solidified by the thirteenth century, with a range of foundational images and texts created between the seventh and thirteenth centuries, and that representations remained unchanged as Islam continued to expand into Europe with the Ottomans during the fourteenth century: ibid., xix.

These latter, fictional representations produced stereotypes that Suzanne Conklin Akbari relates to Edward Said's *Orientalism*, an interpretive framework that explains how human agency circumscribes the East and its occupants in order to define the West.[5] However, Akbari also notes that some rather significant disparities emerge in a comparison of medieval with modern Orientalism: despite all its differences, the Middle Ages' East existed as a point of origin for the whole world (in the Garden of Eden) and as a physical and temporal end (during the Apocalypse).[6] When reevaluating *Orientalism* himself in 2001, Said noted that Islam cannot readily be located as an external other; it emerged within the geographical borders formed by classical antiquity.[7]

Eastern locations appear throughout John Gower's fourteenth-century *Confessio Amantis*. To begin with, the poem's depicted religions and valued intellectual traditions take root in the East, and yet the *Confessio* largely vacates this foundational land of its medieval occupants. In place of Muslims, Gower's poem primarily represents ancient peoples. Chaucer's 'Prioress's Tale' makes a similar temporal swap of eastern inhabitants, which prompts Sheila Delany to note the tale's 'conspicuous' absence of Islam.[8] The same conspicuous absence haunts most of the lengthy *Confessio*, but Gower's extensive replacements have not yet garnered the same attention. Even Akbari's magisterial study of eastern representations consigns the *Confessio* to the footnotes, except when discussing how the poem provides conventional maps of the earth, a standardised mapping tradition that I have elaborated on elsewhere.[9] As

---

5   Suzanne Conklin Akbari, *Idols in the East: European Representations of Islam and the Orient, 1100–1450* (Ithaca NY, 2009), 1–2; Edward Said, *Orientalism* (New York, 1979).
6   Akbari, *Idols in the East*, 3.
7   Edward W. Said, 'The Clash of Ignorance', *The Nation* 273.12 (22 October 2001), 11–13 (13): 'the West drew on the humanism, science, philosophy, sociology and historiography of Islam, which had already interposed itself between Charlemagne's world and classical antiquity. Islam is inside from the start, as even Dante, great enemy of Mohammed, had to concede when he placed the Prophet at the very heart of his *Inferno*.' See also the discussion of Sharon Kinoshita, 'Deprovincializing the Middle Ages', in *The Worlding Project: Doing Cultural Studies in the Era of Globalization*, ed. Rob Wilson and Christopher Leigh Connery (Berkeley CA, 2007), 61–76.
8   Sheila Delany, 'Chaucer's Prioress, the Jews, and the Muslims', *Medieval Encounters* 5.2 (1999), 198–213 (205).
9   Amanda Gerber, 'Earthly Gower: Transforming Geographical Texts and Images in the *Confessio Amantis* and *Vox Clamantis* Manuscripts', in *Gower in*

Akbari's footnoting suggests, the *Confessio*'s representations of Muslim peoples barely merit mention because they barely appear.[10] The poem's patterns of omission and replacement seem especially notable, given how many of its tales occur in the East and how frequently and variously the poem defines eastern terrain.

In place of Islam, the *Confessio* relies on alternative means of defining the East. This essay follows suit by retracing Gower's sundry geographical, astronomical and genealogical representations of the region, each of which offers a different outline. I propose that the poem makes few efforts to coordinate the East's divergent boundaries. Gower instead voraciously consumes many disparate intellectual histories about the region's various ancient incarnations, retaining the pluralist perspectives from which his information came. The *Confessio*'s variable accumulations of Easts often obfuscate his primary sources for them. As Gowerians have established, the *Confessio*'s Greco-Roman lore tends to derive from Ovidian commentaries, its biblical information from Peter Riga's *Aurora* or *Biblia versificata*, and its encyclopaedic sciences from Brunetto Latini's *Li Livres dou Trésor*. Nevertheless, the poem's depictions of the East often deviate from these three primary sources, sometimes obscuring their true point of origin. In place of seeking to identify particular sources, this essay often reverts to general information known to circulate in Latin Christendom, including the medieval manuscripts that disseminated Lucan's *Pharsalia*, sciences attributed to Islamic scholar Abu' Ma'shar, and biblical information outlined in the genealogies of Peter of Poitiers. Rather than offering previously unattributed sources for Gower, the following pages illustrate a range of disparate premodern textual conversations about the East. However Gower may have accessed them, he duplicates these conversations with a similar variety of eastern depictions.

To systematise Gower's variegated compilations, this essay first outlines the *Confessio*'s disparate maps of the East, maps regularly reorganised by historical conquests, sexual encounters and the scholars who record them. The second half of the essay focuses especially on the sexual encounters recorded in genealogies for both Abrahamic and Greco-Roman lineages, which originate from and proliferate in the East. With various maps and perspectives, the *Confessio* repeatedly makes and

---

Manuscripts and Early Printed Books, ed. Martha Driver, Derek Pearsall and Robert F. Yeager (Cambridge, 2020), 89–112.
10   Akbari, *Idols in the East*, 45–8.

breaks eastern borders, using metaphors of sex and conquest that have the capacity to permeate otherwise impermeable boundaries of history. I argue that the *Confessio* compiles disparate worldviews beyond the strict hierarchies imposed by his Orientalising contemporaries, and even superseding his own earlier views of Islam. Admittedly, the *Confessio*'s numerous eastern depictions could result from the many years that Gower spent writing the compendious text. However, Gower repeatedly omits Muslim inhabitants from these numerous eastern depictions, and such prolonged consistency may be taken as a hallmark of intention. Instead of assuming that the *Confessio*'s omissions result from sloppy disregard, this essay explores how a synoptic representation of the East did not serve a poem that compiled worlds alongside its lore and then re-divided its stories based on sins, which supposedly transcended religious and geographical borders. Overall, the poem's readings of the East prove fragmentary, contradictory and manifold, often refusing to follow one inherited sense of the East to its logical ends. The ultimate ideal might have been a unified global empire, such as the poem's accounts of ancient empires that supposedly spread across the world, yet the reality of these worlds proves just as fractious as the human sins that divide the *Confessio*'s books.

Where is Gower's East?

I am not the first to note that a late medieval writer could both acquire and complicate Orientalist attitudes. Simon Gaunt and Kim Phillips make similar claims about late medieval European travel writers, whose diverse attitudes reflected the disparate peoples that they encountered in both the Near and Far East.[11] Medieval representations of the East can accommodate an Orientalist framework because Said himself refers to the concept as a collection of interdependent definitions, not a singular, essential concept. For Said, anyone who studies, teaches or writes about the Orient from outside the Orient is an Orientalist.[12] Nevertheless,

---

11   Both add the far East to the conversation; Gaunt observes that Marco Polo's attention to the East includes far more than xenophobic stereotypes: Simon Gaunt, *'Le Devisement du Monde': Narrative Voice, Language and Diversity* (Cambridge, 2013), 153–77; and Kim Phillips, *Before Orientalism: Asian Peoples and Cultures in European Travel Writing, 1245 –1510* (Philadelphia PA, 2013), 4–5.
12   Said, *Orientalism*, 2–3.

there are certain narrowing features, especially the understanding of human agency and power dynamics that Europe systematically employed to discipline and manage the East.[13] Said's capacious definition of Orientalism as a system of representation has made it a particularly fruitful avenue for medievalists, and yet as Kinoshita notes, the historical complexity of the Middle Ages complicates its monolithic and monologic 'Othering' of the East.[14] In fact, as I aim to demonstrate, the *Confessio*'s representations of the East focused more on interconnected lands than exoticised inhabitants, and even the land acquired several different borders because of Gower's several different sources. Intellectual history from Latin Christendom offered writers like Gower a wealth of eastern portrayals. The poem's encyclopaedic Book VII alone provides three distinct maps of an East, the first of which appears to introduce a region that sometimes encompasses multiple disparate territories and sometimes exists as a province of an overarching ancient inheritance.

The *Confessio*'s Prologue introduces the East as part of a unified antiquity, but also as antiquity's most prominent fissure. To introduce this complex historical terrain, Gower narrates Nebuchadnezzar's dream of a statue with a head of gold, breast of silver, arms of brass, legs of steel and feet partially of earth.[15] When interpreting the dream, Daniel associates the different materials with the Ages of Man, a Greco-Roman model of history that begins with the Golden Age followed by eras of successively degraded qualities: in the *Confessio*, silver, brass and steel.[16] Ancient Roman texts like Ovid's *Metamorphoses* represent such degrading materials as reflections of humanity's push towards societal decay.[17] Gower's knowledge of Ovid cannot be doubted,[18] yet his own

13 Idem.
14 Kinoshita, 'Deprovincializing the Middle Ages', 66. Similarly, Celia M. Lewis suggests that binary religious identities often fractured as personal experiences prompted some to challenge the hegemony encouraged by polemical and popular texts: 'History, Mission, and Crusade in the *Canterbury Tales*', *Chaucer Review* 42 (2008), 353–82 (354).
15 John Gower, *Confessio Amantis*, ed. Russell A. Peck, 3 vols (Kalamazoo MI, 2004–6), 1: Prologue 604–24.
16 The first seminal account appears in Hesiod, *Works and Days*, in *Homeric Hymns and Homerica*, trans. Hugh Evelyn-White (London, 1914), 109–201.
17 Publius Ovidius Naso, *Metamorphoses*, ed. Richard J. Tarrant (Oxford, 2004), Book I.
18 See, for example, Andrew Galloway, 'Gower's Ovids', in *The Oxford History*

version demonstrates more ambivalence about what the decreasingly valuable materials represent. By his account, the Age of Steel concludes the ages of humanity and encompasses tyranny, bloodshed, greed, and the 'fals' Emperor Leo.[19] Nevertheless, Gower also acknowledges that steel, the hardest metal, represents the mightiest Roman empire and introduces defenders of the Christian faith, such as Emperor Constantine and Charlemagne.[20]

Gower's complex evaluations respond to ancient histories' changeable borders and faiths. Gowerians have already observed the latter, noting how the *Confessio* evaluates historical religions chronologically. R. F. Yeager points out that Gower adopts a recognisable Greco-Roman model of history to depict non-Christian religions chronologically: Chaldeans, Egyptians, Greeks and Jews.[21] Yeager refers to this model as the Chain of Being, also called *Scala naturae*, which derives from Plato's idea that nature ascends like a ladder from inanimate objects like rocks to plants up to humans. Medieval adaptations added the supernatural world to accommodate angels and finally God. Unlike the traditional Ages of Man, Gower's Chain of Being observes religious development in reverse order, with the earlier chronological religions being further removed from God. For Gower, some of the Chain of Being criteria prove independent of chronology, such as Egyptian idolatry, which, as Ethan Knapp points out, attracts the *Confessio*'s most virulent attacks even though Egypt founds many western principles.[22] Attacks against Egyptian beliefs indicate a fundamental conflict in any

---

of *Classical Reception in English Literature*, Vol. 1: *800–1558*, ed. Rita Copeland (Oxford, 2016), 435–64.
19 Gower, *Confessio Amantis*, Prologue, line 739.
20 Ibid., Prologue, lines 733–55.
21 The order Gower uses for these religions differs from his primary sources, especially the *Vita Barlaam*, which notes Chaldeans, Greeks and then Egyptians. G. C. Macaulay was the first to note Gower's use of *Vita Barlaam* while also acknowledging Gower's own additions. See R. F. Yeager, 'Gower's Religions', in *The Routledge Research Companion to John Gower* (New York, 2016), 62, n. 41; G. C. Macaulay, *The Complete Works of John Gower* (Oxford, 1901), III:515, note to line 729; Masayoshi Itô, 'Gower's Use of *Vita Barlaam et Josaphat* in *Confessio Amantis*', *Studies in English Literature* (Japan) 56 (1979), 3–18; and *Barlaam and Iosaphat: A Middle English Life of Buddha*, ed. John C. Hirsch (London, 1986), 120.
22 Ethan Knapp, 'The Place of Egypt in Gower's *Confessio Amantis*', in *John Gower, Trilingual Poet: Language, Translation, and Tradition*, ed. Elisabeth Dutton, with John Hines and R. F. Yeager (Cambridge, 2010), 26–34.

simple chronology for Gower's ancient histories. Idolatrous ancient religions and occasional tyrants interfere with all attempts to depict a linear historical progression or decline.

The *Confessio*'s version of ancient histories instead embraces variability, with Julius Caesar's ancient Rome offering a brief reprieve from otherwise divisive historical tendencies. Daniel's interpretation of Nebuchadnezzar's dream explains this exemplary moment of Roman cohesion in the Prologue:

> The noble Cesar Julius,
> Which tho was king of Rome lond,
> With gret bataille and with strong hond
> Al Grece, Perse, and ek Caldee
> Wan and put under, so that he
> Noght al only of th'orient
> Bot al the marche of th'occident,
> Governeth under his empire,
> As he that was hol lord and sire,
> And hield thurgh his chivalrie
> Of al this world the monarchie,
> And was the ferste of that honour
> Which tok the name of Emperour. (Prologue, lines 714–26)

Julius Caesar's Rome acknowledged divisions, but ones that he removed by conquering beyond them. His conquests of Greece, Persia and Chaldea connect territories that each had their own significant ancient empire. The *Confessio* also mentions the peoples attached to these territories at several points, including the Chaldeans who begin Gower's Chain of Being and the Persians who initiate earthly divisiveness with the reign of Cyrus.[23] In fact, Daniel explains to Nebuchadnezzar that the city of Babylon subjected all the world until King Cyrus and his son Cambises conquered Babylon, killing King Balthazar to initiate the Silver Age. The Silver Age then ends with Persia's Darius, whom Alexander overthrew with the Greeks to inaugurate the Age of Brass.[24]

Governing these three ancient empires together grants Julius Caesar dominion over East and West, creating one empire out of 'al this world'. The entire known Earth becomes a singular empire, whose control renders Julius Caesar a 'hol lord', connoting his undisputed, undivided

23 Gower, *Confessio Amantis*, Prologue, lines 601–700.
24 Ibid., Prologue, lines 663–99.

control. In this regard, East and West combined represent a 'hol' empire, an undivided Earth once ruled in Rome's name. This unified era did not belong to the Golden Age in Gower's account of the Ages of Man, nor the Christian Age in Gower's Chain of Being. The complete, undivided earthly empire instead existed as an ancient Rome that connected East to West. However, no sooner does Gower acknowledge this ancient unity than he dismantles it, alluding to it only as part of a dream about history's changeable nature. According to Gower's Prologue, earthly divisions took root in Paradise and again with Noah's Flood and the Tower of Babel – all three resulting from human sin.[25] Ancient empires provided rare moments of cohesion in human history, leaving Gower's pagan narrator Genius to grapple with the resulting world maps.

The poem's most explicit maps of the Earth appear in Book VII, perhaps not coincidentally from the perspective of Aristotle, a supposed educator of Alexander the Great – one of the poem's two imagined rulers of an undivided Earth. Book VII's first map includes the simplest, most frequently repeated premodern depiction of the Earth. The curriculum begins with a tripartite *mappamundi*, or map of the world, comprised of three continents: Asia, Africa and Europe. When addressing this tripartite world design, Gower describes Asia's borders in the following terms:

> Wher as the flod which men Nil calleth
> Departeth fro his cours and falleth
> Into the See Alexandrine,
> Ther takth Asie ferst seisine
> Toward the West, and over this
> Of Canahim wher the flod is
> Into the Grete See rennende;
> Fro that into the worldes ende
> Estward, Asie it is algates,
> Til that men come unto the gates
> Of Paradis, and there ho.
> And shortly for to speke it so,
> Of Orient in general
> Withinne his bounde Asie hath al. (VII. 561–74)

Tripartite world maps, such as the one Gower describes here, tend to use bodies of water for borders. This passage mentions the Great Sea

---

25 Ibid., Prologue, lines 1002–28.

(meaning the Mediterranean) into which the 'Canahim' (meaning the Tanais (now the Don River)) runs. The quotation also mentions the Nile, which leads to the 'See Alexandrine' – most likely the Red Sea. The outline primarily corresponds with Gower's primary source for Book VII, Latini's *Trésor*. Gower duplicates Latini's watery boundaries, including those of the Nile and the Great Sea, as well as the earthly Paradise course for the Tanais. He also repeats Latini's 'mer en Alixandre', by which Latini means that the Nile leads to the sea in Alexandria, rather than what Gower names the sea.[26] Gower's conflation relates to his general omission of cities within the three continents. He focuses only on the watery outline here, removing many of Latini's subsequent city details, like Babylon and Cairo in Egypt, details that help distinguish Asia from Africa.[27]

Gower's reduced Asian geography correlates with the commonly reproduced T-O, or *orbis terrarum*, maps that appear in a wide range of medieval manuscripts. As I have noted elsewhere, illustrated Gower manuscripts feature similar tripartite orbs.[28] T-O maps permeated medieval manuscripts, including copies of Ovid's *Metamorphoses* (a significant source for Gower's Greco-Roman tales)[29] and copies of another ancient author who featured commonly in medieval curricula, Lucan.[30] T-O maps depict the three known continents trisected by the Nile, Mediterranean Sea and Tanais, just as Gower mentions. Like Gower's description, T-O maps typically label the Nile beneath Asia on the bottom right side to separate the continent from Libya, or Africa. The Tanais, also like Gower's account, separates Asia's bottom left side from Europe. Gower's Nile, however, does not run straight; it veers

26 For more about Gower's use of Latini, see especially Seb Falk, 'Natural Sciences', in *Historians on John Gower*, ed. Siân Echard and Stephen H. Rigby (Cambridge, 2019), 495, n. 15; George L. Hamilton, 'Some Sources of the Seventh Book of Gower's "Confessio Amantis"', *Modern Philology* 9 (1912), 323–46.
27 Brunetto Latini, *Li livres dou tresor: edition d'après les manuscrits*, ed. Polycarpe Chabaille (Paris, 1863), I.123.1.
28 Gerber, 'Earthly Gower', 89–112.
29 For more about Gower's well-attested use of the *Metamorphoses*, see especially Galloway, 'Gower's Ovids', 435–64; Amanda Gerber, *Medieval Ovid: Frame Narrative and Political Allegory* (New York, 2015).
30 For more about curricular authors, see esp. Vincent Gillespie, 'The Study of Classical Authors: From the Twelfth Century to *c*.1450', in *The Cambridge History of Literary Criticism, vol. 2: The Middle Ages*, ed. Alastair Minnis and Ian Johnson (Cambridge, 2005), 145–235.

into the 'Alexandrine' Sea, which directs Asia's property westward. The Tanais in T-O maps also leads to the Great, or Mediterranean, Sea. T-O maps, including Gower's description, lack realism. These maps depict the Don River, which flows through modern-day Russia, connecting to the Mediterranean Sea. The near-mythic proportions of the waterways lead Gower to mention the Mediterranean Sea's trajectory as leading to the 'worldes ende', a phrase that could have both geographical and temporal significance, referring to the end of Asia's geographical space as well as the end of time. In such T-O maps, the East extends to the end of the geographical and historical Earth: it encompasses the beginning of human time with Creation and Paradise, and the last conquered territories of global emperors, exemplified by Gower's Aristotle's Alexander the Great.

Greco-Roman T-O maps reappear as Abrahamic ones with the same watery boundaries. Gower's Aristotle addresses this overlap when describing each continent's connection to one of biblical Noah's three sons. As in many medieval encyclopaedias, the *Confessio*'s account claims that Noah's three sons each founded his own continent, beginning with the East:

> Asie, which lay to the sonne
> Upon the marche of Orient,
> Was graunted be comun assent
> To Sem, which was the sone eldeste;
> For that partie was the beste
> And double as moche as othre tuo,
> And was that time bounded so (VII. 554–60)

Noah's eldest son, Shem, receives Asia, half of the whole post-fluvial Earth. As the largest inheritance, Shem's Asia receives more lines of description within the *Confessio* than the other two continents. Gower describes the continents in terms reminiscent of T-O maps, allotting the longest description to Asia. Book VII devotes twenty-one lines to the continent,[31] while Africa and Europe combined receive eight lines.[32] This uneven attention matches the regions described. In particular, the Nile boundary expands Asia to incorporate large portions of Egypt and, by extension, most geographical settings for Abrahamic histories. Some T-O maps also add Egypt to Asia. Following biblical and Greco-Roman

---

31 Gower, *Confessio Amantis*, VII.554–74.
32 Ibid., VII.575–82.

precedents, the East surrounded the Levant, which Said also considers part of the Orient as a result of biblical and scholastic traditions.[33] The passage then associates the vastness of the terrain with the vast Greco-Roman and Abrahamic histories that occurred within them: Asia occupies one half of the tripartite Earth, and it houses most of the events that Gower recognises as ancient.[34] The comparative age of the region's origins especially resonates when identifying the East as the gateway to Paradise, the location of Earth's first inhabitants.[35]

Saturn's Disoriented 'Orient'

T-O maps circulated extensively and authoritatively, providing a widely accepted model for how the ancient Greco-Roman and Abrahamic worlds overlapped. Akbari both explains that the tripartite medieval map challenges Orientalism's simple geographical binary, and identifies that the *Confessio* also divides East from West in a tradition established by Augustine, Isidore, Hrabanus Maurus, Vincent of Beauvais and Bartholomaeus Anglicus.[36] The East/West model actually belongs to a four-quadrant design that Gower attributes to Abu' Ma'shar, and it is not the only additional map of the East that the *Confessio* supplies. Within the same Book VII that describes Shem's Asia, astronomy offers additional, competing outlines of the East that use both planets and zodiacal signs to divide the Earth. The former divides the Earth into seven parts based on the seven supposed planets, three of which influence separate portions of a T-O map's Asia: Mars exerts control over the Holy Land, Jupiter over Egypt, and Saturn over a generalised 'Orient'.[37] The Holy Land, Egypt and generalised East all belong to Asia

33 Said, *Orientalism*, 4.
34 According to Gower's account of Nebuchadnezzar's dream, the five ages of man were Babylonian, Persian, Greek, Roman and post-Carolingian (Prologue, lines 738–880). More than the first half of this history focused on the East. Charles L. Regan, 'John Gower and the Fall of Babylon: *Confessio Amantis*, Prol. ll.670–86', *English Language Notes* 7.2 (1969), 85–92 (92).
35 Bruce S. Eastwood explains that medieval European maps accordingly orientated maps with East (or Subsolanus) at the top: *Ordering the Heavens: Roman Astronomy and Cosmology in the Carolingian Renaissance* (Leiden, 2007), 163. See also Alessandro Scafi, *Maps of Paradise* (Chicago IL, 2013).
36 Akbari, *Idols in the East*, 3, 46–7.
37 Gower, *Confessio Amantis*, VII.721–954.

in the T-O design, but this part of Book VII's planetary geography delves deeper into some portions of the region.

The generalised East especially merits mention because of how many disparate depictions of the region circulated in late medieval England, including planetary depictions. According to the *Confessio*'s Book VII, Saturn produces a cold, cruel complexion for the East:

> The heyeste and aboven alle
> Stant that planete which men calle
> Saturnus, whos complexion
> Is cold, and his condicion
> Causeth malice and crualté
> To him the whos nativité
> Is set under his governance.
> For alle hise werkes ben grevance
> And enemy to mannes hele,
> In what degré that he schal dele.
> His climat is in Orient,
> Wher that he is most violent. (VII.935–46)

Saturn, the melancholic planet, governs the unspecified East. People born under this last, highest planet are prone to malice and cruelty. The planet itself proves inimical to people's health, as a mythological and planetary opponent to Jupiter. As Raymond Klibansky, Erwin Panofsky and Fritz Saxl have pointed out, this characterisation of Saturn derived from a convoluted ancient history merging lore about ancient Rome's agricultural god Saturn with ancient Greece's Kronos (the castrated son of Uranus overthrown by Zeus) and Chronos (the god of time). The original Roman Saturn only existed as a mythological god, not a planet.[38] References to the planet's age derived from its thirty-year revolution, longer than any other planet's.[39] These astronomical and mythological (henceforth astro-mythic) traits circulated in Gower's medieval world

---

38 The resulting characteristics of these combined figures varied, even in terms of climate, which could be moist or dry; nevertheless, Saturn's cold, dry characteristics gained traction with Epigenes of Byzantium, a protégé of the Chaldeans who claimed that the planet's great distance from the Sun and the god's advanced age resulted in its coldness. See Raymond Klibansky, Erwin Panofsky and Fritz Saxl, *Saturn and Melancholy: Studies in the History of Natural Philosophy, Religion, and Art*, new edn (Montreal, 2019), 133.

39 Regarding Saturn's revolution, see, for example, Johannes Sacrobosco, *The Sphere*, trans. Lynn Thorndike (Chicago IL, 1949), 120.

through the likes of Cicero's *De natura deorum*.[40] Although Gower likely only received his Ciceronian information second hand, his *Confessio* mentions the same astro-mythic opposition between Jupiter and Saturn, a planetary relationship based on the mythological significance of Chronos, whom Zeus/Jupiter overthrew. Thus, Gower's Saturn inspires malice, cruelty and, as the most violent of planets, strife.

Saturn's humoral traits as the old, cold, melancholic and malevolent planet gained consistency in the Middle Ages,[41] whereas his location and planetary impact retained more of his convoluted astro-mythic history. Gower's primary source for Book VII, Latini's *Trésor*, also refers to Saturn's cold influence,[42] yet Gower connects this influence to eastern locales. In fact, Latini never mentions the regions over which Saturn exerts its influence, only the planet's general influence and path through the zodiacal signs.[43] Saturn's geographical influence instead derives from other widespread ideas, with a history dating back to ancient Greece. In Ptolemy's *Tetrabiblos*, Saturn and Venus govern the southeast quadrant of the known world.[44] Some late medieval sources distinguish a separate portion of a Saturn-influenced East. For example, thirteenth-century Roger Bacon claims that Saturn controls India, whereas Jupiter exerts control over Babylon.[45] The *Confessio* acknowledges the general areas mentioned by the likes of Ptolemy and Bacon, but the poem leaves this third region of Asia as an unspecified cardinal direction.

The direction instead of a place name here leaves space for ambiguity. The *Confessio* elsewhere demonstrates Gower's awareness of India, mentioning it four times, including 'Ynde the superior' as the last

---

40 Klibansky, Panofsky and Saxl, *Saturn and Melancholy*, 132, 137; and Lucius Annaeus Seneca, *Naturales quaestiones*, Vol. 2, trans. Thomas H. Corcoran (Cambridge MA, 1972), VII.4, 2; and Marcus Tullius Cicero, *De natura deorum*, trans. H. Rackham (Cambridge MA, 1933), II.119.
41 See Olaf Pedersen, 'In Quest of Sacrobosco', *Journal for the History of Astronomy* 16 (1985), 175–221; Roger Beck, *A Brief History of Ancient Astrology* (Oxford, 2007), 77; and Sacrobosco, *The Sphere*, 209, 216, 213.
42 Latini, *Trésor*, I.3.111.
43 Ibid., I.109, I.111.
44 Ptolemy, *Tetrabiblos*, F. E. Robbins (Cambridge MA, 1940), II.3.64; and Beck, *A Brief History of Ancient Astrology*, 115.
45 Roger Bacon, *Opus Maius*, Vol. 1, ed. John Henry Bridges (Cambridge, 2010), IV.276 –78; and Akbari, *Idols in the East*, 275, n. 37. Bacon even extends this model to religion, claiming that Saturn exerts influence over Jewish people: *Opus Maius*, 287; see Akbari, *Idols in the East*, 275.

territory Alexander the Great conquered before turning back towards his home in Macedonia.[46] Gower even mentions this final destination of Alexander's conquest as the moment when 'al the world he overran',[47] suggesting that Alexander's final empire covered the entire inhabitable earth, not unlike Julius Caesar's dominion over East and West. India's place as the final conquered territory locates it at the edge of the Earth, which perhaps explains why Gower subsequently calls the region a desert when introducing the location of Hercules's two brass pillars.[48] However, ancient traditions tend to place Hercules' pillars at the western-most point of his travels. Ancient Greek Strabo, for instance, locates the pillars in Gades, now southern Spain.[49] Conversely, ancient Romans Pliny and Seneca identify the pillars as the remnants of Atlas's mountain, through which Hercules smashes to create the Strait of Gibraltar and the pillars in North Africa.[50] The ancient Greek and Roman traditions orient Hercules' pillars on two different sides of the Strait of Gibraltar, both sides at the opposite end of Alexander's empire from India. Any side of Alexander's empire could have a desert climate. However, Gower's planetary map mentions Saturn, which, according to the passage above and authorities like Abu' Ma'shar, has a cold complexion.[51]

Gower's disparities multiply in Book VII as he provides another map of the East still. His zodiacal division of the earth, unlike his seven-part planetary division and his three-part continental map, divides the Earth into quadrants:

> bot in his degré
> Albumazar yit over this
> Seith, so as th'erthe parted is
> In foure, riht so ben divised
> The signes tuelve and stonde assised,
> That ech of hem for his partie

46 Gower, *Confessio Amantis*, III.2445–51.
47 Ibid., III.2445.
48 Gower, *Confessio Amantis*, IV.2054–7; the poem's other two references to India appear at V.1001–100 and V.1901–200.
49 Strabo, *Geography*, Vol. 2, trans. Horace Leonard Jones (Cambridge MA, 1923), III.5.5.
50 Pliny, *Natural History*, Vol. II, trans. H. Rackham (Cambridge MA, 1942), III.4; and Seneca, *Hercules Oetaeus*, trans. Frank Justus Miller (Cambridge MA, 1917), line 1240.
51 Abu' Ma'shar, *The Great Introduction to the Science of the Judgments of the Stars*, trans. Benjamin N. Dykes (Minneapolis MN, 2020), 151–2.

Hath his climat to justefie.
Wherof the ferst regiment
Toward the part of Orient
From Antioche and that contré
Governed is of signes thre,
That is Cancer, Virgo, Leo (VII.1238-49)

In this passage, Gower acknowledges the earth's revisable boundaries, attributing this final version to illustrious Muslim scholar Abu' Ma'shar, called here by his Anglicised name, 'Albumazar'.[52] Gower claims that Abu' Ma'shar re-divided the earth into quadrants related to the twelve zodiacal signs. The redistribution results in four climates, as opposed to a zonal map's five or seven, and as opposed to a T-O map's three continents or a planetary map's seven parts.

In this so-called Abu' Ma'shar zodiacal map, three zodiacal signs influence each of the four regions. Gower states that Cancer, Virgo and Leo influence the East, and Abu' Ma'shar does indeed refer to Cancer, Leo, Virgo as a quadrant with its own climate – the driest and hottest of the four.[53] Abu' Ma'shar also classifies the twelve zodiacal signs according to the four cardinal directions; however, his eastern quadrant houses Aries, Leo and Sagittarius, meaning that Gower only correctly credits Abu' Ma'shar as a source for Leo in the East.[54] These three zodiacal signs instead derive from Gower's primary source for Book VII, Latini's *Trésor*. Within a *mappamundi* entry, Latini mentions the zodiacal signs, but he does not attribute them to Abu' Ma'shar.[55] The map quadrants instead likely originate from Chalcidius's commentary on Plato, which does in fact group Gower's named signs together in the bottom left quadrant of a seasonal map.[56]

The *Confessio*'s use of multiple designations for the East mirrors what Kathy Lavezzo's *Imagining a Medieval English Nation* uncovers

---

52   Gower then concludes the astronomy/astrology section by citing his source as Abu'Ma'sar's *Introductorium in astroniam* (granted, George Hamilton cites the source as the *Secretum secretorum* section that cites Abu'Ma'sar). Hamilton, 'Some Sources for Book 7', 342.
53   Abu' Ma'shar, *The Great Introduction*, II.7.22.
54   Ibid., VI.25.
55   Latini, *Trésor*, I.4.123.
56   For more about Chalcidius's diagrams, see Bruce Eastwood and Gerd Graßhoff, *Planetary Diagrams for Roman Astronomy in Medieval Europe, c.800–1500* (Philadelphia PA, 2004), esp. 73–5.

about medieval England's self-perception. Lavezzo concludes that the combined concepts of the nation defy any subsequent monolithic mythologies produced by nationalistic projects.[57] Gower's Book VII, not to mention the rest of the poem, challenges attempts to create a monolith of the East with its three distinctly different divisions of the Earth: the tripartite map with Asia extending to the middle of the world and including Paradise and Egypt; the seven-part planetary map that separates Egypt and the Holy Land from the East, with the last influenced by cold, militant Saturn; and finally, the four-part zodiacal map that places ancient Greece in the East and ancient Rome in a newly formed North, whereas the Prologue suggests that Rome begins in the West and incorporates the whole world by conquering the East. Gower's geographical borders for these zodiacal quadrants notably expand the East from Antioch, a city in ancient Greece, now Turkey. With Antioch, the East absorbs a centre of ancient Greece. The West then stretches from Armenia, likely the western border of modern-day Turkey. The South begins from Alexander the Great, a person instead of a place, and one known for conquering disparate lands and lending several cities his name.[58] Gower's North ends with 'londes [...] diversed', an unspecified location that leaves its northernmost borders open. The southernmost border of the North claims Constantinople, now Istanbul. The city was a capital of ancient Rome and became the last territory maintained by the Byzantine Empire, until absorbed by the Ottoman Empire in 1453. The city border claims ancient Rome as North, a significant relocation effort, considering that the *Confessio* mentions Rome more than 100 times: it is by far the poem's most common geographical reference, and the centre of Julius Caesar's whole-Earth empire.

---

57   Kathy Lavezzo, *Imagining a Medieval English Nation* (Minneapolis MN, 2003), xix.
58   According to Gower, Alexander eventually conquered the whole world. The reference might hint at the significance of Alexander for medieval Muslims, although, even when citing Abu' Ma'shar, Gower does not mention Islam. See Faustina Doufikar-Aerts, 'Alexander in Medieval Arab Minds: Archetype of Kings, Magnificent Warrior, and Custodian of Philosophy and Divine Principles', in *A History of Alexander the Great in World Culture*, ed. Richard Stoneman (Cambridge, 2022), 308–33.

Who Occupies the Confessio's East?

By juxtaposing different geographical orientations, Gower draws attention to the people who define the regionalities of the East, not just the borders produced. These peoples prove just as diffuse and variable as their geographical borders. Only two moments within the *Confessio* acknowledge late medieval Latin Christendom's conflict with the Islamic East, and both appear in responses to the tales, rather than within the tales themselves. First, at the end of 'The Tale of Alexander and the Pirate', Amans asks Genius about going to kill the 'Sarazin', a reference to Christian warfare against non-Christians for which Gower's *Mirour de l'omme* had previously expressed enthusiasm.[59] However, as Lee Manion suggests, the *Confessio*'s references to 'Saracens' might reflect crusading rhetoric, but without qualifying the poem as a crusading romance.[60] To begin with, Gower's Genius forbids murderous warfare, citing scriptural morals from one of the Gospels.[61] Timothy Guard connects such injunctions against killing to literary conventions that expressed ambivalence towards knightly codes during the second half of the Hundred Years War and periods of papal schism.[62] The altered attitude reflects what Celia Lewis has called Gower's growing dissatisfaction with crusading slaughter.[63] Lewis supposes that changing opinions might not have been an unusual outcome of personal interactions, such as those afforded by Richard II's multi-religious court.[64] These conflicted beliefs perhaps explain Amans's need for reiteration, as Amans repeats the question about killing 'Sarazins' after Genius concludes a tale about Jephtha's daughter.[65] Whatever Amans might understand about the 'Sarazin' lesson, Genius here reduces the geo-political problem to a simple Christian injunction against killing. The injunction, however, only simplifies the question of

---

59 Gower, *Mirour de l'omme*, in *The Complete Works of John Gower*, ed. G. C. Macaulay, vol. 1 (Oxford, 1899), lines 23,895, 23,901–3, 23,951–2, 23,961, 23,969, 24,037–8; see Marcel Elias, 'Chaucer and Crusader Ethics: Youth, Love, and the Material World', *The Review of English Studies* 70 (2019), 629.
60 Lee Manion, *Narrating the Crusades: Loss and Recovery in Medieval and Early Modern English Literature* (Cambridge, 2014), 13, 109.
61 Gower, *Confessio Amantis*, III.2489.
62 Timothy Guard, *Chivalry, Kingship and Crusade: The English Experience in the Fourteenth Century* (Woodbridge, 2013), 377 –8.
63 Celia M. Lewis, 'History, Mission, and Crusade in the *Canterbury Tales*', *Chaucer Review* 42 (2008), 353–82 (358).
64 Ibid., 357.
65 Gower, *Confessio Amantis*, IV.1679.

religious warfare, not eastern inhabitants' representations. The resulting eastern inhabitants exhibit characteristics ranging from hypersexuality and blood-thirsty barbarity to enlightenment and magnanimity. Rather than using characteristics or geographical locations to divide them, the *Confessio* differentiates subjects by means of the ethical categories to which the poem devotes its books.[66]

In a similar fashion to Chaucer's 'Prioress's Tale', Gower's *Confessio* tends to conflate 'Saracens' with Jewish people.[67] 'Saracens' anachronistically populate Gower's tales about Gideon and Solomon's multiple wives, which originated in the Hebrew Bible and which Gower accessed through Riga's commentary.[68] Gower's tale begins with kings arriving to destroy the kingdoms of Judah and Israel before Gideon leads a company of 30,000 to defend God's people.[69] Gower then explains how Gideon asks God's counsel:

> And God, which wolde he were war
> That he schal spede upon his riht,
> Hath bede him go the same nyht
> And take a man with him, to hiere
> What schal be spoke in his matiere
> Among the hethen enemis;
> [...]
> Be nyhte tok toward thilke host,
> Which logged was in a valleie,
> To hiere what thei wolden seie;
> Upon his fot and as he ferde,
> Tuo Sarazins spekende he herde (VII.3688–93, 3698–702)

---

66 Suzanne Akbari, 'Alexander in the Orient: bodies and boundaries', in *Postcolonial Approaches to the European Middle Ages: Translating Cultures*, ed. Ananya Jahanara Kabir and Deanne Williams (Cambridge, 2005), 105–26; Chris Chism, 'Saladin and Richard I', in *The Cambridge Companion to the Literature of the Crusades*, ed. Anthony Bale (Cambridge, 2019); and Jeffrey Jerome Cohen, 'On Saracen Enjoyment: Some Fantasies of Race in Late Medieval France and England', *Journal of Medieval and Early Modern Studies* 31 (2001), 113–46.
67 Sheila Delany, 'Chaucer's Prioress, the Jews, and the Muslims', *Medieval Encounters* 5.2 (1999), 198–213.
68 Judges 6–8.
69 Gower, *Confessio Amantis*, VII.3628 –39; Judges 6:20–5; and Peter Riga, 'Liber Iudicium', in *Aurora: Biblia Versificata, A Verse Commentary on the Bible*, ed. Paul E. Beichner (South Bend IN, 1965), I: 83–228.

The two speaking 'Sarazin' enemies identify the five leaders of their camps as 'Madian', 'Amalech', 'Amoreie', 'Amon' and 'Jebuseie'.[70] Although Riga does not specify the location or even the names of the five enemy camps, the Book of Judges places all five kings somewhere in West Asia, including Midianites, descendants of Abraham's son Midian, whose religious beliefs are now unknown. Amalekites, descendants of Esau, resided in southern Israel. Amon, a descendent of David, became king of Judah; and finally, Amorites and Jebusites inhabited lands of Canaan around modern Syria and Jerusalem. Like the medieval religious conflations Delany and Akbari note, 'Sarazin' here becomes a generic designation for the Israelites' various ancient enemies, the same as heathens or unbelievers. Gower's primary Riga source does not use the label here. The closest word within Riga's commentary might be 'antichristus',[71] a reference that inspires Gower to create one continuous branch of righteous monotheists versus everyone else. In doing so, Gower follows a fourteenth-century tradition of using *heathenesse* to refer to non-Christian regions in the Mediterranean, Balkans, Iberian peninsula and the Baltic.[72]

Such conflations abound in medieval Latin Christendom, as is implied by Sarah Salih's observation that all pagans, which included Muslims, are ubiquitously represented as idol worshippers.[73] Gower's Genius explicitly conflates the two later in Book VII when introducing the biblical tale about the counsel of Balaam:

> Hou Amalech the paien king,
> Whan that he myhte be no weie
> Defende his lond and putte aweie
> The worthi poeple of Irael,
> This Sarazin, as it befell,
> Through the conseil of Balaam
> A route of faire women nam,
> That lusti were and yonge of age,

---

70 VII.3710–12. Gower's Latin headnote (trans. Andrew Galloway) also identifies these enemy camps as the kings of the Midianites, Amalachites, Ammonites, Amorites and Jebusites.
71 If Gower is in fact translating from Riga here, he takes several liberties. Riga, 'Liber Iudicium', *Aurora*, 167, 210.
72 Ibid., 1.
73 Sarah Salih, *Imagining the Pagan in Late Medieval England* (Cambridge, 2019), 139–72.

And bad hem gon to the lignage
Of these Hebreus (VII.4408–17)

Gower again positions Sarazins against Israelites, with the latter signifying a 'worthi people' who resist the pagan Amalech's attempts to subject them. Gower elsewhere distinguishes between pagans and Muslims, especially when Amans twice asks Genius about the crusading agenda to kill 'Sarazins'; however, within his biblical tales, 'Sarazins' become amorphous opponents to ancient Israelites. As in the tale of Gideon, Gower's tale of Balaam differentiates enemies from allies according to blood lines: Gideon's enemies belong to tribal descendants, and Balaam's resolution for Amalech involves marriageable women with 'Hebrew' lineage. Hebrew lineage and opponents both occupy territories that Book VII's maps place in the East, leaving beliefs and lineage as the sole means for separating 'Hebrews' from other occupants of the ancient East.

The *Confessio* distinguishes between beliefs historically, such as in the Chain of Being from Book V, outlining the history of pre-Christian religions. Furthermore, as Yeager has pointed out, Gower consistently distinguishes between Hebrews in a pre-Christian sense and Jewish people in the Christian era.[74] As a result, Gower's religious borders fluctuate over time, just as geographical borders do after conquests. Lineage, on the other hand, aims to cross historical boundaries. For example, Book VIII, the final book in the poem, repeats the T-O map of Noah's sons to explain how early humanity's population spread:

> Sem, Cham, Japhet, of these thre,
> That ben the sones of Noe,
> The world of mannes nacion
> Into multiplicacion
> Was tho restored newe agein
> So ferforth, as the bokes sein,
> That of hem thre and here issue
> Ther was so large a retenue,
> Of naciouns seventy and tuo (VIII.83–91)

Gower's 'muliplicacion' reiterates a medieval perception of the Hebrew Bible's emphasis on procreation, and relates this biblical proliferation

---

74 R. F. Yeager, 'Gower's Jews', in *John Gower: Others and the Self*, ed. Russell A. Peck and R. F. Yeager (Cambridge, 2017), 190.

ANCIENT GEOGRAPHIES AND GENEALOGIES IN JOHN GOWER 189

to making 'a retenue' and 'mannes nacion'.[75] The former equates the population increase with a type of royal company, the latter with political states – and yet neither appears within the *Confessio*'s many maps. The seventy-two 'naciouns' prove more genealogical than geographical or astronomical.

Emphasising the genealogy of tribes, the *Confessio* uses historical heredity just as it did religions in its Chain of Being.[76] Chaldeans supposedly initiated religious observation before Egyptians further developed their beliefs. Gower presents this chain of religions in terms of inheritance, as a genealogy of belief. His religious distinctions follow an Augustinian model,[77] and his biblical information is elsewhere derived from Riga's *Aurora*.[78] However, Riga's exegesis of Genesis rarely works to define the geographical and genealogical boundaries adopted by the *Confessio*. Gower's information instead reiterates details emphasised in Peter of Poitiers's copiously copied genealogical reading aid for the Hebrew Bible, although there is no evidence Gower directly encountered Peter of Poitiers's genealogy, the *Compendium Historiae in Genealogia Christi*.[79] Rather than subdividing Noah's sons' continents, Peter upholds a simple boundary between East and West, emphasising Asia as the central line of biblical inheritance, a line that extends from the first inhabitants of eastern Paradise, Adam and Eve, and concludes with Christ.

Gower also repeatedly emphasises eastern descendants at moments of rapid population growth. For example, his account of Cain and Abel initiates the first proliferation:

---

75 Gower's 'mannes nacion' biblically refers to non-Christian peoples: *MED*, s.v. 'nacioun, n.' (2).
76 Yeager, 'Gower's Religions', 62.
77 Gower presents Christianity as the 'rational solution' to the problem of 'irrational belief' of past religions: Yeager, 'Gower's Religions', 65–6.
78 As with Book VII, Riga's *Aurora* is used to add encyclopaedic information to biblical lore, such as identifying the twelve zodiacal signs when commenting on the Book of Hester. The *Aurora* also repeatedly mentions the reign of Alexander the Great, as does Book VII. Riga, *Aurora*, *Liber Hester*, 12, 17–34 and *Liber Machabeorum*, 1; and Paul E. Beichner, 'The Old French Verse *Bible* of Macé de la Charité, A Translation of the *Aurora*', *Speculum* 22 (1947), 226–39 (234–5).
79 N.b., Latini's *Trésor* also includes passages about biblical genealogies, but Gower truncates them, as he does Latini's geographical landmarks. Peter's genealogy offers a more schematic approach to biblical genealogy, one that resembles Gower's own account.

> Thus was mankinde to beginne;
> [...]
> To Chain was Calmana betake,
> And Delboram hath Abel take,
> In whom was gete natheles
> Of worldes folk the ferste encres.
> Men sein that nede hath no lawe,
> And so it was be thilke dawe
> And laste into the Secounde Age,
> Til that the grete water rage,
> Of Noe, which was seid the flod (VIII.67, 71–9)

Gower and Peter both trace original Creation with Adam and Eve from the East. Humanity begins from Paradise in the East and increases at traceable singular historical moments centred in the East, from where the Earth's few occupants emerged. The first 'encres' derives from the pairings of Adam and Eve's four children: Cain and Calmana, Abel and Deborah. The second population expansion begins again from a singular family line, initiating the second age of humanity from Noah's post-fluvial family. Gower refers to these moments as lawless, more specifically as not needing law, by which he means papal laws forbidding incest.

Gower effectively streamlines the numerous descendants of this Abrahamic family according to their more ancient roots. He especially devotes attention to moments when the ancient Abrahamic tree branches out, such as Jacob's twelve sons' becoming patriarchs of the Twelve Tribes of Israel. This tree, commonly depicted in medieval art as Jacob's Tree, introduces Gower's final tale as part of humanity's origin story. According to Book VIII, Eve's children serve to replace the population of angels lost to Hell as part of Lucifer's 'court'.[80] Such origin stories typically appear at the beginning of his source texts, but Gower presents Creation at the beginning of his final book, where Jacob's extensive family tree appears:

> His sone Jacob dede also,
> And of Laban the dowhtres tuo,
> Which was his em, he tok to wyve,
> And gat upon hem in his lyve,
> Of hire ferst which hihte Lie,

---

80   VIII.22–36.

Sex sones of his progenie,
And of Rachel tuo sones eke:
The remenant was for to seke,
That is to sein of foure mo,
Wherof he gat on Bala tuo,
And of Zelpha he hadde ek tweie.
And these tuelve, as I thee seie,
Thurgh providence of God Himselve
Ben seid the Patriarkes tuelve;
Of whom, as afterward befell,
The tribes tuelve of Irahel (VIII.120–36)

This passage beginning with Jacob ends with the Twelve Tribes of Israel. As with Eve, Jacob begins with incest, enhancing the cohesion of the family's branches that result in the Twelve Tribes.

Scholars such as Diane Watt and Larry Scanlon have also noted the *Confessio*'s interest in Abrahamic law in Book VIII. They have explored how Gower describes the Hebrew Bible's allowances for incest, recognising the early historical imperative to breed through incest to populate and repopulate the earth from a limited number of inhabitants.[81] Gower uses these incestuous unions resulting in the Twelve Tribes of Israel as a pre-Christ practice that papal law then forbade; papal law appears as a turning point in the history of genealogical generations.

The Abrahamic East is not Gower's only historical East to move, reinvent itself, or even rely on incest. Gower's ancient Greece initiates the eastern quadrant of his zodiacal map from its Antioch capital. According to Gower's Genius, Greeks and Romans had the same beliefs, although

---

81 David Benson, 'Incest and Moral Poetry in Gower's *Confessio Amantis*', *Chaucer Review* 19 (1984), 100–9; Victoria Blud, *The Unspeakable, Gender and Sexuality in Medieval Literature, 1000–1400* (Cambridge, 2017), 162; María Bullón-Fernández, 'Confining the Daughter: Gower's "Tale of Canace and Machaire" and the Politics of the Body', *Essays in Medieval Studies: Proceedings of the Illinois Medieval Association* 11 (1994), 75–85; Georgiana Donavan, 'Taboo and Transgression in Gower's Apollonius of Tyre', in *Domestic Violence in Medieval Texts*, ed. Eve Salisbury, Georgiana Donavin, and Merrall Llewelyn Price (Gainesville FL, 2002), 94–121; Larry Scanlon, 'Speaking the Unspeakable: Alain de Lille, Sexual Regulation and the Priesthood of Genius', *Romanic Review* 86.2 (1995), 213–42; Larry Scanlon, 'Gower, Lydgate, and Incest', in *John Gower: Others and the Self*, ed. Russell A. Peck and Robert F. Yeager (Cambridge, 2017), 156–82; and Diane Watt, 'Gender and Sexuality in *Confessio Amantis*', in *A Companion to Gower*, ed. Siân Echard (Cambridge, 2004), 197–213.

he refers to the gods by their Roman names (part of his view that the 'Latins' translated all worldly knowledge into Latin).[82] By creating human genealogies for Greco-Roman gods, the *Confessio* extends its lack of differentiation to Greek and Roman peoples, despite ancient Rome's Constantinople initiating the northern quadrant of Gower's zodiacal map. The Greco-Roman conflation, like the ancient Abrahamic tabernacle, moves beliefs across borders. As with his depiction of Abrahamic peoples, Gower's Greco-Romans have their own genealogy for populating the East.

Within the *Confessio*'s Chain of Being, Gower describes Greek beliefs in the manner of his Abrahamic trees. He begins by tracing connections from the ancient records' first progenitors, in this case, Roman-named gods Saturn, Jupiter, Neptune and Juno. Gower's genealogy recognises the interbreeding that mythologically resulted from the limited pantheon. Gower presents the gods conventionally, as humans, claiming to uncover the 'sothe' of their Greco-Roman depictions.[83] This truth is a genealogy that identifies Venus as Saturn's daughter,[84] and mother of 'diverse children':[85]

> Nou on be this, nou on be that.
> Of hire it was that Mars begat
> A child, which cleped was Armene [*Harmonia*]
> Of hire also cam Andragene [*Androgynus (Hermaphroditus)*],
> To whom Mercurie fader was.
> Anchises begat Eneas
> Of hire also, and Ericon
> Biten begat, and therupon,
> Whan that sche sih ther was non other,
> Be Jupiter hire oghne brother
> Sche lay, and he begat Cupide. (V.1395–405)

Ovid provides the same genealogy of Hermaphroditus;[86] and in his fourteenth-century mythic *Genealogia deorum* Giovanni Boccaccio

---

82 Gower, *Confessio Amantis*, V.1304–7.
83 V.1386. Regarding Gower's euhemerised, or 'demythologised', approaches to the gods in Books V and VII, see esp. Theresa Tinkle, *Medieval Venuses and Cupids: Sexuality, Hermeneutics, and English Poetry* (Stanford, 1996), 178–97.
84 Genius explains that she has graced diverse men with love and lust: V.1393–405, V.1430–51.
85 V.1394.
86 Ovid, *Metamorphoses*, IV.274–388.

makes the other lines from Venus more explicit.[87] Gower also notes the well-attested account of Anchises and Venus' begetting of Aeneas, the origin story for Virgil's *Aeneid*. These widespread accounts of her family tree lend her an extensive impact on ancient history, including the seminal Virgilian account of Aeneas founding Rome.

However, the begetting of Cupid from her brother Jupiter lacks the same widespread confirmation. Roman literature sometimes refrains from identifying Cupid's father, and other accounts such as Seneca's attribute his siring to Vulcan, whereas Cicero offers multiple fathers for different Cupids.[88] Cicero inspires Boccaccio's own account of multiple Cupids and Venuses, a multiplication practice that helped accommodate the many sources for and meanings of Greco-Roman gods. In particular Venus, like her father Saturn, represents a goddess, a planet and a historical person. Having a Greek and a Roman inheritance resulted in contrasting accounts that only multiple identities could accommodate.[89] As Theresa Tinkle points out, Venus gained even more identities because she functions as a 'literary-amatory convention, a historical woman, a planet, an anthropomorphized force of sexual desire, or fortune's twin'.[90] Venus's literary and anthropomorphic features inspire an evaluation that differs from her Abrahamic counterparts. Unlike Eve and Calmana, Venus appears fickle and inconstant, a prolific procreator with multiple sexual partners.

Venus's sexuality, like the Chain of Being and Ages of Man, undergoes perpetual revision. Gower presents these perpetual sexual revisions as a law that Venus imposes on the land:

> And sche, which thoghte hire lustes fonde,
> Diverse loves tok in honde,
> Wel mo thane I thee tolde hiere;
> And for sche wolde hirselve skiere,
> Sche made comun that desport,
> And sette a lawe of such a port,
> That every womman mihte take

---

87 Giovanni Boccaccio, *Genealogy of the Gentile Gods*, ed./trans. Jon Solomon (Cambridge MA, 2011), II.63.4, III.21.1.
88 Lucius Annaeus Seneca, *Octavia*, in *Tragedies, vol. 2: Oedipus. Agamemnon. Thyestes. Hercules on Oeta. Octavia*, ed. John G. Fitch (Cambridge MA, 2018), line 560; Cicero, *De natura deorum*, III.59–60.
89 Tinkle, *Medieval Venuses and Cupids*, 4.
90 Ibid., 190.

What man hire liste, and noght forsake
To ben als comun as sche wolde. (V.1421–9)

According to Gower, Venus's 'diverse' sexual conquests prove too numerous to list. Rather than accept condemnation, she turns her desires into law, making them 'comun', normalising female conquest of any man she chooses. Venus thus formalises women's sexuality in martial terms: whereas men like Caesar and Alexander take whatever lands they choose, women take whatever men they choose. This law of sexuality appropriates and reverses established courtly love, or *fin' amor*, practices, which render amorous activities masculine by adopting conquest metaphors characteristic of battlefields. Gower not only feminises the metaphoric conquest of love here, as do other medieval romances,[91] but also legalises the process, formalising the law of love as a law of the land.

Her laws as well as her progeny render Venus's signification manifold and complex, just like the East from which she hails. She follows the same models as Abrahamic progenitors, and she begets a significant historical lineage. As the patroness of the poem, her sexual exploits escape some of the traditional moral denigrations. In terms of religion, Yeager suggests that the *Confessio* deems pagan religious practices, such as the incest of Cupid and Venus, as ignorant and foolish rather than as sinful – at least from the perspective of the pagan priest of Venus. Yeager relates this view on pagan incest to Gower's treatment of the Chain of Being, by which religions historically supplant one another as their beliefs encounter more rational developments.[92] Gower hesitates to condemn the sexual proclivities of Venus, whom his tale collection claims to serve. The poem also hesitates to condemn the sin she personifies, delaying the seventh sin of lust after devoting each of the first six books to the other deadly sins. Book VII instead provides encyclopaedic information, and Book VIII finally turns to the subject, but in a limited fashion, providing only one complete tale that addresses incest, rather than dissecting various sexual activities or desires.

Nevertheless, Venus's pagan incest attracts a distinctly different tone than used to describe her Abrahamic counterparts. Whereas Book

---

91 See, for example, Sarah Kay, 'Courts, Clerks and Courtly Love', in *The Cambridge Companion to Medieval Romance*, ed. Roberta L. Krueger (Cambridge, 2000), 81–96.
92 Yeager, 'Gower's Religions', 62–3.

VIII explains the historical imperative of population replacement, Venus's genealogy here presents her procreative practices as dilettantish, flitting from one partner to the next regardless of familial connections. Venus's incest and sexual activities spread a different type of legacy through ancient history. According to Gower, Venus also initiates the genealogy of Semiramis, the Babylonian wife of Ninus, Assyria's king and conqueror of Asia:

> Sche [*Venus*] was the ferste also which tolde
> That wommen scholde here bodi selle.
> Semiramis, so as men telle,
> Of Venus kepte thilke aprise,
> And so dede in the same wise
> Of Rome faire Neabole,
> Which liste hire bodi to rigole;
> Sche was to every man felawe,
> And hild the lust of thilke lawe,
> Which Venus of hirself began [...]
> Se nou the foule miscreance
> Of Greks in thilke time tho,
> Whan Venus tok hire name so. (V.1430–39, 1444–6)

Gower refers to Venus not only as the world's first sex worker, but also as the world's first madame, or instructor for other women pursuing sex work. The result is not pure moral condemnation of Venus, who, as Watt has explained, shares the blame with Cupid for spreading infectious lust.[93] Nevertheless, Gower's version traces a sex-worker lineage as a preamble to the mystery of Greeks turning Venus into a goddess. This lineage spreads across disparate lands, including Semiramis of Babylon as well as 'Neabole' of Rome. The latter presumably denotes Niobe, wife of Amphion and mother of fourteen children, whose pride in her procreative power earned the ire of goddess Latona.[94] Niobe's mythography also occasionally divided her into separate personalities; Boccaccio's *Genealogia* variously identifies Niobe as the daughter of Phoroneus and mother of Apis with Jupiter, as well as the daughter of Tantalus and mother of twelve or fourteen children with Amphion, depending on whether one trusts Homer or Ovid.[95] Gower reunites

---

93   Watt, *Amoral Gower*, 89–90.
94   Ovid, *Metamorphoses*, VI.146–312.
95   Boccaccio, *Genealogy of the Pagan Gods*, II.iv.1, V.xxx.4, V.xxxi.1–2.

historical figures whom mythographies had separated into multiple characters with the same name: namely, Niobe, Venus, Semiramis and even Cupid each become one character in the *Confessio*. His poem might recognise various maps of the Earth, but he streamlines its many populations into almost linear genealogies.

Gower had many mythographic models for presenting such figures as multiple people, but he chose instead to unify them, even while recognising that Venus and Saturn have both mythographic and planetary significations that do not always agree. Even within the same commentary, the planetary gods can acquire multiple meanings. Pierre Bersuire's *Ovidius moralizatus* allegorically identifies Saturn as an avaricious influence, a boon for sowers of fields, a violent tyrant, and a sign of sagacity.[96] Gower's Genius makes Venus's sole legacy her sexuality, source of all ancient worlds' sexuality. He was not alone in this; medieval mythographers ranging from Fulgentius to Thomas Walsingham emphasised her life focused on gratification and carnality.[97] Bersuire also notes her role in inspiring infidelity.[98] Boccaccio expands upon this picture to claim that after the death of her two husbands, Venus established the world's first brothels and public prostitution to make her lasciviousness appear less abominable.[99] Gower adopts an account of Venus related to Boccaccio's, similarly attributing her sex-work to a desire for social acceptability. In the *Confessio*, Venus forces this acceptance by rendering her sexuality a type of 'law', and one that proves uniquely capable of transcending traditions. Sex-work alone enters disparate eastern worlds. It crosses from ancient Greek to ancient Roman Venus, and then moves again to Babylonian Semiramis, 'infecting' an Abrahamic world that the poem renders otherwise impervious to neighbouring contexts, like Islam.

---

96 Pierre Bersuire, *L'"Ovidius Moralizatus" di Pierre Bersuire*, ed. Fausto Ghisalberti (Rome, 1933), 91–3.
97 Fulgentius, *Fulgentius the Mythographer*, trans. Leslie George Whitbread (Columbus OH, 1971), 66–7; Thomas Walsingham, *Archana Deorum*, ed. Robert van Kluyve (Durham NC, 1968), I.xi.1–8.
98 Gower, *Confessio Amantis*, V.1452–4.
99 Boccaccio further claims that Venus forced married women to enter her brothels, a practice he deems detestable and related to the Cypriots: Giovanni Boccaccio, *Famous Women*, ed./trans. Virginia Brown (Cambridge MA, 2001), VII.8–11. Nevertheless, he comes to other, less condemnatory conclusions about two separate Venuses elsewhere: *Genealogy of the Pagan Gods*, III.22–3.

Conclusion

The *Confessio* unifies its historical cast of characters, forging Venus, Niobe, Semiramis and Cupid each into one character, rather than several historical figures with the same names. Reuniting a character like Venus with her multiple mythological sexual partners perhaps also inspires Gower to retain some medieval commentary practices of condemning pagan sexuality by calling prolific pagans sex-workers.[100] As a cast of characters hailing from the East, these sex-workers likely relate to Gower's changed opinions about religious warfare against the East. According to Elias, Gower's *Vox clamantis* represented the period's more controversial crusader values, with chivalric codes fixated on love rather than morality.[101] In this framework, Gower's *Confessio* follows the condemnation of chivalric amor, yet his geographical and genealogical histories also include lustful laws that prove just as amorphous as the East's perpetually reorganising borders. Even when reducing historical signifiers, such as the conflation of 'Sarazins' with Israelites and all *heathenesse*, the *Confessio*'s lineages cross traditions. In fact, the representations of peoples prove more consistent than their borders. The *Confessio*'s peoples from Greco-Roman and Abrahamic traditions as well as from all directions retain the same signifiers while geographical, religious and astronomical borders transform around them.

Gower's eastern boundaries end up resembling his versions of ancient histories, in that neither follows a linear progression, even when their peoples do. Histories of ancient populations followed multiple cycles of victory and destruction, with population replacement occurring multiple times and along incestuous lines. According to Gower, incest fulfilled a historical imperative for humans to multiply, responding to original Creation as well as mass extinction events like the Flood. However, the *Confessio* disparages the same incestuous practices in a parallel ancient history. Venus's incestuous lineage gives birth to global lust, contaminating other peoples, rather than branching into the population diversity characteristic of Noah's three sons, Adam and Eve, or Jacob's Tree. These distinct outcomes for the same behaviours in the same East demonstrate Gower's complex attitude towards the region that he believes covers half of the occupied Earth, the most important inheritance of Noah, from where human diversity emerged.

100 Bersuire, *Ovidius Moralizatus*, 96.
101 Elias, 'Chaucer and Crusader Ethics', 623, 630.

The *Confessio*'s resulting portrait of the East offers multiple complex views that recognise the region as the centre of human histories and the linchpin for global cohesion, the heart of Julius Caesar's and Alexander the Great's empires. These global empires rely on conquering the opposite sides of the Earth, an approach that the *Confessio* mirrors by compiling disparate lore. He appropriates multiple Easts, but ones that omit many of their sociopolitical contexts to create a global, bookish empire. The *Confessio* results in multiple historical worlds whose varying fortunes radically redesigned boundaries at regular intervals. The Flood, for instance, forced humanity to begin anew. Scholars also repeatedly began anew with their various maps of the Earth. Gower's approach creates space for competing borders and competing intellectual histories, ones that might overlap with contemporaneous histories, such as the conflicts between Latin Christendom and the Muslim Near East, yet in pre-Christian terms. 'Sarazins' become opponents for Israelites more than Christians, preserving battle lines recounted in ancient histories even when accommodating more contemporary medieval scholarship attributed to Abu' Ma'shar. The results form multiple genealogies for multiple Easts with disparate outcomes, such as a Chain of Being account of religions' increasing in rationality, against the Ages of Man decreasing in value. The *Confessio* compiles both historical models despite their mutual contradiction; the poem also accumulates more disparities within them, such as Egyptians having the most aberrant beliefs, rather than the supposedly original Chaldeans. Additionally, the final Age of Steel integrates Christian defenders. In place of linear progressions or regressions, Gower's ancient histories unfold as clustered activities, moments that branch out from a central East just like the genealogies attached to their lore.

Nevertheless, the resulting genealogies of antiquity, just like the *Confessio*'s geographies for them, multiply. By compiling maps and family trees, Gower avoids forcing interpretive singularities onto disparate climes, peoples and historical sources. Gower multiplies the region just like its prolific original populations who repeatedly and diversely repopulated the Earth from its centre. Monumental conquerors like Alexander the Great and Julius Caesar offer occasional historical cohesion, but the rest of history succumbs to fractious tendencies. Competing maps and genealogies should perhaps not surprise any reader who recognises Gower's own tangential relationship to the maps and genealogies he describes. His native North does not appear until, according to the *Confessio*, Abu' Ma'shar reorganises the Earth to add its quadrant.

Gower's native England exists on a distant shore from the ancient histories that he narrates. Nevertheless, this distant view gives him a vantage point for the description of incessantly changing histories and borders. Paradise, Noah's Flood, Jacob's Tree, Venus's incest, Alexander's and Caesar's conquests all changed the world map. All these events create divergent pathways to multiple Easts, where all his changeable histories began. Gower thus collects branches of ancient Easts, juxtaposing their proliferations to compile ancient histories anew.

7

Arthur in the Mountains: The Multivalency of Mont-Saint-Michel and the St Gotthard Pass in the Alliterative *Morte Arthure*

Stephen De Hailes

> The king covers the crag   with cloughes full high,
> To the crest of the cliff   he climbes on loft,
> Cast up his umbrere   and keenly he lookes,
> Caught of the cold wind   to comfort himselven.[1]
>
> Now he moves his might   with mirthes of herte
> Over mountes so high,   those marvelous wayes,
> Gos in by Goddard,   the garret he winnes,   *Mt. Goddard watchtower*
> Graithes the garnison   grisly woundes!   *Deals garrison*
> When he was passed the height,   then the king hoves
> With his hole batail   beholdand about,
> Lookand on Lumbardy   and on loud meles:
> 'In yon likand land   lord be I think!'
>
> (3103–9)

In the Alliterative *Morte Arthure*, a poem composed in English by an anonymous poet at the turn of the fifteenth century, the above two passages describe Arthur's experience of what we would today term 'mountaineering': the physical act of climbing a mountain or promontory.[2] The brevity of these passages, in contrast to the ever-expanding

---

1   *King Arthurs's Death: The Middle English Stanzaic Morte Arthur and the Alliterative Morte Arthure*, ed. Larry D. Benson, rev. Edward E. Foster (Kalamazoo MI, 1994), lines 940–3. All further references are to this edition. Translations and marginal glosses are my own but with recourse to this edition.
2   *OED*, s.v. 'mountaineer', v. The earliest use of this term in reference to the act of climbing appears in a letter by Samuel Taylor Coleridge in 1802. Prior to this, the noun *mountaineer* implied an individual who lived or worked in the

body of literature on mountain ascents since the advent of Alpinism, is one example of the radical shift in our attitude towards mountains in recent centuries. For many in the modern world, mountains are a source of pleasure, excitement, wonder and escape, in a way that would seem alien to our medieval forebears. And yet mountains and hills are as much a part of the medieval world as they are our own, linked to worship, military strategy, defence, geopolitics, agriculture, industry, travel and commerce. In art and literature, they serve as sites of contemplation, as figurative embodiments of worldly and spiritual power, and as otherworldly landscapes associated with monstrosity and otherness. In the specific context of the medieval Arthurian tradition, the primary focus of this essay, they are also linked to the figure of King Arthur.

The Alliterative *Morte Arthure*, building on Geoffrey of Monmouth's twelfth-century *De Gestis Britonum* (and later vernacular translations by the likes of Wace and Laʒamon), tells the story of Arthur's campaign in Europe against Lucius the Emperor of Rome, Mordred's usurpation of Arthur's throne, Arthur's return to England, his war with Mordred, and his mortal wounding in the battle of Camlann. Mountains and hills are a consistent feature of the poem, appearing regularly as landmarks that define key moments in Arthur's advance across the continent. Two such instances stand out as examples of the centrality and significance of mountain landscapes within the text: Arthur's battle with a giant on Mont-Saint-Michel in Northern France, and his crossing of the Alps via the St Gotthard pass into Italy.[3] While both of these moments have their origin in Geoffrey's *De Gestis*, the poet of the Alliterative *Morte* develops the events that transpire on and around each peak to an extent that far exceeds what we find in any of the poem's antecedents.

Drawing on these two examples, but with reference to the appearance and function of mountain landscapes throughout Arthur's campaign in Europe, this essay argues that the mountains of the Alliterative *Morte* are fundamental to the construction of meaning in the poem, and a crucial component of the poet's combined celebration and interrogation

---

mountains, rather than one who visited for pleasure: *OED*, *s.v.* 'mountaineer', n. & adj. See Simon Bainbridge, *Mountaineering and British Romanticism: The Literary Cultures of Climbing, 1770 –1836* (Oxford, 2020), 3–5. For the dating of the Alliterative *Morte Arthure*, see *Morte Arthure: A Critical Edition*, ed. Mary Hamel (London, 1984), 53–8.

3 In reality, Mont-Saint-Michel sits just 92 m (302 ft) above sea level. However, the *Morte*-poet clearly intends for the Mont to feature as a much grander mountain landscape in the poem, as will be shown later in this essay.

of Arthur's status as king. The moral dimension of Arthur's campaign has long been a subject of scholarly debate, particularly when it comes to the violence that is a consistent feature of the poem, and the parallels that can be drawn between Arthur as noble warrior king and the giant of Mont-Saint-Michel as a corrupted image of imperial governance.[4] However, Arthur's developing relationship with the mountain landscapes that he encounters is an equally important means of examining his exercise of power. Mountains are landscapes that disrupt. They are both real-world locations and otherworldly settings; they are linked to spiritual and secular power while simultaneously associated with monstrosity, outlawry and the foreign other; they are uncultivated spaces, devoid of civilisation, and yet tied to medieval ideas of vision, insight and forethought. Their very nature as obstacles to be overcome ensures that they are identified as spaces of trial, particularly in the context of romance convention, but this also connects them to allegories of fortune and the rise and fall of individuals.

Building on a nascent trend in literary mountain studies and premodern ecocritical theory, this essay argues that the mountains of the Alliterative *Morte* encapsulate a range of literal and metaphorical interpretations that broaden and complicate our understanding of Arthur's campaign and his precarious relationship to power. In doing so, it challenges a widespread consensus in literary mountain studies which argues that mountains in premodern literatures tend to be incidental, background features of a work, or derived exclusively from clichéd and unimaginative literary convention. In essence, the mountain of the medieval mind is a more nuanced object of enquiry than many modern commentators have acknowledged. By examining their centrality within the Alliterative *Morte Arthure* and considering their role as part of the cultivation of meaning within the poem, this essay argues that there is much more to be said on the subject of mountains in the medieval English imagination.

---

4   See, for example, Jeffrey Jerome Cohen, *Of Giants* (Minneapolis MN, 1999), 153; Patricia DeMarco, 'An Arthur for the Ricardian Age: Crown, Nobility, and the Alliterative *Morte Arthure*', *Speculum* 80 (2005), 464–93 (466); Robyn Thum-O'Brien, 'The King, the Giant, and Time: Temporality in the Encounter at Mont Saint Michel in the Alliterative *Morte Arthure*', *Arthuriana* 32.1 (2022), 82–94 (83).

Allegory and Actuality: A Dialectical Approach

As a result of English literary mountain studies' emphasis on works of the Romantic period or later, very little has been written on mountains in medieval English literature. The focus on poets such as Percy Bysshe Shelley, Lord Byron and William Wordsworth is a result of the clear interest in mountain landscapes that develops in English literature during the eighteenth century, an interest that is commonly defined within the context of the Sublime, and the increasing emphasis in this period on the emotional and often euphoric impact that landscape can have on the individual. Mountains, as Simon Bainbridge identifies, were objects that astonished, both in terms of their intimidating size and because of their potential for spectacle.[5] By contrast, critical and popular opinion on the status of mountains in the premodern imagination has been shaped in large part by a single work: Marjory Hope Nicolson's *Mountain Gloom and Mountain Glory* (1959). For Nicolson, the personal and emotional response that Romantic poets like Byron, Shelley and Wordsworth experienced around mountains, and the urge to put pen to paper to acknowledge them, would not have occurred to anyone in the classical, medieval or renaissance periods.[6] There is, as Nicolson writes, nothing to compare in the poetic works of earlier ages to the likes of Shelley's *Prometheus Unbound*, a poem that engages in detailed description of mountain landscapes in a way that would seem alien to figures such as Chaucer, Gower and the *Gawain*-poet, a point that she illustrates with the following extract:

> And far on high the keen sky-cleaving mountains
> From icy spires of sunlike radiance fling
> The dawn, as lifted Ocean's dazzling spray
> From some Atlantic islet scatter'd up,
> Spangles the wind with lamp-like water-drops.
> The vale is girdled with their walls, a howl
> Of Cataracts from their thaw-cloven ravines

---

5   Bainbridge, *Mountaineering and British Romanticism*, 81–4. An aesthetic appreciation for mountains that links closely to their power to astonish can be found in *Critical Essays from the Spectator by Jospeh Addison*, ed. Donald F. Bond (Oxford, 1970), 178–81; and Edmund Burke, *A Philosophical Enquiry into the Origin of Our Ideas of the Sublime and Beautiful*, ed. Paul Guyer (Oxford, 2015), 47–8.
6   Marjorie Hope Nicolson, *Mountain Gloom and Mountain Glory: The Development of the Aesthetic of the Infinite* (New York, 1963), 8–9.

Satiates the listening wind, continuous, vast,
Awful as silence.[7]

Nicolson reads Shelley's description of the Caucasus, along with Alpine verses in the likes of Byron's *Manfred* and Wordsworth's *Prelude*, as invested in the idea of 'grand Nature', landscapes that shatter old artistic ideals of 'pattern, regularity, symmetry, restraint, proportion' and instead replace them with 'diversity, variety, irregularity, […] indefiniteness and vastness'.[8]

Conversely, mountains in premodern literatures are characterised as hostile and dangerous spaces, landscapes of trial and necessary obstacles to overcome in the course of travel. Medieval mountain descriptions, in particular, are seldom considered as anything more than incidental background features of a work, serving as part of a broader metaphorical conceit. Nicolson argues that with few exceptions (she identifies *Beowulf* and *Sir Gawain and the Green Knight* as worthy of special mention when it comes to detailed descriptions of wilderness), 'the dominant tendency of medieval literature was toward abstraction and moralisation, so far as most nature imagery was concerned'.[9] In Nicolson's view, the emphasis that medieval and renaissance authors placed on allegory was so overwhelming that even as late as the seventeenth century, realistic descriptions of mountains were entirely overshadowed by what she describes as 'no more than a series of conventional stereotypes' that were at best unimaginative and at worst designed to repulse and induce fear.[10]

Nicolson's work has had a significant impact on our sense of the division between premodern and modern attitudes toward mountain landscapes. Bainbridge, for instance, calls *Mountain Gloom and Mountain Glory* the 'major study of the change in the aesthetic response to mountains'; Dawn Hollis, writing in 2019, observes that Nicolson's sixty-year-old monograph continues to be cited across academic disciplines from landscape history to the philosophy of aesthetics, to literary studies and works on mountaineering.[11] This influence has also

---

7 Percy Bysshe Shelley, *Prometheus Unbound: A Lyrical Drama in Four Acts, With Other Poems* (Cambridge, 2013), II.iii (78).
8 Nicolson, *Mountain Gloom*, 12, 16.
9 Ibid., 47.
10 Ibid., 50.
11 Bainbridge, *Mountaineering and British Romanticism*, 1; Dawn Hollis, '*Mountain Gloom and Mountain Glory*: The Genealogy of an Idea', *ISLE* 26.4 (2019), 1038–61 (1038).

penetrated the popular imagination. One of the more commonly cited examples is Robert MacFarlane's history of mountaineering, *Mountains of the Mind*, a work that identifies premodern mountains as 'aesthetically repellent', 'dangerous places to be' and 'the habitat of the supernatural and the hostile'.[12] However, MacFarlane's popularity perhaps places him unfairly in the spotlight, as this tendency to emphasise the fear that mountains provoke in premodern civilisations is a strikingly standard feature of contemporary nature writing and landscape history. Simon Ingram's *Between the Sunset and the Sea*, an account of the author's experience of summiting sixteen mountains across England, Scotland and Wales, argues that 'those early people who settled beside mountains didn't see them as objectives, or assets; they feared them'.[13] Similarly, Stephen O'Shea begins *The Alps*, his human history of the European mountain range, as follows: 'MOUNTAINS WERE FEARED. Dragons and ogres prowled their summits. They rudely got in the way of travel to important places, like Rome. They were God's punishment for man's sinfulness. They were useless.'[14]

Scholarship on the medieval environment has developed significantly from the late twentieth century alongside (if perhaps slightly behind) a broader interest in environmental and ecological humanities.[15] However, it is only quite recently that work relating to the study of premodern and early modern mountains has begun to challenge the widely held belief that the eighteenth century marks a clear dividing line in the way that authors, artists and poets defined and conceptualised these landscapes. The most notable English-language contribution to

12 Robert MacFarlane, *Mountains of the Mind: A History of a Fascination* (London, 2003), 15. See Bainbridge, *Mountaineering and British Romanticism*, 10–11; Hollis, 'Mountain Gloom', 1056, n. 5.
13 Simon Ingram, *Between the Sunset and the Sea: A View of 16 British Mountains* (London, 2015), 55.
14 Stephen O'Shea, *The Alps: A Human History from Hannibal to Heidi and Beyond* (London, 2017), 6–7.
15 See, for example, Derek Pearsall and Elizabeth Salter, *Landscapes and Seasons of the Medieval World* (London, 1973); *The Medieval World of Nature: A Book of Essays*, ed. Joyce E. Salisbury (New York, 1993); Rebecca Douglass, 'Ecocriticism and Middle English Literature', *Studies in Medievalism* 10 (1998), 136–63; Sarah Stanbury, 'EcoChaucer: Green Ethics and Medieval Nature', *Chaucer Review* 39 (2004), 1–16; Gillian Rudd, *Greenery: Ecocritical Readings of Late Medieval English Literature* (Manchester, 2007); John Aberth, *An Environmental History of the Middle Ages: The Crucible of Nature* (London, 2013); Richard Hoffman, *An Environmental History of Medieval Europe* (Cambridge, 2014).

the field so far is Dawn Hollis and Jason König's *Mountain Dialogues from Antiquity to Modernity*, which argues that the 'gloom-glory model leads to a vastly oversimplified image of premodern mountain engagement, and to a systematic failure to understand what we can gain by exposing texts from different centuries to the same questions within a comparative framework'.[16] The collection helps to identify the complex interweaving of attitudes towards mountain landscapes from Antiquity, through the Middle Ages, and into the Early Modern period and beyond, drawing attention to the intersections between real and imagined mountains, to attempts by premodern authors to define mountain landscapes and, in turn, to the use of mountain landscapes in literature to navigate human concerns and values. For Hollis and König, the problem of the 'continuing tendency to think in terms of a sharp dichotomy between premodern and modern responses' is twofold: first, it underestimates the similarities that exist between modern and premodern responses to mountains; and second, it undervalues the differences that are found in earlier works.[17] This seemingly paradoxical statement is, they argue, part of the point. By downplaying the role of mountains in premodern literatures through constant reference to their devalued status in relation to later approaches to mountain writing, we limit our sense of the importance and complexity of these landscapes for premodern commentators. As evidence of this, Hollis and König cite Petrarch's 'Letter from Mont Ventoux', one of the most frequently cited examples of medieval mountain literature. The famous account of the poet's ascent of the Provençal mountain on 26 April 1336 appears as part of his *Epistolae familiares* (compiled in the late 1350s) and has been used to identify Petrarch as a man ahead of his time: a medieval

---

16 *Mountain Dialogues from Antiquity to Modernity*, ed. Dawn Hollis and Jason König (London, 2021), 3–4. See also *Heights of Reflection: Mountains in the German Imagination from the Middle Ages to the Twenty-First Century*, ed. Sean Ireton and Caroline Schaumann (Rochester, 2012); William M. Barton, *Mountain Aesthetics in Early Modern Latin Literature* (London, 2016); V. della Dora, *Mountain: Nature and Culture* (London, 2016). Scholarship in English is a little behind work from the continent (particularly France) on this topic. See *La montagne dans le texte medieval: entre mythe et réalité*, ed. C. Thomasset and D. James-Raoul (Paris, 2000); *Montagnes médiévales: XXIV congrès de la SHMES*, ed. Société des historiens médiévistes de l'Enseignement supérieur public (Chambért, 23–5 mai 2003) (Paris, 2004); N. Carrier and F. Mouthon, *Les communautés montagnardes au Moyen Age* (Rennes, 2011).
17 Hollis and König, *Mountain Dialogues*, 4–5.

poet with modern, humanist sensibilities.[18] However, as Hollis and König suggest, Petrarch's engagement with mountain landscapes is not unique, as has often been suggested, and the tendency among critics to single out this work as an early exemplar of an environmental humanist outlook comes in large part from the surface similarities that the letter shares with modern mountain literatures, rather than its function as a medieval Christian allegory concerning man's relationship to the Divine. Petrarch's ascent of Mont Ventoux is a key source in relation to our understanding of medieval attitudes toward mountain landscapes (one that will be returned to later in this essay), but we also need to be able to consider this work in the context of the broader traditions of mountain writing that emerge throughout the Middle Ages in order to fully appreciate the multivalent quality of these settings for medieval authors and audiences.

Mountains, broadly defined, appear regularly in medieval literatures related to the Matter of Britain – the history and legends associated with Arthur and his knights – and in the folkloric and geo-cultural traditions that proliferate across Britain and the continent. Even the earliest literary sources to mention Arthur associate him with mountains and hills. In Nennius' ninth-century *Historia Brittonum*, the first text to identify Arthur as an historical (or at least pseudo-historical) figure, he single-handedly fells 960 men in a charge on Mount Badon, the culminating achievement in a series of twelve victories against the Saxons.[19] Geoffrey of Monmouth's *De Gestis Britonum*, the first detailed account of Arthur's life, likewise features passages that link Arthur to mountainous or hilly terrain, including Arthur's charge against a Saxon army encamped on a summit near Bath (derived from Nennius) and his encounter with a giant on Mont-Saint-Michel (the earliest surviving source for this story).[20] In Thomas Malory's *Le Morte D'Arthur*, and in many other Arthurian romances, mountains are identified as landscapes of trial or otherworldly spectacle for the knightly protagonists who ascend them.[21]

18 For a discussion of this, see Peter H. Hansen, *The Summits of Modern Man: Mountaineering After the Enlightenment* (Cambridge MA, 2013), 12–7.
19 Nennius, *History of the Britons (Historia Brittonum)*, trans. J. A. Giles (Cambridge, Ontario, 2000), 23.
20 For the connection between Badon and Bath in Geoffrey's *De Gestis*, see Merlin's prophecy to Vortigern: Geoffrey of Monmouth, *The History of the Kings of Britain*, ed. Michael D. Reeve, trans. Neil Wright (Woodbridge, 2007), *Prophetiae*, 143–4.
21 See, for instance, the 'fynde' that Perceval encounters on a 'wylde mounteyne'

And in the context of Arthur's relationship to the landscapes of Britain and Europe, there are multiple examples of his folkloric connection to real-world locations, including Arthur's Seat in Edinburgh, Pen-y-Fan in the Bannau Brycheiniog (Brecon Beacons), Yr Wyddfa (Snowdon) in North Wales, and even Mount Etna in Sicily.[22]

The intention of this essay is to add nuance to our understanding of medieval mountain literature in such a way as to reframe Nicolson's claim that premodern mountains are 'no more than a series of conventional stereotypes'. In many ways, this will involve extending and complicating what Nicolson has to say, moving the argument away from an either/or debate to one where different interpretations of the value of mountain landscapes can exist side by side. For instance, she suggests that medieval and early modern mountain literatures consistently draw on one of two clichés: mountains and hills may serve an allegorical function linked to virtue, truth, fortune, or learning; or hilltops may be associated, through a Christian lens, with pride and ambition in contrast to the humble setting of the valley.[23] These conceits are present in the Alliterative *Morte*, both in relation to mountains as sites associated with

---

during the quest for the Sankgreal: Thomas Malory, *Le Morte Darthur, or, The hoole book of Kyng Arthur and of his noble knyghtes of the Rounde Table: Authoritative Text, Sources and Backgrounds, Criticism*, ed. Stephen H. A. Shepherd (London, 2004), 525–5. For further examples, see Guillaume le Clerc, *The Romance of Fergus*, ed. Wilson Frescoln (Philadelphia PA, 1983), 2019–264; *Melion*, in *French Arthurian Literature IV: Eleven Old French Narrative Lays*, ed. Glyn S. Burgess and Leslie C. Brook (Cambridge, 2007), 436–66; and *The Wars of Alexander*, ed. Hoyt N. Duggan and Thorlac Turville-Petre, EETS s.s. 10 (Oxford, 1989), 4842–5032.

22   Arthur's connection to the volcanic outcrop in the centre of Edinburgh is well known. For reference, see Mary Bateman, *Local Place and the Arthurian Tradition in England and Wales, 1400–1700* (Cambridge, 2023), 129, 263. For Pen-y-Fan, see Rebecca Thomas, 'Kaerarthur, Cathedra Arthuri: Enwau Hanesyddol Pen y Fan', *Studia Celtica* 57.1 (2023), 1–14. Arthur's connection to Snowdon is expressed through its Welsh name, Yr Wyddfa: identified in Welsh folklore as the tomb of the giant Rhitta Gawr who was slain by Arthur on the mountain's summit: James MacKillop, *A Dictionary of Celtic Mythology* (Oxford, 1998), 372. For Arthur's connection to Mount Etna (identified as a possible site of Arthur's tomb by Gervase of Tilbury), see Roger Sherman Loomis, *Wales and the Arthurian Legend* (Cardiff, 1956), 69–71.

23   Nicolson, *Mountain Gloom*, 50–2. The latter derives from Isaiah 40.4: 'Every valley shall be raised up, every mountain and hill made low.'

vision and forethought and (simultaneously) in terms of their figurative embodiment of Arthur's rise and fall.

Of particular note is the connection that Nicolson establishes between mountain tops and the allegorical figure of Fortune.[24] In doing so, she is drawing on Howard Rollin Patch's *The Goddess Fortuna in Medieval Literature*, which identifies a high mountain as the traditional setting for Fortune's home. This connection can be traced back to Boethius' *De consolatione philosophiae*, and appears across the Middle Ages in works that include Alanus de Insulis' *Anticlaudianus* (the primary source for medieval adaptations of this allegory), the *Roman de la Rose* and Lydgate's *Disguising at London*.[25] Arthur's dream of the Wheel of Fortune in the Alliterative *Morte Arthure*, a sequence that appears soon after his crossing of the St Gotthard pass as he travels across Italy toward Rome, is an integral feature of the poem's broader thematic and ideological function.[26] The *Morte*-poet's familiarity with the connection between Fortune and mountains is briefly highlighted in the description of the landscape that forms the backdrop for the dream. Arthur passes through a forested valley filled with wild and dangerous animals before reaching a beautiful meadow 'with mountaines enclosed' (3238) from which Fortune herself seems to appear: 'Then descendes in the dale, down fro the cloudes, / A duchess dereworthily dight in diapered weedes (richly dressed in patterned clothes)' (3250–1). In the dream, Arthur observes the Wheel of Fortune with eight figures clinging to its circumference, six descending and two ascending (3270–337).[27] Fortune lifts him onto a silver chair situated at the wheel's highest point, identifying herself as the source of his prosperity in war (3342), but as midday arrives her

---

24   Ibid, 51.
25   Howard Rollin Patch, *The Goddess Fortuna in Medieval Literature* (Cambridge MA, 1927), 123–9. See also Stanley Leman Galpin, 'Fortune's Wheel in the Roman de la Rose', *PMLA* 24 (1909), 332–42.
26   See Larry D. Benson, 'The Alliterative *Morte Arthure* and Medieval Tragedy', *Tennessee Studies in Literature* 11 (1966), 75–87; Mary Hamel, 'The Dream of a King: The Alliterative *Morte Arthure* and Dante', *Chaucer Review* 14 (1980), 298–312; Anke Janssen, 'The Dream of the Wheel of Fortune', in *The Alliterative Morte Arthure: A Reassessment of the Poem*, ed. Karl Heinz Göller (Cambridge, 1981), 140–52.
27   The *Morte*-poet links the traditional image of the Wheel of Fortune (derived from Boethius) to the popular medieval description of the Nine Worthies, a combination that appears to be unique to the poem: see Hamel, *Morte Arthure*, 43.

temperament changes and she 'whirles the wheel', crushing Arthur beneath it (3389–91). Here, the *Morte*-poet associates height with power followed by an inevitable decline in three distinct ways: through the image of the wheel itself; through the shift in Fortune's behaviour at noon, and in relation to the mountain setting which, in the context of Arthur's crossing of the St Gotthard pass a little earlier in the poem, establishes a link between his campaign in Europe and the allegory of the dream. The mountains that appear in this dream sequence are a background feature of the scene, but when considered in the context of their relationship to Fortune and her wheel, they play a part in linking the *Morte*'s moral message to a distinctly Boethian warning about the perils of ambition. In Book II (poem four) of the *Consolation*, Boethius writes:

> The prudent, steady man who wants a lasting place, immune from blasting winds and dangerous waves, should avoid high mountain peaks and the shore's shifting sands. For the mountain tops are lashed by terrifying gale-winds; and the loose sand on the beach will not bear his weight. Leave then the dangerous places of delight, and make your home safely on the low rocks. Though the wind trouble the sea with threats of destruction, you will live a serene life, happy for having built a strong house in the quiet valley, and laughing at the wrath of the elements.[28]

For Boethius, those who seek the windswept heights of mountaintops are destined to fall. Arthur, in the course of the Alliterative *Morte*, scales both Mont-Saint-Michel and the St Gotthard pass in pursuit of his goals, but in doing so he is also setting himself up for the inevitable decline that comes as a result of achieving these heights. As the example of the mountain setting in the Dream of Fortune demonstrates, the Alliterative *Morte* draws heavily on the kinds of convention that Nicolson describes as unimaginative, but these allegorical motifs are an integral part of the hermeneutic process for the reader, particularly, as we shall come to see, because this brief description represents just one of many examples of mountain landscapes serving to define Arthur's relationship to power.

A reliance on convention does not preclude a rich and detailed engagement with mountain landscapes. This has been demonstrated, for instance, by Marianne Vos in relation to the mountains that feature in *Le Chanson de Roland*. As Vos argues, mountains are not a dominant motif within the poem in the way that betrayal, heroic conquest or references

---

28 Boethius, *The Consolation of Philosophy: Authoritative Text, Contexts, Criticism*, ed. Douglas C. Langston (London, 2010), 24.

to 'sweet France' are, but through an examination of the geographical and topological features of the poem, she suggests that images of mountains influence the broader meaning of *Roland* in three distinct ways: through their overarching role as a setting for the events of the poem; in relation to the poet's presentation of the high-altitude fortress of Zaragosa; and encoded in the 'Munjoi (Mount Joy)' battle cry used by the French.[29] For Vos, the mountains that feature in *Roland* represent real-world locations, but they also serve to historicise and allegorise the poem, particularly in the way that descriptions of the Battle of Roncevaux Pass interact and intersect with the mountains of Scripture, and with the text's broader exploration of the human condition.

The meaning is rich and dense, never only literal or allegorical. The mountain *is*; it is not *like* anything else. It is concretely itself and something other. The landscape is conceived of in such a way that it is at once Spain, the land of the Psalms and that of Israel. In addition, it is not only *the same as*, but it *is* the human condition struggling to emerge from deep despair.[30]

Drawing on the work of Albert Cook, Vos argues that the mountains of the *Chanson de Roland* constitute a 'visible background to the action' that nonetheless encapsulates 'une expression littérale et immédiate du combat (a literal and immediate expression of the battle)'.[31] The poet's understanding of the historical, geographical and geo-political realities of the Pyrenees intersects with biblical and allegorical interpretations of mountain landscapes in a way that enhances the meaning of the poem.

Likewise, the mountain landscapes that appear in the Alliterative *Morte Arthure* function as more than just metaphorical constructs

---

29 Marianne Cramer Vos, 'Le paysage montagneux dans l'épopée, Le chanson de Roland', in *Ce nous dist li escris... che est la vérité: Études de littérature médiévale offertes à André Moisan par ses collègues et amis*, ed. Miren Lacassagne (Aix-en-Provence, 2000), 56–64 (57).

30 Vos, 'Le paysage montagneux', 61: 'La signification en est riche et dense, jamais seulement littérale ou allégorique. La montagne *est*; elle n'est pas *comme* quelque chose d'autre. Elle est concrètement elle-même et autre chose. Le paysage est conçu d'une façon telle qu'il est à la fois l'Espagne, le terrain des Psaumes et celui d'Israël. De plus, il n'est pas seulement *pareil à*, mais il *est* la condition humaine qui lutte pour émerger d'un profond désespoir' (author's italics).

31 Ibid., 58; Albert Cook, *The Classic Line: A Study in Epic Poetry* (Bloomington IN, 1966), 40.

that serve to mirror the protagonist's growth and decline. The text's relationship to these landscapes is dialectical in nature, emphasising an interplay between reality and allegory. While many of the clichés that govern the appearance and function of mountains in medieval literature are present in the Alliterative *Morte*, this is also a text that is capable of recognising the sensorial, environmental and geo-political realities of these spaces. For the reader, the introspective moral focus that governs Arthur's mountain encounters interacts with the realities of these settings in such a way as to elevate their role in shaping the poem's discursive approach to kingship.[32] Mountains, by their very nature, are closely connected to the notion of Arthur's rise and fall, but their function as evocative landscapes that help to chart the progress of Arthur's campaign both through geographical space and along a moral continuum is worthy of closer examination.

Mont-Saint-Michel and the 'Mountain Gloom' Topos

There is no escaping the tendency of medieval English literature to identify mountains as dangerous and inhospitable spaces. They are, to use a term familiar to medieval authors and audiences, desert landscapes: wild, uncultivated spaces that exist beyond the bounds of human society.[33] As Rebecca Douglass observes, the term 'desert' in Middle English might just as easily apply to a forest as to a barren and arid landscape, and has more to do with its symbolic status as a place 'void of human culture', somewhere that is ultimately 'useless', than with its ecological make-up.[34] Lord Bertilak's isolated castle 'Hautdesert' (2445) in *Sir Gawain and the Green Knight* is one example of this

---

[32] Arthur's comprehension of the significance of these mountain ascents is not emphasised, but he lacks the foreknowledge of his fate that both author and audience possess. Even after the Dream of Fortune and the revelation of Mordred's betrayal, his focus is on revenge and the eradication of his enemy (3559, 4006, 4296-8, 4320-3) rather than moral reflection.

[33] MED *desert n* 1a.

[34] Rebecca Douglass, 'Ecocriticism and Middle English Literature', *Studies in Medievalism* 10 (1998), 136-63 (149-50). This definition is not exclusive to archaic forms of English. Janice Hewlett Koelb argues that the Greek ὄρος encompasses more than the English 'mountain', and contains within it the idea that such spaces are heights beyond the bounds of civilisation. As such the Egyptian desert can be considered an ὄρος that is distinguished by its separation from the cultivated lower Nile valley: Koelb, 'Erudite Retreat: Jerome and Francis in the

definition, a setting that Gawain comes to after passing 'Bi a mounte', 'Into a forest ful dep, þat ferly watz wylde' with 'Hiȝe hillez on vche a halue' (740–2).[35] Similarly, *Genesis and Exodus* recognises the close link between mountains and desert in the description of Moses' journey to Mount Sinai: 'He bar his gerde (rod) forth in is hond / And nam a weie bi deserd lond; / To mount synai forth he nam' (2581–3).[36] And in John Trevisa's fourteenth-century translation of Bartholomaeus Anglicus' *De Proprietatibus Rerum*, he records that 'Places of wodes and of mounteyns þat ben nouȝt ysowe ben yclepid desertes'.[37]

In the Alliterative *Morte Arthure*, mountains are identified as hostile and dangerous landscapes from the outset. The poem begins at Christmas with the arrival of a senator of Rome in Arthur's court, who summons Arthur to pay tribute to the Emperor Lucius. Arthur instead declares war, and the senator and his knights make all haste to leave Arthur's lands, fearing for their wellbeing if they linger (484). The poet spends relatively little time describing their journey back to Rome, but one interesting detail that does appear here is a brief reference to their crossing of the Alps via the St Gotthard pass, a route that is identified as 'full grevous' (496). This is the first of many references to this particular pass, which features in the poem as one of the primary means of crossing from central Europe to the Italian peninsula, and thus also as one of the key strategic obstacles that Arthur must overcome if he is to conquer Rome.[38] When Lucius is advised to look to his borders to prepare for

---

Mountains', in *Mountain Dialogues from Antiquity to Modernity*, ed. Hollis and König, 109–30 (109).

35 *Sir Gawain and the Green Knight*, ed. J. R. R. Tolkien and E. V. Gordon, rev. Norman Davis, 2nd edn (Oxford, 1967).

36 *The Middle English Genesis and Exodus re-edited from MS CCCC444 with introduction, notes and glossary*, ed. Olaf Arngart (Lund, 1968).

37 *On the Properties of Things: John Trevisa's Translation of Bartholomæus Anglicus De Propietatibus Rerum. A Critical Text*, ed. M. C. Seymour et al., 3 vols (Oxford, 1975), 2:vix.721.

38 The question of why the Gotthard pass features so prominently in the Alliterative *Morte* is an intriguing one. No substantive study of this particular feature of the poem has been carried out since George B. Parks' 'King Arthur and the Roads to Rome', *JEGP* 45.2 (1946), 164–70. Parks bases much of his reasoning on the now-outdated assumption of a mid-century composition for the *Morte*, but his suggestion that the poem's familiarity with key sites between St Gotthard and Rome may imply a personal connection to pilgrimage (either by the author or an informant) is nonetheless interesting. The earliest evidence of a British traveller crossing the Gotthard pass is Adam of Usk, who describes

Arthur's imminent invasion, he declares that he will assemble 'Many giaunt of Gene (Genoa)' and 'jousters full good' to 'meet him in the mountes' (558–9):

> There shall upon Goddard   a garret be rered   *Mt. Goddard watchtower*
> That shall be garnisht and keeped   with good men of armes,
> And a becon aboven to brin   when them likes,
> That none enmy with host   shall enter the mountes.
> There shall on Mount Bernard   be belded another,
> Busked with bannerettes   and bachelers noble.
> (561–6)

The building and manning of fortifications on both the Gotthard and Bernard passes is the first indication of the defensive role that mountain landscapes play within the poem, but there is also an extent to which these landscapes are subject to a process of supernatural and foreign othering.[39] The reference to giants from 'Gene' guarding the mountain passes serves to foreshadow the appearance of the giant of Mont-Saint-Michel, who is likewise identified as originating from Genoa. However, the presence of Genoese giants in Lucius' ranks, both here and during the final battle between Lucius and Arthur (2087, 2111, 2133), also enhances the foreign and otherworldly qualities of Lucius' army. Foreignness is a trait that the poet, building on his ultimate source in Geoffrey of Monmouth's *De Gestis*, clearly associated with Lucius, as demonstrated by the letters that Lucius sends requesting military support from rulers of the Near East, Middle East, Africa and Asia (569–608).[40] The poet identifies 'este marches (eastern countries)' (576) – including Arabia, Egypt, Persia and Syria – and mythical locations – 'The flowr of the fair

---

his passage in March of 1402 (an early time of year to be making the crossing) in the following terms: 'I was drawn in an ox-wagon half dead with cold and with mine eyes blindfolded lest I should see the dangers of the pass': *Adam of Usk's Chronicle*, trans. Sir E. M. Thompson, K. C. B., ed. M. S. F. Johnston (Malvern, 2023), 146.

39 The supernatural and foreign other are not, of course, mutually exclusive in medieval thought, and can be seen in multiple examples of geographically distanced monstrous races (skiapods, blemmya), associated with Africa and the East. See John Block Friedman, *The Monstrous Races in Medieval Art and Thought* (Syracuse NY, 2000); and Stephen T. Asma, *On Monsters* (Oxford, 2009).

40 The description matches, with some variation in detail, that found in Geoffrey's *De Gestis*, X.1–11.

folk of Amazonnes lands' (583) – as those willing to side with Lucius in his war against Arthur's distinctly Western European empire (25–46). Lucius' mountain garrisons, then, are defended not just by giants but by the 'jousters' and 'good men of armes' of foreign lands. From the outset, mountains are identified in relation to their distance from the centralised society of Arthur's court and their potential as dangerous obstacles for Arthur to overcome.

A similar process of othering can be identified in relation to Mont-Saint-Michel. Arthur first learns of the giant who inhabits the Mont's summit when his fleet lands at Barfleur on the coast of Normandy. Arthur is approached by a Templar knight who informs him of a 'grete giaunt of Gene, engendered of fendes' (842) who has devoured more than 500 people in and around the Cotentin peninsula. The knight also tells Arthur that the giant has kidnapped the Duchess of Brittany and taken her back to the Mont, where he intends to 'lie by that lady ay whiles her life lastes' (854). More than 500 men pursued the giant, but the giant's ascent of the Mont signals the point at which the pursuit is given up as hopeless:

We followed o ferrome	mo than five hundredth	*from afar*
Of bernes and of burges	and bachelers noble,	
But he covered the crag;	sho cried so loud	
The care of that creature	cover shall I never.	*recover*
	(855–8)	

It is clear that the poet of the Alliterative *Morte* has no personal knowledge of the landscape surrounding Mont-Saint-Michel, nor is he particularly interested in providing accurate topographical descriptions of the area. This is demonstrated most obviously by the Templar knight, who achieves the impossible by pointing to 'yon forland (the Mont)' (879) from the king's camp at Barfleur, a distance of more than seventy miles spanning the full length of the Cotentin peninsula. Rather, the poet's interest is in juxtaposing the hostile landscape of the Mont with the relative safety of the lowlands that surround it. Arthur, distraught at the news of the captured Duchess, decides to act quickly and sets off that very evening for Mont-Saint-Michel with two accompanying knights, Sir Kay and Sir Bedivere. Here, the poet takes a moment to describe the landscape that Arthur and his knights pass through on their way to the Mont:

> Then they rode by that river   that runned so swithe,
> There the rindes over-reches   with real boughes;   *trees; stately*
> The roe and the reindeer   reckless there runnen,
> In ranes and in rosers   to riot themselven;   *bushes; amuse*
> The frithes were flourish   with flowres full many,   *woods*
> With faucons and fesauntes   of ferlich hewes;
> All the fowles there flashes   that flies with winges,
> For there galed the gouk   on greves full loud;   *cuckoo; in thickets*
> With alkine gladship   they gladden themselven;
> Of the nightingale notes   the noises was sweet;
> They threped with the throstels   three hundreth at ones!
> That whate swowing of water   and singing of birds,   *swift sound*
> It might salve him of sore   that sound was never!
> (919–31)

The passage serves to pre-empt the poet's description of the Mont. By drawing on recognisable conventions of a *locus amoenus* – flowers, singing birds, running water, life and abundance – the poet establishes a sense of the verdant and bountiful lowland space as desirable.[41] The transition from lowland to highland, and the increased hardship that is implied by this shift, is marked in the final two lines of the passage. The restorative effect that birdsong and flowing water has on Arthur as he moves through this landscape is lamented as a passing pleasure – 'that sound was never (i.e. never again)' – and the passage as a whole speaks to Arthur's apprehension of the trial that is to come and his yearning to remain within the more hospitable lowland setting.

Accordingly, the top of the Mont is identified as a desolate space associated with grief and death. As is fairly typical for mountains in Middle English literature, there are no detailed descriptions of the Mont's landscape to compare with Arthur's journey through the lowlands. This presents an obvious problem when attempting to identify the value of these landscapes for medieval authors and audiences, but what the passage lacks in topographical and ecological detail it makes up for in other ways. For instance, Arthur's first encounter on the summit is with a grieving widow found weeping over a freshly dug grave, who warns him of the threat posed by the giant:

---

41 This juxtaposition of highland and lowland is identified, although not examined in detail, in Cohen's *Of Giants*, 154. For more on the conventions of the *locus amoenus* in medieval art and literature, see Howard Rollin Patch, *The Other World* (Cambridge MA, 1950), 134–74.

> A wery woful widow   wringand her handes,
> And gretand on a grave   grisly teres,   *weeping*
> New merked on molde,   senn mid-day it seemed.   *dug in the earth*
> He salued that sorrowful   with sittand wordes
> And fraines after the fend   fairly thereafter.   *asks*
> Then this woful wife   unwinly him greetes,   *unhappily*
> Coverd up on her knees   and clapped her handes,
> Said: 'Careful, careman,   thou carpes too loud!   *man*
> May yon warlaw wite,   he warrays us all!   *warlock; attacks*
>   (949–57)

Of particular note is the poet's interest in sound, or rather the lack of it. While the lowland landscape is linked to birdsong and running water, the widow is quick to rebuke Arthur for making too much noise on the summit lest the warlock (giant) finds them and attacks. The need for silence serves as a strikingly oppressive quality of the Mont, and helps to illustrate the disparity between spaces in a way that singles Arthur out as an intruder within this landscape. As the widow notes, 'Weryd worth the wight ay that thee thy wit reved, / That mas thee to waife here in these wild lakes! (Curse the man who stole your wits from you to make you wander here in these wild lakes!)' (958–9). The setting is far removed from the safety of Arthur's court, or even from his army camped close by at Barfleur. The widow's reference to 'wild lakes', likely an allusion to the natural springs that are identified as flowing from the Mont's summit (see lines 881, 946), draws our attention to landscape in a way that further emphasises the remoteness of the setting.[42] In this moment, the relatively small promontory of Mont-Saint-Michel becomes an expansive mountain range – capable, it seems, of containing large bodies of water – and Arthur's attempt to locate the giant is briefly envisaged as a quest that extends over a wide landscape made up of challenging terrain.

The grave, we discover, is for the Duchess of Brittany, whom Arthur is too late to rescue. On top of this, the widow's estimation of Arthur's

---

42   The description brings to mind Gerald of Wales' account of the lakes found in Eryri (Snowdonia), North Wales. He writes of two lakes in particular, situated at the very top of the range: 'One has a floating island, which moves about and is often driven to the opposite side by the force of the winds'; the second 'abounds in three different kinds of fish, eels, trout and perch; all of them have only one eye'. Gerald of Wales, *The Journey Through Wales and The Description of Wales*, trans. Lewis Thorpe (London, 1978), 194–5.

ability to defeat the giant is doubtful – 'Such six were too simple to semble with him one (Six such as yourself would be insufficient to attack him alone)' (966) – and this sense of futility is further exaggerated when the poet comes to describe the giant's appearance. He is 'the foulsomest freke (foulest man) that formed was ever', with 'grisly tuskes', a face and forehead like the 'fell of a frosk (skin of a frog)', a hide like a 'hound-fish (i.e. small shark or dogfish)', a hooked nose like a hawk's, 'Bull-necked', and 'Brok-brested as a brawn (spotted like a boar's breast)' (1061–93). His monstrous appearance is only further compounded by his intimidating size. The poet describes him as 'five fadom long' (1103): thirty-foot high or roughly equivalent to a three-storey building. Here, we are dealing with well-established conventions of knightly combat with giants. In the context of the *nanus contra gigantum* topos, giants are corporeal beings, aggressive combatants and figures of supernatural strength and size who provide extreme tests of a hero's martial ability.[43] Giants are also linked to an exploration of selfhood and othering by virtue of their uncanny appearance and behaviour. They are, as Jeffrey Cohen notes, creatures that lurk on the 'threshold of the hall', both recognisable and alien at the same time.[44] The fearsome and terrible appearance of the giant serves primarily to enlarge the glory and status of the protagonist whose destiny it is to defeat him. At the same time, the giant's aggressive, martial character and his mirroring, particularly in works of romance, of many of the trappings and customs of knightly culture, establishes him as a rite of passage and links his defeat to a 'political, sexual, social coming of age' for the young knightly protagonist.[45]

What is particularly striking about the *Morte*-poet's take on the giant of Mont-Saint-Michel is the extent to which the giant is presented as a grotesque amalgamation of various animals that, while familiar to the lands and coastlines of Britain and France during the fourteenth century, represent a diverse range of species from an equally diverse range of ecological biomes. The clearest example of this is lines 1091–3, where the

---

43   Cohen, *Of Giants*, 66.
44   Ibid., 28. As Kateryna Schray has argued, the natural rock formation of Mont-Saint-Michel serves to parallel the description of the 'Giauntes Towr' (244) where Arthur's war council takes place at the beginning of the poem, emphasising the giant's function as a perversion of Arthur's monarchical power and authority: Kateryna A. Rudnytzky Schray, 'The Plot in Miniature: Arthur's Battle on Mont St Michel in the Alliterative *Morte Arthure*', *Studies in Philology* 101 (2004), 1–19 (3).
45   Cohen, *Of Giants*, 66.

poet shifts our attention from the giant's fat, dolphin-like body to the lips on his face that seem to quiver and twist like the head of a wolf:

> Grassed as a mere-swine   with carkes full huge
> And all faltered the flesh   in his foul lippes,
> Ilke wrethe as a wolf-heved   it wrath out at ones!

There is something truly bizarre and horrific about the mixture of terrestrial and marine animals that contribute to the giant's physiology, particularly regarding the way that such references work to blur the boundary between land and sea.[46] The description of the giant calls attention to the liminal qualities of the tidal island on which he resides. The effect is to associate the Mont with uncertainty, a point that is further reinforced by the poet's repeated acknowledgement that this is also a mountainous space. Indeed, the Mont is frequently identified in terms that seem to imply a much higher promontory than exists in reality. There are multiple references to the giant's refuge as a 'mount' (937), a 'mountain' (853) or even plural 'mountes' (873, 965).[47] During Arthur's ascent of the Mont, the poet describes its size as 'full high' (940). This is fairly commonplace language – the phrase is used again just four lines later to mark the height of the two fires that are blazing on the summit – but the description is clearly intended to emphasise the difficulty of Arthur's climb up the Mont's steep 'cloughes (cliffs)'. Likewise, the shift in temperature, marked by the 'cold wind' on the Mont's summit as well as earlier references to a 'cold well' that flows from the 'crest of the crag' (881), serves as a sensory indication of the transition from lowland to highland.[48] This, coupled with descriptions that emphasise the relative silence of the Mont and the 'wild lakes' on its

---

46 For John Finlayson, the description of the giant has its closest parallels in depictions of demons in medieval art. In this respect, the giant represents more than just a romance antagonist, instead becoming an enemy to Christendom itself: Finlayson, 'Arthur and the Giant of Saint Michael's Mount', *Medium Aevum* 33.2 (1964), 112–20.

47 The references to multiple mountains comes from the Alliterative *Morte*'s sources, which identify a second hilltop near Mont-Saint-Michel, the slightly-smaller Tombelaine. See Geoffrey of Monmouth, *The History of the Kings of Britain*, X.43–5; *Le Roman de Brut de Wace*, ed. Ivor Arnold, 2 vols (Paris, 1940), 11333–44; Laȝamon, *Brut*, ed. G. L. Brook and R. F. Leslie, EETS o.s. 277 (Oxford, 1978), 12844–5.

48 Thomas Malory draws directly on the Alliterative *Morte* for his own description of Arthur's ascent of the Mont: 'Than the Kynge yode up to the creste

summit, aids in further highlighting the desolate and liminal quality of the landscape and its primary occupant.

In this respect, the Mont's role is comparable to the uncultivated environments that are frequently found in romance narratives. As Gillian Rudd has argued, wilderness in works such as *Sir Orfeo* and *Sir Gawain and the Green Knight* is characterised by its unknowability, but at the same time these spaces can be populated by the kinds of supernatural entities (fairies, the Green Knight) that function as reflections of, and challenges to, the moral and social values of medieval courtly society.[49] Like the forests regularly entered into by questing knights in romance, the Mont blurs the boundary between worlds, destabilising the reader's sense of the established order of the poem which has, up to this point, shown Arthur to be a figure of supreme power and authority.[50] The Mont becomes a landscape of trial in which Arthur must overcome seemingly insurmountable odds in order to demonstrate his right to govern.[51] In the context of the Alliterative *Morte* as a whole, the passage functions as a precursor to Arthur's war with Lucius, establishing the King's credentials as a warrior capable of individual feats of heroism.

It would seem, then, that in many ways the poet's depiction of Mont-Saint-Michel does conform to the 'mountain gloom' model identified by Marjorie Hope Nicolson. The poet draws heavily on the dangerous and inhospitable quality of mountains in order to cultivate a space that is suitably foreboding, thus allowing Arthur's triumph over the giant to shine all the brighter. However, we might tentatively identify a degree of realism intermixed with the poet's engagement with established literary convention in this scene. This is particularly noticeable in the way that Arthur's experience of summiting the Mont is closely tied to sensory stimuli. The cold conditions and reduced noise serve to emphasise the hostility of the landscape, but they also speak to the reality of being at altitude. Arthur's actions on the summit – 'Cast up his umbrere (visor) and keenly he lookes / Caught of the cold wind to comfort himselven'

---

of the cragge, and than he comforted hymself with the colde wynde' (*Le Morte Darthur*, ed. Shepherd, 122).

49 See Gillian Rudd's chapter on 'Wilderness' in *Greenery*. For a discussion of the dramatic shift in audience expectation that is generated by encounters with liminal or otherworldly settings, see Aisling Byrne, *Otherworlds: Fantasy and History in Medieval Literature* (Oxford, 2015), 22.

50 Of particular note is the opening passage of the poem listing Arthur's military conquests (25–46).

51 Finlayson, 'Arthur and the Giant of Saint Michael's Mount', 115.

(942–3) – emphasise his experience of the landscape through vision and touch in a way that feels similarly realistic. Of course, this is not to argue that the Alliterative *Morte*-poet can be heralded, as Petrarch often is, as some kind of proto-mountaineer. It is, after all, only necessary to glance up at snow-capped hills in winter to see such spaces as colder and less habitable than the lowlands that surround them.[52] However, it seems similarly reductive to argue that the author and his audience were only capable of relating to hilly or mountainous terrain through literary topoi, with no recourse to their existence as real-world topographies.[53]

The poet is also elevating the importance of Mont-Saint-Michel to an extent that far exceeds what we find in the Alliterative *Morte*'s sources.[54] While the text does not indulge in lengthy descriptions of the mountain environment, the Mont's role within the context of Arthur's encounter is of far greater significance than in Geoffrey, Wace or Laȝamon. This is apparent in Arthur's defeat of the giant, a moment that the Alliterative *Morte*-poet transforms from a brief battle on the Mont's summit to a dramatic sequence in which both Arthur and the giant tumble down the side of the mountain, locked in combat:

> Yet is that warlaw so wight   he welters him under;   *topples*
> Wrothly they writhen   and wrestle togeders,
> Welters and wallows over within those buskes,   *toss and turn; bushes*
> Tumbelles and turnes fast   and teres their weedes,
> Untenderly fro the top   they tilten togeders,
> Whilom Arthur over   and other while under,
> Fro the heghe of the hill   unto the hard rock,
> They feyne never ere they fall   at the flood marches[.]
>
> (1140–7)

---

52   See, for instance, the opening to Chaucer's *The Clerk's Tale*, which identifies Monte Viso as 'Vesulus the colde': Geoffrey Chaucer, *The Canterbury Tales*, in *The Riverside Chaucer*, ed. Larry D. Benson, 3rd edn (Oxford, 2008), IV.58.
53   Region will of course play a significant role in terms of the level of familiarity that can be assumed here. For the poet of the Alliterative *Morte Arthure*, we can draw attention to the likely provenance of the text in the general region of the North Midlands, where there is some proliferation of hilly and mountainous terrain; while this does not in itself constitute evidence of the poet's familiarity with such landscapes, it is at least interesting to note the correlation. For more on the text's provenance, see Hamal, *Morte Arthure*, 62; Ian Cornelius, *Reconstructing Alliterative Verse: The Pursuit of a Medieval Meter* (Cambridge, 2017), 7.
54   Finlayson, 'Arthur and the Giant of Saint Michael's Mount', 113.

The poet showcases a clear interest in the Mont as a landscape that enhances the tension and dynamism of the encounter through the danger posed by the fall.[55] It is not enough to say that the mountain top functions solely as a conventional (and interchangeable) romance wilderness because, in this instance, gradient plays a key part in the action. This encounter could not play out in the same way if Arthur ventured into a woodland or a cave, or onto an island.

The giant's fall is also figured in metaphorical terms in a way that seems briefly to link him to Arthur. Indeed, when they land at the foot of the Mont, Kay's first reaction is to assume the worst, declaring 'Alas! We are lorn (lost)! My lord is confounded, / Over-fallen with a fend! Us is foul happned!' (1153-4). Kay's grief is quickly passed over when Arthur is revealed to be alive and well, but the conflation of Arthur with the giant at the instance of the giant's fall is a revealing moment, particularly in terms of our foreknowledge of Arthur's own inevitable decline at the poem's conclusion.[56] Mountains, by their very nature, are sites of impermanent occupation, spaces that can only be visited, or 'conquered', with significant effort.[57] Their unsuitability as sites of regular habitation brings us back to Boethius' assertion that the 'prudent, steady man' should 'avoid high mountain peaks', but the familiarity of this idea for medieval authors and audiences is likewise represented in the romance convention of the uncultivated mountain desert, or even in the real-world practice of transhumance that governed the seasonal movement of livestock from lowland to upland pastures throughout the Middle Ages and later.[58] For the poet, Mont-Saint-Michel functions as both literary

---

55 For the battle as it appears in the Alliterative *Morte*'s sources, see: Geoffrey of Monmouth, X.78-95; Wace, 11469-560; Laȝamon 12998-3032. Laȝamon's *Brut* includes a moment where Arthur and the giant run round a tree three times (13008-9), but otherwise they are comparatively static affairs that culminate in Bedivere removing the giant's head on the Mont's summit.

56 As I discuss below, the tumble from the Mont also foreshadows Arthur's crossing of (and descent from) the St Gotthard pass, a moment that is tied to his hubristic desire to conquer all of Lombardy (3108-9).

57 The notion that mountains must be 'conquered' is largely a reflection of the colonial era in which mountaineering as a leisure pursuit took hold, but there is more that could be said about the ubiquity of the connection between mountains and conquest in both medieval and post-medieval literatures. For a detailed discussion of mountain conquest in classical literature, see Part III of Jason König's *The Folds of Olympus: Mountains in Ancient Greek and Roman Culture* (Princeton NJ, 2022).

58 See Eugene Costello, *Transhumance and the Making of Ireland's Uplands,*

convention and allegory, simultaneously providing a landscape of trial and a physical embodiment of the giant's (and subsequently Arthur's) rise and fall, but he is also engaging with mountains as real-world settings. Most notably, the poet acknowledges the topology of highland landscapes, and incorporates this into Arthur's battle by emphasising the heightened challenge to combat that gradient and altitude present.

Furthermore, as Christopher Pipkin has observed, the poet ties together spiritual and secular imagery in the way that he sets up Arthur's battle with the giant, particularly when it comes to the Mont's connection to St Michael.[59] The link between the fictional giant's abode and the real abbey on Mont-Saint-Michel can be traced back to Geoffrey's *De Gestis*, which describes how Mont Tumba, the site of the encounter, was later renamed for the archangel.[60] However, as Pipkin notes, the *Morte*-poet takes this a step further. Arthur himself has an anachronistic knowledge of the connection between the Mont and Saint Michael.[61] We first see this in his stated intention to 'seeken a saint by yon salt stremes, / In Saint Michel mount' (897–8). Pipkin writes that 'to the *AMA* poet and his audience, the place is no longer a diabolical locale that must become a holy mountain one day, but a holy mountain already dedicated to the archangel Michael despite being controlled by

---

1550–1990 (Woodbridge, 2020), 14–17.
59 Christopher Lee Pipkin, 'Monster Relics: The Giant, the Archangel, and Mont-Saint-Michel in the Alliterative *Morte Arthure*', *Arthuriana* 27.1 (2017), 95–113.
60 See Geoffrey of Monmouth, X.33–6; Wace, 11293; and Laȝamon, 12808. The legend linking St Michael to Mount Tumba (tied to the founding of the first chapel on the summit by Bishop Aubert of Avranches) was well known throughout the Middle Ages. Versions can be found in the *South English Legendary*, and in Jacobus de Voragine's *Legenda Aurea*, which survives in 800 manuscripts as well as Italian, French, German, Dutch and English translations. See Richard F. Johnson, *Saint Michael the Archangel in Medieval English Legend* (Woodbridge, 2005), 49–70.
61 The first religious sanctuary on Mont Tumba was not established until the early eighth century, long after the events of the Alliterative *Morte* are meant to have taken place (Johnson, *Saint Michael the Archangel*, 41–5). In the *Morte*, Arthur founds the Church that sits on the Mont's summit (1219). In Geoffrey's *De Gestis*, it is the smaller Mont Tombelaine that is the site of the chapel (X.109). This second promontory was well known for its Marian convent in both Geoffrey's and the *Morte*-poet's time (see Pipkin, 'Monster Relics', 106), but the poet of the Alliterative *Morte* makes no real distinction between the two peaks, effectively conflating them.

an incarnate devil'.⁶² Arthur demonstrates a prophetic familiarity with the Mont's status as a holy site, while also playfully conflating the figures of the giant and the archangel.

This joke is repeated again when Arthur and the giant tumble down the side of the Mont. If Kay's first reaction is concern that Arthur is 'Over-fallen with a fend', then Bedivere's response can be characterised as more light hearted:

> 'Now certes,' says Sir Bedvere,   'it seemes, by my Lord,
> He seekes saintes but selden,   the sorer he grippes,
> That thus clekes this corsaint   out of thir high cliffs,   *drags; holy body*
> To carry forth such a carl   at close him in silver;   *to enclose*
> By Michel, of such a mak   I have much wonder   *fellow*
> That ever our soveraign Lord   suffers him in heven!
> And all saintes be such   that serves our Lord
> I shall never no saint be,   by my fader soul!'
>
> (1162–9)

Bedivere's joke compares the giant's body to the relic bones of a saint, using the comparison as a facetious acknowledgement of the giant's monstrous appearance. However, as Pipkin argues, we need not necessarily treat Bedivere's statement as deliberately subversive or politicised, but rather as evidence that the poet is allowing for an interaction between two narrative systems, those interested in pilgrimages to shrines and those that feature the killing of giants. Drawing on Barbara Newman's *Medieval Crossover* and her 'hermeneutics of both/and', Pipkin draws attention to the way that Bedivere's joke encourages the Alliterative *Morte*'s audience to contemplate the multivalent levels of interpretation available to us in this scene, without necessarily forcing an explanation.⁶³ For Pipkin, the Mont itself plays an important role in allowing for these opposing functions to coexist within a single space:

> The most important 'relic' involved in this account is [...] the mountain called 'Tumba', upon which the abbey of Mont-Saint-Michel was founded. This distinctive and impressive landmass is itself both an island and a mountain, depending on the tides; it is, in other words, a prodigy, and it evokes supernatural associations at once monstrous and holy.⁶⁴

---

62 Pipkin, 'Monster Relics', 99.
63 Ibid., 98–9; Barbara Newman, *Medieval Crossover* (Notre Dame IN, 2013).
64 Pipkin, 'Monster Relics', 104.

Pipkin argues in favour of the Mont's otherworldly and timeless qualities that allow the poet to establish a connection to Arthurian legend, to the founding of the cult of the archangel and to the Mont as real-world site of pilgrimage, in a way that enables all three to exist simultaneously in this one scene.

It is, therefore, the multivalent quality of Mont-Saint-Michel that constitutes its primary value for both author and audience in the Alliterative *Morte Arthure*. There is more going on here than the straightforward transference of an existing setting from earlier chronicle sources, as evidenced by the number of inventive ways that the poet is expanding on these texts to offer a more complex, nuanced, and detailed engagement with the Mont. The hostile nature of the landscape predominates here, but it is also not quite as straightforward as identifying this space as representative of the kinds of interchangeable wilderness settings commonly found in romance. The *Morte*-poet is clearly thinking of Mont-Saint-Michel as a mountain, identified through scale, gradient and Arthur's sensory reaction to the upland environment, and while there is a certain amount of interweaving between literal and figurative elements in the way that this space is presented, this further contributes to a setting that cannot be reduced to a single interpretation based on clichéd literary convention.

'Over mountes so high': Arthur's Rise and Fall

The example of Mont-Saint-Michel relates to a broader trend in the way that mountains operate in the Alliterative *Morte Arthure*, as landscapes that allegorise changes in Arthur's power and authority, but also as spaces that cannot be restricted to a purely metaphorical reading. In the immediate aftermath of Arthur's clash with the giant, his journey through France is marked by the ease with which he and his army are able to traverse the land. The march south is defined by Arthur's 'blithely (joyfully)' departing from Barfleur, his army spread out along 'blithe (bright/calm) stremes' as they make their way through 'a fair champain (country) under chalk hilles' (1223–6). Natural barriers are easily mastered by Arthur's advancing forces as they traverse this landscape: 'The king fraistes a furth (seeks a ford) over the fresh strandes, / Foundes (goes) with his fair folk over as him likes' (1227–8). Arthur's transition from a romance-inflected battle with the giant to the continuation of his European campaign is marked by a renewed emphasis on his supreme regnal authority. He is in control of his surroundings and in harmony with the landscape: a direct contrast to Lucius, whose march north, described by a messenger just a few lines later, is linked to the felling of forests and plundering of the land (1247).

Arthur's battle with Lucius is likewise presented in the context of his mastery of the mountainous terrain that surrounds the city of 'Sessoine'.[65] When Lucius' forces enter the valley, they discover Arthur and his men arrayed across the surrounding landscape, inhibiting any attempt at escape:

> [Arthur] had the citee for-set upon sere halves,   *besieged; many sides*
> Both the cleves and the cliffs with clene men of armes, *narrow valleys*
> The moss and the morass with mountes so high   *moorland*
> With grete multitude of men to mar him in the ways.
> (2012–15)

The 'grete multitude of men' adorning the mountaintops in this passage presents a very different image from that of Arthur's lone ascent of Mont-Saint-Michel, but there are still similarities here in the way that the *Morte*-poet is using mountain landscapes to elevate Arthur's status as king. Within the context of the poem, Arthur's manoeuvre represents a masterstroke in strategic military planning, a point that Lucius himself is forced to concede: 'Here is no way, iwis, ne no wit else, / But fight with our fomen, for flee may we never' (2020–1). The poet places particular emphasis on the narrow valleys, moorlands and high mountains that encircle Sessoine as an explanation for Arthur's dominance over Lucius' forces in this moment.[66] The passage as a whole thus serves to emphasise Arthur's status as a military commander by demonstrating his mastery of a difficult but strategically defensible landscape.[67] The mountains are

---

65 Once again, there is a lack of specificity when it comes to regional geography here. Larry Benson's edition identifies 'Sessoine' as Soissons which is, in reality, situated in a relatively low-lying region of France roughly sixty miles northeast of Paris. This fits with other locations listed in this section of the Alliterative *Morte*, including Paris, Chartres and the province of Champagne, but it represents a departure from the *Morte*'s sources, which locate this part of the narrative closer to Langres, situated further southeast. See Geoffrey of Monmouth, X.235–42; Wace, 12282–6; and Laʒamon, 13648.
66 The passage clearly derives from Laʒamon, who describes dales, downs and hills lined with the helms of Arthur's men, but the emphasis in the *Brut* is on the shining armour and fluttering standards of the stern warriors (13652–7).
67 The strategic value of higher ground is such a universal reality of warfare,

not an obstacle for Arthur to overcome, as Mont-Saint-Michel is, but an asset in service to his cause. In conjunction with the description of Arthur's easy passage through the chalk hills south of Barfleur, this section of the poem functions as a literal expression of Arthur's authority over the land. We might even go so far as to argue that Arthur's encounter with the giant on Mont-Saint-Michel grants him the ability to thrive in mountainous terrain, an experience that he combines with his existing knowledge of military strategy to great effect. Arthur, having survived the Mont, is now more attuned to operating within these highland settings.

However, as the poem progresses, Arthur's relationship to mountains develops in a way that seems to align these landscapes with his increasingly tyrannical approach to power. There has been considerable debate on whether Arthur in the Alliterative *Morte* represents an idealised or a flawed vision of kingship, a question that is closely tied to the poem's presentation of warfare and one that, as Patricia DeMarco recognises, 'has generated diametrically opposed interpretations of the status of violence in the poem'.[68] For DeMarco, the poet's overwhelming interest

---

identified by everyone from Sun Tzu to Obi Wan Kenobi, that it hardly requires mention. However, in using landscape to his advantage, Arthur is adhering to a military tactic outlined in the most commonly cited treatise on warfare in the Middle Ages, Vegetius' *De re militari*: 'Good generals are acutely aware that victory depends much on the nature of the field of battle. [...] The highest ground is reckoned the best. Weapons thrown from a height strike with greater force; and the party above their antagonists can repulse and bear them down with greater impetuosity, while they who struggle with the ascent have both the ground and the enemy to contend with': Vegitius, *De Re Militari: Complete Official Edition* (Dubai, 2019). For the original text, see *Vegetius: Epitoma Rei Militaris*, ed. Michael D. Reeve (Oxford, 2004), III.xiii.

68 Patricia DeMarco, 'An Arthur for the Ricardian Age', 466. See, for example, William Matthews, *The Tragedy of Arthur: A Study of the Alliterative Morte Arthure* (Oakland CA, 1960); Juliet Vale, 'Law and Diplomacy in the Alliterative *Morte Arthure*', *Nottingham Medieval Studies* 23 (1979), 31–46; Karl Heinz Göller, 'Reality versus Romance: A Reassessment of the Alliterative *Morte Arthure*', in *The Alliterative Morte Arthure: A Reassessment of the Poem*, ed. Karl Heinz Göller (Cambridge, 1981), 15–29; Elizabeth Porter, 'Chaucer's Knight, the Alliterative *Morte Arthure*, and Medieval Laws of War: A Reconsideration', *Nottingham Medieval Studies* 27 (1983), 56–78; Rebecca S. Beal, 'Arthur as the Bearer of Civilization: The Alliterative *Morte Arthure*, ll. 901–19', *Arthuriana* 5.4 (1995), 32–44; and Richard J. Moll, *Before Malory: Reading Arthur in Later Medieval England* (Toronto, 2003), 97–122. See John Burrow, 'The Fourteenth-century

in Arthur's campaign, which far exceeds that expressed in other versions of the Brut narrative, raises questions about authority and governance that closely tie the poem's critique of Arthur to the late fourteenth-century crisis of leadership under Richard II. In particular, DeMarco argues that changes in military practice during this period challenged the traditional ethos of the chivalric aristocracy. This helps us to interpret certain moments in the poem – Arthur's battle with the giant on Mont-Saint-Michel, and his ability to lead his knights in recapturing the English coast – as indicative of the poet's nostalgia for an era in which military practice serves to unify the King and his court.[69] In effect, DeMarco argues that the poem presents Arthur in a positive light as a capable ruler (particularly in matters of war) in direct contract to the weak leadership of Richard.

For others, though, Arthur's perpetuation of acts of violence in the Alliterative *Morte*, including his battle with the giant of Mont-Saint-Michel, serves to illustrate the damaging and all-consuming nature of his aggressive campaign. Dorsey Armstrong has argued that the martial focus of the poem is undercut by an alternative reading that seems to promote a more peaceful agenda, presenting Arthur's campaign in distinctly negative terms. The secondary, latent narrative that emerges from this is, therefore, 'one of secure succession and genealogical continuity, of consolidation, defence, and maintenance rather than aggression, conquest, and conflict, and it haunts the narrative as surely as Saracens, giants, Romans, Saxons, and kin treason do'.[70] In this context, the Mont-Saint-Michel encounter, while clearly intended as a positive display of Arthur's martial abilities, is still indicative of the way that

---

Arthur', for a summary of the debate that ultimately identifies Arthur as a positive model of medieval kingship: *The Cambridge Companion to the Arthurian Legend*, ed. Elizabeth Archibald and Ad Putter (Cambridge, 2010), 69–83 (70–2).

69 DeMarco, 'An Arthur for the Ricardian Age', 493.

70 Dorsey Armstrong, 'Rewriting the Chronicle Tradition: The Alliterative *Morte Arthure* and Arthur's Sword of Peace', *Parergon* 25.1 (2008), 81–101. For an argument that emphasises the cyclical nature of war and peace in the Brut tradition, see Andrew Lynch, '"Peace is Good After War": The Narrative Seasons of English Arthurian Tradition', in *Writing War: Medieval Literary Responses to Warfare*, ed. Corinne Saunders, Françoise Le Saux and Neil Thomas (Cambridge, 2004), 127–46. See also Steven P. W. Bruso, 'The Sword and the Scepter: Mordred, Arthur, and the Dual Roles of Kingship in the Alliterative *Morte Arthure*', *Arthuriana* 25.2 (2015), 44–66.

Arthur and his retinue place too much emphasis on war while giving too little attention to peace.[71] Of particular note is Arthur's sarcastic claim that he seeks the giant 'To trete with that tyraunt for tresoun of landes / And take trews for a time, til it may tide better' (877–8). As Armstrong notes, there is no such recourse to peaceful negotiation when Arthur eventually encounters the giant. Indeed, Arthur's 'deliberately mocking use of terms associated with peaceable activities' pre-empts his later aggressions and hostilities – including sending the body of Lucius back to Rome as the 'tax and the tribute of ten score winteres' (2344) and his wholesale destruction of Metz (3038–43) – emphasising that Arthur's warlike nature places him on narrow ground when it comes to the divide between brave hero and cruel, despotic tyrant.[72]

For Gillian Adler, a comparison between Laȝamon's *Brut* and the Alliterative *Morte* reveals that while the former depicts Arthur as a model for justice, the latter presents Arthur in terms of hyper-masculinised violence, a flaw in his character that ultimately leads to the destruction of any hope for dynastic continuity.[73] Adler places particular emphasis on the tension between duty and pride, arguing that Arthur's defeat of the giant at Mont-Saint-Michel represents something of a turning point towards his becoming an increasingly reckless tyrant:

> The king's triumph over the Giant invites praise from his knights; for one, Sir Bedivere wishes to place the Giant's destroyed body into a relic-like encasement as proof of the king's honor. However, the scene featuring Arthur's success also hyperbolizes the correlation between knightly violence and self-destruction. Wishing to defeat the Giant independently, Arthur privileges the quest for personal renown. His desire to receive individual distinction, rather than displace chivalric recognition onto the knights Kay and Bedivere, foreshadows a progressive loss of self-awareness at the cost of the greater chivalric community.[74]

---

71   Armstrong, 'Rewriting the Chronicle Tradition', 93. Armstrong also notes that Arthur's Wheel of Fortune dream towards the end of the poem highlights how each of the Nine Worthies adheres to an ideology of war and conflict, and that Arthur's eventual fall is not a consequence of fate but of his own actions: his decision to align himself with those figures by climbing onto the wheel (97).
72   Ibid., 93.
73   Gillian Adler, '"Æit þat traytour alls tite teris lete he fall": Arthur, Mordred, and Tragedy in the Alliterative *Morte Arthure*', *Arthuriana* 25.3 (2015), 3–21.
74   Ibid., 11.

For Adler, as for Armstrong, Arthur's violent actions on Mont-Saint-Michel go some way to prefigure his later fall. However, in the case of all three critics – DeMarco, Armstrong and Adler – the encounter with the giant on the Mont signifies more than just a brief inter-generic excursion, an isolated example of a romance-inspired quest narrative. Rather, the giant and the Mont are bound up in determining the poet's attitude towards kingship, and his presentation of Arthur's fallibility as a figure of supreme power and authority.

The argument that Arthur and the giant are identified with one another is a well-established one. As Cohen has shown, the poet of the Alliterative *Morte* has a tendency to conflate the monarchical and the monstrous.[75] Perhaps the most striking example of this is the ritual act of shaving that Arthur and the giant demand of their subjugated foes: the giant requires the 'berdes of burlich (noble) kings' of 'fifteen rewmes' (1002–5) as a form of tribute and Arthur, following his victory over Lucius, commands that two senators of Rome be shaved as a sign of their supplication (2330–5). For Cohen, the 'kirtle (gown/cloak)' (998) that the giant fashions from the beards he collects 'undermines the ideological purity of Arthur's vision of forcibly uniting disparate realms under British sovereignty, materializing Arthur's own ambition of empire into a costume with which to clothe a monstrous body'.[76] There is even something eerily reminiscent of the giant's taste for human flesh and his butchering of men and children like beasts (1041–52) in the description of Arthur weeping over the body of Gawain during his campaign against Mordred:

> Then sweltes the sweet king   and in swoon falles,   *fainted*
> Swafres up swiftly   and sweetly [Gawain] kisses   *staggered*
> Til his burlich berde   was bloody berunnen,
> Als he had bestes brittened   and brought out of life[77]
>   (3969–72)

Gawain, the last in a line of knights to fall in service to Arthur – including Kay, Lionel and Bedivere – is a victim of the consuming nature of Arthur's war. Indeed, regardless of whether we look on Arthur's campaign as just or unjust, the deaths of Arthur's knights on the battlefield are a reminder that the power Arthur wields comes at

---

75 Cohen, *Of Giants*, 153.
76 Ibid.
77 'As if he had killed and dismembered many animals.'

a cost. Arthur's violence is more chivalrous (and so more acceptable) than the giant's, but it is nonetheless another indication of the centrality of violence in the poet's interpretation of regnal authority. With these examples, our understanding of the boundary that exists between man and giant, king and monster, righteousness and corruption becomes increasingly unstable. The giant effectively serves to embody the worst possible attributes of power sought through might.

However, while the giant's role in prefiguring Arthur's downfall has been well attested, there is more to say here about the way that mountains contribute to our understanding of Arthur's developing relationship to power. Far from being abstract, background features of the poem, they are, in fact, integral to our estimation of Arthur's character. The section of the poem that establishes the greatest affinity between Arthur and the mountains is thus the point at which his power and authority stretches the furthest. Indeed, the scene that appears to present mountain landscapes in the most positive light comes at the moment of one of Arthur's most destructive acts: the siege of the city of Metz. Arthur's decision to besiege Metz is linked to its importance as a stronghold of the Duke of Lorraine. While Arthur identifies Lorraine as a traitor and an ally of Lucius, a man 'Redy ay with Romanes to riot my landes' (2403), his actions in this moment are fuelled in large part by his own coveting of Lorraine's lands: 'The lordship is lovely, as ledes me tells (as men tell me); / I will that duchy devise (divide) and dele (i.e. deal out) as me likes' (2399–400).[78] The moment represents a subtle but significant shift in the focus of Arthur's campaign, a movement away from war in defence of lands subjugated by an invading tyrant, to a campaign of territorial expansion.

During the siege of Metz, which culminates in a destructive barrage of the city that employs engines to level monasteries, hospitals, chapels, private dwellings and inns (3032–43), Arthur instructs Sir Florent and a band of his French knights (accompanied by Gawain) to 'founde to the felle and forray (forage in) the mountes' (2489). The description that follows is both striking and unusual when compared to the conventions of the mountain gloom topos. Instead, it has more in common with the lowland paradise that Arthur passes through on his way to Mont-Saint-Michel:

---

78 In the context of the poem, Lorraine is identified as a German territory (2387), reflecting its fourteenth-century status as an autonomous Duchy of the Holy Roman Empire.

Now ferkes to the firth   these fresh men of armes,   *hasten*
To the felle so fawe,   these freshlich bernes,   *colourful/bright; eager*
Through hoppes and hemland,   hilles and other,   *valleys; borderlands*
Holtes and hore woodes   with heslin shawes,   *grey; hazel thickets*
Through morass and moss   and mountes so high,
And in the misty morning   on a mede falles,
Mowen and unmade,   mainovred but little,
In swathes sweppen down,   full of sweet flowres;
There unbridels these bold   and baites their horses.[79]
To the gryging of the day   that birdes gan sing   *dawning*
Whiles the sours of the sun,   that sande is of Crist,   *rising; messenger*
That solaces all sinful   that sight has in erthe.   *i.e. who witness it*
(2501–12)

Here, our understanding of mountains as hostile and alien landscapes has been replaced by a description of an idyllic pastoral setting. Once again, a large part of the poet's emphasis is on sensory stimuli. Just as the Mont-Saint-Michel sequence emphasises vision, sound (or its absence) and temperature as integral to Arthur's experience on the summit, there is a specific focus here on the beauty of this mountain setting as expressed through sweet flowers, singing birds and the visual spectacle of dawn breaking across the landscape, a moment that is described in sacral terms. Given the bleak nature of the summit of Mont-Saint-Michel and the frequency with which mountains are identified as hostile landscapes in medieval literature, the poet's identification of the 'felle (mountain)' as a colourful or bright space is particularly striking.[80]

An explanation for the emphasis placed on scenic beauty in this instance can be found in what follows. Gawain jousts with Sir Priamus, a prince of Africa, who warns Gawain of a hostile foreign army concealed in a nearby forest, replete with knights from Lorraine, Lombardy, the Lowlands, Westphalia, Saxony, Syria and the garrison who guard the Gotthard pass (2650–7). The subsequent battle in the mountains is hard-fought – Priamus identifies 'Sixty thousand and ten' (2659) of the Duke's forces against 'at the ferrest (most) not passand five hundreth'

---

79 'And in the morning mist that falls on the mown meadows, amidst rows of swept and unstacked cuttings full of sweet flowers, the bold men unbridle their horses and let them graze.'
80 Based on the time of day, it is tempting to imagine one side of the mountain lit up orange by the dawn light, an image that is consistent with the Middle English definition of 'fawe' as particoloured: *MED*, s.v. 'fou'.

ARTHUR IN THE MOUNTAINS

(2741) of Arthur's men – and the conflict is marked once again by continual reference to the foreignness of the opposing force, including the appearance of several more Genoese giants (2889, 2908) and a passage describing the Duke of Lorraine charging into combat on a dromedary (2941).[81] However, the outcome is an overwhelming victory for Arthur's knights. In comparison to Arthur's earlier battle against Lucius' forces, the only casualty of note is Gawain's ward Chastelayne, a loss that pushes Gawain into a battle frenzy that helps to bring about their final victory (2952–88).

Compared to the Mont-Saint-Michel sequence, the shift in the role that mountain landscapes play in this scene is in part a consequence of genre. While Arthur's battle with the giant draws heavily on the conventions of romance to establish an alien and otherworldly setting, the emphasis here more closely draws on epic conventions. The bucolic surroundings that form the backdrop to this encounter are used to emphasise the glory and virtue of Arthur's knights at the height of their power. When Arthur first instructs Sir Florent to head into the mountains, the poet places emphasis on the clement conditions – Florent is first summoned when 'the sun has a flethe yolden (i.e. sent forth a flood of light)' (2482) – and the bountiful harvest that can be obtained from the highlands to help sustain Arthur's forces (2491–2). After Gawain's fight with Sir Priamus, the two knights return to Sir Florent's foraging party, who have remained resting at their leisure, laughing or sleeping as they listen to the singing birds (2668–77). Here, the poet is drawing attention to the difference between Arthur's knights and those of the Duke of Lorraine who, despite outnumbering Arthur's men considerably, remain hidden 'in yon huge holtes' (2650) while Arthur's men roam freely across the mountain meadows.[82]

Not long after this encounter, Arthur crosses the Alps via the St Gotthard pass into Lombardy. At this point in the poem, all opposition to Arthur's advance has been removed.[83] The garrison that Lucius

---

81 The poet in this moment seems to be evoking Crusader narratives, as evidenced by an earlier reference to a battle that takes place in the vale of Josephat in the *Fuerre de Gaderes*: see Benson, *King Arthur's Death*, note to 2876.
82 Vos makes a similar argument in relation to *Roland*: Charlemagne's men ascend into the mountains, taking their rest beneath pine trees (evergreen, linked to Christ's eternal salvation), while the pagans head further towards the bottom of the valley, representing their spiritual destruction: Vos, 'Le paysage montagneux dans l'épopée', 61–2.
83 Geoffrey, Wace, and Laȝamon all cause Arthur to turn back from his

assembles to 'meet [Arthur] in the mountes' (559) has already been partially defeated in the previous battle, and so the passage of the pass is instead marked as a joyous and triumphal moment in which Arthur crosses 'mountes so high' via 'marvelous wayes' (3103).[84] Arthur's temperament is characterised by his 'mirthes of herte' (3102) as he 'Graithes the garnison (deals the garrison) grisly woundes' before setting his sights on the unconquered lands of Lombardy:

> When he was passed the height,   then the king hoves
> With his hole batail   beholdand about,
> Lookand on Lumbardy   and on loud meles:
> 'In yon likand land   lord be I think!'
>
> (3106–9)

Of particular note is the emphasis that is placed on Arthur's anticipation of future triumphs. The poet's use of the verb *hoven*, a term that appears regularly in the *Morte* to signal a character, or characters, waiting in readiness (1260, 2475, 3074), here takes on additional meaning that relates to its other common usage in both Middle and Modern English: to hover.[85] The description imbues Arthur with raptor-like qualities, suspended high above the lands that he surveys and poised in readiness to strike. Unsurprisingly, then, his descent from the pass into Italy is marked by another example of the increasing brutality of his campaign. When he reaches Como, he once again sends some of his French forces forward as an advance party. At this point, the poet switches perspectives and introduces us to the townsfolk of Como as they emerge from their city to graze their livestock in the surrounding countryside:

> Then ishewes out of that cite,   full soon by the morn;
> Sleyly discoverers   skiftes their horses;   *stealthy scouts; spread out*
> Then skiftes these scowerers   and skippes on hilles,   *disperse; searchers*
> Discoverers for skulkers   that they no scathe limpen.[86]
> Poverall and pastorelles   passed on after   *peasants; shepherds*

---

campaign in Europe and return to Britain before he is able to cross the Alps (see Geoffrey of Monmouth, X.480–4; Wace, 13013–5; Laȝamon, 13969–70, 14088–91).
84 The term *merveillous* is frequently used in Middle English to signify dangerous or supernatural spaces, but here the emphasis seems primarily related to wonder: *MED*, s.v. 'merveillous', 1a, 2, 4.
85 *MED*, s.v. 'hoven' v. (1), 1, 2.
86 'Check for anyone hiding nearby, so that no harm might befall [the people of Como].'

With porkes to pasture   at the pris gates;   *pigs; great*
Boyes in the suburbs   bourden full high   *servants; jest*
At a bore singlere   that to the bente runnes. *lone wild boar; open fields*
                               (3116–23)

The passage is a strikingly rare example of an Arthurian text commenting on the lives and habits of the third estate, and the delight that the townsfolk experience while observing the startled boar is an intimate, curious detail. It is another example of the poet's ability to interlace real-world circumstance and literary convention through an acknowledgement that mountain landscapes and their surroundings are not, in reality, entirely alien and uncultivated spaces, but productive sites of agriculture and commerce.[87]

However, the moment is quickly interrupted when, in the next four lines, Sir Florent and his knights ambush the city and charge through its gates:

Then brekes our bushment   and the bridge winnes, *ambushers*
Braides into the burgh   with banners displayed,   *rush*
Stekes and stabbes through   that them again-standes; *impale; stand against*
Four streetes, ere they stint,   they stroyed forever! *destroyed*
                               (3124–7)

The *Morte*-poet emphasises Arthur's ruthlessness at Como by first introducing us to the pastoral habits and pleasures of the townspeople. With the siege of Metz, these two destructive battles bookend Arthur's crossing of the St Gotthard pass, building a sense of the impact that Arthur's campaign is having on the communities that he passes through. Indeed, within the context of Arthur's descent from the Alps, this scene shares some interesting parallels with the Mont-Saint-Michel sequence earlier in the poem, and the giant's destructive impact on the surrounding land. As we learn from the Templar knight who first informs Arthur of the giant:

In the countree of Constantine   no kind has he leved *Contentin; family*
Withouten kidd casteles,   enclosed with walles,   *outside of well-known*

---

87   See, for example, Kenneth Addison, 'Changing Places: The Cistercian Settlement and Rapid Climate Change in Britain', in *A Place to Believe In: Locating Medieval Landscapes*, ed. Clare A. Lees and Gillian R. Overing (University Park PA, 2006), 211–38; Costello, *Transhumance and the Making of Ireland's Uplands*.

> That he nay has clenly destroyed   all the knave childer,
> And them carried to the crag   and clenly devoured.
>
> (847–50)

Arthur's decision to cross the Alps to conquer new territory is, therefore, one that has destructive ramifications. Like the giant of Mont-Saint-Michel, Arthur descends from the highlands to wreak havoc on those who attempt to venture beyond the safety of their town walls.

Of course, the transition to outright tyrant is not all-encompassing for Arthur: he does not mirror the giant's actions to such an extent that he loses all semblance of humanity. After the attack on Como, Arthur holds court, 'Recounseles the commons (reconciles the common folk)' and selects a knight to govern the city to ensure that 'all the countree and he full soon were accorded' (3128–33); but his ensuing march on Rome is described almost exclusively as a series of violent acts inflicted on the communities of Northern Italy. Arthur tears down walls and towers (3151–3), makes noble widows 'werye (curse) and weep' (3155), and 'Spoiles dispiteously (plunders mercilessly)' (3159) as he moves south with his army. The excess and wastefulness of this part of Arthur's campaign is so extreme that 'Fro Spain into Spruysland (Prussia) the word of him springes / And spekings of his spenses; despite is full huge (and talk of his booty; the bitterness is great)' (3162–3).[88] In light of this, Arthur's crossing of the Alps serves as another example of the poet's subtle conflation of Arthur and the giant, as part of a narrative that seeks to question and destabilise our perception of Arthur's idealised status as king. Indeed, it appears that a comparison between Mont-Saint-Michel and St Gotthard is one that the *Morte*-poet is encouraging us to make. In both examples, the poet presents summiting a mountain as closely related to vision and forethought. These ascents are marked by momentary pauses that draw attention to the heightened perspective (literal and metaphorical) that Arthur is afforded. On Mont-Saint-Michel, he looks both across the landscape and forward in time in anticipation of his encounter with the giant: a rare moment in the poem that emphasises his apprehension for what is to come. While his confidence is more assured during the St Gotthard sequence, both passages identify mountains as viewpoints capable of spanning geographical and temporal dimensions.

---

88   Contra Benson's editorial gloss of 'spending', see *MED*, s.v. 'spens(e)', 1 (e).

The link between altitude and vision in these two examples recalls that most famous account of medieval mountaineering, Petrarch's 'Letter from Mont Ventoux'. The question of whether Petrarch actually climbed Mont Ventoux is disputed, but the value of his account does not lie in its documentary evidence of medieval mountaineering, but in the way that Petrarch conceives of the mountain summit as a space that challenges and redefines the narrator's perspective, particularly as it relates to his conception of self.[89] Petrarch's motivation for climbing the Mont is, he explains, based solely on 'a desire to view the great height of it' but, as Alexander Lee notes, the text's function is quite clearly allegorical in its attempt to encapsulate the conflict between virtue and pleasure, spiritual versus earthly pursuits.[90] At the mountain's summit, Petrarch gazes out at his surroundings, overawed by the sight of clouds spread out beneath him, the rugged and snow-capped peaks of the Alps to the East, the ocean and the Bay of Marseilles to the South, and the Rhône river to the West.[91] However, this momentary 'aesthetic curiosity', as Hans Blumenberg describes it, gives way to a more contemplative introspection when Petrarch takes out his copy of St Augustine's *Confessions*, in which he reads: 'And they go to admire the summits of mountains and the vast billows of the sea and the broadest rivers and the expanses of the ocean and the revolution of the stars and they overlook themselves.'[92] The impact of Augustine's words is to draw Petrarch inwards and then upwards. As Victoria Kirkham argues, 'The route is an itinerary to God: *extra nos, intra nos, supra nos* (outside ourselves, inside ourselves, above

---

89 For Morris Bishop, Petrarch deserves to be recognised as a precursor to Alpinism, 'the first to climb a mountain because it was there': Bishop, *Petrarch and His World* (Bloomington IN, 1963), 104. However, the veracity of Petrarch's *Familiares* has been subject to debate since Vittorio Rossi's 'Sulla formazione della raccolte epistolary petrarchesche', *Analli della cattedra petrarchesca* 3 (1932), 68–73.
90 Francesco Petrarca, *Rerum familiarium libri I–VIII*, trans. Aldo S. Bernardo (Albany NY, 1975), 172; Alexander Lee, *Petrarch and St. Augustine: Classical Scholarship, Christian Theology and the Origins of the Renaissance in Italy* (Leiden, 2012), 32. Albert Russell Ascoli defines this conflict in terms of 'dramatizing the tension between outwardly directed "naturalist" and historicist curiosity and inwardly directed pursuit of spiritual change': Ascoli, 'Epistolary Petrarch', in *The Cambridge Companion to Petrarch*, ed. Albert Russell Ascoli and Unn Falkeid (Cambridge, 2015), 120–38 (122).
91 *Rerum familiarium libri*, 176–7.
92 Hans Blumenberg, *The Legitimacy of the Modern Age*, trans. Robert M. Wallace (Cambridge MA, 1983), 341–3; *Rerum familiarium libri*, 178.

ourselves)'.[93] However, while Petrarch ultimately condemns the desire to stand on mountaintops, here defined in relation to the 'appetites which are exalted by earthly impulses', the mountain itself is integral to Petrarch's rhetorical strategy.[94] The relationship between vision and altitude functions as a catalyst for the poet's contemplation of self, encouraging both narrator and reader (identified as Petrarch's former confessor, Dionigi di Borgo San Sepolcro) to consider the ultimate futility of material pursuits that cause an individual to be caught up in 'vain speculation'.[95]

Like Petrarch, the Alliterative *Morte*-poet conceives of mountain spaces as environments that enhance our perspective, thus prompting a critique of the individual through the context of their surroundings; here that criticism relates to the limits of earthly glory through conquest. While Arthur looks forward to future battles as he pauses momentarily on the high points of Mont-Saint-Michel and the St Gotthard pass, the similarities between these two scenes encourage the reader to glance both forwards and backwards in time, and to identify mountain spaces as central to our understanding of Arthur's inevitable decline. Just as the giant's defeat is described as a literal fall from the summit of the Mont, one in which Arthur and the giant tumble down the mountainside locked in combat, Arthur's descent from the Gotthard pass marks a distinct turning point in the narrative. Indeed, while Arthur's conquest of Italy extends as far south as Viterbo (only fifty miles north of Rome), the noticeable brutality and wastefulness of his campaign on the Italian peninsula seem to pre-empt his eventual fall from power. It is here, after all, that he dreams of the Wheel of Fortune and first learns of Mordred's betrayal.

---

93 Victoria Kirkham, 'A Life's Work', in *Petrarch: A Critical Guide to the Complete Works*, ed. Victoria Kirkham and Armando Maggi (Chicago IL, 2009), 1–30 (14).
94 *Rerum familiarium libri*, 179. For an argument that links the 'gratuitousness of the climb with the gratuitousness of the text', see Lyell Asher, 'Petrarch at the Peak of Fame', *PMLA* 108.5 (1993), 1050–63.
95 *Rerum familiarium libri*, 179. The 'Letter from Mont Ventoux' is not the only instance of Petrarch's apparent interest in mountain landscapes. See also the introduction to the *Tale of Griselda*, which describes Mount Viso in the Apennines (actually located in the Alps) as 'a very high mountain [...] whose summit, piercing the clouds, rises into the pure ether', notable as the source of the river Po. See Francis Petrarch, *Letters of Old Age: Rerum senilium libri I–XVIII*, trans. Aldo S. Bernardo, Sual Levin, and Reta A. Bernado, 2 vols (Baltimore MD, 1992), XVII.3, 656.

Conclusion

As allegorical constructs, mountains embody Arthur's narrative trajectory, not just because they offer a visual metaphor for his rise and fall, but because their very nature challenges the ideology of colonial expansion that drives Arthur's campaign. Mountains are landscapes of impermanent occupation. The giant's fall from Mont-Saint-Michel is evidence of this impermanence and thus a suitable warning for Arthur, who becomes increasingly associated with mountain settings as the poem progresses. However, there is also more going on here than is suggested by Nicolson's 'mountain gloom' topos. While mountains can be dangerous, the poet of the Alliterative *Morte* also draws attention to their potential as bountiful landscapes. They are settings that are rich in both resource and spiritual value, as emphasised by the townsfolk of Como who use the mountain landscape to graze their livestock, or by the knights who venture into 'mountes so high' to gather food for Arthur's army, but end up marvelling at a sunrise that 'solaces all sinful that sight has in erthe'. Likewise, Arthur's defeat of the giant on Mont-Saint-Michel opens up the opportunity for the mountain setting to transform from profane to sacred through the construction of a chapel on its summit, but the Mont is also connected with the wealth hoarded by the giant, to which Kay and Bedivere are encouraged to help themselves after his defeat (1190).[96] To reduce the mountains of the Alliterative *Morte* to negative allegorical constructs is to miss some of their potency as multivalent landscapes that are at once alien and familiar, dangerous and bucolic, literal and figurative. Far from being background features of the poem, they form a consistent and integral part of the poet's cultivation of meaning throughout the text.

All this suggests that our understanding of the value of mountain settings in works of Middle English literature has been simplistic. As growing scholarly interest in the medieval environment continues to broaden our awareness of the actual landscapes and ecologies of the Middle Ages, literary scholars can benefit from attending to mountains as part of the medieval imagination. This essay has sought to argue that there is a richness to the mountains of the Alliterative *Morte* that goes far beyond the clichés and overused motifs that have so far been recognised

---

96 Malory places more emphasis than the *Morte*-poet on the treasure that can be found on the summit of the Mont, suggesting that Kay and Bedivere are able to retrieve 'tresoure oute of numbir' when they climb the Mont to gather the giant's club and coat (*Le Morte Darthur*, ed. Shepherd, 125).

as the medieval period's foremost contribution to mountain literature. This is not a case of trying to reframe medieval approaches to mountains to fit with a post-eighteenth-century shift in our aesthetic appreciation for these landscapes, but an attempt to consider their function in a way that is attuned to medieval literary convention, natural philosophy and biblical exegesis, while also recognising their role as real-world sites of economic, spiritual and geo-political importance.

Printed in the United States
by Baker & Taylor Publisher Services